Praise for Dermot Bolger

'A fierce and terrifyingly uncompromising talent ... serious and provocative.'

Nick Hornby, *The Sunday Times*

'Bolger does it masterfully, as always. He has been prying open the Irish ribcage since he was sixteen years old.... Pound for pound, word for word, I'd have Bolger represent us in any literary Olympics.'

Colum McCann, *Irish Independent*

'Bolger is to contemporary Dublin what Dickens was to Victorian London: archivist, reporter, sometimes infuriated lover. Certainly no understanding of Ireland's capital at the close of the twentieth century is complete without an acquaintance with his magnificent writing.'

Joseph O'Connor, Books Quarterly

'Joyce, O'Flaherty, Brian Moore, John McGahern, a fistful of O'Briens ... Dermot Bolger is of the same ilk ... an exceptional literary gift.'

Independent UK

'Whether he's capturing the slums of Dublin or the pain of a missed opportunity in love, Bolger's writing simply sings.'

Sunday Business Post

'Dermot Bolger creates a Dublin, a particular world, like no one else writing can ... the urban landscape of the thriller that Bolger has made exclusively his own.'

Sunday Independent

'A wild, frothing, poetic odyssey ... a brilliant and ambitious piece of writing.'

Sunday Telegraph

'The writing is so strong, so exact ... triumphantly successful – bare, passionate, almost understating the almost unstatable.'

Financial Times

Praise for Tanglewood

'*Tanglewood* is an outstanding piece of work by one of our most mature and courageous writers, one who is unafraid to hack his way through the tangles of contemporary Irish life and write a rare thing in Irish fiction: a serious state-of-the-nation novel.'

The Irish Times

'An absorbing meditation on marriage, masculinity, parenting and the general anxieties of the middle class... Bolger approaches these variegated lives with a wisdom that contrasts sharply with the benightedness of those he depicts. On every page, insight and illumination are found, as might be expected from one of Ireland's most perceptive writers.'

The Times Literary Supplement

'Only a writer of Bolger's precision and suppleness could wade back through the nation's self-loathing into that mess and mine new truths, treasures to be heeded and learned from... Bolger isn't meditating on regret, love, moral fibre, greed and carpe diem – he's setting the record straight on them... This is storytelling that flows deep and soundly, and brims with a hard-earned wisdom... sublime.'

Sunday Independent

'Well-wrought, considered, layered and evocative.'

Irish Examiner

'Bolger is a witty and sensitive writer ... who has always been attuned to social issues... Bolger writes about love and grief particularly well, and it is refreshing to see such an open portrait of the sexual lives of each of the characters, from menopausal Alice to lesbian Sophie, from sexually shy Chris to sexually rampant Ronan... *Tanglewood* makes a critical contribution to contemporary Irish fiction of the post-boom period.'

Sunday Business Post

'Bolger is a gifted storyteller and prose stylist ... a gripping, well-observed examination of the corrosive effects of greed on love, relationships and families.'

Hot Press

'*Tanglewood* is an impressive feat by an author fearlessly interrogating one of the most traumatic moments in recent Irish history. It's a mirror to an age when the party ended.'

The National UAE

About the Author

Born in Dublin in 1959, **Dermot Bolger** is one of Ireland's best known writers. His twelve previous novels include *The Journey Home, Father's Music, The Valparaiso Voyage, The Family on Paradise Pier, A Second Life, New Town Soul, The Fall of Ireland* and, most recently, *Tanglewood*. His first play, *The Lament for Arthur Cleary*, received the Samuel Beckett Award and an Edinburgh Fringe First Award. His numerous other plays include *The Ballymun Trilogy*, which charts forty years of life in a Dublin working class suburb; *Walking the Road, The Parting Glass* and a stage adaptation of Joyce's *Ulysses*, which has toured China. Also a poet, his ninth collection of poems, *The Venice Suite: A Voyage Through Loss*, was published in 2012 and his New and Selected Poems, *That Which is Suddenly Precious*, appeared from New Island in 2015. He devised the best-selling collaborative novels, *Finbar's Hotel* and *Ladies Night at Finbar's Hotel*, and has edited numerous anthologies, including *The Picador Book of Contemporary Irish Fiction*. A former Writer Fellow at Trinity College, Dublin, and Playwright in Association with the Abbey Theatre, Bolger writes for most of Ireland's leading newspapers, and in 2012 was named Commentator of the Year at the Irish Newspaper awards.

www.dermotbolger.com

THE LONELY SEA AND SKY

THE LONELY SEA AND SKY

Dermot Bolger

NEW ISLAND

THE LONELY SEA AND SKY
First published in 2016 by
New Island Books
16 Priory Hall Office Park
Stillorgan
County Dublin
Republic of Ireland

www.newisland.ie

Copyright © Dermot Bolger, 2016

The author has asserted his moral rights.

PRINT ISBN: 978-1-84840-503-5
EPUB ISBN: 978-1-84840-504-2
MOBI ISBN: 978-1-84840-505-9

British Library Cataloguing Data.
A CIP catalogue record for this book is available from the British Library.

Front cover photograph features the crew of the *Irish Poplar* – one of many Irish ships mentioned in this novel – taken by Martin Cunningham in 1945. It is reproduced, with thanks, from Captain Frank Forde's classic work, *The Long Watch: World War Two and the Irish Mercantile Marine* (New Island Books, 2000).

Typeset by JVR Creative India
Cover Design by Karen Vaughan
Printed by ScandBook AB, Sweden

10 9 8 7 6 5 4 3 2 1

In memory of my father,
Roger Bolger (1918–2011)
of Green Street, Wexford town,
who voyaged to Lisbon on the MV Edenvale:
sister ship of the MV Kerlogue.

And remembering his neighbour who took him to sea,
Michael Tierney of Green Street, Wexford town,
who lost his life on the MV Cymric,
sunk in the Bay of Biscay, February 1944.

Prologue

I DON'T OFTEN HAVE THAT same dream, but there are nights when – although I'm now far older than even Myles Foley lived to be – memories come back that I've never told anyone about. How can you talk about that time without folk who didn't live through it making a fuss that blows what we did out of proportion? For the likes of us, there weren't too many options for knocking out a living. My crewmates were ordinary seafarers – no heroics or histrionics. Just banter and slagging and ducking and diving, with a necessary sideline in small-time smuggling, born from the knowledge that shipping companies would dock whatever wages the sailors' families received from the exact moment a torpedo shattered their ship's hull or a Luftwaffe pilot dropped bombs on Irishmen bereft of uniforms or weapons, huddled in a tiny wheelhouse.

They were not at war with anyone – they just had to sail into the midst of everyone else's war. I was only a scared greenhorn that they all took under their wing in their own unassuming fashion. Some days now, when I sit alone, with only the Health Board's emergency pendant around my neck for company, I lose track of the decades that have passed. Why then is that old dream still able to ambush me with its palpable sense of terror? It makes no difference that I've survived to the age of eighty-eight, or whatever age I am now; all it takes is that first avalanche of drenching spray from a Biscay wave to cascade through my sleeping mind and I become a petrified fourteen-year-old cabin boy again.

I stagger across the deck as our small coaster tilts steeply downwards in the trough between huge waves – waves that this ship was never designed to withstand. Myles Foley is too exhausted to acknowledge my arrival beyond granting me a brief nod. The angle at which we ride the next wave is so severe that it feels like the ship may topple over, but this wave brings us within reach of more drowning men. One such man reaches out his right hand but Myles's arm is too short, so I kneel to proffer my outstretched hand instead. A gash across the man's forehead is clotted with blood. His eyes are bloodshot. His face, ravaged by cold, has two days' stubble. But the brass buttons on his midnight-blue jacket display the insignia of a Nazi officer. As the *Kerlogue* rises in the swell of the oncoming wave, I miss his fingers by inches and he disappears from sight.

Myles Foley glares at me. 'You could have reached him.'

'I tried to rescue the Nazi murderer,' I shout back, shocked by my guilty thrill of revenge.

The old man grips my soaked jumper. 'You didn't try hard enough. Before his ship sank he was a Nazi. Now he's a drowning sailor. Out here, we're all sailors. Your father and grandfather understood that about the sea. Are you going to disgrace their memory?'

The brutal force of the next wave hits us, smashing against the gunnel and spraying the deck with icy water. It soaks through our clothes, almost knocking us off our feet.

'These sailors murdered my father.'

'They followed orders,' Myles Foley says. 'If they hadn't, they'd have been put up against a wall and shot.'

'And you want me to follow your orders, is it?' I am so overwhelmed I can barely comprehend what is right or wrong any more.

The ship tilts steeply before the next wave. The German officer resurfaces, his face bleeding even more profusely, having obviously been bashed against the ship's side. Myles Foley leans over the gunnel, trying to reach him. 'I don't give orders,' the old man snaps. 'I'm not following orders either: I'm following my conscience and my conscience tells me to haul this poor bastard out.'

Part One

THE VOYAGE OUT

Chapter One

December 14 1943, the Wexford quays

THE SEA HAD CLAIMED ANOTHER victim. I knew this from the ambulance parked beside one of the small fishing trawlers moored on the Wexford quay, and from the sober demeanour of the fishermen on deck, standing around the sheet of tarpaulin with which they had covered the face of the man when transporting him back to Wexford. Barely a week passed without a Wexford trawlerman retrieving some grim souvenir of the war in Europe: shattered planks from a smashed lifeboat; lifebuoys bearing the name of a missing ship; a sailor's hat bobbing on the waves with only a coloured ribbon to identify the nationality of the young man who had once worn it. Kilmore Quay and Arklow trawler crews had grown accustomed to hauling in lifeless bodies of sailors or airmen. Whether or not these victims were from the Allied or Axis side, the fishermen solemnly knelt in the same way on deck to recite a decade of the Rosary for the dead men's souls before covering their faces with tarpaulin, treating them with the due respect that seafarers afforded to any fellow mariner.

A surge of desperate hope made me want to walk close to the trawler so I could peer over at the body. But Mr Tierney's protective hand landed on my shoulder.

'It's been nine months, Jack,' he said quietly, steering me away from the trawler and towards our intended destination.

'I still want to see,' I replied.

'Trust me, you don't.' He blessed himself. 'When some poor sod drowns out there and finally resurfaces, the sea will have done things to his face that nobody should have to witness. Say a prayer and pass on, Jack. Besides, wherever the trawler found him, it was a long way from Biscay. Only a proper eejit would venture into the Bay of Biscay on a rust bucket as small as them trawlers.'

My neighbour became quiet then, realising the grim irony of his words. Our eyes were drawn to the boat moored at the end of the quay. The *Kerlogue* was barely bigger than the two trawlers tied up alongside it. When the fishermen handed over this latest corpse to the authorities, they would make ready to sail with the tide, joining other Kilmore Quay boats in hunting for mackerel. But even such short expeditions, which barely strayed from sight of the Irish coastline, were not without danger. The Irish Sea could be broody: quick to change mood when storms brewed up. A fishing vessel might strike a mine that floated free from its moorings or find itself dragged beneath the waves if its nets became entangled with one of the hidden U-boats that often lurked in these waters: sharks patiently awaiting their next kill.

The corpse was being loaded onto a stretcher and carried up the gangplank. I turned my face away, comforted by Mr Tierney's hand on my shoulder. I didn't want to think about dead bodies being recovered from the waves. It reignited too many memories of a body never found; a sailor still officially listed as missing, though by now even my mother had accepted that my father was dead. As the ambulance prepared to move off, the fishermen bustled about at various tasks, needing to shout to be heard above the raucous scavenging seagulls. They already wished to disassociate themselves from the horror of what they had retrieved from the waves and distract themselves from the dangers that might lie ahead. But these fishermen would likely encounter little menace this evening and would land their catch safely. In two weeks' time they would enjoy Christmas with their families – a better Christmas than many hungry families in Wexford would know. The tiny ship we were walking towards would be undertaking a more hazardous voyage, right into the wilds of Biscay. If not sunk by U-boats and capsized by storms, it would dock at Christmas in the distant port of Lisbon. My father had often described Lisbon, but I could barely imagine such a metropolis of teeming streets and steep laneways bustling with life.

Allied merchant ships sailed in blacked-out convoys, accompanied fore and aft by armed battleships to offer protection. But the MV *Kerlogue* would sail for Portugal utterly alone, lit up at night in the hope that the Luftwaffe would recognise its Irish flag and respect its neutrality. The fact that the Wexford Steamship Company was reduced to dispatching this patched-up vessel – just a hundred and forty-two feet in length – on such a voyage showed how often aircrews and U-boat captains felt inclined to use solitary Irish vessels for target practice when they encountered them, alone and defenceless, at sea.

My apprehension grew with every step we took. It would require all my courage to embark on this voyage if the Captain could be persuaded to employ me. I would need to gain my sea legs, overcome my fears and learn to share a cabin with men three times my age. But before facing such difficulties, I had to overcome a more pressing obstacle: I needed to become a convincing liar. My neighbour, who lived three doors down from us on Green Street, lifted his hand from my shoulder, indicating that we should walk like two adults. Mr Tierney was Second Engineer on the *Kerlogue*.

Only his wife used his proper name of Maurice; every other adult in Wexford called him Mossy. As we reached the narrow gangplank he paused to look at me, as if this was the stupidest idea either of us had ever dreamed up.

'Mother of God, Jack,' he exclaimed. 'When was your poor mother last able to put a proper feed inside you?'

'I'm not *so* scrawny.' I was too scared to feel insulted. 'Everyone says I'm tall for fourteen.'

Mr Tierney threw his eyes to heaven. Red blotches around his nose betrayed how he had spent much of his shore leave holding up bar counters. 'This isn't a competition to find the tallest fourteen-year-old in Wexford,' he said. 'This is about whether you can pass yourself off to an experienced sea captain as being old enough to sign on for a voyage like this. Now, what age are you?'

'You know my age, Mr Tierney. Didn't your wife help to deliver me?'

He leaned down. 'Listen good to me, Jack Roche: that's the last time you ever call me Mr Tierney. From here on, my name is Mossy. What is it?'

'It's Mossy, Mr Tierney.'

'Mother of Christ, grant me patience.' He shook his head. 'And what age are you?'

'Sixteen on my last birthday, Mossy.'

'Remember that. It's the lie I told the new captain and it's more than my job is worth to lie to him.' His voice softened. 'I've promised your mother I'll mind you if the Skipper is daft enough to sign you on. But I can't be like a father on board. Your poor father was lost on this same route. Sailing to Lisbon won't be an easy voyage for you.'

'Was there ever any easy voyage for him?' I asked. 'Or for you, since Hitler started this slaughter?'

Mr Tierney nodded. 'The sea is no easy life, but what else am I going to do?' He stared past the *Kerlogue* towards the mouth of the River Slaney. 'The sea is in my blood, Jack. When you're a breadwinner like me with nine hungry mouths at home to feed, you duck and dive and do whatever it takes to put food on the table.'

'And if you were forced to sit at home, watching your younger brothers and sister starve, wouldn't you do the same thing, Mr Tierney?'

'You're at it again: calling me *Mister* Tierney.'

'It's hard to break the habit of a lifetime, Mossy.'

'I know.' His voice softened so that he sounded more like the kindly neighbour I knew – the one who never returned from a voyage without bags of boiled sweets to be shared out among every child on Green Street. 'But when you go to sea, you leave your old life behind.' I felt he wanted to ruffle my hair, but such a gesture of affection was out of place on the quayside. 'Listen, Jack, I was rightly fond of your dad. Sean got me out of many a tight scrape in foreign ports when I was stupid enough to let drink run away with my tongue, or some Flash Harry wanted to relieve me of my wages. I'm fond of your mother too: a proper lady. But if Captain Donovan signs you up, you'll be just another shipmate, you understand? Don't come running to me. You must stand on your own two feet on a ship. It's an unforgiving world. Sailors are hard men but generally fair: though being confined to a boat can make anyone ratty and ready to snap for any reason or none. Some men take to the sea like ducks to water, and yet I've seen it destroy other fellows. You'll know seasickness and homesickness and storms when you'll think you'll never see land again. And they're less dangerous than some bars in Portugal, full of girls happy to pluck every penny from your pocket. If you're not careful, waking up with a hangover and an empty wallet will be the least of your problems: you'll need injections in places that a man can't even think about without wincing. And they're only the everyday dangers before we mention the war.'

'The Emergency,' I corrected him. 'In school Brother Dawson beat us with his strap if we called it the war. He ordered us to call it "The State of Emergency" because Ireland isn't officially at war with anyone.'

Mr Tierney stared back towards the town, his voice tinged with unexpected bitterness. 'Is Brother Dawson still alive? He was always fond of his leather strap.'

'He still is,' I said, silently recalling numerous beatings for not knowing an Irish verb, or more often for no reason at all.

'Does he still sew sixpences into his strap to leave an imprint of the coins on your palms?'

I nodded. 'He has such a temper you never know when he's going to explode.'

'Do you know something, Jack? I bet if you met Hitler's Gestapo, they'd be the spitting image of Brother Dawson, only kinder.'

It wasn't the quiet anger in Mr Tierney's voice that shocked me; it was the residue of fear. I found it hard to imagine this sailor once cowering in a classroom while blows rained down on his skull. Mr Tierney spat with slow deliberateness on the quayside.

'Brother Dawson can call it what he likes here in Wexford, where people need only worry about their weekly half-ounce ration of tea. But if the Skipper hires you, you'll be sailing into the teeth of war. So tell me again, where have you spent the past six months, scrubbing pots and mastering the black art of porridge-making?'

'In the kitchens of St Patrick's Seminary, which I've never actually set foot in, helping their cook to prepare meals.'

'And where is the glowing reference the College President wrote, calling you so highly skilled that you're destined to become the head chef in Jammet's Restaurant in Dublin?'

'My mother put it away for safekeeping and she can't find it.'

The one daily train from Rosslare to Dublin slowly shunted past us along the metal tracks set into the quay. We watched it go by, breathing in the billowing smoke that reeked from the damp turf the stoker was using to coax the engine forward. It was growing dark as I looked back at the cramped streets of my native town: medieval roads so narrow that two cars could barely pass each other. Not that you were likely to see two cars with the strict rationing of petrol. This honeycomb of shabby alleyways was the only world I had ever seen, apart from one day when I borrowed a bicycle to cycle the twenty-three miles to Enniscorthy town. In Enniscorthy I had tried to impress the local girls by loudly jangling metal washers in my pocket while swaggering around, hoping to create the impression of being weighed down by half crowns. Instead I was so poor that I had to stop at a roadside stream on my cycle home to slake my thirst and search for berries to take the edge off my savage hunger. It was daunting to leave a town where I knew everyone and everyone knew my seed and breed. Yet I couldn't go home empty-handed. Mr Tierney was shaking his head, exasperated at our threadbare excuse, even though he had invented it in my mother's kitchen last night.

'If we don't say that your mother lost the reference, we'd have to pretend the dog ate it,' he said. 'And when Captain Donovan takes one look at you he'll know the poor woman can't afford to feed her own children, never mind keep a dog.' Mr Tierney glanced up the rickety gangplank as we reached the ship. 'I often think drink is a terrible thing, Jack.'

'Does Captain Donovan drink?'

Mr Tierney shook his head. 'He doesn't, that's the terrible thing. Our best hope was to find a skipper so stocious that he wouldn't even notice your presence until he sobered up, halfway across St George's Channel. But Captain Donovan has never touched a drop, even after nearly losing his life on the *Irish Oak* when the Germans torpedoed it heading home with a cargo of phosphates last May. Before that he was master of the *Lady Belle of Waterford* when she got bombed off the Welsh coast. Let's hope he doesn't need to get lucky with the Nazis a third time. But that won't be your concern. Unless he's suddenly become a full-blown alcoholic, he'll send you hurtling back down this gangplank like a stone from a catapult. I'll be lucky not to get the sack for trying to foster off an infant on him.'

I looked back at the laneways that I never wanted to leave. A boy my own age, Pascal Brennan, came freewheeling down Charlotte Street after making deliveries on his butcher's bicycle. I wanted Brennan to topple over the handlebars and smash his skull. For days I had fantasised about accidents occurring to him, ever since I watched from my bedroom as he called for Ellie Coady to bring her to the Cinema Palace in her best blue polka-dot dress. I knew they went there because I'd followed from a distance, knowing I hadn't enough money to bring Ellie to any film. I had stood outside the Cinema Palace, unable to stop imagining what Pascal and Ellie might be doing in those dark seats until I was driven away by the jeers of other boys eyeing me from across the road. Walking home alone, I had felt like a pauper.

I never liked Pascal Brennan. In school he always sat behind me making snide comments, like he had been doing on my last day in school nine months ago. I didn't know back then that it would be my last day, but that was the day when every woman in Green Street went into a state of terrified paralysis: the day when rumours reached Wexford that the radio station at Valentia Island could get no response to the frantic signals they kept sending to my father's ship. On that night I had put away my school books, unable to concentrate on Irish nouns or worry about Brother Dawson's dangerous mood swings because I didn't know if my father would arrive home – as he often did when delayed on a stormy voyage – or if I suddenly had become the man of the house. Nothing was certain back then; there was no floating wreckage, no survivors found, no official confirmation – just a limbo of waiting in which our hopes slowly petered out. For a long time my mother never referred to my father as being dead. But two weeks after I had stopped going to school, I woke to find that my short trousers were gone from the chair beside the small bed that I shared with my brothers, Eamonn and Tony. My mother had placed my first pair of long trousers there during the night – an unspoken acknowledgement that I had left my childhood behind.

I would have given anything to have Pascal Brennan's job. I would happily even become a telegram delivery boy – the worst job during any war because telegrams almost invariably brought bad news. But there was no shop or builders' yard I hadn't visited a dozen times to ask if any work was going. Every Wexford shopkeeper was sick of my face, and I was sick of the shame of needing to ask the same question when I already knew the answer. But I was even sicker of the famished look in the eyes of Eamonn and Tony and little Lily when I arrived home each evening with one hand as long and empty as the other. If I stayed in Wexford, all I was good for was scrounging scraps of firewood or cinders that rich folk dumped in their rubbish, or walking the cold streets until dusk, eyes scanning the footpath in case I spied a smouldering cigarette butt or a ha'penny dropped from a purse. December was no month to undertake a maiden voyage. But I would sooner wake up in the creaking hull of a ship being tossed about the Bay of Biscay than see my starved siblings try to comfort our mother during her first Christmas as a widow. At the very least I would be one less mouth to feed. These long trousers made me a man.

The gangplank was rickety, without a rope or handrail. Striding past Mr Tierney, I placed one foot on it before I lost whatever courage I could summon. 'Do you know something, Mossy?' I said. 'You do more whinging that the seminarians I used to make breakfast for in St Patrick's. I thought that listening to the bloody cook there moan in his kitchen was bad enough. But in my sixteen years on earth I've never known a greater windbag than you. Now are we going to stand here freezing or talk to this Skipper?'

I had never seen Mr Tierney stuck for words before. He was still standing on the quayside in shock when I stepped onto the deck. Then he scrambled up the wooden gangplank. I turned to face him, unsure if I would receive a slap for my impudence.

'You're Sean Roche's son all right,' he said. 'Just do me one favour: don't call Captain Donovan "Skipper". Call him "Master" or "Captain" or "Sir". If you don't, I'll be joining you in searching for a job down every back lane in Wexford.'

Chapter Two

December 14, the Wexford quays

WHEN I GAZED BACK FROM the ship's deck, only a few feet of water separated me from the quay, but already the view of the town looked different from the small ship. The *Kerlogue* had been built in Holland five years ago for the Stafford family, who owned the Wexford Steamship Company. Yet the ship possessed a haphazard, mismatched feel. The weathered wheelhouse up on the raised forecastle deck seemed to belong to an older ship, but the amidships deck was brand new. It smelled of fresh paint because of the Irish tricolour that had recently been daubed across it to make its markings more visible from the air.

This neutral flag had proved to be no defence six weeks previously when two warplanes machine-gunned the *Kerlogue* en route to Lisbon from Port Talbot in Wales. The original deck was ripped asunder, its radio transmitter shot to pieces and the lifeboats left in smithereens. Mossy Tierney had spent his shore leave telling pub drinkers that he was convinced he would meet his maker when water started to flood his engine room. It was just by the grace of God that the main engine was not hit. This allowed the pumps to continue bailing out enough seawater to keep the ship afloat. But only after the *Kerlogue* abandoned its outward voyage and limped back to Ireland did the crew discover why the ship hadn't sunk: the hold was so densely packed with Welsh coal that the shells

– while destroying the deck – had become lodged in the coal. This prevented them from ripping open the hull. Markings on the shells had proven that, on this occasion at least, the attackers were not German but a Polish squadron of RAF Mosquito pilots who didn't seem to mind attacking a non-combatant ship that was actually carrying British cargo at the time.

Even though the boat wasn't completely destroyed, the *Kerlogue's* original crew had not escaped unscathed from that attack. The Chief Officer was laid up with shrapnel wounds, one sailor was traipsing about Wexford on wooden crutches, while the cabin boy, although unhurt, had not even returned to collect his wages. It was his job I was after. I might have stood more chance if the master of the *Kerlogue* on the day of the attack, Captain Fortune, was still in charge. He was a skipper my father had sailed under and always talked of with respect. But Captain Fortune had spent that attack roving around the ship to ensure his crew's safety; his bravery resulted in compound fractures to both of his legs. It was rumoured that he would never be able to walk unaided again or go back to sea.

Mr Tierney was nervous of the replacement skipper on the *Kerlogue*. As he opened a door in the forecastle buckhead and led the way down the steep ladder to a narrow passageway below deck, his personality changed. He grew more deferential with every step closer to the Captain's cabin. I barely recognised my devil-may-care neighbour who generally ended his tales with a wink, as if he could hardly believe the mishaps that he experienced in foreign ports. Perhaps it was the low ceiling and poor lighting, but he looked smaller. He gave me one last despairing glance before knocking timidly on the Captain's door. I had been too preoccupied with my worries to consider the risks to Mr Tierney's job if this new captain took umbrage at his Second Engineer for trying to deceive him, but I could understand them now. A voice from within instructed us to enter. Mr Tierney opened the door and took a cautious step inside, beckoning me to follow. He didn't want to venture too close to the Captain's desk, but the cabin was so small that we were already on top of the man, who glanced up from the papers piled in front of him.

I had expected Captain Donovan to wear a gold-braided cap, like the ones you saw sea captains wear about the town. He was more casually dressed, but there was no mistaking the quiet authority he exuded. It was an earned authority that had no need to spill over into stern self-importance. Brother Dawson always needed to be the centre of attention. If a boy even glanced down at his copybook when Brother Dawson was talking, he would hear a swish of black robes, like the wings of a hawk bearing down on its prey, and feel that leather strap savagely strike his skull. But as Captain Donovan appraised me with a glance, I felt myself to be in the presence of a different type of authority. I'd always feared Brother Dawson for the pleasure he gained from assaulting anyone weaker than him, but I had never respected him like I immediately respected this man.

I knew nothing about Captain Donovan, beyond the fact that he had already survived two sinkings and was now taking charge of a ship with no earthly right to still be afloat. But I sensed at once that I could trust him with my life. I also knew that I could never fool him. I realised that Mr Tierney sensed this too from how he fidgeted awkwardly – a telltale sign whenever he was trying to bluff his way out of a situation he could no longer control.

'This is the lad I mentioned, Captain,' Mr Tierney began. 'Young Jack Roche, Sir.'

Captain Donovan leaned back to survey us with a weary sigh. 'I heard you were prone to exaggeration, Mossy, but "young" is an understatement.' He addressed me directly. 'Have you any experience at sea, Roche?'

'He has great experience in the kitchens, Captain,' Mr Tierney interjected. 'He worked for the Cook in St Patrick's Seminary. Show the Master that glowing reference from the College President, Jack.'

I felt so paralysed under the Captain's stern gaze that Mr Tierney needed to nudge me before I spoke. 'My mother put it somewhere for safekeeping, Master, and we can't find it, Sir.'

A lesser man might have made a joke at our expense. But Captain Donovan seemed to respect that nobody showed up on a vessel about to undertake a dangerous voyage without good reason. I knew he had already decided not to employ me, but was affording me the courtesy of a proper interview.

'How old are you, Roche?'

'Sixteen on my last birthday, Sir.'

'So your date of birth is…?'

'May 17, 19…' I cursed myself and sensed Mr Tierney damn my slow wits. My hesitation only lasted a second, but was enough to confirm what Captain Donovan already knew. '…1927, Sir.'

'Get away home with you, Master Roche.'

'If I could interject for the briefest second, Captain…' Mr Tierney began. I didn't know what desperate ploy my neighbour had up his sleeve, but a glance from Captain Donovan reduced the Second Engineer to silence. The man behind the desk looked at me directly. His tone was neither angry nor condescending. It was sympathetic, but firm.

'Does your mother know you're trying to sign on, when you're so young you can barely wash behind your ears?'

'She does, Sir.'

'And does she know how often Irish ships get attacked? Every time we sail we need to get lucky. If U-boat commanders don't respect our markings, nobody comes to our rescue. Do you understand this, Roche?

'I do, Sir.'

'This ship has only been tacked back together with a few prayers and a lick of paint. Did Mr Tierney not tell you this?'

'He told half of Wexford, Sir.'

The Captain smiled for the first time. It made him look younger, as if he had momentarily forgotten the responsibilities of the forthcoming voyage. His countryman's smile matched his soft Waterford accent. It was easier to imagine him leaning over a gate into a field on a summer's evening than manning a ship's wheel. 'They're the first true words you've spoken, Roche, and they're only half true. Mossy told the other half of Wexford too, in public houses you're too young to set foot inside.'

Mr Tierney shifted position with a defensive shrug. 'I may as well spin the odd yarn, Captain, seeing as every time we set sail there's a fair chance I'll never get to tell another one. I enjoy a pint, but I've never missed a day's work and no Captain has ever stamped anything less than VG in my Discharge Book when I sign off any ship. When we sail at dawn I'll be present and sober, even if my stomach might need the sort of breakfast young Roche has been helping to serve up for the seminarians in St Patrick's College.'

The Captain's patience seemed on the verge of being tested. 'That's enough guff, Mossy,' he said quietly. 'I've paperwork to finish for the Staffords. When we catch the dawn tide, this lad will be safety tucked up in his bed.' He picked up a pen before addressing me. 'Go home, son. This ship is no place for children. Nobody's saying you're not brave, but nobody knows the meaning of fear until they're at sea and U-boat surfaces and starts to circle them. Do you know how many Irish boats we've lost in this war?'

'A goodly number, Sir.'

'The *Leukos* off Donegal: eleven dead. The *Kerry Head* off Cape Clear: twelve dead. The *Ardmore* off the south coast: all twenty-four crew lost. The *Isolda* sunk within sight of Wexford: six dead. Eleven crew from the *Clonlara*, lost on the same treacherous stretch of the Atlantic where thirty-three souls from the *Irish Pine* now lie. The *Kyleclare*, sunk without trace last February: eighteen crewmen scattered on the ocean floor. I don't know what tales Mossy filled your head with, but can you imagine such a death?'

'I only know about the *Kyleclare*, Sir. Every night when I close my eyes I imagine bodies trapped in the wheelhouse. It's all I think about, though I try to block out such thoughts.' I could feel my cheeks burn and it felt odd to be confessing something to a stranger that I had never even told my mother. She had enough grief without the burden of my sorrow. But often at night, when I told Eamonn and Tony that I would sleep upside-down to give their heads more space on the pillow, in truth it was so that they wouldn't see my tears when I cried silently, imagining my father's corpse after months beneath the waves. Captain Donovan studied me carefully.

'Why makes you think about the *Kyleclare*?'

'My father was lost on it.'

The Captain rose and put out his hand to shake mine. 'I'm truly sorry for your troubles. What was his name?'

'Able Seaman Sean Roche, Sir.'

Captain Donovan nodded. 'I never sailed with him, but I always heard his name mentioned with respect. How is your mother coping?'

'She has good neighbours, Sir, Mr Tierney among them. I didn't mean to get him into trouble. Good neighbours are all she has.'

'She has a fine son.'

'She has three sons and a daughter. My brothers are twelve and ten. Lily is only seven. The nuns wanted to take her but my mother won't let them. I'm the man of the house now, Sir.'

He returned to his seat, shuffling papers to allow himself time to think. He looked up.

'What's your real age, Jack?'

I hesitated. 'Fourteen and a bit, Sir.'

'You seem a mature lad – God knows, you had to grow up quickly. But the sea has taken enough from your mother. Your father's death is only another reason to order you back down that gangplank and away from danger.'

'I'd sooner face any danger than walk home to face three famished faces looking up at me. I can't bear that any more, Sir.'

'You're no use to your family dead, Jack.' Captain Donovan's voice was kind. 'The priests in St Patrick's surely pay you some pittance to work in their kitchens. Knowing your circumstances, they must let you bring home leftover food.'

'I've never worked in a kitchen, Captain. Since my father died I've walked the streets seeking work. I know the Staffords only pay the National Maritime Board rate and that's barely a pittance for a cabin boy. But Mr Tierney says the Irish government tops up the wages of every man willing to sail to Portugal by paying ten pounds a month danger money, regardless of whether you're a captain or a cabin boy.'

'They officially call it war-risk money,' the Captain said. 'It can nearly double an ordinary sailor's wage. It would more than quadruple a cabin boy's wages and shorten his life expectancy to twice that again, which explains why they're right to call it war-risk money.'

'I've good reasons at home why I should take that risk, Sir.'

My reply was respectful, but so stubborn that the atmosphere felt like a Mexican standoff. Then came the sudden sound of voices on the amidships deck, as two sets of footsteps clambered on board. The *Kerlogue* was so small that I could already smell their cigarette smoke. The Captain opened a drawer. He removed some sea charts and then found his leather wallet. He glanced at Mr Tierney.

'Did the men hereabouts have a collection for Able Seaman Roche?'

'As soon as we got word, Sir; or in poor Sean's case, once we realised that we'd never receive word. We dug deep for his widow, but most of us were digging in empty pockets.'

Captain Donovan opened his wallet. Taking out a pound note, he placed it on his desk. 'I was detained elsewhere in a lifeboat and never got to contribute. It was only sheer fluke that I got rescued and didn't share his fate. Excuse the lateness of my contribution, and please send your mother my condolences.'

What he offered was extraordinarily generous. A pound would make a big difference to my mother at Christmas. Some men who went to England were rumoured to earn up to seven pounds a week in the factories that produced munitions around the clock. But in Ireland there were farm labourers who barely got fifteen shillings a week, which was more than Pascal Brennan earned for cycling his butcher's bicycle in all kinds of weather. If I returned home tonight, having used our ration books to get fresh bread and potatoes, Eamonn and Tony and Lily would be more awestruck than if the three wise men arrived with gold, myrrh and frankincense. I knew the depth of their hunger because I shared it. But I couldn't take his money. My mother scrubbed floors in the local doctor's house. She took in washing and I often saw her sit up in the half-light, darning away despite her fingers being almost too numb with cold to work. The one thing she didn't take in was charity. Besides, while the Captain's generosity might help us through Christmas, in January I would be back walking the cold streets and searching for cinders in rubbish tips.

'I appreciate your generosity,' I said. 'But I can't be taking your money.'

Mr Tierney stared at me as if I was an inmate escaped from the County Asylum. He sounded more shocked than if he'd heard me give cheek to a cardinal. 'If the Master is good enough to offer you…'

'I didn't cross this gangplank looking for charity.' I cut across my neighbour's protestations. The two crew members had descended the ladder. I sensed them loitering in the passageway, their curiosity stoked by our voices. Captain Donovan summoned them in. I recognised the ship's cook from seeing him around the town. Beside him a ferret-like man in a cloth cap crowded in through the doorway. There was barely space for us all in the cabin.

'The last provisions are loaded, Captain,' the Cook said. 'Ernie Grogan gave me a hand to carry them up from the town.'

The ferret-faced man nodded. His accent was pure Cockney. 'If they're as heavy in my stomach as they were in that sack I won't complain.'

'Your Cabin Boy never signed back on after the RAF attack?' Captain Donovan asked.

The Cook laughed. 'That scut? The minute we docked, he took off like a scalded cat.'

Ernie Grogan chortled. 'If that dustbin lid ever visits the cinema he'll get barred for doing a jimmy riddle on his seat every time there's an explosion on screen.'

'Are you seeking a new Cabin Boy?' Captain Donovan asked the Cook. 'I've a lad here who can't cook and was never at sea.'

The Cook inspected me like a farmer examining a cow at a mart. His eyes stopped when they reached my face. 'You're a Roche, whoever you are. Are you anything to the late Sean Roche?'

'I'm his eldest son.'

The Cook nodded. 'The Reader Roche we called him: he always had his nose in a book. I sailed with him often. You have his untidy mop of hair and your granddad's eyes. The crew had a collection for poor Sean. I hope your mother got it.'

'She was deeply grateful.'

'I'd say that's all she got. Ireland's a cold country for a widow.'

'How come you took the Cook's money, yet you won't take mine?' the Captain asked. 'It's not charity when a seafarer helps a drowned shipmate's family; it's an unwritten law of the sea.'

'No disrespect, Sir, but you were never his shipmate.'

From Mr Tierney's intake of breath and the terse silence of the Cook and Mr Grogan, I sensed how all three felt that I had crossed a line. Even Captain Donovan seemed taken aback. 'God grant me patience,' he muttered. 'Are you applying to be a cabin boy or to be a Jesuit, splitting hairs about the meaning of words? What do I do with a stubborn mule like you, Roche?'

'Give me a job as a cabin boy, Sir.'

The Captain glanced at the Cook, soliciting his opinion. The Cook addressed me. 'Did Sean tell you never to go to sea?'

' "Get a shop job," he'd always tell me. "Sweep the streets maybe, but don't waste your life on the ocean".'

The Cook nodded. 'I can hear Sean saying that. It's what my father told me and your granddad told Sean. Not that we paid them any heed because there's no sailor to match a Wexford sailor. That's why Wexford schools teach map-reading while Wicklow schools only teach the poor eejits how to herd sheep without falling over. I sailed with your granddad when I was a boy. He took me under his wing and introduced me to bowline knots, woodbines and cheap Spanish brandy.' He addressed the Captain. 'If you sign him on, Sir, I'll knock him into shape. The sea is in his blood. We'll have to say a Novena that cooking comes as natural to him.'

'Mossy was trying to persuade me that the boy singlehandedly ran the kitchens in St Patrick's College,' the Captain said, amused.

'They need to close the churches when Mossy Tierney steps on dry land.' Ernie Grogan interjected. 'That ducker and diver would say mass if he got the chance.'

'What would you know about mass, and you a Protestant?' Mr Tierney replied. 'The only time you ever enter a church is to test the steel chain attached to the poor box.'

'That's enough from you both,' Captain Donovan said. He looked at me. 'Our Chief Engineer, Mr Grogan, is Mossy's superior. Thankfully there's a steel-plated bulkhead between me and the engine room so I can't hear their endless bickering. I may employ you simply to keep the peace between them.'

The Cook put a hand on my shoulder. 'I'll work him hard and teach him all there is to know about cooking. He'd have learnt nothing in St Patrick's. Those seminarians all have cranky, constipated looks. Whoever makes their porridge burns the pot to blazes.' The Cook looked at the Skipper. 'Will you give him a chance, Sir?'

Captain Donovan said nothing. I sensed every man present holding his breath. Then he opened his wallet and added two red ten shilling notes to the pound note on his desk. 'This is not charity any more. Some sailors call it drawing a dead horse, but the proper term is an 'Advance Note' – some of your war-risk money paid up front after you sign the ship's articles. I'll have a contract for you at dawn. You'll need a Seaman's Identity Card with a photograph on it stamped by the police.'

'Leave that to me,' Mr Tierney said. 'A garda sergeant owes me a favour.'

The Captain pushed the banknotes towards me. 'If you sign up, you'll earn every penny. Give most of this to your mother to tide her over Christmas and buy yourself a donkey's breakfast from the balance.'

I looked at him, puzzled. 'What's a donkey's breakfast, Sir?'

Ernie Grogan addressed me for the first time. 'A sack of straw you throw on top of your bunk to have something soft to sleep on. There's no nicer feeling than dumping that blasted sack overboard after a long voyage and knowing that every flea inside it that's been biting you will soon be brown bread.' He wiped his hand on his coat and shook mine. 'Welcome on board, my old mate.'

'He's not on board yet,' Captain Donovan said. 'Sleep on your decision. If you can sleep, Jack. Be here at dawn unless you change your mind. We'll see how you fare on your maiden voyage before deciding if we keep you on. Hopefully your mother has a spare blanket of your father's to save you the expense of a new one.' He picked up his pen as a signal for us to leave, and then gave me one last look. 'I'll not be annoyed if you don't show up. I'll be partly relieved. But don't consider this Advance Note as charity if you decide against sailing. See it as a loan. A betting man would give good odds you'll never need to pay it back if a U-boat stumbles across the *Kerlogue* between here and Lisbon.'

Chapter Three

December 15, Wexford town

I TRIED NOT TO WAKE my mother as I silently got dressed the next morning. The house and the town were still in darkness. Mr Tierney had offered to buy my sack of straw and leave it on the ship. My bag was feather-light, even after I tied a rolled-up old blanket of my father's to it. I had no fear of disturbing my brothers. Once they fell asleep in an untidy tussle of limbs, it would take a Luftwaffe air raid or a hell-and-damnation sermon to wake them.

I crept into the kitchen, remembering my father's homecomings and departures. His homecomings always followed the same ritual. My mother's sixth sense was more trustworthy than any telegram. If the Staffords had employed her to stand looking out to sea she could have told them when their three ships, the *Edenvale*, the *Kerlogue* and the *Menapia,* were crossing St George's Channel. She knew in her bones when a ship was approaching, in the same way as some old men know when a harsh winter is due. Not that she ever made a show of my father by being on the quay to greet his ship. She would be too busy polishing the already spotless house and lighting a fire in our tiny parlour, into which only Da and Ma were allowed on his first night home, sitting like lovebirds, smiling together in the firelight. At some stage during his first night home Da always went down the town for a drink and we children lay awake, listening out for him coming home, not roaring drunk like Mossy Tierney, but flushed and happy.

He'd make a big pretence of having forgotten our treats, but we knew that he had barley sugar or lucky bags in his pockets, with Ma scolding him for letting us jump out of bed to take turns at being swung in his arms. But she would be laughing too, thrilled to see him safely home. His leave-takings were always quieter, they happened when we children were still asleep. But sometimes if their whispers woke me, I'd be allowed to get dressed and walk silently beside him, halfway down the town so that I would be the last person to wave him off to sea.

I hadn't told my mother the full size of the Advance Note Captain Donovan paid me. I had merely pressed the solitary pound note into her palm last night, shocked at how chaffed her shin felt after all those hours of scrubbing other people's clothes. She had accepted the money quietly, deeply appreciative but aware of the cost that it might come at. I intended to bring ten shillings spending money with me, but now I placed the other ten shilling note on the oilskin cloth on the kitchen table to surprise her, in the same way I remembered my father sometimes leaving extra money for her.

I crept about the house like a burglar, though I suspected that she was probably awake. I don't think she had known a proper night's sleep since that day the first rumours about the *Kyleclare*'s disappearance were whispered down every laneway in Wexford, with people initially reluctant to say too much, as if the mere fact of discussing the ship's disappearance aloud would seal the fate of those missing sailors.

Nine months ago it was Ellie Coady who broke this news to me. Everyone in Green Street knew that I was soft on Ellie Coady. We had been inseparable when growing up; there was nowhere within walking distance of Wexford town that we hadn't explored together on summer evenings. But over the past year Ellie had changed – not in any bad way but in a way that showed she was no longer a tomboy and instead a young woman who could turn heads anywhere. The changes occurring within our bodies made us suddenly cautious around each other. I had become less sure of what to say to her, or at least unable to tell her the words I desperately longed to say until I was alone in my bedroom. Then they always came to me in a rush, with only a picture of St Anthony on the wall to hear them.

I had no idea that anything was wrong until I saw Ellie waiting for me outside my school gate last February. I was almost swept past in a ruck of boys before I realised that she was there. I remember my surprise at her presence, knowing she must have needed to race from the girls' school to arrive on time. Her unexpected presence, without a smile or greeting, made me deeply worried. As we walked in an awkward silence among the jostling boys, I was unsure as to why she was present and grew too scared to ask. Then gradually I realised that her silence was not actually silence: it was her way of breaking bad news, of allowing my mind sufficient time to grasp the only possible reason why she would publicly wait at my school gate. Halfway up Green Street she took my hand suddenly. Her grip was strong as we passed her house and reached my front door. Then she spoke for the first time: 'When you go in, you need to stay strong for your mother.'

In the nine months since then I had tried to stay strong. Now the only way to be strong for my mother was to leave quietly without a fuss, so she would not have to relive the ritual of cooking breakfast, like she always did for my father, uncertain if she would ever see him again. If nothing else, my absence might hopefully give her one more ration book to play with for a time. I could not risk peeking in at Lily for one last look because she slept with my mother in the second bedroom.

I touched every familiar item in the kitchen, trying to store up the feel of home. Then I opened the front door silently and did not look back as I stepped onto the deserted street. The night – it still felt like night – was freezing: a white frost coated the street. A light shone in the Tierney house, but otherwise the town was in darkness. I breathed in the silence, remembering how my father once told me there was never silence on a ship, with the throbbing engine and waves breaking against the bow.

I started to walk, but only got a few yards to where Green Street joined Devereux Villas when a figure stepped forward from where she had been sheltering in one of the doorways. To my surprise, it was Ellie. She looked frozen. Her coat was buttoned up to the neck and she wore a headscarf against the cold, or maybe so that nobody would recognise her. The scarf gave her the appearance of an adult, but the way that she shivered, her bare legs blue with cold, made her seem like a child. I stopped, unsure of why she was there.

'You're sailing on the *Kerlogue*,' she said.

'Who told you that?'

'Mossy Tierney is telling half of Wexford how he tricked the new captain into taking you on. You kept your leave-taking very quiet.'

'I only got the job yesterday.'

'It's a big risk you're taking.'

'Maybe I'm not brave enough to stick around and watch Ma try to celebrate Christmas for the sake of the others, when I know she'd sooner be left alone to cry in peace in the parlour.'

'We'll all call in and bring small gifts that won't wound her pride. She must have found it hard this morning, seeing another man off to sea.'

This was the first time anyone had referred to me as a man. I knew that Ellie had used this word deliberately. It was a long way from the terms of abuse she used to tease me with when we were inseparable and running wild. Back then, people teased us about being 'an item', when we didn't properly understand words like 'boyfriend' and 'girlfriend'. The fact that we understood them now had caused this awkwardness between us. It had been up to me to take things to the next step, but a boy without the jangle of coins in his pocket can't take a girl anywhere. I had my pride. I couldn't ask her to simply go traipsing up and down Main Street beside me some evening with every corner boy wolf-whistling after her. I had avoided her since my father's death because I couldn't even afford to pay for her into the cheapest seats in the Cinema Palace.

'I didn't wake Ma,' I said quietly. 'I remember her making breakfast for Da, with the pair of them barely saying anything because they hated being separated. I didn't want her to have to relive that.'

'So you crept off without a word to anyone?'

'I left money on the table, enough to see her through Christmas.'

'And you planned to leave without saying goodbye to me?'

I couldn't stop the hurt from entering my voice. 'I saw you go to the Cinema Palace last week with Pascal Brennan. You had your best frock on.'

Ellie couldn't prevent herself blushing. 'How would you know if that's my best frock?'

'It was the blue polka-dot one you look nicest in. I watched from my bedroom when Pascal called for you, scrubbed to the nines.'

Her voice regained its old teasing quality. 'If you were in your bedroom, how do you know I went into the Cinema Place? Did you follow us down the town?'

'Maybe I just happened to be walking that way.'

'Maybe you're a spy for Father O'Gorman. From his sermons you'd swear that Sodom and Gomorrah are located in the back row of the Cinema Palace.'

'What row did you sit in?'

'Are you jealous?'

'I am not.' This was only a half lie: jealousy was too soft a term for the humiliation I had felt when watching Pascal swagger down Green Street beside her.

'I barely had time to notice the row number. I don't consider that as my best frock any more; I can't wear it without remembering Pascal Brennan's fingers. He was like an octopus. I was barely finished slapping one hand away before the other one came at me in the darkness. I had a battle to still have my frock on before the newsreels ended.'

'What was the film like?' I tried to sound calm when I really wanted to wait outside Synnott's Butcher's and punch Brennan when he arrived for work.

'I can't tell you a thing about it,' Ellie confessed.

'You mean you were too otherwise engaged to watch it?'

Ellie gave me a look of true anger. 'I mean no such thing. You've been crankier than a bag of cats this past year, Jack Roche. I mean that I slapped Pascal Brennan's face so hard I probably burst open half his pimples, and the audience thought there had been a gunshot. I left him sitting alone with a slapped face, and I've a good mind to give you an even harder slap now.'

'What have I done?'

'Damn all for over a year now, and that's the problem. Who else can I go to the pictures with, when the boy who used to be my best friend passes me on the street with barely a glance?'

'I've no money to bring you to the pictures.'

'And what does it cost to walk out the Estuary Road as far as Ferrycarrig any evening?'

'You deserve better than that.'

'I deserve better than you, you thick lump.' She punched my chest. 'You've the courage to sail to Lisbon, but not to walk through the Faythe with a girl. What are you more afraid of, a German torpedo or being seen with me?'

'I've a boat to catch,' I said gruffly, annoyed with myself because, as usual, I couldn't find the words for what I wanted to say. 'Are you out here in the cold just to mock me?'

Ellie Coady glanced down the slope of Green Street to where it turned into Thomas Street and Bride Street, leading to the quay where that tiny boat waited.

'I'm here because I know you inside out,' she said. 'I knew you wouldn't wake your mother, and someone has to see you off on your first voyage. I remember years ago I woke early one morning. Your father was going off to sea. He walked down the street with nobody around but you, holding his hand. I remember thinking the sea must be a great adventure but a lonesome place. You walked him to the corner and stood waving until he was out of sight, as if ... I don't know ... as if seeing him off was your way to ward off bad luck. That moment always stayed with me. So maybe I just happen to be walking this way, but I'll walk as far as the quays if you'd like my company.'

'I'd like that more than anything on earth,' I said, genuinely touched.

Ellie took off her scarf and shook her hair loose. She would feel even colder, but I knew she wanted to look her best for me. There wasn't a sound in the town as we walked down to where Bride Street joined the narrow meandering South Main Street. My footsteps were loud, but I felt that my heart beat even louder.

'Are you scared?' she asked.

'Yes.'

'I'm scared too, and I'm not even the one sailing.'

'I'll bring you back something nice,' I promised. 'American ships dock in Lisbon. Mr Tierney says you can buy anything, even nylon stockings, from US sailors. Would you like a pair of nylon stockings?'

'I'd like you to come home safe to me; that's what I'd like.'

We heard footsteps behind us. I glanced back. It was Mr Tierney nursing a sore head and carrying a kitbag. Ellie took my hand and drew me into a lane to our right, off Main Street, so that Mr Tierney wouldn't see us. I put my bag down at our feet. I couldn't tell if Mr Tierney saw us, but if he did he walked past and pretended he hadn't noticed. This was unlike my neighbour, who rarely resisted a chance to tease anyone. But then I realised that we weren't just neighbours now: we were shipmates, and one shipmate never ratted out another. Ellie had not released my hand. It was so dark in the laneway that I couldn't see her until I felt her lips against mine and she kissed me. For the first few seconds I was too shocked to kiss her back, and then I kissed her deeply, our tongues entwined, eager and deep, until she stepped away.

'You're the biggest eejit on earth, Jack Roche, but you're my eejit. You could have kissed me like that months ago.' She brought my fingers up to her face and kissed them softly. 'But don't get notions that you could have taken too many farther liberties.'

She went to lead me out of the laneway, but we had to step back into the shadows because hurried footsteps were returning up Main Street. A hand reached down to pick up my bag from the laneway entrance. Was my bag being stolen before I even reached the ship? But after a moment the same hand replaced my bag in the exact spot and Mr Tierney – it could only be him – quickly walked away, leaving Ellie with her face pressed against my coat to suppress her giggles. We held each other tight and I stroked her hair. I had never felt anything so soft. Her breasts pressed against me as she leaned up to give me one last kiss. But it was a quick, affectionate peck, like a sister would give. 'We need to hurry or you'll miss the tide,' she said. 'I needn't worry about you keeping your hands off foreign girls. If you're sailing with Mossy Tierney, you'll be doing well just to keep your hands on your own luggage.'

Picking up my bag, I gasped at its extra weight. Mr Tierney had untied my father's blanket and taken it with him, but despite this my bag felt three times heavier. I had no time to ponder this mystery: I wanted to savour every stolen second with Ellie. We walked down the deserted Main Street and turned onto Cinema Lane, every step bringing us closer to saying farewell. When we reached the quays, the town was still in darkness apart from a few lights shining on board the *Kerlogue*. It was the only vessel tied up in the quay now and looked smaller than yesterday, suited only for shunting freight along the Irish coast. Ellie had not released my hand since we left the lane. I loved the warmth of her fingers, even if it brought back memories of being allowed to walk at dawn with my father. Now it was my turn to confront that tough seafaring world which had awaited him. I felt a palpable terror at the sight of the ship. Ellie stopped a hundred yards from the gangplank. We were still hidden by shadows on the far side of the quay. She seemed reluctant to venture closer, and yet equally as reluctant to release my hand as I was to let go of hers. I might never have crossed those cobbles if she had not given me the courage.

'Away with you, you big eejit,' she coaxed softly. 'You've promised me a pair of nylon stockings. They'll not swim here from Lisbon on their own.'

'You'll get your stockings, I promise.'

'Make me a second promise: promise you'll come home safe.'

I risked one final kiss; this one in haste because we were unsure if we could be seen by the crewman at work. Ellie's lips were a world that I was only discovering now when about to sail into the unknown. It felt cruel to have such pleasure quickly taken away from me. Ellie gave me a gentle push. I was halfway across the quay when she called out, half in jest and yet deadly serious, 'If you keep your two promises, then I'll make you a promise. The first time I wear those American nylon stockings, I promise to let you watch me put them on.'

I wanted to wave to her but felt too self-conscious – the sailors up on deck had noticed me approach the ship. They were hard at work, but it was silent work. One nodded to me in a muted greeting. When they looked down at their tasks I turned to wave to Ellie but it was so dark that I couldn't tell if she was still there. I climbed the gangplank. Mr Tierney appeared, giving explanation for his behaviour on Main Street. He just muttered: 'I left your blanket folded on your sack of straw. Go down and dump your bag beside it.'

Captain Donovan emerged from the wheelhouse as I was about to descend the ladder. He was dressed in uniform with his cap on, looking every inch a ship's officer. He nodded down at me in greeting.

'I half hoped you wouldn't show up, Jack. Dump your bag and then report to the Cook: he'll show you your duties. After we sail I'll need you to formerly sign on.'

I descended the steep ladder to the crew's quarters. Four bunks were crammed into each tiny cabin. The officers' cabins were farther down the small passageway. I recognised my father's old blanket on one long sack of straw and placed my heavy bag beside it. Two crewmen moved about in the small cabin I would be sharing. Neither spoke, and I was too shy to address them. I had expected the ship to ring with the banter I always heard from sailors when I passed an open pub doorway. But each man on board this morning seemed preoccupied with his private thoughts. I entered the galley and even the Cook barely greeted me. He simply assigned me a task.

Twenty minutes later the engine started up and I had my first foretaste of the nausea to come as I felt the ship's initial slow movements. Maybe the Cook was worried that I might already be overcome by seasickness down there in the ship's airless depths, or maybe he sensed that I needed to take one last look at the town I had never spent a night away from. But for whatever reason, he told me to go back up on deck. On the way I decided to fetch my thicker jumper from my bag, and found that it had already shed its mysterious additional weight.

I climbed the ladder to stand by the scuppers as the ship slowly pulled away from the deserted quay. The odd light was coming on around the town, people stirring and starting their day's work. Nobody else on deck bothered to look back. Only after we travelled a short distance did I realise that the quay was not deserted. Ellie Coady had remained there waiting all this time. Now that the ship was moving she crossed the train tracks to stand at the bollard where the *Kerlogue* had been moored. I raised my hand and waved, but she did not wave back. She just stood watching, becoming smaller and smaller, until eventually I no longer knew if I could still see her or if she had just become a speck shimmering in my imagination. All I knew for certain was that if I could survive whatever this voyage entailed, then when I arrived home I would finally know the right words to say to her, and I would not be afraid to utter them.

Chapter Four

December 15, St George's Channel

WHEN I SAY THAT THE first leg of our voyage, which took us to Cardiff, wasn't bad, I mean that it didn't kill me entirely. As my father and grandfather had spent decades between them at sea, I always presumed that it would be in my blood. But we were barely two nautical miles beyond Wexford when my illusions were shattered by the first serious lurch of our heavily loaded coaster in a heavy swell. Down in the hot galley, with lids bolted down on the simmering pots to stop them flying off, the Cook took one look at my sickly face and ordered me to run for the ladder that led up on deck.

'This soup tastes bad enough without you vomiting into it,' he said. I was halfway down the swaying passageway when he shouted after me: 'And don't go blaming my cooking, seeing as you've barely tasted it yet.'

I lost track of how many similar lurching runs I made during my first day at sea. In my shame at being surrounded by ten sea-hardened men, the only thing I could take any pride in was how I always made it up the ladder and into the freezing rain before vomiting over the side. My hands would grip the slippery gunnel for balance, especially when heavier squalls pounded the ship. I tried not to look down at the waves as I threw up. After a while I could only retch, having nothing left in my stomach. I knew it was pointless to eat when I couldn't hold down a morsel.

There was something dangerous about those ceaseless swirling waves, especially with my legs so weak that I was at risk of toppling overboard. Still, it was hard not to stare down when I had little else to focus on apart from a grey horizon that became claustrophobic when heavy rain clouds reduced visibility and made me feel utterly hemmed in. We seemed alone in the midst of the St George's Channel, but were we? I had no idea what might lurk in the depths beneath us. Whirling shoals of mackerel and whiting? Rusted hulls of trawlers strewn on the ocean bed? U-boats ready to surface, or not bothering to surface, before unleashing a torpedo to send us to our deaths? I had time to ponder such macabre thoughts because of how often I needed to abandon my work in the galley and retch into the sea.

By and large, my new crewmates left me alone in my private purgatory up on deck. They were busy at their own tasks, but I slowly realised that what I first mistook as indifference was actually a matter of acceptance. Every man had endured a similar ordeal on his maiden voyage: an inescapable rite of initiation. Nobody could help me through it, no more than anyone can help a sobering-up drunk through the *delirium tremens* – or 'the shakes' as Mr Tierney called them.

The *Kerlogue* could manage a top speed of nine knots when the engine was flat out at flank. But in the engine room, Ernie Grogan and Mr Tierney were still cautiously testing each piece of equipment on this, the ship's first outing since being pummelled by that RAF attack. Neither man had a good word to say about the other, but I noticed how Mr Tierney angrily rebuked any crewmate who dared to criticise his fellow engineer, and Ernie Grogan did likewise. They bickered like an old married couple but were dependent on each other's skills. Our engine needed constant coaxing because it was being forced to undertake far more hazardous voyages than it was originally built for. On my first visit to the engine room the two men referred to each instrument as if it possessed a distinct temperamental personality that only they understood. I realised why the crew nicknamed their tiny kingdom 'The Harem', as if the two engineers were sultans, jealously guarding a trove of concubines which only they – and the more junior Third Engineer, Gary O'Leary – were allowed to touch.

As night settled in – the whole world seemingly in darkness apart from our identifying lights on deck – I realised that every man on board was allowing me space to grow accustomed to this constant swaying motion. Yet they each found time to quietly pause beside me on deck and touch my shoulder or murmur words of encouragement cloaked within a throwaway remark. When Captain Donovan, making his final round of the night, ordered me to go down and try to sleep, I did not mind being forced to share a cramped cabin with three men. After all, I had never slept on my own, but always shared a bed with my younger brothers spooned in around me. But it felt strange to sleep among adult strangers. Not that I got much sleep. I had nothing left in my stomach, but lying on that prickly sack of straw increased my feelings of nausea. The tired men fell asleep quickly, the oldest of them, Myles Foley, snoring intensely. But although exhaustion made me drift in and out of consciousness, I was perpetually jolted awake by a lurch of the ship or by a fear of getting sick and choking on my vomit.

It was freezing in the cabin, yet I kicked off my father's blanket, my forehead dripping with cold sweat. I felt fatigued and dizzy. The longer I lay there, the more claustrophobic the cabin became. Had my father been sleeping like this when a German torpedo ripped through the *Kyleclare*? Had he managed to reach the deck, or was his body still trapped in his cabin at the bottom of the Atlantic? This thought caused me such panic that I couldn't lie there any longer. Dressing quietly, I slipped up to the deck, scared that I wouldn't reach the gunnel in time. I gripped the rail on the forecastle deck and retched, feeling utterly nauseous. Lifting my eyes, I saw, in the first stirring of dawn, the distant unlit coast of Wales and heard a knocking on glass. Our helmsman, Thomas Bergin, beckoned me to join him in the wheelhouse. I was friendly with Thomas's son, who played hurling for Buffer's Alley. Thomas saw that I felt too sick to talk, so he took the lead by pointing to our left.

'Before this war we'd have glimpsed the lights of Milford Haven hours ago,' he said. 'Do you believe in God, Jack?'

I nodded feebly.

'If you're bad in this life, God won't send you to purgatory; he'll make you spend a wet weekend in Milford Haven. The only things open there on Sundays are churches. By Sunday evening it's a toss-up as to whether boredom or thirst will kill you first.' Anxious to distract me from feeling seasick, he gestured for me to take the wheel. 'Stand there and you can tell your children you steered a ship into the mouth of the Bristol Channel.'

I grasped the heavy wooden wheel with childish pleasure. 'Where's Bristol?' I asked, so caught up in holding the wooden spokes that I momentarily forgot my seasickness.

Thomas Bergin laughed. 'A long way off. The closest you'll get to England on this trip will be a glimpse of Weston-super-Mare, across the channel from Cardiff. Weston-Super-Mare is so posh that the seagulls wear spats and perch on the cliffs in bowler hats and monocles.'

I laughed at this, but then Thomas Bergin's tone changed. 'Give me back that wheel. I don't mind being shipwrecked, but I'll not be bawled out by a Dublin atheist who thinks himself more of a toff than a Weston-super-Mare seagull.' He nodded towards where Mr Walton – the Second Officer – had appeared on deck. 'Walton's on his dawn prowl. There's no sailor more disgruntled than a man qualified to be a skipper who isn't one.'

'What are Mr Walton's duties?' I asked.

Thomas Bergin shrugged. 'The Second Officer sticks pins in a voodoo doll, hoping that the Captain or Chief Officer get sick so he can get a proper job. Walton isn't the worst, behind his gruffness. I sailed under him when he was a skipper. He surely never thought he'd end up as Second Officer. But he has a hard cross to bear or he wouldn't be reduced to working like this. Still, you'd best step out of this wheelhouse. Just make sure the seagulls don't carry off your scrawny carcass, because you look more dead than alive.'

I was glad to slip out in the freezing dawn air. Mr Walton strode towards me, impervious to the heavy swell. I gingerly reached the gunnel, terrified in case I threw up in his presence. I didn't know his age, but – with the exception of Myles Foley – Mr Walton looked older than everyone else on board. With his white beard and weather-beaten face, Myles Foley looked every inch a sailor, but Mr Walton's confident bearing reminded me of a bank manager or Nicholas Bolger, Wexford's town clerk, crossing the Bullring Square on important municipal business. I gazed towards the grey Welsh coast, unsure if I was meant to address the officer or wait until he condescended to speak first. Mr Walton took several strides past me before he stopped.

'Stomach still queasy, Roche?'

'Yes, Mr Walton, Sir. That's why I came up on deck, Sir.'

He nodded. 'The men in your cabin need their sleep. Every man here has his job to do.' His tone suggested that he didn't include me in their ranks; I was being indulged because the Captain had employed me out of ill-considered kindness. Mr Walton's Dublin accent sounded as out of place as Ernie Grogan's cockney tones among the Wexford and Waterford voices on board. It sounded posher than the other Dubliner on board: Mr Valentine, the replacement for the previous Chief Officer who had been crippled during the RAF attack.

'I'm sure I'll feel better today, Sir.'

He made no reply, but crossed from port to starboard, leaving me unsure if our conversation had concluded. I followed but remained at a respectful distance. He stared out towards the sea. I was unsure if he remained aware of my presence, but then he spoke.

'I left my spectacles in the cabin I share with Mr Valentine. Maybe your young eyes can spy the cliffs.'

'What cliffs, Sir?'

Mr Walton didn't turn. 'We'll pass Lundy Island soon, Roche, with seabirds nesting on every cliff. On misty days you hear Lundy before you see it. It's just a spit of rock at the mouth of the bay, but any Bristol seadog I sailed with always regarded it as his first glimpse of home. On long voyages they had a saying: "Lundy Island at your head, pack your bag and dump your bed".'

He looked down at the waves splashing against the hull. 'When Lundy Island came into view you'd see the sea littered with old straw sacks. You'd hear sailors laughing as they tried to make themselves look presentable to wives or sweethearts they hadn't seen for months. Hardened sailors giddy at the thoughts of simply seeing their homes again.' Mr Walton paused. 'There's no better feeling than the feel of going home.'

His tone was so wistful that the words seemed spoken to himself. Yet I felt that some response was required, though I was out of my depth.

'Did you always intend to go to sea, Sir?'

He turned to look at me. 'My father and grandfather worked all their lives in the Guinness Brewery in Dublin. It was taken for granted that I'd follow them, and taken for granted too that I'd never get promoted beyond a certain point because I was Catholic. It didn't matter if I was a genius or a halfwit: that's how Guinness is run. I started working there aged fifteen. One morning I was summoned to a book-lined office where a company director sat in front of a huge ledger. He never looked up or acknowledged my existence. I was just told that I should turn a page every time he nodded. I did this for four days until he finished examining whatever figures he was auditing. Then he looked up for the first time. But he didn't really look at me, he looked through me. I was waiting for him to say "thank you" or "you may leave", but he just studied me in bewilderment. Then I realised why he was puzzled: he couldn't understand why I was still standing there when he had no farther use of me. Next day I walked along the Dublin quays until I found a sea captain who was a crewman short. I worked my passage for nothing, just to learn the ropes: a dog-rough voyage to La Rochelle in France. But whenever I completed a task well the Skipper praised me and when I made a mistake he cursed me in language you wouldn't wish your worst enemy to hear. But I welcomed his curses as much as his praise, because even when cursing me as a greenhorn he'd the human decency to acknowledge that I existed. It broke my father's heart. He thought I was doing well in Guinness. In all his decades there, he'd never been allowed up into an office to turn pages in a ledger.'

'What would you be now if you'd stayed in Guinness?' I asked.

'The same cowed man my father became. I was in the Chilean port of Valparaiso when news reached me of his death. I don't know if he applied for permission to die, but I know Guinness paid for the telegram. Guinness treats its employees well: provided they tug their forelocks and know their place.'

'Have you a family, Sir?' When I was nervous I always blurted out stupid questions. 'Do you miss being at home?'

He ignored my question. 'You're Jack Roche's son, aren't you? Did your father never tell you not to stick your nose into an officer's business?'

'Did you know my father, Sir? He and I never talked about my going to sea.'

He looked away. 'It's Captain Donovan's business who he signs on.'

'I'll do the best I can, Sir.'

'Did I say you wouldn't?'

'No, Sir.'

'Did your father ever mention my name to you?'

'No, Sir.'

'Are you sure?'

'I am, Sir. I don't know you from a hole in the ground, Sir.'

He glanced at me briefly before turned on his heel. 'You're Roche's son all right. It's a pity you didn't inherit your *paterfamilias*'s sea legs when you obviously inherited his impertinence.'

I watched him descend the ladder, looking more haughty and dismissive than any Guinness director could. Thomas Bergin tapped on the wheelhouse window to beckon me inside.

'What did you say to make Walton stomp off?' he asked when I closed the door.

'I didn't know what to say to him. He wound up calling my da some name in Latin.'

Thomas Bergin whistled softly. 'It's never a good sign when Walton flashes his Latin. They say he reads a page of the dictionary every night. A half-educated man is like a half-wounded animal: you wouldn't know when he might bite. You didn't ask him for the loan of ten bob?'

'I did not,' I said indignantly. 'I asked if he missed his family.'

Thomas Bergin shook his head in disbelief, glancing at the chart to ensure we stuck to our designated route. 'Mother of God, you've a mouth wider than the Bristol Channel. There's only two safe topics of conversation on a ship: the best lodging houses and the

47

loosest women. A sailor's home life is off limits, unless he mentions it himself. Mr Walton's daughter is seriously ill with TB. He's built her a wooden chalet at the end of their garden in Bray so she can live and most probably die at home. His neighbours don't like it – they won't let their children play in their own gardens in case they catch the illness, but at least the poor girl isn't being carted off to a huge sanatorium. Those places are like factories of death: dispensary doctors looking down their noses at waifs fading away before their eyes, and only the good nuns like my cousin to look after them.'

'How was I to know about his daughter?' I asked, mortified.

'You weren't meant to ask. You know nothing about his daughter or that the reason he walks around at this hour is because he's in constant pain with his stomach. He told the Staffords it's a gastric ulcer, but we all know it's stomach cancer. Mr Walton should be on his sickbed. But his daughter needs minding, and to keep her out of the sanatorium he needs to earn money for a doctor to make private calls. And paying a private doctor is like tossing stones into a bottomless pit. Mr Walton was on the *Kerlogue* when the RAF attacked us and it took all of his seacraft to nurse us back to port. I owe my life to that Dublin atheist. Therefore, I know nothing about his cancer and nor do you, because Captain Donovan has the decency not to ask. If he knew Mr Walton was so ill, he couldn't risk signing him on, and Mr Walton is the best navigator you'll ever sail with. Now you know everything about him and you know nothing: do you catch my drift?'

I nodded.

'Good man. A crew needs to rub along together, especially on a boat that's barely the length of a dozen Model T Ford cars parked bumper to bumper. That's why nobody pays any heed to your vomiting: it's no one's business but your own. Now off you go, and learn to keep your eyes peeled for the things you're meant to see and for the things you're meant to turn a blind eye to.'

Chapter Five

December 16, Bristol Channel

IN THE DAWN LIGHT I gingerly made my way down to where the Cook was preparing the porridge, though in truth I was not much help. In that swaying galley I was clumsier than an Eskimo in snowshoes trying to dance the Charleston. The crew arrived in relays, subdued at this early hour. There was little talk. The men seemed more interested in savouring their first Woodbine of the morning than in the meagre breakfast. But any serenity was broken when Ernie Grogan and Mr Tierney briefly entrusted the engine room to the Third Engineer. They both stirred porridge around their plates with equal lack of interest. Ernie Grogan lit up a Woodbine and inhaled deeply before unleashing such a torrent of coughing that he nearly filled the spittoon at his feet with clots of grccn phlcgm. Mr Tierney swallowed a hearty spoonful of porridge, disdaining to look at his fellow engineer as he spoke.

'May I merely observe that, by mutual agreement, the second half of that fag belongs to me?'

Ernie Grogan stopped coughing long enough to address a reply to the row of tightly secured pots on the wall.

'And may I observe that I haven't finished smoking the blasted first half yet?'

49

Mr Tierney looked at him directly. 'And if you're greedy enough to take another drag, you'll cough up your entire innards and I'll need to prise whatever remains of my fag from between the fingers of a corpse.'

Ernie Grogan picked up the spittoon and placed it on the table beside his porridge. 'You're talking through your bottle and glass as usual. That's honest phlegm that any Christian should be allowed to cough up in peace in the morning, to leave a bit of space in his lungs for God's fresh air.'

This time the Cook intervened. 'I don't care if it's caviar that the Tsar of Russia was saving for Christmas before his plans got rudely interrupted by a Bolshevik's bullet. Get that spittoon off my table. Go and feed your phlegm to the seagulls.'

'I'm going topside for a gypsy's kiss.' Ernie Grogan rose and lifted up the spittoon. 'This is worse than trying to have a cup of rosie with the Spanish Inquisition.'

'Not so fast.' Mr Tierney deftly plucked the cigarette from Ernie Grogan's fingers. 'I never met a seagull who smoked and this isn't the time to be teaching the poor creatures bad habits.' He savoured a long drag, which resulted in an equally violent fit of coughing, and directed a voluminous glob of phlegm into his porridge. 'No disrespect to the chef,' he said, 'but that cockney scoundrel made off with the only spittoon. Did you ever have the misfortune to sail with a more contrary blowhard?'

The Cook angrily picked up Mr Tierney's bowl of soiled porridge. 'I did not,' he said. 'But I've the double misfortune of having to sail with his twin.'

Mr Tierney stood up. 'I was making a general observation,' he replied. 'I wasn't soliciting anyone's opinion about the excellence of the engineers who keep this tub afloat.'

'If you could keep us afloat a bit quicker you might both earn your keep.' The Cook emptied the bowl into the slops bucket. 'I've a good mind to get young Roche to swim on ahead to order our provisions in Cardiff. The grocer would have them stacked on the dockside by the time you bilge rats get us there.'

Mr Tierney tapped the smouldering cigarette tip against the door frame until it was extinguished. Placing the unsmoked butt behind his ear for later, he looked at me. 'Did Brother Dawson ever beat Shakespeare's *Julius Caesar* into you with his Gestapo strap?'

'No.'

'In it, Caesar tells Cassius: "I am constant as the Northern Star". That was Shakespeare summing up our Cook in one line.' Mr Tierney winked as he took his leave. 'He's a man who is as constant in his ignorance of engineering as in his ignorance of the rudiments of cooking.'

The galley door closed swiftly before the steel ladle flung by the Cook collided with it. It splattered the wall with particles of hardening porridge. I grabbed a cloth and set to work cleaning off the wall in silence. When I risked turning around, the Cook had regained his composure.

'Did you hear tell of a ship named the *Mary Celeste*, Jack?'

'My father often told me it was discovered with a full cargo on the Atlantic and no one on board after the crew mysteriously abandoned it. He used to call it the greatest seafaring mystery ever.'

The Cook pointed towards the dishes, indicating that I should wash them. 'There was no mystery. The ship's engineer was a Tierney from Wexford. His crewmates fled in a lifeboat, leaving him so busy pontificating that he never noticed they were gone.'

I stacked the dishes, careful not to use too much of the scarce hot water. 'Then how come the rescuers never found his body on board?'

'Didn't I say he was a Tierney?' The Cook added ingredients to the pot of stock he kept on the boil. 'He was so full of hot air that he self combusted.'

We both laughed, but I soon regretted this as the act of laughing set me off retching again. Racing down the passageway to climb the ladder up onto deck, I tried to vomit over the side but had nothing left to throw up. However, after taking deep breaths of freezing salty air, I felt strong enough to resume my duties in the galley. The Cook showed sufficient pity to keep me as far away from the simmering food as possible, knowing that even the sight of boiling cabbage would turn my stomach. When he could find no more tasks he sent me up on deck with an unnecessary query for our boatswain, the Dazzler Kehoe.

The Dazzler stalked every inch of the ship, responsible for supervising all tasks. He was his own man and while he listened with respect to instructions from officers, he gave the impression of looking up to no man and looking down on no man either. The Dazzler was a hard taskmaster when the ship entered port and repairs needed to be carried out. His nickname came because he ended every instruction with the words, 'and make it shine until it dazzles, lads.' While the men grumbled at times, they didn't grumble about him because he never asked a sailor to do an unnecessary task, or one he wasn't willing to help with. The Dazzler played along with the Cook's charade by inventing tasks to create the impression that I was hard at work and to keep me up in the fresh air.

All day our progress was slow as we shunted up the Bristol Channel, past Tenby and Swansea. We were the smallest vessel using the well-fortified shipping channel and given the lowest priority. We frequently had to halt to let larger vessels pass. It took us an age to pass Port Talbot with its frenzied activity on the quays there. After another lengthy delay we passed Barry Port, and I finally saw the sprawl of Cardiff in the dim late-afternoon light. The engine's slow chugging as we turned inland made my stomach worse, and I leaned on the gunnel to throw up more green bile. It was freezing on deck, and yet I broke out in a cold sweat. Shay Cullen – at twenty, the crewmate closest to my age – paused to lean alongside me.

'You're some eejit.' He used the term affectionately. 'Any lad who picks December to make his maiden voyage is not the full shilling.'

'I had my reasons.'

'Aye: no man signs on without reason. I thought I was being clever when I signed on for my first voyage during a mild September with the sea like glass.'

'You were lucky,' I said.

Shay Cullen glanced behind him to ensure that Mr Walton wasn't scrutinising us from the wheelhouse as he steered the vessel into Cardiff Bay. 'It made no difference; I was sick as a dog for days. I'd never known a noise to go through me like the throb of the ship's engine. On my third night I left my bunk when I thought the crew were asleep and settled down, wrapped in a blanket in the lifeboat. I was breaking rules, but it was the only way I could sleep, with sea air around me. I was so exhausted that I never heard the crew come up on deck. A Welsh engineer tucked a doll under my arm that he was bringing home to his daughter. The Stoker had purchased lipstick for his missus and gave me the reddest pair of lips this side of a Shanghai knocking shop. The blasted Cook even rubbed a red paste onto my checks as rouge. I saw the doll after I woke and knew some codology had gone on, but the crew kept me so busy that I never had a second to glance in a mirror until dusk.'

'What did you do?' I asked Cullen.

'I went to wash myself and I knew from the sudden silence that every man was watching me glance into the broken mirror pinned to the cabin wall. I spun around, ready to punch the first man who laughed. But not a soul looked up, every man was suddenly so engrossed in reading old newspapers – even lads who couldn't read – that all I could do was stand there, fuming. Then the Welsh Engineer said, without looking up: "If you've no farther use for the doll, my daughter would love discover it on her pillow when I get home". "I'll smash the doll over your blasted skull," I shouted, and the Stoker piped up. "Keep the lipstick you're wearing," he said. "It looks prettier on you then on my missus." That set the crew off laughing and I could only join in, knowing that it must have near killed them to rein in their laughter all day. I called them every name, but it was the first time I felt a part of them. You see, it wasn't just mischief; it was their way to look out for a crewmate. Our Captain was a sour geezer. If he'd caught me breaking regulations by sleeping in a lifeboat, he'd have blackened my discharge papers and I'd have had trouble signing on another ship. That's the way with crews: there's always some codology, a daft rite of initiation.'

This sentence scared me. It was bad enough feeling seasick without the threat of an initiation. 'Do you mean the crew will play a prank on me when I'm asleep?'

He laughed. 'We'd have our work cut out, seeing as you haven't slept a wink since leaving Wexford.' He stopped laughing and studied the concrete wharves we were slowly approaching in the dusk. 'You need no initiation after what happened to your da, God rest his soul,' he said quietly. 'My best mate drowned with him on the *Kyleclare*: Jimmy Sinnott. No man on this ship hasn't lost a friend to the Nazis and doesn't hate their guts. You can sleep sound, when you finally get to sleep. No one will lift a hand against you, even in jest. Mossy Tierney has threatened to punch the daylights out of any man who does, and Mossy has us scared witless.'

'Are you frightened he'll punch you?'

Shay Cullen moved off to resume his work. 'Are you daft? We're frightened that the lump of lard will give himself a heart attack if he starts to swing his fists. Then we'll never see a penny back from the loans he's cajoled from us all.'

I went down to the galley where a mountain of pots waited to be scrubbed. The Cook sounded more brusque, as if suggesting that it was time I found my sea legs. Although weak from lack of food, I set about each chore with as much vigour as possible, confident that at least there was nothing left in my stomach to throw up. In that cramped galley every utensil needed to be strapped with bars into its rightful place. The Cook had vouched for me when Captain Donovan seemed undecided. I obeyed his instructions, but had not yet managed to hold a proper conversation with him. My conversation with Mr Walton had ended disastrously. In school you never questioned a teacher unless you wanted the sting of a strap. With shopkeepers, I had kept my head down, knowing that Ma only sent me into some kind-hearted grocer's when too ashamed to go herself and plead for a loaf of bread on tick. I wasn't used to talking to adults and certainly not as an equal. But 'equal' was the wrong word on a ship where every man had to stick to his duties. Even if U-boats were about, the engineers could not get distracted from carrying out their jobs, despite not knowing if the terse quietude they worked in might be shattered by an explosion. My thoughts were disturbed by Mr Tierney's arrival in the galley.

'We're close to shore,' he told the Cook. 'The Harbour Master may allow us to dock or tell us to hold our position until dawn, but while there's light left we should let Jack catch his first glimpse of a foreign port.'

The Cook snorted. 'You'd swear it was Casablanca,' he said, and then relented. 'Away with you, Jack. You've every surface so spotless that it's only fair to give the Bombay runners a sporting chance.'

'What are Bombay runners?' I asked.

'Cockroaches. Now be gone before I change my mind.'

An hour before, the Welsh coast had been clearly visible. But now when I climbed up on deck the shoreline had disappeared with the onset of dusk.

'There's nothing out there,' I told Mr Tierney, who stood beside me at the gunnel.

'Trust me, Jack, there's a vast city, but the blackout is strictly imposed. Air Raid wardens patrol the streets. Woe betide any poor woman who lets a glimmer of light escape through her blackout blinds, because there's nobody looks more self-important than a retired bank manager in a tin hat.'

'No one looks more ridiculous either, strutting about like Third Officers playing at being Captains.'

Myles Foley's voice was so quiet behind us that it took us both by surprise. The old man leaned against the rail to stare at the blacked-out city.

'It must be a queer clatter of years since you first sailed into Cardiff,' Mr Tierney said.

Myles Foley chuckled. 'A bishop wouldn't even ask me that in confession.' He glanced at me. 'You and I are in the same boat, Jack lad: questions about our age are decidedly unwelcome on this trip.'

It was hard to imagine ever reaching Myles Foley's age, let alone still being at sea in fifty or even sixty years' time. Yet I sensed a generosity in his comparison: it was his way of making me feel welcome.

'It was the queerest thing to pass the port of Barry and not see a single light,' he added. 'There was a time when I'd often convince myself that I could make out the lamp shining in the front window of Mrs Boss's lodging house.' He looked at Mr Tierney. 'Did you tell young Roche about Mrs Boss?'

'Sure the lad's barely a wet day at sea.'

'We were all once barely a wet day at sea. Do you want him to spend his life sleeping in rough seamen's hostels that smell like the bowels of Hades if no one gives him the knowledge?' Myles Foley turned to me. 'If you ever get paid off a ship in Barry, Mrs Boss keeps a good lodging house on Jewel Street. She'll let you stay on tick until you sign on a new ship and can settle your slate from your Advance Note. No sailor would ever do a runner on Mrs Boss. Her house is such a home from home for sailors down on their luck that if you left her a penny short you'd have an enemy in every port. Am I saying the truth, Mossy?'

Mr Tierney nodded beside me in the gloom. 'You're saying devil the word of a lie. The sea is no place for saints, Jack, and a sailor must survive on his wits. Landlords and publicans want our money but half of them think that we're just a necessary evil: the lowest of the low. Mrs Boss judges no man by how he earns his crust. That's why no honest seafarer would ever swindle her out of a farthing.'

I was listening to them, but in truth I was barely taking the words in. Only two days out from Wexford, I was already as sick of the sea as I was by its constant motion. The world they described didn't feel like it could ever have anything to do with me. Myles Foley sensed this and leaned in close.

'You think you've only signed on for a few months to get your mother over a hump,' he said. 'But that's what we all think on our first voyage. There's no sailor who hasn't at some stage sworn never to set foot again on a ship. But the sea gets into your blood. You're barely home before you're itching to leave again.'

'He's telling the truth, Jack,' Mr Tierney observed quietly. 'You've always felt you've belonged in Wexford, haven't you?'

'I do belong there, Mr Tierney.'

He took a last drag on a cigarette stub that was almost burning his fingers and tossed it into the waves.

'What have I told you about my name?'

'It's Mossy. I keep forgetting.'

'Your pals in Wexford will be agog for tales of your travels when you get back. And you'll enjoy telling them and asking about local news until, after a few days at home, you'll discover the queerest thing: you've nothing much left to say to old friends, and they've nothing much to say to you. Once your horizons change you never fit back into a world where everyone pries over everyone else's shoulder and anyone not born in the town is regarded as a foreigner. So as they yap away you'll find yourself closing your eyes to imagine every port you ever docked in.'

'That's the God's truth,' Myles Foley agreed. 'And that's how you learn the knowledge. A sailor can't remember every street in every port, so it's vital to remember one place there where you'll feel safe.'

'Like a sanctuary.' The lights that had illuminated our deck since we left Wexford were not permitted to be lit so close to port, and so I could only see the two men in silhouette.

'That's a grand word for it,' Myles Foley murmured so appreciatively that I realised, at his age, this was how he saw this ship, no matter what danger we were sailing into.

Mr Tierney nodded. 'He has a way with words, young Jack.' He turned to me. 'Now say you were stranded in Swansea, where would you go?'

'I haven't a clue.'

'Exactly,' Myles Foley said. 'And that's why we're giving you the knowledge. Ask directions to Spanish Joe's Café on Wind Street: under the railway bridge arches. It's nothing fancy, but stranded sailors have survived for days on bowls of Spanish Joe's pea soup, with an extra hunk of bread if you look famished.'

'Spanish Joe would never turn a sailor out into the rain,' Mr Tierney agreed. 'He'd let you sit all day at the long wooden tables, listening for news of ships hiring crews. I remember sitting there, when I was barely older than you. Fancy free: no wife and kids back then – my only care was to post my mother home part of my wages before they vanished in the nearest grog house. I'd had no work for weeks when two shipping clerks burst in to announce that the *Trongate* of Whitby was taking on a crew bound for Buenos Aires and bunks were going a begging on the *Cragmore,* sailing to Halifax, Nova Scotia.'

'Which one did you take?' I asked.

'I had my mind set on sailing for Nova Scotia because it paid better when an old Arklow schooner man nudged me. "Are you daft, sonny?" he said. "I don't know what ailments you'll catch in Buenos Aires, but the only ailment you'll catch in Nova Scotia is frostbite." I sailed for Argentina on the *Trongate*.'

'They're wise men, Arklow sailors,' Myles Foley agreed.

'That's where you must be from so, a shrewd old seadog like you,' Mr Tierney probed. 'You never did tell any of us.'

Myles Foley shrugged non-committally. 'Maybe I am or maybe my father was a parish priest from Arklow. I'll tell you one thing though: I'll never forget any time I sailed to Buenos Aires.'

Mr Tierney laughed. "I had my eyes opened there in ways I never dreamt of when sitting shivering in Spanish Joe's Café.'

'What ways were those, Mossy?' I asked in all innocence.

He turned to me as a glow appeared in the twilight: the barest flicker of a lantern on the bow of a small tugboat chugging out to inspect our papers before we were steered to our allotted berth. 'In ways I swore to your mother your eyes won't get opened by some floozy in a Lisbon bar, and I'm a man of my word, Jack.'

Our ship was in darkness, but I saw one red blink of light from the wheelhouse as a signal to the approaching tug. The wheelhouse door opened. Captain Donovan appeared, dressed in full uniform.

'What's Cardiff like?' I asked, embarrassed now and anxious to change the subject.

Mr Tierney lowered his voice. 'There's Welsh squaddies fighting through the Burmese jungles tonight who find it so tough that they think they're fighting their way out of Tiger Bay on a Saturday night.'

'Where's Tiger Bay?'

'It's a strip of paradise or purgatory – depending on your purse – which separates the Bute Docks from the respectable parts of Cardiff. Red-brick streets crammed with sailors looking for ships and sailors that no captain would look at. Am I right, Myles?'

'You're not wrong,' the old man replied. 'Take a walk there, Jack, and you'll hear a babble of tongues day and night: Greek and Spanish and Norwegian and lingos from parts of Africa that I've no names for.'

'I hear there's some streets where people speak a language only spoken in Somalia and the Yemen. I don't suppose even you know much Somali, Myles?'

'Only enough to say my prayers in,' Myles Foley replied in a tone so deadpan that I couldn't tell if he was serious. He was old enough to have been a seasoned deckhand before even my grandfather went to sea. I wanted to ask him if he had ever sailed with my father and yet I was afraid to mention his name in case I was ambushed by grief here, peering towards a port that my father must have known so well.

'Cardiff has its share of Irish too,' Mr Tierney added. 'My Aunt Peggy among them. She had the sharpest tongue in Wexford until God answered our novenas and she married a dour Welshman and moved over here to inflict misery on him. Peggy used to be able to toast bread just by breathing on it, the malevolent old dragon.'

'The whole world washes up in Tiger Bay,' Myles Foley said. 'There's kips and clip joints and dosshouses and ladies of the night on street corners and dog-rough pubs that a heavyweight boxer wouldn't enter. I've often stood in back lanes there and I couldn't tell if the food being cooked was from India or China.'

'Not that you're to wander down any back lanes,' Mr Tierney warned. 'If sailors get beaten up or murdered in such places, the culprit is rarely caught because he generally sails on the next tide for Algeria or Le Tréport. The police pay little heed because there's one law for the Welsh who live in Cardiff proper and another law for the poor sods fighting for any bit of space in Tiger Bay.'

The tugboat drew up alongside us. Captain Donovan told Shay Cullen to lower an accommodation ladder, though in truth we were so laden down with agricultural produce that our deck was only a foot above the waterline. The uniformed customs' officials ignored the ladder and clambered over the gunnel to greet Captain Donovan at amidships with a salute. One boarding officer glanced sharply up in Mr Tierney's direction as if trying to recognise him in the dark. Mr Tierney turned away, leading me towards the ship's bow. I realised that Myles Foley had already slipped away into thin air at the first sight of a uniform.

'Steer clear of them fellows,' he muttered sourly. 'The three things to avoid in life are slow horses, fast women and uniformed men in oversized hats. Anyway, you'll see Tiger Bay for yourself tomorrow.'

'The way you describe it, I'm not sure I want to.'

'It's all changed since the war.'

'What's it like now?'

Mr Tierney gazed at the dark shoreline. I had never known darkness to be so foreboding. Across this stretch of water a city was hiding in blackness, every window covered. The few cars nosing about were only allowed to steer by pinpricks of light emanating from their headlights, which were covered over by cardboard. It was a city that looked to be asleep, but which never slept. It was perpetually alert for air-raid sirens.

'Tiger Bay is awash with children,' Mr Tierney said quietly.

'That sounds nice.'

'Children you see and children you don't. There are so many swarms of kids playing in bomb craters that you'd swear no child is missing at all. Then you see a parent sitting by a pile of rubble, staring into space. They're not Greek or Somali or Chinese now; they're aching bundles of grief. You've more chance of finding your father, God rest him, than those parents have of finding the children they've lost under collapsed buildings when Hitler sent his warplanes to party above the Bute Docks.' He stopped and looked at me. 'And when you see them sights, Jack, that's when you lose your innocence, and after that you'll never fit properly back into Wexford again.'

Mr Tierney made for below deck and left me alone, staring in apprehension at the brooding darkness behind which a city was trying to hide from danger.

Chapter Six

December 17, Cardiff

THE NEXT MORNING IT FELT good to be on a ship that was moored and anchored. We were the smallest vessel berthed on a wharf teeming with workers. At dawn our hold was opened and dockers set to work, unloading crates of vegetables and meat transported from Ireland. A British Ministry of Food official stood nearby, itemising every crate of rationed foodstuffs to ensure that nothing disappeared into the black market. The dockers treated him with a wary disrespect. Our hold was barely empty before more dockers set to work, preparing to refill it with three hundred and thirty tonnes of Welsh coal, bound for Lisbon's electric power plant.

This detour to Cardiff added additional danger to our voyage, but before being allowed to venture into the Bay of Biscay, Captain Donovan needed to obtain a Navicert from the British authorities. This document set out specific routing instructions for our voyage to Lisbon. If Captain Donovan deviated from them by straying into the prohibited area, 12° west in Biscay, then Allied aircrafts were permitted to sink us on sight. Our Navicert specified that the sole cargo we could carry from Cardiff was British coal, sold in advance to the Portuguese government. As Portugal was also neutral, we would in theory be carrying cargo belonging to another neutral nation, with Britain using us to continue its coal trade by proxy. The Navicert also bound Captain Donovan to a solemn oath to dock again in Wales during our homeward journey to allow British customs to inspect whatever cargo we collected in Portugal to bring back to Ireland. In return for accepting these conditions, we were allowed to bunker enough fuel to get us to Lisbon.

Captain Donovan was too busy analysing our designated route with British officials to pay any heed to the crew's comings and goings. I was up on deck, savouring the buoyancy of the ship with its empty hold, when Mr Tierney appeared behind me and glanced at the stockpile of coal waiting to be loaded. 'You don't want to be here when these dockers start work,' he said. 'Otherwise you'll find soot on parts of your body that never see the sun. The Dazzler will have you working the hoses and scrubbing brushes all day tomorrow just to get this deck shipshape again. So better stretch our legs while we can, Jack.'

Last night I had looked forward to exploring a new city, but there seemed something sinister about Cardiff in the morning light. I could spy gaping holes in the terraces of houses where bombs had landed, and felt anxious about venturing through such unfamiliar streets.

'I might rest up on the ship,' I said.

'Rest up?' Mr Tierney snorted. 'Your cheeks are a pale as a ghost's. It's fresh air you need. Lucky for you, you have your personal guide to Cardiff and I won't even charge a ha'penny for a tour of the sights.'

Mr Tierney refused to take no for an answer, yet he seemed reluctant to leave the ship alongside me. Therefore, I left first. Two harbour policemen at the end of the gangplank took my name, briefly quizzing me before I was allowed to walk past the dockers at work. I had never seen men with such muscles. Most ignored me, but one old man acknowledged me with a curt nod.

The quayside noise was overwhelming: a cacophony of steel hammers, huge cranes, whirling machinery and the shunting of steel wagons loaded with coal from the Taff Valley siding. Most vessels were ten times the size of any ship that I had ever seen docked in Wexford. I was standing there, trying to absorb the frenetic activity, when I heard a shout of pain. I turned to see that Mr Tierney had stumbled on the final slat of the gangplank and landed on the cobbles. When the harbour policemen reached down to help him up, his anguished shout turned into a string of oaths, as if they had deliberately tampered with the gangplank.

Their concern was replaced by irritation, obviously now considering him to be drunk. But how could anyone drink enough whiskey to lose their footing in the few minutes since he coaxed me to descend the gangplank? Mr Tierney's abuse became more personalised, as if the policemen were old adversaries who had done him some grievous wrong. I was tempted to walk back to act as a peace broker when I saw an object hurtling towards me through the bright winter sunshine. Instinctively I put out my hands to catch it, though the weight nearly knocked me over. It was my kitbag, as heavy again as when I had struggled to carry it on board in Wexford. Glancing up, I saw that Shay Cullen had thrown it from the stern of the *Kerlogue*. He raised a finger to his lips, cautioning me to quickly walk on.

The dockers observed Shay's actions, though none looked likely to inform the harbour policemen now sharply telling Mr Tierney to be on his way. I didn't look back at him; I knew I wasn't meant to. I didn't look at the huge ships moored nearby or at the faces of the sailors and harbour officials I passed. I knew what role I had been press-ganged into playing: I had to pretend to be an inconspicuous Cardiff cabin boy strolling home on shoreleave. But I was furious with Mr Tierney and Shay Cullen. I hadn't agreed to this and had no idea what trouble I might be in if searched. Nor had I any idea what I was smuggling out from the docks, but I knew that it was contraband destined for the black market. I nodded to two bored-looking policemen guarding the entrance to the docks, and kept walking through the small streets of Tiger Bay until Mr Tierney caught up with me.

'Slow down, Jack,' he panted. 'You're in a fierce hurry, wherever you're going.'

'I'm going to wring your bloody neck.'

'That's no way to address a neighbour,' he scolded.

I thrust the kitbag into his hands. 'You're no neighbour. You said that if Captain Donovan took me on I'd need to stand on my own feet, because the sea is a tough, unforgiving world.'

'There was devil the word of a lie in that.'

'I'm not even a shipmate, I'm just a stupid kid you think you can use as you like.'

'That remark is out of order,' he protested.

'Then tell me,' I asked. 'Is there any other shipmate you'd pull such a scam on?'

'Of course not.' he looked at me as if I was an imbecile. 'They wouldn't get past the harbour police. You've the gift of an innocent face, Jack. You could walk out of the Tower of London with the Crown Jewels and the guards would only stop you to make sure you had the bus fare home to your mother. You were our one hope. Shay Cullen, the Cook, the Dazzler and Myles Foley all have shares in that kitbag. You'll get a cut of the profits too.'

'I didn't ask for a cut,' I said angrily. 'I never asked to be involved in this crime.'

Mr Tierney rolled his eyes to heaven. 'We're not meeting Al Capone's men with machine guns. We're meeting a harmless butcher who wants to keep a few customers happy. Your kitbag contains baked hams and roast beef, not gelignite. You're a sailor now. It's time you realised that while sailors can survive shipwrecks and storms, the one thing no sailor can survive on is his wages.'

'Are you saying my da was a smuggler?'

Mr Tierney handed me the kitbag. 'Your father was a decent, honourable man. Now you've strong shoulders and my back is wrecked. Carry this and, if you're good, we'll visit Cardiff Castle. If you're bad we'll visit my dragon of an Aunt Peggy down in Blackstone Street.'

I slung the kitbag over my shoulder and Mr Tierney tousled my hair, anxious to be friends again.

Soon he had me laughing because as we walked through Tiger Bay Mr Tierney had a story about every pub we passed, even pubs no longer standing. He instinctively knew his way but I was soon lost: entire streets were missing or individual red-brick terraces had collapsed midway down narrow roads. Often the only thing left to denote where a street corner had once existed was a pile of rubble. Mr Tierney stopped at one crossroads, the buildings flattened on every side.

'A pub stood on every corner here once,' he said. 'Four rough houses. Sailors called this spot the Four Corners of Hell.'

'Was it really like hell?'

'No. But if you were left standing out on the street without money to enter one of them it was like purgatory.' He studied the devastation. 'God help the poor blighters who lived around here. It would take more than an Anderson Shelter to save them from what Hitler sent raining down.'

We walked on. Occasionally I saw a single house that was totally demolished and yet on both sides of it the houses were so untouched that there might be no bombing raid. On other streets whole terraces were buttressed up with wooden beams. Some homes were without doors and windows, yet were still occupied by families living in impossible conditions. Soon even Mr Tierney ceased telling yarns, as if overawed by the scale of the destruction. I felt increasingly uneasy – it was unlike anything I had ever imagined. I only needed to close my eyes to envisage sirens blaring at night, the terrifying noise of bombs falling; footsteps stumbling through the dark to air-raid shelters; huddled figures illuminated by flashes of explosions and the sudden spurt of flames.

This was the stuff of nightmares, but you could wake from the worst nightmare to find that life was the same. It was hard to imagine life ever being the same here. I had often imagined the horror that must occur during a blitzkrieg, but I had never envisaged its mundane aftermath, with children walking to school past rubble where classmates lay buried. What surprised me was the normality of everyone's behaviour: women with ration cards gossiped as they queued outside shops and men strolled past shattered terraces without a glance. A gang of children swarmed out from a massive bomb crater, carrying sticks as make-believe weapons in games where they chased imaginary German soldiers. I didn't like this city. I wanted to be back in the ordered world of our ship, ready to sail with a full cargo for Portugal.

Mr Tierney was starting to walk at a distance in front of me. At first I thought that I was dallying too much, but then I noticed how his stride lengthened each time mine did. He remained a constant distance ahead: near enough to ensure that I was following him but not enough to make it obvious to passers-by that we were together. This distance lengthened when we turned a corner and I noticed a police constable approaching. Mr Tierney's stride increased as he brusquely brushed past the constable. My face obviously betrayed a look of panic as the policeman stopped when we drew level. Mr Tierney never glanced back but ducked into an alleyway, leaving me on my own. The constable stared into my face and then at the kitbag on my shoulder.

'That's a heavy load, laddie. You look lost. You're not from these parts, are you?'

There was no point in pretending to be home on shore leave. I could no more attempt a Welsh accent than impersonate Humphrey Bogart.

'I'm from Wexford, Sir. I'm visiting my aunt.'

'And where does she live?'

I racked my brains to remember the road Mr Tierney had mentioned. 'Blackstone Street.'

He leaned his head sideways to better observe – or interrogate – me. 'What number?'

'I'm not rightly sure, Sir. I just know she lives there.'

'The Luftwaffe didn't leave much of Blackstone Street standing when they tried to flatten all of Cardiff. I was three days helping to pull bodies from the rubble there. What's your aunt's name?'

My mind went blank. 'I don't know, Sir.'

He glanced suspiciously at my kitbag. 'How can you not know your aunt's name? What's in the bag?'

Panic made me concoct a wild story. 'She's my mother's sister. I don't know her married name, because she ran off and married a Welsh Presbyterian. My family never mention her, because of the scandal involved. No offence if you're a Presbyterian yourself.'

'I'm a Baptist. We don't take offence easy, or suffer fools gladly.'

Having started lying, I was so nervous I couldn't stop. 'My mother asked me to bring her over a few presents from the farm, but not to tell my father. My father has a fierce temper.'

'He's a farmer, your father?'

'He owns sixty-two acres and has grazing rights leased on another five.'

He nodded, pretending to be suitably impressed. 'And how did you arrive here from Wexford?'

'On the MV *Kerlogue*, Sir. We sail again for Lisbon. My mother asked me to find her sister – it's two years since she's heard from her.'

'And what did she last hear?'

'That Peggy's husband's ship was sunk by Germans when crossing the Atlantic. It's hard on a widow, Sir.'

His tone hardened. 'How would you know in Ireland, living on the fat of the land on your father's sixty-two acres?'

'I know exactly what it's bloody well like.'

My vehemence surprised him.

'I think that's the first honest thing you've said.'

'I don't care what you think,' I replied hotly. 'I know what it's like to lose someone in this war and what it's like to go hungry too.'

He stepped back to appraise me, any cynicism stripped from his tone.

'I didn't mean to mock, laddie. We're just trying to stamp out smuggling from the docks. It's not fair on decent folk who queue for hours to know that rich folk with money needn't queue at all.' His voice grew kinder, which only made matters worse. 'Who did you lose?'

'That's my own business.' I looked away, blinking to prevent tears forming. Grief was a succession of unexpected ambushes and I had stupidly walked myself into one with my own lies. My abrupt tone didn't anger the constable.

'Did you lose a brother?' he asked quietly. 'My brother is in the Welsh Guards. His battalion is thronged with volunteers from Éire. I've no respect for your cowardly government, but I've huge respect for the Irish lads in the Welsh Guards. My brother was conscripted, but those Irish lads volunteered to fight against Hitler and get dog's abuse back in Ireland for doing so. Was it your brother you lost?'

'It's my business who I lost,' I said. 'I'm no black-market smuggler. I've presents for my aunt. If you don't believe me, take my bag down to Blackstone Street and find her yourself. Or divide it up among your chums in the police station. But I'll not stand here being made a fool of.'

I held out my kitbag, crammed with Mr Tierney's contraband. It was so heavy that I could barely hold it upright. Once the constable grasped it he would know that I'd been lying. Mr Tierney would kill me, but just then I didn't care about Mr Tierney. I hadn't publicly cried for my father since the day I donned long trousers, but my stupid cock-and-bull story about a rich father felt like a betrayal. The closer I came to tears the angrier I looked. I didn't know what trouble would lie ahead if the policeman opened my bag. I just knew that I wouldn't let him arrest me. I'd kick his shins and run, even though he knew my ship's name and the harbour police would be waiting there. But my bottled-up grief was threatening to spill out and I was too proud to be caught crying in front of a grown man.

The constable stretched out his hand – not to seize my bag but to pat my shoulder. 'I didn't mean to upset you, laddie. Is this your first voyage?'

I sighed. 'Yes, and it will probably be my last as well. My stomach can't hold any food down and I'll most likely end up at the bottom of Biscay if Hitler gets his wish. It's all a cod, me pretending to be a sailor. I get seasick just looking at a glass of water. Tramping the streets penniless was better than this.'

He glanced down the deserted street. 'I saw a man walking in front of you, with a sailor's gait and a red nose hardly acquired from sunburn. Were you in his company?'

'I've nothing to do with him.'

'What's your name?'

'Jack.'

'A word of advice, Jack: steer a wide berth from men like him.' He looked around self-consciously and undid the top button on his tunic. Reaching in, he produced a ribbon from around his neck. 'One night two years back I left my post digging out the dead and wounded in De Burgh Street to help stem the fires threatening Llandaff Cathedral. I surely looked half-dead when I paused at dawn to try to rid my lungs of smoke as I slumped on the cathedral steps. A tiny Catholic nun appeared from nowhere and put this around my neck to keep me safe. I don't share her creed but maybe that makes no difference. I just know this St Christopher medal has kept me safe since then. I hope it keeps you safe, all the way to Lisbon and back.'

He placed it around my neck and then tucked it in under my jumper so that it was hidden. 'I'm don't know if it helps with seasickness. But may it bring you fair winds and a following sea. Now, if you are really looking for Blackstone Street, swing left at the next corner and walk for half a mile. You'll recognise the street, because half of it is missing. Once the women realise there's food in your bag they'll all claim to be your Aunt Peggy. They may well even take the clothes off your back. Hang on to that St Christopher medal; it could be the only thing keeping you warm when you flee back to your ship.'

I fingered the medal through my jumper. Maybe it was foolish, but I felt safe already. 'Thank you,' I said. 'I'll wear it at all times.'

'Don't even take if off when having a wash,' he winked. 'Otherwise your red-nosed friend will swipe it to sell for drink.'

I stood watching him until he disappeared from sight. Then I walked on and was almost past the alleyway when Mr Tierney pulled me in beside him.

'Is the peeler gone?'

'He is.'

'Were you rehearsing a play by Shakespeare? I'm frozen to death waiting for you.'

'You could have come out from skulking here and helped me,' I said.

'I know his sort of narky copper. They've no time for my kind except to cause trouble and stick their noses in where they're not welcome. Did he get his greedy claws on anything in our kitbag?'

'When did it become *our* kitbag? I didn't see you claim ownership when I was being interrogated!'

Mr Tierney shifted uncomfortably. 'A few harmless questions is hardly an interrogation. We're in this together, Jack. I promised your mother I'd look after you.'

'Take this blasted bag then, and may the weight break your back.'

I pushed the kitbag towards him and angrily stepped onto the street. He followed me for a few paces, bent under the weight of the kitbag, and anxiously glancing towards where the constable had vanished. 'Jack, you don't know your way – you'll get lost entirely.'

'I'll take my chances.'

'Jack, I promised your mother…'

'Mention my mother again and I'll brain you.'

'I should never have been persuaded into taking you to sea – you're already nagging me worse than a wife.' As I walked away he called after me one last time. 'I've to meet a man in the Coldstream Pub on Dispenser Street. You can't miss it – there's nothing left standing on that corner beyond the pub and a butcher's shop next door. If you can't find your way back to the ship, ask for directions to it.'

Chapter Seven

December 17, Cardiff

I WAS PLANNING TO VISIT no pub with Mr Tierney that afternoon. I felt used and miserable and homesick and glad just to be alone for a time after spending much of the past two days confined to the ship's dark airless cabins where there was never any space to be on your own. I wanted to get the hell out of Cardiff and yet I was already dreading setting to sea again. Mr Tierney was the only crewman I knew and now I had fallen out with him. I was so lost in self-pity that I wasn't sure how far I had walked when a clod of muck struck my neck. A cheer arose. I turned to spy the gang of children I'd noticed earlier. They were playing in another bomb crater, so deep that I could barely see their muddy faces.

'A direct hit,' the tallest yelled. 'I took out a Jerry tank single-handed with one mortar.'

He was my age and had the same easy-going grin I had once possessed when playing on the streets in Wexford. The other children didn't seem unfriendly as they clambered up through a gap in the barbed wire surrounding the crater, where a sign read: 'Danger. No trespass.' The tall boy extended his hand to help a girl of around fourteen climb out. She accepted his hand, despite being so nimble-footed that she had no need of it. Once she set foot on the remnants of the pavement, she pushed him away. Some children seemed to be only seven or eight years old and had been obviously foisted onto their older siblings with instructions to mind them. I didn't know what imaginary games the young children were playing, but I sensed how this older boy and girl were playing a more adult game: the unspoken battle of risk and reward which Ellie Coady and I had played when we first became aware of being attracted to each other in new and unsettling ways.

'I'm Gareth,' the tall boy said. 'Do you want to play?' The others seemed to instinctively accept him as their leader.

'What's the game?' I asked.

'We hunt down Jerries and kill them.'

'Real Germans?'

'Are you daft? Any real Germans living in Cardiff got put in internment camps when the war started. We have to make do.'

'With what?'

Gareth gazed around as if he was a general surveying his troops. 'Sympathisers, slackers, fifth columnists: the enemy within, as they say on the wireless. Whoever we decide is German. Anyone who lives in Butetown for example; they're all half-breeds down there.'

'And anyone from Pontcanna,' the girl who had brushed away Gareth's hand added.

'Where's that?' I asked.

She jerked her head to indicate a district a few streets away. 'When the bombs dropped around here, none landed on Pontcanna. It's as if the Germans like them.'

'My aunt lives in Pontcanna,' one small boy said, indignantly. 'The German's wouldn't like her.'

'That's true, Jimmy,' the girl agreed. 'Nobody likes your aunt.'

'Go to hell, Bronwyn,' Jimmy said.

'I take it back.' The girl – Bronwyn – winked at me. 'All the sailors like her.'

The small boy angrily tried to kick out at her and Gareth held him back. 'Go easy, Jimmy,' he laughed. 'The sailors couldn't afford your aunt.' But his laughter had an edge. He had spotted Bronwyn's wink and didn't like it being directed at me: an alien who had strayed into his territory.

'Where are you from?' Gareth asked. 'And why are you hanging around here?'

'I'm a sailor,' I said, 'from Ireland.'

Bronwyn laughed. It was the damaged laugh of someone far older, someone who had already witnessed far too much in life. This made me concerned for her but also deeply cautious. 'Run back to the aunt, Jimmy, and tell her to slap on more rouge. There's a new sailor in town. And tell her to paint a seam down the back of her leg with an eyebrow pencil, to pretend she owns a decent pair of nylons.'

'Leave my aunt alone,' Jimmy said, near tears. 'She works her fingers to the bone making dresses. She has nothing to do with sailors – unlike your mum and sisters.'

'This gringo is no sailor.' Gareth stepped towards me, anxious to stop Jimmy revealing any more insights into Bronwyn's family. 'He's just a kid. What are you really doing here? Spying?'

'Why would I be spying?'

'Then have you come to gloat over your handiwork? My father says that every Irish harbour is lined with U-boats refuelling and your hotels are crammed with German commanders wolfing down steaks. You Irish are making a fortune as collaborators with the Nazis.'

'That's a goddamn lie,' I said. 'We've nothing to do with the Nazis. We barely have enough fuel to run our own trains.'

'You beg fuel from us and flog it to the Nazis at ten times the price. You don't even have a blackout at night – you leave on your street lights to give Germans pilots directions when they fly over you to bomb Liverpool. All Irishmen are Nazi lovers: my dad says so. But you've come to the wrong place. *Comprende*, Himmler?'

'My dad was killed by a Nazi U-boat,' I said angrily.

Gareth snorted, anxious to impress Bronwyn. 'Your dad is a Nazi. I bet he wears a swastika.'

'Mention my dad again and I'll burst you,' I said. But I took a step back. Every child began to advance on me, emboldened now. Instead of clods of mud, they were selecting stones from the rubble. I knew enough about street-gang warfare to sense that the moment of all-out attack had not yet arrived. I might still have a chance to talk my way out of this standoff. My dispute had nothing to do with most of these famished-looking children: the boys shivering in short flannel trousers and the girls freezing in old gabardine macs or threadbare cardigans buttoned up for warmth over short dresses. The only girl with nothing covering her dress was Bronwyn. Her dress had padded shoulders, its thin material best suited to a summer's day. It was a dress handed down after being taken in at the sides and having its hem shorted to just below the knee.

Any conflict was between Gareth and me, with Bronwyn the cause of this tension. She was the one who was really in control of the situation, savouring her sense of power in being able to make us fight. I sensed how much Gareth liked her: he eyed me with the same hatred I had felt at watching Pascal Brennan bring Ellie Coady to the pictures. Therefore I knew that the moment to run had arrived when Bronwyn smiled sweetly at me and said: 'Leave him alone, Gareth. He's so cute you'd just want to give him a *cwtch:* like a young Gary Cooper with those dove eyes.'

'Nazi spy!' I recognised the jealous cocktail of emotions in Gareth's furious shout. 'Irish collaborator!'

I ducked instinctively as the rock he hurled just missed me. The smaller children had better aim. I glanced back once, to see how Bronwyn was the only person not holding a stone. She was laughing. Yet her eyes were deadly serious: she was enjoying being able to manipulate Gareth. But there was nothing triumphant in her look – it was the wounded look of someone used to always being hurt and let down in the end. Then I had no more time to look back – the stones hurt as they struck my back, though I tried to duck as I ran. Despite two days of constant seasickness, my legs felt strong as every instinct learned on the streets of Wexford propelled me forward. I could outrun most gangs, but they had two advantages. Firstly, an unbridled hatred spurred them on. I didn't know how many had fathers fighting overseas or had seen their mothers open a front door to be handed a telegram containing bad news. Everything Gareth said about Ireland was a lie, but to them their game had turned real and they were chasing a real Nazi. Secondly, I had no idea of where I was going. If I accidently turned down a street blocked by fallen buildings, I was done for. The only thing that could save me from a serious beating at that stage would be if Bronwyn decided to farther demonstrate her powers by ordering her knight to call off his ragtag army.

I tried to run into open spaces, but this allowed them to spread out and gather more ammunition amid the bombed desolation. The street rose slightly and I became conscious of two solitary buildings standing amid the rubble, but I only realised that I had located the Coldstream Pub by fluke when I heard Mr Tierney's shout. He had emerged from the pub alongside a butcher in an apron. They had stopped to light cigarettes. The butcher also shouted at the children but made no other effort to intervene. In contrast, Mr Tierney dropped my kitbag and charged forward. When he reached me he didn't stop. 'Make for the pub,' he said as he rushed past, panting.

I ran on a few paces and then stopped to watch him. One stone caught him above the eye but he didn't flinch, even when other stones rained around him.

'Which of yous wants to challenge the boxer who boxed twelve rounds against Freddie Mills for the British Light-Heavyweight title in the King's Hall in Manchester? The first gouger I catch will feel the left hook that floored Mills in the third round.'

Most of the children stepped backwards, confronted by the sight of Mr Tierney. Only Gareth stood his ground, holding a rock which could have knocked the middle-aged sailor unconscious. It was ludicrous to imagine Mr Tierney in a boxing ring, yet he seemed to pump himself up so that he looked as if he possessed a manic strength. He was only yards from Gareth when the boy glanced back and realised that Bronwyn had disappeared. He dropped the rock and ran after the others. With the enemy scattered, Mr Tierney bent over, holding his stomach as he gasped for breath. I heard the butcher's voice behind me. He placed at my feet the kitbag which Mr Tierney had dropped.

'He'll need these bits and bobs on his travels. He might also need a stiff whiskey.'

'Did Mr Tierney ever box against Freddie Mills?' I asked.

The butcher shrugged. 'There are lies and white lies and then there's the gospel truth according to Mossy Tierney.'

The butcher disappeared back into his shop. Mr Tierney recovered his breath and walked towards me. There was a bloody gash above his eye where the rock had struck him. He didn't ask how I got into trouble, nor did he seek thanks for having saved me. We were shipmates and shipmates looked out for one another.

'Thinking about it in the pub, I realised I shouldn't have left you alone to deal with that copper on the street,' he said apologetically,

'No, you were right to stay out of sight,' I replied. 'I'd more chance of talking my way out of trouble on my own.'

He nodded, as if respecting my wisdom. 'All the same, it wasn't fair.' He gestured towards my kitbag. 'No money changed hands, you should know that. Instead we've made a wee profit through a bit of gumshaw artistry: good, honest, illegal bartering. Our wages are damn all if you take out the war-risk bonus and if we're blasted to high heaven between here and Lisbon, even that will get stopped from the exact moment the ship is lost. A sailor needs to squeeze a bit of extra profit wherever he can, and a bit of extra pleasure too. I've two pounds of proper white flour here for your mother, not the brown muck rationed out in Wexford that tastes like sawdust. It's the type of flour your father always smuggled home, like every sailor does for his family.'

I closed my eyes and recalled the smell of baking filling our house after my father arrived home on shore leave: miraculous white loaves that my mother would proudly place on the table, made from flour that I never thought to inquire about when smearing the hot bread with butter. I opened my eyes and examined Mr Tierney's face.

'You're bleeding,' I said.

He shrugged. 'I've nicked myself worse when shaving. You'll have your share of bruises tomorrow.'

I grinned. 'Sure they'll take my mind off the seasickness.'

He raised a finger to his face and took it away, surveying the amount of blood there.

'We should get that seen to,' I said.

He rubbed his hands together in the cold. 'Only a bandage will make this bleeding stop.'

'Where will we get a bandage?'

'The harbour police keep a first-aid kit in their hut. Walk a few paces behind me until I fall in their arms, mumbling about being attacked by ruffians in Tiger Bay.' He nodded for me to pick up the kitbag, now even heavier than before. 'Your crewmates would be most obliged if you could discreetly slip past them and up the gangplank when I'm so concussed that it takes all their full attention to hold me upright.'

'Is it not sore?'

Mr Tierney looked back at the Coldstream Pub. It was approaching dusk. Two barmen lowered the blackout blinds. 'One small Scotch is the best painkiller known to man.'

'We need to get back to the ship,' I said, thinking about the journey back through shattered unlit streets.

'Don't worry, Jack, I won't be two minutes.' Mr Tierney felt the lump forming above his eye and winced slightly. 'It may be Scotch whisky, but it's served in Welsh measures.'

Chapter Eight

December 21, Morning Watch, Bay of Biscay

SHAY CULLEN'S STORY ABOUT SLEEPING in a lifeboat on his maiden voyage planted the notion in my head. On the next two nights after leaving Cardiff, when I was sure that the men in my cabin were asleep, I would stop twisting on my straw sack, dress quietly and slip up into the fresh air on deck. I didn't risk lying down in our tiny lifeboat. For one thing it was too cold, though, mercifully, frost never formed on the deck as I crouched there, wrapped in my father's blanket, with an insidious chill colonising my bones until I feared that the blood circulating in my veins would freeze.

On both nights Myles Foley was on watch in the wheelhouse. Myles's sight was so bad that he could barely see beyond the prow but the crew trusted his instinctive sense for danger. I hadn't spoken to Myles since the evening we docked in Cardiff, but he paid no heed to me up on the forecastle deck beyond acknowledging my presence each night with a brief nod. He said little at the best of times and had bigger dangers than me to look out for. I associate those nights with the image of him peering ahead, wrapped in his old peacoat. Ships possessed a strict hierarchy but I was learning one unwritten rule. What I did up here at night under the gaze of this solitary helmsman would never be mentioned below deck. No ship as small as the *Kerlogue* could have private space, but

Myles Foley afforded me the unspoken privacy that all sailors sometimes need to prevent them from going crazy. If I wished to silently cry with homesickness up here at this late hour, this was my business alone.

It felt longer than six days since I had left home. I still felt constantly queasy but I no longer needed to suppress a desire to gag when helping Cook serve out greasy breakfasts. Since leaving Wales I had managed to hold down small quantities of porridge and soup. But all I was doing was subsisting: my body having passed beyond exhaustion and into survival mode. During my working day I obeyed every command of the Cook. But an inner voice also commanded me to eat just enough to keep my body active and ordered me up on deck at night to gain some rest so that I would possess enough strength to function the next day. I had learnt to stop thinking and just do whatever my survival instincts told me. There was a sheltered spot behind the wheelhouse where heat emanated from the engine throbbing below. The arc lights illuminating the deck were in shadow there and it offered respite from the chilly winds spraying salt water across the amidships deck. If not happy up here alone on deck, hunched beneath my blanket in the night air, I was happier there than down in the stuffy cabin, and I sometimes managed to black out and snatch a few hours of fragmented sleep.

On our second night after leaving Cardiff – huddled up on deck beneath the stars with my blanket tight around me – I felt in no danger of falling asleep and being discovered there at dawn. I trusted my instincts to tell me when it was time to go below deck and feign sleep on my sack of straw before the sailors who shared the suffocating stale air in my cabin began to stir.

But I must have blacked out because suddenly I looked up to discover Captain Donovan kneeling down to observe me. I had no idea how long he had been there. I felt embarrassed and scared. Even if not breaking any of the numerous regulations in my signing-on papers by being up on deck at this hour, my presence here surely proved that I did not possess the ability to be a proper sailor.

'Are you still vomiting?' the Captain asked quietly.

'No, Sir. I always feel like I want to be sick but I no longer feel that I need to be.'

'Are you sleeping?'

I looked around, aware that Myles Foley was deliberately keeping his back turned, scanning the horizon. I hoped I had not got him into trouble by being up here. 'I didn't mean to break any rules, Captain. My stomach just feels more settled in the fresh air.'

'I'm not worried about rules,' Captain Donovan replied, 'I'm worried about you catching pneumonia. Dawn will be breaking soon and it's brass monkey weather – you must be chilled to your bones.'

'I've known colder evenings in Wexford, Captain. Walking the streets and gazing in at warm shops, putting off going home because with no fire lit our house felt colder than the streets outside. At least here I'm earning a wage and I know there's a fire in my mother's grate and some food for my family. I swear I've not caught any class of cold that might prevent me from working. I'll go below deck now, though we're bucketing about so much that I can't guarantee I won't throw up. But I need this job, Sir.'

'No one's taking your job away.' The Captain stood up and rubbed his stiff back. 'Take a stroll with me. This morning it seems that we're two of a kind.'

I rose with difficulty – one leg had gone numb. The air felt colder standing up, even with my blanket wrapped around me. To the east a creeping greyness indicated the approach of dawn.

'How are we two of a kind, Sir?' I asked, falling into step beside the Captain.

'We're cursed by the same complaint, Jack, a lack of sleep. I can't sleep because I've a dozen fears preying on my mind.'

'Are you afraid of dying, Sir?'

Brother Dawson would have viciously slapped any boy with the impudence to ask him such a personal question. But Captain Donovan didn't appear to mind. In fact, he gravely pondered his reply before answering.

'I don't rightly know, Jack,' he replied finally. 'No sane man wants to die. No sound is more terrifying than a torpedo cutting through a boat. When a U-boat sank the *Irish Oak* last spring I scrambled for safety and feared for my life as our tiny wooden lifeboat bobbed about. But I grew oddly calm during the hours drifting out there with no seeming chance of rescue. I've lived a full life, Jack, with hopefully more years to come. But if that lifeboat had capsized, I was ready to meet my maker for two reasons.'

'What reasons, Captain?'

He stared out towards the sea. 'Firstly, because, looking back, I felt that I'd made the most of the years God gave me. But secondly and more importantly was the fact that I was only the Second Mate on the *Irish Oak* when it went down.'

We walked past the wheelhouse. Myles Foley gave the Captain a silent, respectful greeting: halfway between a countryman's nod and a sailor's salute.

'What difference did it make being only the Second Mate?' I was straining so hard to grasp his meaning that I forgot to address him correctly as 'Sir'.

'Every man on the *Irish Oak* survived because, by a miracle, the *Irish Plane* located our SOS call. But if any of them had drowned, then, as Second Mate, it wouldn't have been on my watch. Not that our Captain was at fault. If a U-boat decides to sink you, there's nothing anyone can do. But the Captain was in charge. Do you understand, Jack?'

'I think so, Sir.'

'Do you know what SOS stands for?'

'A cry for rescue, Sir, but I don't know what the initials mean.'

He lit a cigarette, after offering me one. I politely shook my head.

'Those initials actually have no hidden meaning. They were chosen because they're unmistakeable when transmitted: three dots, three dashes and three dots. But sailors swear that the initials stand for "Save Our Souls". A captain's responsibility is to save souls. It's one thing to face your own death in a lifeboat, but another thing to know that a crew might face a watery grave because of something you might have done differently. That responsibility is a terrible burden. I worry about lots of things. I worry that the sea may get too rough this far out into the Western Approaches. I worry that if our navigational instruments malfunction we'll steer into the Allied Shoot on Sight zone. I worry that when we reach Lisbon our cargo from America may not have arrived. If so, I'll need to scour the docks to find a cargo of convenience to hopefully cover the cost of our voyage or the Staffords will be waiting to sack me. When not worrying about big things, I worry about the corns on my toes because my old boots are torturing me. But what worries me most is having the death of any sailor on my conscience. I don't want to fail in my first duty, which is to save their souls.'

It was the most solemn speech any adult had ever addressed to me. Even at my father's memorial mass – there was no funeral because his body was never recovered – most grown-ups had merely muttered trite expressions of sympathy. I didn't know how to reply, so I blurted out the first response to enter my head: 'Is there anything I can do for you, Captain?'

The notion that I could do anything for this man was so preposterous that I expected him to laugh. Instead he placed a hand on my shoulder.

'You could do two things, Jack,' he said kindly.

'I'll do anything I can, Sir.'

'Firstly, try to ensure that Cook doesn't burn my breakfast. Secondly, ask yourself why you haven't thought about feeling seasick during this time we've been talking.'

'You're right, Sir, I haven't.'

'Your mind was on other matters, despite us being stuck in this heavy swell until we pass Finisterre and can cut in towards the Spanish coast. Our chat didn't cure your seasickness but it made you forget it. With every day that passes you'll lose your fear of getting sick, until the ocean feels like a second home. I know this for a fact, because I only recall one boy who did more vomiting than you.'

'Who was that?'

He smiled. 'He became a sea captain, tortured by corns because his old boots are killing him.'

I couldn't stop myself from smiling back. 'I can't imagine you being seasick, Sir.'

'Can you imagine me being angry?'

'I've never seen you angry, Sir.'

'You will unless you skip down that ladder and get some rest.'

'I will, Sir. Thank you, and goodnight, Sir.'

'It's a bit late saying goodnight – dawn is breaking. Now down to your bunk!'

This was said with such authority that I scuttled across the deck and would never have glanced back if it had not been for Myles Foley's shout. The Helmsmen had opened the wheelhouse door to point out to sea. The Captain stood beside him, shielding his eyes to peer into the grey and slowly growing half-light. They spoke in low, urgent tones. Captain Donovan glanced back and beckoned for me to join them. I felt uneasy, sensing their anxiety. If they had spied a U-boat rising from the waves, I didn't wish to see it. I knew how a torpedo could tear a hole in our hull at any moment, but it seemed too cruel to have to watch the spray of water being tossed up as it sped towards us. Yet my Captain had summoned me, so I crossed the deck. I tried to pray, but in my terror I couldn't remember the prayers I had recited every night during the family Rosary. Instead, two lines came to me from an old hymn:

Mother of Christ, Star of the sea,
Pray for the wanderer, pray for me.

When I joined the silent men at first I could see nothing amid the waves, not even the jutting tip of a periscope getting a fix on our position. The sea looked empty and immensely lonely. Then the Captain flicked a switch in the wheelhouse so that the lights illuminating our deck went out. We were enveloped in the drizzly greyness stretching across an unbroken expanse of drab waves. But as my eyes adjusted to the unfolding dawn light, I made out a tiny bobbing object in the distance. It was no periscope: a periscope could remain steady, anchored by the sinister weight of a submarine. Whatever this object was, it drifted about at the mercy of wherever the waves took it.

'Is it a mine?' I asked, remembering Irish ships that had been sunk by accidentally brushing against mines.

'That's no mine,' Myles Foley said grimly. 'You only get mines on the approaches to harbours. Even if they drift loose of their moorings, they wouldn't make it this far out.'

'What is it then?'

'With your young eyes we were hoping you might be able to tell us,' Captain Donovan replied. 'Take a gander through these.'

He reached for the powerful binoculars hanging in the wheelhouse. Ordinarily, gazing through them would have been fun, but this was no game: the only thing certain about this object was that it should not be out there. The Captain showed me how to adjust the lenses.

'My eyes are shook,' he said. 'The flash when the *Irish Oak* burst into flames left me nearly as blind as Myles. You needn't tell the Staffords, mind you. See if you can get a fix on it before it drifts away from us.'

The sea looked different through the binoculars – vast and unknowable. I heard footsteps of other sailors sleepily ascending the ladder to start their work: men who paused when they saw us and then walked quietly over to stand behind me. I had given up hope of glimpsing anything when I caught sight of the wooden prow of a tiny boat. I lost it again under the crest of a wave and then it reappeared. It was barely bigger than the rowing boats I often saw elderly fisherman use within sight of the Wexford shore on calm evenings to check lobster pots drifting on ropes.

'It's a rowing boat,' I said. 'And it's empty except for an oar sticking out over the side.' Another wave obliterated my view so that it took a moment to locate the craft again. 'Wait, that's no oar,' I cried. 'It's a man's hand and he's faintly waving.'

The binoculars were taken from my grasp. I turned to watch Shay Cullen expertly train them out to sea. He homed in on the tiny craft drifting away from us. 'The lad is right,' he said grimly. 'Or half right. Please God, the man is waving, but I think the poor blighter has gone to meet his maker.'

'I saw his hand wave,' I protested.

'Maybe you're right, Jack,' Shay Cullen said gently. 'But I think he stretched out his hand with his dying breath and it's been swaying about over the side as the boat got tossed in the waves ever since. But maybe he is alive and unconscious or just too weak to move.' He glanced at the Captain. 'We can't just leave him out there, Sir.'

'Who is he?' I asked.

'He's a sailor: dead or alive,' the Captain replied. 'We're not leaving him to drift alone there.'

The Captain took command of the wheel with Shay Cullen beside him, initially tracking the rowing boat through the binoculars as we altered course to try and reach the tiny boat that kept disappearing amid the towering waves. The Third Engineer went down to relieve Mr Tierney, who had worked the night shift. My neighbour came up on deck and stood beside Ernie Grogan, both men too conscious of the gravity of the moment to exchange their customary abuse. All the crew were silent, with even the Cook making a rare appearance up on deck. It was freezing, however, and the Cook sent me below to brew a huge urn of tea, with instructions to make it strong enough for a mouse to trot across. Sailors drifted down to accept a mug of scalding tea from me in silence, preoccupied with their private thoughts, perhaps remembering drowned men they had sailed with.

I brought up two mugs for the Captain and Shay Cullen in the wheelhouse. The boat bucketed about so much that I scalded my fingers repeatedly. Both men accepted the tea with silent nods of thanks. I rejoined the other sailors gathered in the bow. Mr Tierney held a grappling hook attached to a rope, which he hoped to hurl seawards to catch the wooden side of the rowing boat and draw her in close. But the hook looked so heavy and the distance so far that this seemed unworkable. The boat was almost parallel with the *Kerlogue* but kept getting pushed away in the wake created by our engines. We could see a body stretched on the planks. Perhaps other survivors had scrambled into it with this sailor from some sinking ship. We would never know, and never know how long he had bobbed about in the waves, because, even to me, it was obvious that he was dead. I couldn't stop staring at him across the twenty yards of heavy waves that separated us. Not only was it my first time to see a corpse, but it was also the first time that I had ever glimpsed a black man.

I said this to Mr Tierney who was making a third attempt to fling the grappling hook towards the boat, which was in danger of drifting past. The hook fell well short and Mr Tierney looked at me as he hurled back in the wet rope.

'I've sailed with black sailors out of Swansea,' he said. 'Fine seamen: fearless and good company. The only thing I can tell you about this poor sod is that he's not black. This is what weeks of exposure to the sun does to a man.' He turned to Captain Donovan who had joined the knot of men, several of whom softly prayed aloud for this man's soul. 'We're losing him, Captain. Without someone in that rowing boat to catch the rope, I don't see us getting close enough to reel him in.'

'I can swim, Sir,' I said.

The Captain put a hand on my shoulder. 'You can swim in the River Slaney, no doubt. Biscay is so icy cold, Jack, that your limbs seize up the moment you enter the waves. I've seen strong swimmers fall overboard and become paralysed with shock. The cold shuts down their bodies and saps their strength. You'd sink like a stone or get crushed between our hull and that boat.'

'We can't leave him out there.' This time I was addressing the Captain, man to man.

'I'm sorry for the poor blighter, Jack, but he's beyond our help and it's not worth risking your life.'

'He's a shipwrecked sailor, like my father was.'

What I did next wasn't rational, but I wasn't thinking rationally. I pulled off my boots and grabbed one end of the longest rope coiled up on the deck. I balanced for a second on the bulwark and then was gone over the side, ignoring the Captain's shouted command and the panicked cries of the other men. Captain Donovan was right: nothing could prepare me for the shock of that freezing water. The ferocity of the waves threatened to sweep me under. For ten seconds – which felt like an eternity – I was too paralysed to do anything except sink into an unlit underwater world. Saltwater stung my eyes and filled my mouth when I was forced to give an involuntary gasp. The water weighted so heavily on my clothes that the sea felt like an iron fist violently dragging me down. Then I focused on the inexcusable ridiculous hope I had harboured in my heart since first glimpsing that boat on the waves. There was no logic in the thought, but one part of my brain was convinced that just maybe – by some miracle – this corpse might be my father. My father was nine months missing and nobody could survive so long in these pitiless waves. This sailor looked nothing like my father, though I couldn't bear to imagine what a castaway might look like after nine months adrift. As I floundered in those icy waves, I knew that my father was beyond rescue, but I could make a gesture of amends by recovering this man's body instead.

I needed to breathe: my lungs were bursting from a lack of oxygen. Summoning what strength I could, I crested the waves, gasping for air in the dawn light, and kicked out with the same instinct for survival which had made me tightly grip the rope wound around my left hand when I jumped. A strong wave turned my body around and I was shocked to discover how far from the *Kerlogue* I had been swept. I could see the crew gesturing and shouting but no sound reached me. Then another wave swept me around to face the small boat, only yards away. Straining every muscle, I swam towards it, unsure if the rope was long enough. I was terrified of feeling a sudden tug when only inches from the boat. I would then have to either abandon this man or let go of the rope to clamber into the boat and share his fate. My clothes felt heavier than a suit of armour. I stretched my right hand towards the rowing boat and scraped my knuckles against the wood when my reach wasn't long enough. A trail of blood in the water was my only clue that I had cut myself – my hands were too frozen to feel anything.

The rope was so tight around my numb left hand that I feared the blood was cut off from it. I let the next wave drag me closer to the boat before I lunged forward in a last desperate attempt. This time my right hand managed to grip the prow. I was held steady, or at least as steady as that tiny boat was amid the waves. I wasn't sure I had enough strength to clamber into the boat or if I would capsize it in my efforts to do so. But my body felt so icy that I could not hold on to the prow for much longer. Summoning some reserve of strength, I hauled myself upwards. The boat swayed viciously, unbalanced by my weight. It seemed about to capsize and trap me underneath. But instead, the violent swaying dislodged the corpse, which fell forward, as if rushing to greet me. As I hauled my feet free of the waves and collapsed awkwardly into the half-flooded boat I discovered that the dead man was now lying on top of me. Horrified, I pushed him away and tried to rise. I quickly realised the foolhardiness of this – any sudden movement could tip over the boat.

I couldn't bear to look at his sun-blistered face. In truth I couldn't bear being this close to the corpse. So I simply lay in the flooded bottom of the boat until I felt a tug on the sodden rope. It was still so tightly embedded around my lifeless fingers that I struggled to unwind it with my right hand. When it came loose, my left hand was numb, but I somehow managed to secure the rope to a metal oarlock. I fell back, too exhausted to move. The sun was now low in the sky, though it gave me no warmth. The sky was becoming an unearthly blue and the only sounds I could hear were the waves and the loud beat of my own heart. I closed my eyes and then I heard Shay Cullen shout: 'Two more pulls and we have him.'

Mr Tierney was shouting too, though I was too disorientated to make out his words. But I sensed the concern in his tone, and something akin to love. He was the biggest rogue I knew but an intonation of his voice told me that he would kill any man who laid a hand on me, and do anything to help me if I was in danger. I heard a thud of wood colliding with the ship's hull. Someone jumped into the rowing boat. I opened my eyes to see Shay Cullen pick me up, holding me aloft so that other sailors could reach out to take me and lay me down on the amidships deck. I was in shock from the freezing waves, unable to stop shaking. Hands stripped me naked and I hadn't the strength to fight them off. I felt myself being lifted into a sitting position. Blankets were pressed around my shoulders to try and get me warm. The Captain knelt, holding a tin mug.

'Drink this!' he ordered.

I took a sip and gasped.

'What is it, Sir?'

'Brandy.'

'I don't drink, Sir.'

'You'll do what you're bloody well told.'

His tone was so sharp that I drained the remaining brandy in one gulp. It carried such a kick that it felt like someone had punched me. My throat burnt with the raw aftertaste, yet it warmed my insides like a kindled fire. The alcohol went straight to my stomach but also straight to my head. I felt dizzy and my vision blurred. But I mainly felt terror at being confronted by the furious Captain.

'You could have drowned,' he said. 'Don't say you didn't hear me ordering you to stop. Never in my days at sea did I see such an act of open insubordination.'

'I'm sorry, Sir.'

'You should be.' Behind him I could see some men lifting the dead sailor onto the deck with solemn reverence. Other crew members stood around the Captain, gazing anxiously down at me, Mr Walton among them. Captain Donovan poured another measure of brandy.

'You should be discharged from this ship once we reach Lisbon.' He looked back at his Second Officer. 'What do you say, Mr Walton?'

'He has his father's insubordination,' Mr Walton replied quietly, 'and the same man's courage.'

The Captain held out the mug to me. 'You're a cheeky scut, Roche.'

'Does that mean you're going to sack me, Sir?'

'It means you're going to drink this and get some warmth inside you.'

'I can't drink any more, Sir, my head is spinning.'

Mr Tierney touched the Captain's shoulder respectfully.

'Begging your pardon, Sir, but do you know the Latin phrase *in loco parentis*?'

'I wouldn't have mistaken you for a Latin scholar, Tierney,' Mr Walton said.

'And you'd be right, Mr Walton. I was a poor scholar at everything. But unless I'm mistaken, Captain, it means to take on the burden of responsibility of a parent.'

'What's your point, Mossy?' the Captain asked, bemused as to where this conversation was leading.

'My point is that I promised Jack's mother to mind him and my nerves are shook. I am very much in *loco parentis* here. I won't beat about the bush, Sir. While the boy mightn't need the brandy, I'm shaking so bad that I'll accept it on his behalf.'

Without farther ado, Mr Tierney took the mug from Captain Donovan's grasp and drained it in one gulp, while I stared groggily past him at the growing circle of men kneeling around the dead body on the deck.

Chapter Nine

December 21, First Dog Watch, Bay of Biscay

I DON'T KNOW IF IT was the shock of the cold water, the brandy, or pure exhaustion, but that morning, after the Captain ordered me below deck, my sack of straw felt like the softest mattress. I'm not sure if my crewmates left me undisturbed or occasionally tiptoed into the low-roofed cabin to check on me but I just know that no sound woke me during the hours when we sailed to within sight of Cape Finisterre – the rocky peninsula that the Romans once regarded as the furthest end of the earth. At this, the most western tip of the Iberian Peninsula, our Navicert allowed us to gain some relief from Biscay's waves by hugging the Spanish coast until we reached a position of 40° north, when we were permitted to swing inland towards Lisbon.

When I finally woke, dusk had closed in around the ship and the captain was ordering our identifying lights to be switched on. Somehow I felt older in myself, with an inkling that one day I might fully belong to this seafaring world. But I also sensed how far I had to go before being able to count myself as truly belonging to this crew. Strangely enough, I no longer felt seasick. I knew enough about sailors to know that no man could go out of his way to praise my earlier actions, but when I climbed up on deck the crewmen there rewarded me with quiet nods of respect. Having finished a shift in the engine room, Mossy

Tierney was savouring the butt of a cigarette at amidships. He took a last drag of such intensity that I feared he would burn his fingers, and then tossed the tiny remnant out into the waves. He turned, holding the smoke in his lungs before exhaling pleasurably.

'Never play cards with a Flash Harry who can blow smoke rings,' he said. 'That was some sleep you had. The Captain and I took the precaution of glancing in. Count John McCormack could have sung arias at your bunk and you wouldn't have stirred.'

It felt disconcerting to imagine two grown men watching over me while I slept.

'Did we find any papers on the sailor we rescued?' I asked.

'If he had any, they were washed away,' Mr Tierney replied.

'So we'll never know who he is?'

'He had a Royal Navy identity dog tag around his neck, engraved with his rank, service number and name: Eoin Deasy. And his religion: RC – Roman Catholic.'

'Deasy is an Irish name,' I said.

Mr Tierney nodded. 'There's thousands of Irish fighting in this war: fighting to keep Ireland out of it.'

'Should we be in it?' I asked.

'Hitler is a bowsie,' he said. 'I never boxed twelve rounds against Freddie Mills. But if I had to get into a ring with him, I'd try to survive as long as possible by ducking and diving and boxing clever. That's what you must do against a bully, a hundred times stronger than you. I used to hear IRA men in pubs sing Hitler's praises, so blinded with hatred for England that they swallowed the fairytale that, if we throw in our lot with Hitler, he'll give us back Northern Ireland and let us live happily ever after in a United Ireland, flying both the tricolour and the swastika. Thankfully I no longer have to listen to those buck-eejits bellyaching.'

'Did they enlist in Hitler's army?'

'They did not.' Mr Tierney snorted in derision. 'The Irish government interned them before Hitler could make use for such stooges.' Mr Tierney sounded more serious than usual: his camouflage of jokes stripped away. 'But it's only twenty years since a different IRA fought our way to the negotiating table to try and gain independence. My older brother Tom was in the IRA back then. If I rarely mention him it's because I don't like remembering how British Black and Tans tortured him and left his mutilated corpse on a road outside Enniscorthy. Tom was a hothead who would have accepted nothing short of a full republic. But we were never offered the full republic we all wanted. Instead, at that negotiating table Britain foisted a three-card trick on us called a Free State, promising a declaration of full-scale war if we declined their kind offer. Do you know what a Free State actually is, Jack?'

'Not really,' I replied.

'Neither do foreign governments – they don't know if we're fish or fowl; an independent nation or still just a British dominion, tied to the King's apron strings. That Treaty foisted on us in 1922 locked us into their Empire and set Irishmen at each other's throats in a brutal Civil War. Our governments have done damn all to make life any better for the likes of you and me, but they've spent two decades slowly untangling us from Britain's apron strings: abolishing their Oath of Allegiance and passing our own constitution. Churchill wants to starve us into joining this war, but maybe we're fighting a different one. If we can prove our neutrality, then other countries will have to accept that we acted as an independent nation and treat us as one.'

'So neutrality is how we prove we're tied to nobody's apron strings?'

He nodded. 'I remember the Black and Tans burning down Cork City in 1920, looting shops and leaving families homeless.

Before that, they left Balbriggan a smouldering ruin and bayonetted locals to death. Bad things were done by every side in that War of Independence – and my brother, God rest him, was no saint. The British are a fine people and there's little support for Hitler in Ireland, but our country is barely twenty years old, with an army too poorly equipped to last more than two days against any invasion from either side and people would find it impossible to see British soldiers on our streets so soon again if we joined the Allies.'

'So what do we do?'

'Box clever until forced to show our cards. That's what all nations do: it's why the USA never showed their true hand until the Japs attacked them. The IRA can believe any nonsense they like, but Hitler is only biding his time before he sends his jackboots marching in to invade us. When that happens, we'll fight him for as long as we can. But until then, this ship is Ireland's front line, despite having no weapons and no protection beyond a painted tricolour. But we're showing the world that we can sail our own course. The poor fellow whose body you recovered, like thousands of other Irish lads, joined the British army to fight Hitler because he's an evil bowsie. But they're also fighting for our right to remain neutral as an independent nation.'

'What if Hitler wins?'

Mr Tierney spat into the waves. 'Then we're rightly screwed and mankind is screwed with us.' He looked at me. 'You did a foolhardy thing, but a brave thing. We'll never know if that sailor had a Cork or Waterford or coventry accent. But at least his family will know that his body was found. Now, can you sew as well as you can swim?'

I was unsure if Mr Tierney had resumed his old jocular manner. 'My mother never taught me to sew: she saw it as women's work.'

'At sea all work is a sailor's work. Go down to the kitchen. The Cook probably needs your help.'

Below deck, the Cook looked up when I entered the galley, his hands white with flour. 'I've emptied two sacks of flour,' he explained. 'But we'll need to empty this last sack too. Give me a hand to lift it after I cut it open so we can pour the flour gently in on top of what's already inside this steel drum. I could have used your help to scrub this drum dry, but you were snoring so loudly that whales kept scattering in fright.'

'I didn't mean to sleep so long,' I said.

He shook his head. 'You earned your kip, son. Now help me lift this sack so we don't spill a teaspoon of flour. It took a lot of bartering to get my hands on good flour in Cardiff. I hope to have one sack left when we get back to Wexford. If I do, I'll be like a film star with all the women hanging off me.'

'What are we baking now that we need all this flour for?' I asked, helping him to empty the third sack into the drum.

'It's not the flour we need, son.' He shook the sack softly and a gentle explosion of flour filled the air, entering my nostrils and sticking to my hair. It made the Cook's face so white that he might have looked comical had his expression not become so sombre. Handing me the empty sack, he pointed to the two empty ones. 'Wash these out so that every trace of flour is gone. Then slit the sides with a knife and tell Myles Foley they're ready for him.'

Puzzled, I did as instructed and found Myles Foley kneeling by his bunk. At first I thought he was praying, but then I realised that he was selecting a needle and thread from a sewing box in his kitbag. Even with his bad sight, Myles was our 'chippy', or ship's carpenter. His white beard made it impossible to guess his age, especially as while he moved around the ship in a slow, unhurried fashion, he did so with surprising agility. I had never seen him lose his temper, raise his voice or criticise another sailor. He observed his crewmates' exaggerated banter with an amused smile which often gave the impression that his thoughts were elsewhere. It was like he lived in two worlds: the crowded and occasionally quarrelsome world of this ship and the secretive world of his memories, which he rarely talked about and into which none of us were invited.

Myles nodded when I told him about the sacks and quietly asked if I wished to join him at his work in the kitchen. I wasn't sure what his work entailed but I did know that he had no need of my help. Perhaps he simply wanted company or maybe there are occasions when any man – no matter how taciturn his nature – needs to break his silence. Perhaps a death at sea reminds any old sailor about how quickly they will be forgotten when they die.

The kitchen was empty. Myles Foley climbed up onto the table and sat there, at ease in a cross-legged position, oblivious to the violent movements of the ship. He beckoned for me to hand him the sacks.

'I bet you think I've spent my whole life at sea,' Myles said.

'You look more like a sailor than any man on board.'

He smiled. 'And you look the least like a sailor.'

It was no jibe, just a statement of fact. 'Do you think I'll ever look like one?'

Myles nodded. 'One day you'll get a big wage packet and pay a tailor to make your first proper suit: an oversized jacket with big lapels and broad shoulders and the trousers tapering down to the ankles. Suddenly you'll look the part and then you'll start to act the part. Townsfolk in ports will think twice before blocking your path and greedy publicans will eye you as you swagger past their premises, because any sailor in a good suit looks like a man with money to spend. The suit makes the man. I should know: for years I was a man who made suits.'

'You were a tailor?' I asked.

He nodded again. 'I was many things I don't talk about it in case the crew make a cod of me, but I served my time as a travelling tailor. I'd have never eked out a living near big towns, but I had my own circuit of tiny villages, some barely more than a crossroads: just one pub serving as a grocery and haberdashery too. You could buy everything in them from a needle to a scythe: with the same shopkeeper dabbling in auctioneering and being the local undertaker too. Tight-fisted men, but they didn't mind me sitting cross-legged on their kitchen table because every old farmer who wandered down with a suit for mending or every girl wanting me to make a frock based on a picture in a magazine put cash in that shopkeeper's till while waiting for me to finish stitching. I was their travelling newspaper too: carrying gossip and news of weddings and funerals and scandals not talked about till the young ones were tucked up in bed.'

'How long did you spend tailoring?' I asked.

His fingers moved with swift dexterity as he sewed the sacks together. 'Too long. My bones still feel the winter journeys over mountains to find no work waiting, because a tea chest of old clothes was sent home from America and half the village were dressed like Yankees in Time Square. No tailor with a few bales of cloth can compete with clothes sent from Brooklyn. Folk fed me decent and made me up a bed by the fire, but I needed to move on or else overstay my welcome. I'm thirty years at sea now and I still don't much care for the ocean. But no matter how mountainous the waves look, they're not real mountains that I need to cross in the rain, with bales of cloth near breaking my back.' Myles Foley examined the three sacks now neatly woven together. 'I made going-away suits for farmers' sons who wanted their sons properly attired on the ship to New York. But I never thought I'd be using flour sacks to make a going-away suit for any man, God rest his soul.'

Only now did I realise the intended use of the flour sacks. Myles Foley handed them to me. 'Take these to the Captain,' he said. 'It will need a final seam of stitches down one side but I'll do it when the time comes.'

I went up on deck. Every sailor must have been listening for my footsteps because, by the time I climbed up towards the wheelhouse, I could hear men's footsteps ascending the ladder behind me. I walked past the funnel to the bow of the ship. I saw the dead sailor's body lying there, covered with tarpaulin. It was after dusk and the deck was lit up at amidships. The steel doors down into the hold were open. Captain Donovan emerged from the wheelhouse in full uniform. The other men were dressed in their Sunday best. I gave the sackcloth to the Captain who handed it to Shay Cullen and Thomas Bergin. They pulled back the tarpaulin. Many crewmen had donated an item of clothing to the dead sailor. I recognised the shirt on the corpse as one that Mr Tierney had intended to wear to Christmas mass in Lisbon. The Rosary beads entwined between his fingers were a set that I had seen our First Officer, Denis Valentine, silently pray with one evening. Shay Cullen and Thomas Bergin spread out the sackcloth and lifted the corpse to place in it. A last pair of footsteps joined us: Myles Foley's. All hands were now assembled on deck. I glanced at the Captain.

'Is he to be buried at sea, Sir?'

'It would be a Christian burial, and more than he might have expected when dying alone on the waves. But Lisbon has a tiny British cemetery: St George's. We'll send word to the British ambassador after we dock. At least in Lisbon he'll be lying among comrades and the embassy can send word to his family. Even in their loss, that would be a great comfort.' He paused. 'You know the truth of it more than any of us. I thought we'd say the Glorious Mysteries of the Rosary for him. Would you lead us off by saying the first decade: The Resurrection of Jesus?'

One perk of life at sea was avoiding the nightly ritual of the family Rosary which my mother always insisted on us kneeling down to recite. I associated the Rosary with boredom and sore knees and Lily, Eamonn, Tony and myself risking a slap if we giggled. Repetition had robbed those prayers of any meaning. But now, as I led the first decade and saw how all my assembled crewmates – with the exception of Mr Walton – had dropped onto one knee to recite the responses, the words became infused with meaning. I was praying with men who knew the dangers of the sea and were paying their respects to an unknown man who was undeniably one of their own – not because of his Irish-sounding name but because he was a fellow seaman.

When I had finished the first decade, Mr Tierney took up the Second Mystery: The Ascension of Jesus. Other crewmates followed suit until all five decades were recited. Then the Captain led us in the Hail Holy Queen:

> *Hail Holy Queen, Mother of Mercy,*
> *Hail our life, our sweetness and our hope.*
> *To you we cry poor banished children of Eve…*

I wasn't sure if the captain would make a speech to lend this occasion extra gravitas. But maybe there was nothing that he could say. Priests are trained to trot out platitudes to conclude ceremonies. But platitudes are hollow. The *Kerlogue* was too small a ship, and his weathered corpse too stark a sight, for the truth to be softened by trite phrases. His fate could befall us all. At a nod from the Captain, Shay Cullen drew the loose end of the sackcloth over the man's face and Myles Foley knelt beside him to quickly stitch together the two sides so that the corpse was now enclosed in a makeshift shroud.

Shay Cullen and Thomas Bergin respectfully carried the body down towards the open hold. But it was Mr Walton who made a point of climbing alone into the hold, where his clothes would be destroyed by coal dust. He held out his arms, signalling for them to lower the body to him. For a moment he stood there, cradling the weight of the dead man in his arms. He had not joined in our prayers, but this seemed to be his way to pay his respects. Slowly he knelt and placed the body down carefully on top of the coal. It was no place to leave a body but our ship was so small that there was nowhere else to lay him to rest. Mr Walton climbed up and Shay Cullen and Thomas Bergin closed over the heavy hatches. For a moment the crew stood about, unsure of what to do or say next. Then the Captain issued orders brusquely, telling men which tasks needed to be done now and which needed to be carried out at first light. His tone was authoritative, yet no man objected to being spoken to like this. They welcomed his instructions: it banished the sombre mood and brought them back to reality. The sailor in the hold might be dead, but they were alive and needed to be alert to danger from the sea or the skies. The knot of men dispersed; each one reminded of his allotted duties on this voyage to the port that Mr Tierney called, with an almost holy reverence, the White City.

Part Two

LISBON

Chapter Ten

December 23, Belém, Lisbon, First Watch,

FOR THREE DAYS WE DIDN'T stray from our designated route of 12° west, which kept us outside the Allied Shoot on Sight zone. On the third afternoon we finally reached the navigational point of 40° north. Mr Walton and the Captain checked our position and the crew breathed a sigh of relief: our Navicert now permitted us to swing landward and begin our approach to Lisbon. In the fading light our first sight of land was the deserted beaches of Praia do Guincho and the distant splashes of massive waves thrown up in heavy swells caused by the predominantly easterly breezes. The *Kerlogue* lurched about heavily, but while I occasionally needed to grip onto the rail for balance, I no longer felt sick. The moment when I dived into the Biscay waves seemed to mark my baptism with the sea. I still feared the ocean and its lurking dangers, but I had grown so accustomed to the ship's constant motion that my legs would only feel peculiar again after we docked and I readjusted to walking on solid ground.

We passed the lights of Estoril but needed to journey farther up the Tagus River before Lisbon came into view. By then it was late at night but it was not dark, because how could anyone contemplate darkness when confronted by this city of blazing light? It felt as if I had been sent into blacked-out Cardiff purely to appreciate this spectacle. Lisbon resembled a cliff-face of dazzling lights that climbed up from the water's edge to culminate at a vast height on streets so steep that only a mountain goat could climb them. This was no ordinary city: it was a metropolis so stupendously bright that I needed to shade my eyes to take in its glistening majesty.

I wasn't alone in being overcome. After our dangerous voyage, even hardened sailors, normally unimpressed by any sight, felt compelled to linger beside me on deck and contemplate this pulsating wall of light that came from the huge floodlit buildings and the enormous neon advertising signs that flashed rhythmically off and on.

'Who would believe it?' Myles Foley paused at my elbow, his voice infused with wonderment. 'It's astounding.'

'I've never seen anything more astounding than Lisbon,' I agreed.

'Lisbon?' The old sailor shrugged. 'Lisbon is grand, but I've been sailing into this port since before you were born. What's astounding is how this rust bucket actually got us here.'

'There's nothing astounding about it,' Mr Tierney said, stopping alongside us to survey the view, his voice tinged with pride and indignation. 'This ship's engine has the heart of a lion.'

Myles Foley stepped back from the gunnel. 'Maybe it does, Mossy, but it's trapped inside the body of a sardine.'

I laughed, and the old man placed a hand on my shoulder. It was a fatherly touch, out of keeping with his normally reserved nature. The unexpectedness of the gesture brought home the fact that, to my knowledge, Myles did not have any family. Maybe he owned a cabin down a back lane or maybe all he possessed to call his home was a shared room in a lodging house with a suitcase of personal possessions stored under a bed. I knew nothing about his life when not on this boat. But his simple act of grasping my shoulder with undisguised affection made me realise that he was undertaking this hazardous voyage for a different reason than the rest of us. The older crewmen had dependants relying on the extra danger money to be earned on this trip. For a young man like Shay Cullen the sea represented an escape from poverty and a way to see the world. But Myles Foley was so long at sea that he was on board because he had nowhere else to be. No man wanted to hear the heart-stopping whoosh of a torpedo, but maybe such a swift death was preferable to slowly coughing your last breath in a row of iron bedframes in a ward in the County Home.

Myles slowly relinquished his grip on my shoulder. 'You've come through your first voyage, young Roche,' he said. 'You're one of us now. So get some sleep, son. If you thought the Biscay waves were high, wait till you see the height of Lisbon's hills.'

He disappeared down the ladder. Other sailors followed as they tired of gazing at this labyrinth of light. Finally I stood alone, knowing I should go below and yet unable to drag myself from the mesmerising sight. A small tugboat was coming out from the port to guide us to our allotted docking berth. It was manned not only by a pilot but by four armed soldiers.

We were close enough to the dockside now for me to make out individual buildings. We were passing an ancient fortified tower on the water's edge: its elaborate turrets decorated with stone carvings of exotic animals and high-domed watchtowers on every corner. The wheelhouse door opened. I turned to see Mr Walton behind me.

'That's the Belém Tower,' he said. 'The first time I saw it I remember thinking that I'd never see anything as beautiful again. It was built with the riches that Vasco da Gama brought back. Have you heard of da Gama?'

'I'm afraid not, Sir.'

'It's not your fault, boy.' His tone was gentler than usual. 'The Christian Brothers can barely see beyond their own noses. Da Gama was the world's greatest sailor. Four hundred years ago his crew spent a night at prayer with monks in a dilapidated old hermitage in this spot before setting sail in four ships to find a new route to the Orient.

It took ninety-six days before his crew sighted land and only a quarter of them made it home alive. But they brought back spices and gold and new sea routes that made Portugal a great nation.'

'Is it still a great country, Mr Walton?'

Mr Walton watched the armed soldiers observe us unsmilingly from the tugboat. 'Don't let the dictator who pays the wages of those goons overhear you, but it's not. If you think you've seen poverty then wait till you see the back lanes here. Lisbon glows magically from a distance but all that glistens isn't gold. Still, it has magnificent sights. Look past the tugboat. Have you ever seen a more extraordinary building?'

Mr Walton was right. We were approaching an extravagantly ornate edifice that resembled a church, but if you placed every church in Wexford in a row they still would not equal its length.

'Is it a cathedral, Sir?' I asked.

Mr Walton shook his head. 'This was once the shabby hermitage where da Gama's men prayed before setting sail. It shows you what gold can build. Gold flooded in here during the Age of Discovery. This Jerónimos Monastery and the whole city was built on foundations of gold. It's all changed now.'

'What is Lisbon built on now, Sir?'

The Second Officer discreetly glanced at the wheelhouse where Captain Donovan was steering, with Denis Valentine in watchful attendance. Unbuttoning his greatcoat he produced a hip flask. 'Did your first experience of brandy give you a taste for it?'

'It burned my throat, Sir. And I was so drenched after being pulled from the waves that I could barely think straight afterwards.'

'That was just a medicinal dose to ward off pneumonia.' Mr Walton took a sip from his flask and handed it to me. 'This is your first glimpse of a great port. It calls for a toast. You won't refuse a drink with an officer, will you, boy?'

I couldn't refuse his offer or indeed fathom his behaviour. I raised the flask and held it to my lips for a few seconds. Then I stepped back and gasped, like I had been punched. The lining on my stomach felt as if it had been set alight.

'What are we drinking to, Sir?'

Mr Walton took the hip flask and held it aloft as if saluting the soldiers eyeing us from the tugboat. 'To something which dictators hate: democracy.' He took another long slug and insisted on me doing likewise before putting the flask back in his pocket. 'Today Lisbon is built on fear: a fear of police cells, beatings and unmarked graves.'

The quayside had initially seemed to be deserted but now I noticed solitary figures appear amid the mist creeping in from the river. One man in a white suit and matching Panama hat paused on his late-night saunter to lean on a walking cane and observe our progress. 'Spies,' Mr Walton said quietly. 'Information is a currency here: every boat that docks here is watched. There's always a price for information and for gold.'

'Does gold still come into Lisbon, Sir?'

Mr Walton nodded. 'In big quantities and small quantities. The big quantities come in looted gold bars that the Nazis use to purchase tungsten ore to keep their murder machine working. The little quantities come in wedding rings and heirlooms sold for a pittance by poor Jewish refugees crowding in here from across Europe, all hoping for a safe passage to America.' He turned to me. 'How do you feel, boy?'

'Groggy from the brandy, Sir. Tipsy is the word my mother would use.'

He smiled. 'Tipsy: that's a good word. I'd hate to see brandy wasted.' He buttoned up his coat. 'Away to your bunk and that's an order. Sleep well and sleep long, Jack.'

Chapter Eleven

December 24, Alcântara, Lisbon

I SLEPT SO WELL THAT when I woke the sailors who shared my cabin were long gone about their tasks. I was surprised that none had woken me: they were normally loud when moving about and surely knew that the Cook expected me to help him serve breakfast. My throat was scalded and I had a headache caused by Mr Walton's unwelcome generosity with his hip flask.

There was a bucket of cold water for us to wash with. Kneeling down, I plunged my face into its depths. Quickly lifting my head from the water I gasped at the icy shock, shaking my hair like a drenched dog before I grabbed my father's old towel and rubbed it dry. My cheeks stung with cold but the arid dryness was stripped from my tongue and my headache seemed to have eased.

I felt invigorated and intensely alive, eagerly anticipating the chance to explore this city. Then a foreboding permeated my consciousness – a dread which my hangover had blocked out. For the previous three days I had made a sign of the cross every time I passed the hatches to the ship's hold, imagining that poor sailor's body stitched into sackcloth in the darkness there. How was it that I had found the courage to instinctively dive into the ocean to recover his body? For days I had been dreading the moment when the hatches would be unsealed and I would have to watch his corpse being brought forth. I was terrified that the Portuguese police would cut open the sack and force me to stare again at his ravaged face. My euphoria vanished. With my hair half-dry I made my way to the galley. The Cook barely looked up when I entered.

'A hungry shower of horses stampeded through here at dawn. They almost ate the plates and all, but I saved you something for breakfast, though you're two hours late reporting for work.'

'I'm sorry,' I said. 'I'm not really hungry.'

'Sit down,' he ordered, bringing over a small plate of food. 'The last time you weren't hungry you were in your mother's womb. They say you were snoring as loudly as a sea captain. Nothing tickles the vocal chords like brandy.'

'I said I'm not hungry,' I repeated defensively.

'And I told you to eat.'

Sitting down, I stared glumly at the plate. Seeing my hesitation, the Cook sat down beside me. 'That business is over and done with, Jack,' he said quietly.

'What business?'

'Do you think we haven't seen you shiver every time you walk past the hold? Men from the British Consulate arrived at dawn to take away his body. He'll be buried in St George's Cemetery.'

'How did the Captain get word to them so quick?'

The Cook laughed. 'News travels fast in Lisbon. Every scrap of information is constantly being sold. The Captain only had to mention it to the tugboat pilot last night. Within an hour, both the British and German consulates knew everything there was to know. The great thing about information here is that a tugboat pilot can sell it twice. The Portuguese police showed up before the British Consulate officials. They weren't interested in his body; they were looking for any documents in his pockets that they could flog to the Germans. They wanted to question you, but Mr Walton said that you were asleep and told them they could go to hell in a basket. Being Mr Walton, he said it more diplomatically, but in a menacing tone. Something in Mr Walton's manner makes officials who take bribes nervous. They wonder what a man like him is doing on a ship like this. They can't tell if he's spying for the Allies or the Axis powers, or if he's supplying information to both sides.'

'Is Mr Walton a spy?'

The Cook laughed. 'Mr Walton is resolutely his own man. He doesn't suffer fools gladly. Unfortunately some shipping companies are owned by fools, which explains why he switched ships so often. Anything he does is for his own reasons and he serves no other master.'

The Cook's words made sense of Mr Walton's actions in getting me drunk last night. The whole crew must have known of his plan to shield me from seeing the body being taken away. The Cook patted my shoulder as he rose.

'No man on board thinks you're a coward. But you know too much about death already. Now finish that grub and wash these pots because they won't wash themselves. I want this galley so clean that any Bombay runner will trundle down the gangplank and find another ship to infest. Then, when you finish your work, I don't want to see you until dark. Do you get my drift?'

I nodded in gratitude. Looking down at my plate I was suddenly so ravenous that I could have eaten the meagre breakfast there ten times over. I barely tasted it in my haste to get my work finished. I only had one thought: to get off this ship and explore Lisbon.

Chapter Twelve

December 24, 11 a.m. Lisbon

THE IMAGES GLIMPSED LAST NIGHT of the Belém Tower and the Jerónimos Monastery were so sumptuous as to create an illusion of sailing into a dream-like landscape. But any impression of having docked in paradise was shattered by the piercing warning sirens of the numerous mechanical cranes at work along the dockside. There was a continuous hubbub of activity as dock workers and officials swarmed about. Up on deck Mr Tierney recommended the best shop to buy Portuguese currency with what cash remained from my Advance Note. He warned me to keep my identity papers safe and my wits about me at all times, and most especially when passing through an area called Cais do Sodré. Once I got beyond Cais do Sodré I should follow the river and tram tracks until I reached a plaza called Black Horse Square, and then I would be in the real heart of Lisbon.

'How will I know when I've reached Black Horse Square?' I asked.

'Sure, hasn't it a statue of a horse in the middle of it?' he replied.

'A black horse?' I asked, still fearful of getting lost in this metropolis that looked a hundred times bigger than Wexford.

'Of course it isn't black,' he said, as if addressing an eejit. 'It's bronze but it looks blacker than the Devil's boots when you first see it from a distance on a ship sailing up the Tagus. That's why sailors call the plaza Black Horse Square.'

'What do Portuguese people called it?'

'How the hell would I know?' Mr Tierney seemed impatient to get on with conducting whatever illicit bartering he had planned. 'Now get away into the fresh air. If Captain Donovan tracks down this American cargo ship we're meant to meet, we'll have sailed again before we even get a chance to acquire a Christmas hangover.' He saw me hesitate. 'What's bothering you, Jack?'

'It's embarrassing.'

He looked me in the eye. 'We're shipmates: what happens on this ship stays on the ship.'

I held out what little money I possessed. 'Will I have enough to buy a pair of American nylon stockings?'

'Would these stockings be a Christmas present for a certain Miss Ellie Coady?'

Despite my best efforts, I blushed until my face felt like a furnace. 'What happens on board stays on board,' I reminded him. Mr Tierney tried to maintain a serious face.

'Trust me,' he said. 'Unless the money-changer rips you off entirely, not only have you enough to buy a pair of nylon stockings, but you'll be able to treat yourself to any young lady willing to model them.' Mr Tierney paused, fearing he had overstepped the mark, and then hastily added: 'Not that you're to entertain any such thoughts. I made a solemn vow to your mother. Maybe hang on till I'm ready and we can walk up through the town together.'

I assured him I would be fine and descended the gangplank before he could summon me back. Having been enlisted as his illicit pack mule in Cardiff, I had no intention of enduring any similar type of interrogation from a Portuguese policeman.

Dock workers were starting to unload our cargo of coal. But another cargo caught my attention farther down the cobbled wharf at Alcântara: a cargo of shivering people who looked like they had queued all night at the berth where a passenger liner was moored. The lucky ones possessed winter coats, but some children wore only light summer dresses, with blankets around their shoulders to try and stay warm. It didn't feel cold by the standards of December in Wexford, but a strong breeze whipping in from the river stole most of the warmth from the sun in the clear sky. These people looked as if coldness had colonised their bones during the long hours spent queuing on this quay. Some sat mutely on cardboard suitcases, while others shuffled from foot to foot, trying to keep the blood circulating in their bodies.

Some children ran about in the long queue because children find a way to play in any circumstance. But they never strayed far from where their parents patiently waited, even though there was no sign of movement on the passenger liner they queued alongside. It was the only ship where there was no gangplank lowered, as if its crew feared that the sight of a gangplank would provoke a stampede. Three policemen in elaborately braided hats kept order: the only people in good form, smiling indulgently at the children playing on the cobbles. They possessed the satisfied look of men who had enjoyed a fine breakfast before starting their shifts. Occasionally they chatted to the queuing passengers and smiled while shrugging their shoulders as if to show that the interminable delay was equally baffling to them.

As I walked down past the queue I heard a bewildering babble of languages. Passengers seemed to share nothing in common beyond a hard-learned patience and an air of exhausted desperation. I didn't know what lands they came from but instinctively knew that they were not Portuguese, not that I had any idea of what Portuguese people looked like. The only Lisboetas I had seen so far were dock workers unloading ships, uniformed officials patrolling the wharf and local women hurrying away towards the city with heavy baskets of fresh fish adroitly balanced on their heads. Other local women were trying to entice buyers for sardines being grilled on makeshift barbecues near the steps that led up to the city. I sensed the divide that existed between these locals and the exhausted queue of travellers whose clothes were originally far more expensive than those worn by local people, but which now looked ragged and shabby. Many men wore double-breasted suits that had fitted them before hunger wasted away their bodies. The queuing women's faces were equally pinched: their once fine dresses similarly tattered and patched. Not one piece of jewellery was on display, as if everything of value had been sold or bartered.

I felt disconcerted by how people in this queue stared at me. Their threadbare clothes could not disguise how most of them had once been prosperous. They belonged to a higher social class than the shopkeepers who often brushed past me on the streets at home as if I didn't exist. Or if some doctor's wife did condescend to glance at me in Wexford, her expression betrayed pity at my ragged clothes or glacially reminded me that I was a corner boy who belonged among the lowest of the low. I was used to being looked down upon by what my mother termed 'professional people'. But I had never experienced the looks of undisguised envy which came from this queue that watched my unhindered progress and knew I could stroll back up the *Kerlogue's* gangplank whenever I wished. While they fretted about their papers being in order in case they were turned away when the queue was finally permitted to board the America-bound liner, I could leave Lisbon whenever Captain Donovan gave the word.

I showed my Irish Seaman's Identity Card to a harbour policeman who waved me on. But I paused on the steep steps to watch women deftly turn over their sardines on the sizzling barbecues. I had never seen fish cooked this way before or smelt anything more appetising than the smoky aroma arising from the charcoal. One woman smiled, encouraging me to purchase. I felt hungry, despite the breakfast the Cook had squirrelled away for me. But I was too shy to try and buy anything, or too overcome by the sway of strangers milling around me. I didn't know if the sardine seller would accept my Irish coins or how to communicate when I lacked a single word of Portuguese. I was still a small-town boy, and what scared me most was the risk of publicly making a fool of myself. Besides, I had resolved to buy nothing else until I purchased the nylons for Ellie.

So I ascended the steps to discover a farther set of steps which led to a plaza crammed with more people than on the dockside. Other queues had formed here – longer and more quarrelsome – outside the offices of various shipping companies. The weary passengers down on the wharf might endure a long wait before the gangplank was lowered but at least they possessed tickets to travel. The hordes who thronged this plaza possessed no tickets and vented their frustrations on hapless shipping clerks whose faces I could glimpse through metal grilles. These clerks avoided eye contact with the people they directly addressed, but were unable to prevent themselves from peering out at the endless line of families – many of whom looked as if they had slept under the stars to keep their place in a slow-moving queue.

Everyone looked so stressed that I was anxious to walk on in the direction that Mr Tierney had advised. I climbed more steps up onto a road where the atmosphere was utterly different. Here were Lisboetas going about their ordinary lives as if the anguished queues outside the shipping companies belonged to a different world. Although I was still a foreigner I felt more at home than on the dockside. I couldn't understand local people up here but I sensed that they were engrossed in the same everyday conversations as people in Wexford, hurrying to jobs or gossiping loudly. Fuel was so scarce in Wexford that motor cars were rare. But here taxies whizzed past, honking horns to alert the shoals of cyclists and the old men on horse-and-carts who ignored them. Every few minutes the high-pitched ringing of a bell announced the appearance of a packed, wooden trolley-tram that loudly rattled along iron tracks cut into the road. I had found

Cardiff oddly quiet, but Cardiff had been bombed. Here there was constant bustle beneath the huge flags draped from buildings.

After a few minutes I saw even more red-fringed flags across the wide street: this time being carried by young standard-bearers leading a marching procession of boys younger than me, dressed in green short-sleeved tunics decorated with badges and epaulets. Every boy wore beige trousers and a military-style khaki side cap. Most wore highly-polished black shoes, though some children towards the rear marched in their bare feet. The standard bearers at the front stood out by wearing a darker green shirt. Although barely older than the other boys, their haughty bearing exuded power and authority. One blew shrilly on a whistle and the children behind him obediently broke into fervent song. This marching seemed like fun, but also felt sinister. I remembered Gareth leading his ragtag followers around bomb sites in Cardiff. But they were innocent children, led by an older child they chose to look up to. There was nothing ragtag about this procession. Yet no matter how much the standard-bearers strutted, they were not the true leaders like Gareth had been. I knew little about politics, but I sensed that these children had been conscripted by an adult for his own purposes: to be dedicated child-soldiers acting as his eyes and ears in every home in Lisbon.

Any pleasure I felt at seeing the colourful procession vanished with this thought. I walked on, discreetly following three women who had been in front of me since I left the docks, chatting away with baskets of fish balanced on their heads. Surely they were heading towards the city centre to sell fish on street corners. But because I couldn't be certain of directions, I politely stopped a well-dressed woman strolling towards me, holding her young daughter's hand. Her daughter carried a small wooden crib. Her excited face reminded me that my own sister, Lily, would now be giddy with anticipation about Christmas, although she'd have precious few presents to open tomorrow morning. The woman smiled patiently as I struggled for the words to seek directions. Black Horse Square might mean nothing to her if this plaza was called another name in Portuguese. Then I remembered the area which Mr Tierney had told me I needed to pass through.

'Cais do Sodré?' I pointed in the direction from which she just come.

Her smile disappeared. Her gaze became a mixture of hostility and suspicion. '*Marujo?*'

My expression betrayed that I didn't understand this word. She repeated it in English: 'Sailor?'

I nodded. 'Sailor,' I announced proudly and pointed ahead. 'Cais do Sodré?'

The woman pulled her daughter closer and walked past, refusing to look at me. I felt myself blush, though I didn't know what to be ashamed of. Mr Tierney had told me to follow the river but when I reached a junction where a street sign read 'Largo de Santos', I couldn't resist exploring a series of side streets to my left that might lead more quickly to the real heart of the city. I intended this as only a small diversion, but I quickly got lost in the maze of narrow streets. Every time I turned a corner a remarkable new vista appeared and my curiosity led me farther astray.

Everything was on a grander scale than in Wexford, yet everything was shabbier too. At one time these splendid streets surely radiated wealth, but that time was long past. Now each four-storey building housed numerous families, judging by the number of children stampeding through open doorways. Glancing into bare hallways that reeked from the stale odours of cooking and damp clothes, I spied steep wooden staircases where many spindles had fallen off the shaky banisters or been sawn down for firewood. The fanlights above each doorway had been constructed with delicately wrought metal but the panes of glass were either missing or spider-webbed with cracks. The upper-storey windows opened out onto small wrought-iron balconies where copious quantities of hanging washing could not disguise how rust-eaten these neglected railings were. Most window frames were equally neglected: paint peeling away and sackcloth used to block the wind blowing in through any broken windowpanes. The buildings had originally been ornately tiled but strips of tiling had fallen off to reveal bare cement. The tiles that remained in place were smudged with streaks of sandy dirt washed down from rooftops during heavy rain, with no guttering left in place to protect the walls.

I was so mesmerised by everything around me, even the elaborate mosaic of tiny pavement tiles, that I quickly lost any sense of direction. I just knew that I had never climbed so many steep stone steps before. In some places the roads grew so narrow that daylight had difficulty breaking in. Then I would turn a corner to find that the next street, set at a different angle, was a blaze of shafting light. Every available sunlit space was occupied by someone: old shawled women seated on low walls with baskets beside them or groups of old men at tables outside shabby cafes gesticulating in heated conversations. Often they paused to observe my progress with an indifferent curiosity, mutely puffing away on pungent cigarettes.

Eventually the streets widened out, winding uphill in wide loops, with an old church or some other elaborate building on every bend. The steps up to each church displayed elaborate nativity scenes. I was following a set of tram tracks, hoping they would lead into the city centre. These tracks led up a hill so steep that my legs struggled to ascend the tiny steps built into the narrow pavement. I found it hard to imagine a tram being able to ascend this steep incline. At the top I savoured the breathtaking view and then ran excitedly down the centre of the equally steep street on the far side. There were no pavement cafes here: the road growing so narrow that I could touch the buildings on either side by just one leap to my left or right. Every inch of space overhead was filled with clothes drying on wires suspended from balconies. So many white sheets fluttered in the breeze that it felt like watching a flotilla of three-masted schooners at full sail.

I was so busy gazing up that it took the urgent clanging of a bell to alert me to the appearance of a wooden tram that had managed to crest the steep hill behind me. The tram careered downhill, the driver warning me to move from the centre of the road. But this street possessed no grandiosely tiled pavement; it hardly possessed any pavement. There was just a narrow step: two-foot high and barely a foot wide. I mounted this but even then I felt scared: the road was so narrow that there seemed barely room for the tram to hurtle down the single set of tracks. I prayed that nobody would emerge from a building because they would surely be mown down. The closer the tram came, the more anxious I grew that it might not have sufficient space to pass without crushing me. I tried to gain an extra inch of space by pressing my back against the peeling paintwork of a doorway. The tram was only yards away: the driver ringing his bell, warning me not to move. Its single carriage was packed on the inside, with more passengers standing up than could squeeze into its wooden seats.

But people were not just inside of the tram. As it approached I spied a girl, barely older than myself, precariously balanced on the running board of the back step. She clung onto the door handle by the fingertips of one hand. Hitching a lift on the back of a vehicle without the driver's knowledge was known as scutting in Wexford. But this was different: this girl made no effort to conceal herself. The driver who could see her through his side mirror seemed unconcerned by the presence of an extra illicit passenger. I heard her voice over the loud clicking of the steel handle that the driver used to operate the motor. She was playfully conducting an animated conversation through the glass panels on the rear door with passengers pressed against the far side. She leaned back to laugh at something someone said. Her hair streamed out behind her, as did her white dress. I was terrified that she would crack her skull against the buildings the tram was flashing past. But she seemed to possess a sixth sense about the narrow streets she was being carried through, instinctively knowing when to tuck in her head as the tram passed a protruding window ledge.

It was as if she knew the exact location of every obstruction without needing to look up. I knew that she was aware of me too – a new and unexpected obstacle – because, as the tram reached me, she did not lean in towards the safety of the glass but trailed out her free arm to let her long hair and fingertips brush against my face as I pressed against the doorway. She turned towards me and laughed; lips inches from mine, her eyes enjoying my startled expression, her skin glowing with the carefree joy of being young. She allowed her free hand to caress my cheek one last time as she smiled. I wanted to shout a warning about a windowsill inches behind her. But without taking her eyes off me she tucked in her head at the last second. The tram bustled on down the hill and around another severe corner with a clamorous ringing of its bell.

I let out a deep breath, feeling shaken and yet exhilarated. I could still feel the swish of her hair against my face, her fingertips playfully caressing my cheek. Her laughter had been intoxicating. I wanted to shout and dance on this back street of a foreign city where I felt so free and completely and utterly alive. Nobody here knew me: there were no prying eyes like in Wexford where every shopkeeper knew to the exact penny what my mother owned them. To the Lisboetas I was just another foreign sailor – a *marujo* – passing through. This description stripped away my poverty. Here I possessed no identity. This didn't feel lonely: it felt liberating. I ran down the street after the tram, knowing that I would never be able to catch it. But I longed to see this girl in the white dress again. I fantasised about jumping up onto the back step of rickety trams to journey through these streets with her, sharing the vibrant thoughts that filled my head.

Chapter Thirteen

December 24, Lisbon

THEN I TURNED THE CORNER and I was stopped, utterly still, in my tracks. The girl stood waiting in the centre of the street, as if expecting me to chase after her. My onslaught of excited thoughts shuddered to a halt. I had never expected to catch her. The swish of her long hair against my face had possessed a dreamlike quality. Now that she stood before me – having hopped down off the running board at a nearby tram stop – my new-found confidence evaporated. I retreated back to being the tongue-tied boy who could never find the right words to say to Ellie Coady. The girl smiled, enjoying my surprise. But her smile contained no mockery. It was friendly and undamaged. This seemed like a strange word but it was the word that came to me. Her open expression made me realise how damaged the last girl to smile at me had been: Bronwyn in Cardiff, shivering in a summer dress with padded shoulders that was too grown up for her.

The girl laughed. 'If you run after something you catch it.'

I didn't know what to say. Then I realised that this was alright: she was not expecting me to automatically be funny or sophisticated. Nor was she judging me with the sharp appraisal of most Wexford girls, who could instantly work out – to the pound, shilling and pence – whether your father was better off than theirs. This girl seemed amused and genuinely curious about me. We had encountered each other by chance. If I wished to talk she seemed happy to talk. But if I just walked past her, she would instantly forget me and jump onto the back of the next tram to journey on towards her next adventure. This is what she made our encounter feel like: an adventure.

'I'm Jack,' I said simply. 'Jack Roche.'

She laughed. 'Like cockroach?'

I laughed too. 'Just call me Jack.'

Pointing to herself, she said: 'Kateřina.'

'Katherine?'

She repeated it more slowly. 'Ka-teři-na.'

'You speak English?'

'At school I study English. And in this city some men teach me new words. But sometimes they pretend that a word means one thing and later I find out it is not a nice word but has a rude meaning. Some men play tricks: are not always nice.'

'But you speak good English for a Portuguese,' I said, pronouncing each word slowly. Throwing back her head, she laughed with good-natured incredulity.

'You think I am Portuguese?'

'I heard you joking in Portuguese to the tram passengers.'

'They tease me. I know enough Portuguese to tease back: enough to survive. Also some English, German and a little French and Italian. My Spanish is no good: all I know to say in Spanish is "the pink horse is blue". It is the most useless phrase: no horse is blue and especially not a pink one.' Kateřina laughed, but it sounded like she was laughing at herself. 'Words fly around my head in different tongues, like birds trying to escape. Sometimes the wrong birds fly out in the wrong tongue.'

'I think it's great,' I replied in genuine admiration. 'I can only speak English.'

She looked perplexed. 'Why come?'

'You mean "how come". I speak English because it's what we speak every day in Ireland.'

'No: I do mean "why come". Why come here? Ireland is not at war, so why flee?'

'I'm not fleeing; I'm a sailor.' I remembered the Portuguese word the woman used earlier. '*Marujo*.'

This time Kateřina's laugh was teasing. 'You no *marujo*, you *menino*.' She made a rocking motion, as if cradling a child. 'Your captain was surely drunk to mistake a *bambino*, *le gargon*, a *děcko* like you for a sailor?'

'I'm not so young,' I protested, furiously trying to stop blushing. 'I'm sixteen.'

'Sixteen? You?' Kateřina counted out the number on her fingers. 'In Ireland the years must be short, maybe a year is only ten months long in Ireland. Maybe you are sixteen in Ireland years: but in real years you are only a *bambino*. Maybe your captain is not drunk but blind.'

Her mockery contained no malice, but I felt hurt at being cut down to size.

'I'm a sailor who has just crossed the Bay of Biscay.' She looked amused at my attempt to make my voice sound deeper. 'What do you do?'

'Me?' She paused and, for the briefest instant, I caught a flicker of unhappiness in her expression. Then she shrugged self-deprecatingly. 'My job is not exciting: I work in a café not far from Rossio. If you find my café I will serve you coffee as my treat.'

'I'll track you down,' I promised. 'There can't be that many cafés in Lisbon.'

Kateřina smiled. 'All Lisbon has is cake shops and spies. And people trying to get out.'

'Are you trying to get out of Lisbon?'

Her eyes became guarded and she looked more vulnerable. 'Do you not believe I work in cake shop?'

'Of course I do. I wasn't trying to pry.'

'What is "pry"?'

'It means to spy.'

'You no spy,' she said with conviction. An element of teasing re-entered her voice. 'I know what a real spy looks like.'

'How do you know the real spies who come into your cake shop?' I tried to tease her back.

'They pass notes hidden inside *pastel de nata*.' She laughed at my bewildered look. 'Inside the little custard cake you see in café windows on every street corner.'

I grinned ruefully. 'Not the street corners I've seen. I got lost. I had to ask a woman for directions but she stomped past like I was dirt.'

'What did you ask her?'

'For directions to Cais do Sodré.'

Kateřina tossed back her hair with a renewed peal of laughter. 'Cais do Sodré is the red district.'

'Red?' I was confused. 'You mean like communist?'

She threw her eyes to heaven. '*Bambino, le gargon*, a *děcko*. Cais do Sodré is red-light area: where real sailors go to buy women's body. You are not a real sailor: I think you are not ready to buy a woman's body.'

'I wasn't trying to buy a woman's body,' I said, embarrassed. 'I was hoping to buy something entirely different.'

'What you want to buy?'

I blushed again, acutely mortified. I had no idea where to buy nylon stockings, but I wasn't going to make a fool of myself by asking this girl.

'I got lost,' I said gruffly. 'My home town is a hundred times smaller than Lisbon.'

'I get lost here too,' Kateřina said. This time her tone contained neither gaiety nor mockery. She spoke from the heart and, in that moment, looked younger than me. 'Lisbon is an easy city to get lost in or to disappear with no question asked.'

'Where are you from?'

'Czechoslovakia.'

'I don't even know where that is,' I confessed.

'It no longer exists since the Nazis marched in,' she said. 'We packed what we could in a suitcase and fled.'

'Did you want to leave home?' I asked.

'Leaving was better than the other option.'

'What was that?'

'To be herded up and killed.'

I didn't know how to reply. Her voice was so low I barely made out her words. I wanted to put my arms around her, but not in the way that I had held Ellie Coady in the lane off Main Street. I wanted to comfort Kateřina for what she had been through and yet I had no understanding of what she had experienced. We stood in silence. The street was ablaze in sunlight but it felt cold. Then the peal of a bell broke the silence and we stepped onto the pavement as another tram manoeuvred its way around the corner, wheels groaning on the tracks. We watched it pass and let the silence settle back.

'I don't know about such things,' I said then. 'They censor all news about the war in Ireland and, even if they didn't, I can't afford to read any papers, unless I find old copies in bins. But the Irish ones are only about hurling matches and rationing. All I know are things my father told me, and he's dead now.'

'What happened to him?' Kateřina asked quietly.

'The Germans sank his ship when he was en route back to Ireland from Lisbon. But the Irish papers are not even allowed to print this: they just say that his ship is missing. That's why I'm here, trying to earn a wage for my mother. You're right: I'm no real sailor. I'm fourteen and a half and so lost that I don't even know where to change my money into Portuguese currency.'

Kateřina linked her arm through mine. It felt like the way a big sister would do. 'I show you and make sure you are not cheated. Then as thanks, you can buy me coffee.'

'I'd like that.'

'You like coffee?'

'I don't know.' I confessed, unsure if she would laugh. 'I've never tasted proper coffee. We only drink tea in Wexford and even that's rationed when my mother can afford it.'

Chapter Fourteen

December 24, Lisbon

I HAVE NO IDEA HOW Kateřina navigated so quickly through the maze of side streets but after a few moments she led me out onto the widest street I had ever seen, with trees and statues lining its centre. Cinemas, swanky hotels and restaurants stretched along both pavements.

'You wouldn't see the like of this even in Dublin,' I said, awestruck.

She laughed. 'They rebuilt this avenue after an earthquake. People say it is modelled on Paris but this is no Paris.'

'You lived in Paris?'

'Only little while.'

'What's Paris like?'

'Far grander but not impressed by its own grandeur: Paris takes itself for granted. It has everything.' Kateřina paused. 'Even Nazi troops on its streets.'

'Are they why you left Paris?'

'They are why I ended up in Paris.' Anxious to change the subject, Kateřina pointed to a statue on a roundabout at the top of the avenue.

'If you turn left at that monument you reach Hotel Aviz, where the rich sit out this war. The richest man on earth lives there. I saw him once.'

'Salazar?' I asked, thinking of the dictator.

Kateřina laughed. 'Salazar lives like a monk. In newspaper pictures he sits in his bare office, with pictures of the Pope and Mussolini on his wall. Salazar is too much dimwit to enjoy luxury like Hotel Aviz. It is Calouste Gulbenkian I once saw in there, eating alone at a table in the restaurant. Two secretaries sat in silence at the next table, waiting like dogs in case he summoned them. Or maybe he just did not like being alone, though he looked like the loneliest person on earth.'

I didn't know whether to believe her. 'What were you doing in such a swanky hotel?'

Kateřina stood up to her full height, fixing me with a glacial, autocratic stare. 'If we try to walk in there now the doormen will stop you, but not me.'

'I can't help how I'm dressed.' Her unflinching gaze made me acutely conscious of my shabbiness. 'I've only two sets of clothes and these are my good ones.'

Her disdainful look vanished. She touched my shoulder apologetically.

'I do not mean to make you feel bad. I am just showing how actors act. It is not your clothes that count, but how you glare at people. If you act like you belong, if you have a haughty look, no doorman ever dares ask your business. It is easier for a girl. The secret is never to smile. Instead I give the doormen a snooty look, waiting for them to hold open the door. My gaze so unnerves them that they never notice my clothes ... they bow and let me in.'

'What happens then?'

Kateřina shrugged ruefully. 'Nothing except that I savour each minute until I get thrown out. It is just a game where I pretend to look like I belong. But I get caught quick because you would fool a judge quicker than a hotel concierge. Concierges notice everything but they hate fuss in their foyers. Their stare soon lets me know that they know I have no business there. If I leave quiet they do nothing, but remember my face for next time. But often I can steal four, five minutes and peer into the restaurants in each grand hotel. I mingle with guests at Hotel Tivoli, waiting for cars to take them to the casino at Estoril. I have sat in the Avenida Palace Hotel where the less nasty German officials like to stay, because its back door allows informers to slip away back to docks.'

'Where do the really nasty Germans stay?'

'Hotel Metropole at Rossio.'

'Have you seen inside there?'

Her tone became abrupt and guarded. 'I never set foot in that hotel.'

'I was only asking,' I said. 'I meant no offence.'

'No offence taken.' She smiled. 'Let's go and look at the posters outside the cinema: I rarely have money to go inside but I love staring at movie stars.'

I didn't care where we went: I just loved being with her. I wasn't sure when the Cook expected me back. The coal was probably unloaded by now, the dockers hurrying home to prepare for Christmas Eve celebrations with their families. I didn't know how long it would take for the Captain to arrange the loading of our American cargo. Today might be the only day I had to explore Lisbon. But even if I was due back on board, I would have risked Captain Donovan's wrath for the chance to wander these streets with this girl.

Kateřina enjoyed my stunned reaction to the extravagant buildings we passed. We chatted about everything and then at other times we didn't speak at all, but there was nothing strained in our companionable silences. Maybe it was because I was so removed from my normal world, but it felt like the most natural thing to walk alongside this girl, laughing as we invented outrageous occupations for prissy-looking passers-by. I had never experienced a holiday, beyond one or two afternoon family jaunts by train to Rosslare Strand. But surely this was what a proper holiday felt like? We reached a packed square that Kateřina told me was called Rossio. She ordered two tiny coffees at a café there, laughing when I wanted to pour milk into mine and becoming even more amused when I scrunched up my face at the sourness of the drink, which tasted as thick as tar.

'It is called espresso,' she said. 'When you lie on bunk tonight and cannot sleep, it is because of espresso and not because of me.'

I blushed. For some reason this also made her blush. Kateřina looked away and I saw, directly behind her across the square, a sign for the Hotel Metropole. I could not tell if she had chosen her seat deliberately so as not to have to look at that hateful place decked in Christmas decorations. She insisted on paying for our coffees, though I sensed she had very little money. I saw her carefully count out coins from her purse when she slipped past me up to the counter. I couldn't have paid anyway as I still needed to change my money into escudos. When I mentioned the exchange bureau that Mr Tierney had suggested, Kateřina threw up her eyes to heaven. She claimed that its owner was a bigger gangster than Calouste Gulbenkian himself, who funded his suite at the Aviz by paying elderly refugees a pittance for any jewels they managed to salvage before fleeing to Lisbon.

She brought me to a small shop, down a side street near the river, and haggled with the trader until satisfied that I had received a fair rate of exchange. I offered to buy her a small gift to express my thanks, but when we walked outside she was distracted by an office window across the street. She walked across to peer in, so lost in thought that a taxi needed to brake to avoid hitting her. The driver beeped his horn and shouted through his open window but Kateřina barely heard him. I walked over to join her. The building had a more modern feel than the small shops nearby: the words Pan American Airlines were painted in gold-leaf letters on the plate glass. No customers were inside but a woman in an air hostess's uniform busied herself with papers at a desk. I could not tell if she was working or simply avoiding Kateřina's gaze.

'If you wish to buy me something,' she said dreamily, 'buy me a ticket for Boeing clipper flying boat. It flies from the Azores to New York. Imagine landing at dawn on the Hudson River by Manhattan.'

'If I'd the money to buy you a ticket I would,' I said. 'I swear.'

The Pan American attendant rose and walked over to the glass door, where she placed a sign which read *Este escritório está fechado* and, in smaller letters, *This office is closed*. Kateřina's eyes never left her but the woman refused to acknowledge her presence. Behind us, the exchange bureau owner was also busily locking up, closing early to hurry home to his family. The hours leading up to midnight mass on Christmas Eve were the centrepiece of celebrations here. Yet despite many shop windows containing cribs, I found it hard to remember in this sunshine that we were on the cusp of Christmas. Or maybe I didn't want to think about it in case I was overcome by homesickness, imagining Green Street, where hopefully my brothers would scavenge enough wood to get a decent fire blazing in the kitchen. I wondered how Kateřina's family would spend tomorrow. She turned to me.

'I believe that if you had the money – even if it costs you all you own – you would buy me that Pan Am ticket. You have a good heart. But there are refugees in Lisboa who owned mansions once and even they will never have enough money to enter that booking office. Don't mind my silly talk about seaplane. I gaze in the window of Pan Am like I enjoy sneaking into lobbies of grand hotels. I like to dream and to dream costs nothing.'

'Does it make you sad, being stranded here?'

She shook her head. 'Why would I be sad? In Lisboa I am safe. I have my job, my family, my friends. Today I even have handsome escort.'

'You're teasing me.' I blushed.

'I compliment you. You never compliment me.'

137

I went to speak and for the first time all afternoon I became tongue-tied and embarrassed. Kateřina took pity on me.

'If I dream too long at this window I get sad,' she said. 'I must go to work soon.'

'I want to buy some Christmas presents,' I replied. 'Trinkets for my brothers and sister. My father always did that.'

Kateřina smiled. 'I know a good shop. I would enjoy if you let me help you to pick.'

She led the way, as excited as if buying gifts for her own siblings. But I noticed that she crossed to the other footpath to avoid one particular shop and then, after we passed it, crossed back again. I was shocked to see that it was a German propaganda store, with Nazi insignia arrayed in the window alongside magazines and books. The centrepiece of the display was a newspaper called *Der Stürmer* with an ugly anti-Semitic cartoon on its cover. I was horrified by the grotesque material and fascinated by the bland indifference of passers-by. But from the cut of Kateřina's shoulders I knew that she would be hurt if I lingered to stare any longer. A few doorways down from it, we entered a toy shop. The owner was closing up but happy to let us browse and examine small items on the wooden shelves.

Kateřina laughed at my poor selection of presents for Lily and insisted on suggesting gifts that, although no dearer than my choices, perfectly matched what a girl of Lily's age would like. Two shelves were devoted to religious statues and I picked a small statue of Our Lady of Fatima, which I knew my mother would treasure. I selected small items for my brothers and hoped that I still had enough money left to buy those precious American nylon stockings.

We emerged into the sunshine and passed beneath an archway that led into a huge square. Three sides were lined with imposing red-bricked buildings. The fourth side had steps leading down to the

Tagus River. The centre of the square was dominated by a lavishly decorated plinth, topped by a statue of a man on horseback.

'I know where we are.' I was pleased to finally display some local knowledge. 'This is Black Horse Square.'

Kateřina stared at the statue and laughed. 'The horse is bronze.'

'Yes, but it looks black when you're passing by on a ship.'

'How you know? How often have you seen this horse from a ship, you salty jack-tar?'

She pronounced each word with such an outrageous mock accent that I couldn't stop smiling. 'How did you learn so much slang?'

'From English sailors in the café. Often I wonder who could follow their odd words. When my aunt taught me English … she was … what you say … very strict about grammar. I imagine her frown, trying to understand words like…' Kateřina again impersonated an old sailor's accent. ' "The rain it bucket so hard, my old salt, them bigwigs made us batten the hatches, but when we entered Biscay there be just enough blue in the sky to make a pair of sailor's trousers."' She looked at me. 'Who makes trousers from cloud?'

'I haven't a clue,' I confessed ruefully. 'I never set foot on a ship until last week.'

'This square is Praça do Comércio. Try to say it.'

'Teach me some Czech instead.'

'*Jste sladký mladý muž.*'

'What does that mean?'

Kateřina smiled. 'That for me to know.'

'Can I say it back to you?'

She shook her head. 'It is not appropriate.'

'Do you mean that it's rude?'

'I would not appreciate being called a sweet boy.'

I looked away, embarrassed. She stepped sideways to observe me better.

'You blush easily,' she teased.

'I don't,' I said, blushing even more furiously now.

'Your face is like red apple. What is English word for bright red?'

'Leave me alone.' I turned my back, even more self-conscious.

'You are not used to girls teasing you?'

I looked back at her. 'I'm not used to girls at all.'

'No sweetheart?'

I didn't know how to reply. Could I call Ellie my sweetheart? Maybe Ellie only walked me down to my ship at dawn from pity, knowing there was a chance I might not come back alive. 'I might have one,' I said. 'It depends.'

'On what?'

'On whether I find a pair of American nylon stockings to bring home to her.'

Kateřina laughed, like this was the funniest sentence she had ever heard.

'What did she promise you for nylons?'

'She promised me nothing.' I blushed so furiously that I felt my face would explode. 'It's nothing like that ... well, actually she promised I could watch her put them on.'

'You have never seen a girl put on pair of stockings?' Kateřina sounded amused, probing farther. 'Or seen a girl take off pair?'

'Ellie isn't like that,' I said.

'What is she not like? Not flesh and blood? Does she not like to be kissed? What sort of girl does not like to be kissed?'

'I promised to bring her back nylons. But I'd be too embarrassed to ask for them in a shop.' I looked at Kateřina. 'Will you help me buy stockings?'

'For another girl?'

'If I've enough money, I'll buy you a pair too.'

Kateřina smiled. 'I do not want your stockings: I only tease you.' She paused. There was a sudden wistfulness in her voice that I could not even begin to fathom. 'I like normal things … a boy and girl teasing each other as they walk … like it was an ordinary day at home.'

'If your home was Wexford then you wouldn't be seen walking with the likes of me.'

'Why not?'

'It's obvious you come from moneyed folk. I bet you even had servants.'

'We had only one servant,' Kateřina said defensively. 'Also a cook and gardener. But we were not rich.'

'That sounds rich in Wexford.'

'We are no longer in Wexford or Prague. Maybe it is you who is now snob, Jack.'

'Sure what have I to be snobbish about?'

'If you do not want to walk with me, walk away.' Kateřina turned her face and I saw she was genuinely upset.

'Why wouldn't I want to walk with you?'

'You talk about things that no longer matter. Maybe you never have a maid but you never hid under rags in the boot of a stopped car, listening to hobnail boots … guards at border crossings. You never walked all night through a wood, starving but too scared to stop to pick berries because you are listening always for soldiers with dogs. It is no matter who we once were: what only matters is who we now are. I am now a girl who lives in the smallest room on top floor of the shabbiest street on Bairro Alto. In my old house in Prague one whole room was given to books in my father's library. My father never stopped me reading any book. Now if I wish to read a book I must sneak into second-hand bookshop close to where I live. It full of books in languages that owner cannot recognise. He knows I have no money to buy anything, so often I am too ashamed to enter shop. All I can do is stand outside and stare at books in window. That who I am now: you are the rich one. When your captain wishes to sail, you can leave.'

I didn't know how to reply: the events she described were beyond my limited experience of life. So I just intertwined my fingers with hers. 'All I own are the two sets of my father's old clothes that my mother cut down in size. But even if I was richer than whoever this Gulbenkian guy is, I'd still be proud as punch to be seen walking anywhere with you.'

Kateřina looked down at my fingers and squeezed them. 'You are not so poor.' Her tone was gently mocking but I sensed she was touched by my words. 'You have the price of a pair of American nylon stockings.'

'I hope so,' I said. 'I haven't a clue what nylons cost.'

'Nylons are like everything in Lisbon: they cost what people are willing to pay. Most shops are closing now for Christmas Eve but you don't need to find a shop: you need find American sailor drinking in *tasca*. American sailors have everything – nylons, Lucky Strike cigarettes, chewing gum, bourbon, Hershey chocolate bars – and know the price of everything. Or the two prices: the price they ask for and the price they accept when you barter them down.'

'I'm no good at bartering,' I said, savouring the warmth of her fingers.

'I am,' Kateřina replied. 'I need to be.'

'Will you talk to a sailor for me?'

'I do not talk to sailors.'

'You're talking to me.'

She laughed: her good humour restored. 'You only a *menino*, a *bambino*, schoolboy.'

'If I was a real schoolboy I'd pull your hair.'

'You would not dare try.'

Her defiant taunt could only have one outcome. Kateřina knew it, which was why she pulled her hand free and ran through the crowds thronging the square, certain that I would chase after her. Respectable passers-by were irritated by our antics, but we didn't care. In that moment we were neither Irish nor Czechoslovakian. I was simply a boy chasing a girl, so fleet-footed that she was confident of eluding my clutches until she consented to allow herself be caught. Several times my stretched fingers came within inches of her hair before she nimbly switched direction to dart between people. But I sensed her deliberately slow down. She turned to face me, moving backwards, but only at walking pace. Her face was flushed with the exertion of running but also the exhilaration of the chase: her eyes alive with flirtatious mockery. She stopped suddenly so that I nearly bumped into her, her face so close to mine that it seemed to invite a kiss.

I might have kissed her too, intoxicated by the moment, had I not glanced beyond her shoulder. I saw an ornate sign for the Café Martinho da Arcada looking out onto the square. Most tables were inside but some stood outside: covered in white cloth and arranged along the flagstones underneath high porticos which guarded the entrance. The clientele at these outdoor tables were exclusively male. They conducted loud conversations over cigarettes and tiny cups of coffee or read the newspapers supplied by the café, held together by bamboo canes to prevent the pages blowing away. Only one man sat alone at a table, holding an English-language newspaper which he had been so immersed in that he barely seemed to notice the ragged shoeshine boy vigorously polishing his shoes. But this solitary man was no longer reading his paper: I sensed that for several minutes he had been watching me. Mr Walton saw me stare back in shock. He raised his Fedora hat in a silent greeting and handed the shoeshine boy a few coins for his work, which, judging by the boy's delighted reaction, represented a generous payment.

Kateřina touched my shoulder, concerned that my expression had changed. 'You look like you see a ghost.'

'It's worse: I've seen a ship's officer. He'll tell the crew that I was making a holy show of myself in public and they won't be long telling all of Wexford.'

'What is *holy show*?' she asked. 'Is it *holy show* to snatch a moment of happiness? I thought you nice, now I think you are stupid.'

'Why are you calling me stupid?'

'You cross a dangerous ocean, yet you have not travelled at all. You still can only think of everywhere as being like Wexford.'

'That's not fair.'

'It is true.'

'I just don't like Mr Walton. Let's go somewhere where I can't feel his eyes watching me.'

But the carefree intimacy between us was broken. Would I really have kissed her and might she have kissed me back? It wasn't what I had been seeking, but I knew so little about girls that I was more lost in this encounter than if Captain Donovan, halfway across Biscay, had asked me to steer without a compass. Maybe a kiss might have ruined everything, but I just knew that I loved Kateřina's company and didn't want to be parted from her yet. I pointed towards a municipal building being besieged by crowds. 'Let's go in there,' I suggested, hoping to get away from Mr Walton's scrutiny.

'I do not like in there.' Kateřina's tone was subdued, as if the sight of Mr Walton had reminded her of figures of authority from her past. 'I must go to work soon.'

'I thought everywhere closed early on Christmas Eve.'

'Some cafés stays open. Also hotels and *tascas* that sell wine and food. With so many sailors and refugees, there is money to be made even on Christmas Eve, and money scarce in Lisboa.'

'Don't leave yet,' I pleaded. 'We'll just slip into that building and slip out again. What is it?'

'The main post office.'

I walked towards it. Kateřina hesitated and then reluctantly followed. I sensed her anxiety. Her mood grew increasingly apprehensive as we pushed our way into the jammed building. Long queues stretched everywhere. Even more people leaned against the walls or stood in small clusters, looking like they had been there since the building opened.

'What are they all doing?' I asked.

'Waiting,' Kateřina replied.

'For what?'

'For something or nothing: for a letter that might arrive, addressed to them here, because nobody in the outside world has any other address for them. Or because they hope a relation who reached America might finally be able to place a phone call to this building and their name will be called out. Imagine how terrible it would be to wait here, day after day, and then, on the day you are not here, your name is paged and the caller has to hang up by the time people have run to find you, in another queue instead, looking for any news at the Shaaré Tikvah.'

'What is the Shaaré Tikvah?'

'The Gates of Hope.' She saw my puzzled expression. 'That is the name of the Lisbon synagogue. The synagogue is small and can give little aid, so most people wait here. They hope to catch sight of a face from the past who might have news about the loved ones they are separated from. Or maybe they wait because the streets are cold and they have no money for a café. Maybe it feels better to be among others waiting for nothing to happen than to sit alone in the cubbyhole they call home. In a post office everyone has an excuse to wait.'

'From the opposite side of the crowded marble concourse I saw a woman glance across at Kateřina with a surprised glance of recognition. Kateřina looked towards the doorway. I could not tell if she was deliberately avoiding the woman's gaze.

'Do you ever wait in here?' I ask.

'I am finished with waiting,' she said quietly. 'Who would send a letter to me when nobody outside Lisboa knows I am alive?' She looked at me impatiently. 'Please, let's leave here.'

'Are you frightened that someone you know will see you?'

She reached out to stroke my face. I couldn't tell if this was a gesture of affection or an act to show that she was not alone, done for the benefit of the woman who had noticed her and was taking a hesitant step in our direction. I barely heard Kateřina above the hubbub of foreign accents. 'Only children can afford to be frightened.'

We pushed our way through the incoming crowd, back out into the cold air. I sensed Kateřina's anxiety to be gone now.

'Will you promise to help me buy those stockings?' I asked.

She smiled sadly. 'I make no promises.'

'Can I even just meet you tomorrow?'

'Find the café where I work.'

'I wouldn't know where to look for it.'

'Near Rossio. We pass it earlier. Find that café and I help you buy the stockings that Ellie says she will let you watch her put on. That is my promise.'

Crowds pushed against us: people entering the post office and others trying to exit. Kateřina leaned forward and lightly kissed me on both cheeks. Then before I had time to say or do anything, she disappeared among the throng of passers-by. I was left standing there, alone and confused but determined to find her again.

Chapter Fifteen

Christmas Eve, Bairro Alto, Lisbon.

I SHOULD HAVE RETURNED TO the ship but I wandered the streets instead, carrying my sack of presents, watching as shops closed and locals went home for family festivities. I told myself that I was seeking a *tasca* where American sailors might have goods for sale, but in truth I was hoping to catch a glimpse of Kateřina at work in her café. By seven o'clock my legs were exhausted from walking through dimly lit laneways, when I heard my name shouted. I turned to see Shay Cullen smoking in the doorway of one of the few small *tascas* still open. He was spruced up: his hair slicked back with half a bottle of Brylcreem, his clothes as dandy as if dressed up to go a jazz dance on a Saturday night. He nodded towards the open door, through which I heard accordion music.

'The whole crew are inside,' he said. 'They're serving cheap wine and decent grub, if you like fish stew and queer-tasting sausage. If you don't like the taste, there's mounds of white bread. Join the Christmas feast, Jack. We've even acquired a ship's officer we can't get rid of. Mr Walton is drunker than Tommy Bergin, and Bergin can put his booze away. I rarely get two words out of Mr Walton on board: now we can't get two seconds of silence from him.'

I was starving, having lost my nerve every time I had peered into one of the narrow eating houses that stretched back forever:

places where I could not read a word of the menu. But at the same time I was savouring this freedom to explore the city. So despite my hunger, I might have still walked on with a wave if Shay Cullen hadn't shouted in through the doorway. Mr Tierney appeared in response to his call. I needed to look away for fear of laughing: it was obvious who had used the rest of Shay Cullen's bottle of Brylcreem. The attire that Mr Tierney had managed to assemble made him resemble a cross between a New York gangster and a prosperous cattle dealer. If I had a camera, drinkers in Wexford pubs would have paid a fortune for a photograph of him dressed like this, just for the chance to slag him.

'We thought we'd have to send out a search party,' Mr Tierney scolded. 'Are you not joining your crewmates on Christmas Eve? We've a stool kept for you.'

There was no point in arguing, especially when I had no intention of revealing that I wanted to keep walking to find a café where a girl was working an evening shift. So I went inside, unable to resist a verbal dig.

'What happened to your hair? Did the Cook spill grease on it?'

Mr Tierney gave me a playful clip across the ear. 'My hair always looks this well and if you tell any *menina bonita* that it doesn't I'll make you swim back to Wexford.'

'What's a *menina bonita?*'

He snorted. 'You should know, seeing as you spent the afternoon chasing after one.'

I blushed and pretended not to understand. His sly remark shrank Lisbon back down into the narrow prism of Wexford town. Even here, where I imagined I was utterly free, prying eyes had caught me out. Mr Tierney wouldn't be slow about using this information when needing to wheedle favours from me, subtly threatening to inform Ellie Coady that I had been seen with another girl. Not that my feelings for Kateřina echoed what I felt for Ellie. I had known Ellie all my life and the only word to describe my feeling for her was love; even if, so far, that word had proved unsayable. But Kateřina was revealing a wider world beyond my previous imagining and – I suspected – beyond Ellie's comprehension too: how could anyone in Wexford know about such experiences? My father and grandfather had frequented foreign taverns like the one I was entering. But my mother had never even visited Dublin. The furthest she ever travelled – a train journey of thirty-seven miles still mentioned with pride – was what she referred to as: 'The day I saw the cathedral in Waterford'. I might as well try and talk to Ellie about Neptune as talk to her about Czechoslovakia. But I didn't want to discuss Kateřina with anyone, and especially not with my crewmates, crowding around a long wooden table in the *tasca*, who acknowledged my arrival by tipping their caps with a finger or by an almost imperceptible nod.

Myles Foley sat quietly beside the Dazzler Kehoe, with Thomas Bergin next to him, the worse for drink. The Cook sat beside Thomas at the end of the table, chewing a piece of sausage meat, his face displaying a professional scepticism as if it didn't meet his exacting standards. On the opposite side of the table, Mr Walton sat with Ernie Grogan. There was a free stool beside Ernie. Mr Tierney told me to sit there and help myself to whatever food remained. Shay Cullen came back inside and sat on the stool beside me, leaving the last stool free for Mr Tierney who wandered up to the bar with a relaxed, proprietorial stride that came naturally to him in all licensed premises, as if every foreign bar was merely an extension of his local pub.

He passed a stack of wooden casks piled almost to the ceiling. An elderly man leaned against the casks, playing an accordion softly. His vacant gaze as he swayed suggested that he was blind. In what free space remained on the tiled floor, an old couple danced to his tune: the man wearing a buttoned up overcoat and hat, the red-faced, plump woman smiling up at him. They seemed to exist in a different world to the other drinkers who sat at tables or lined whatever free space remained against the walls: locals engaged in loud conversations and yet taking a discreet interest in everything that occurred at our table.

'Where's Gary O'Leary?' I asked, noticing the Third Engineer's absence.

'I'll give one you clue,' Ernie Grogan replied. 'Somewhere where a mother forgot to lock up her young bricks and mortar.'

'Never mind O'Leary, where were you?' the Cook asked. 'Are you a cabin boy or a fly boy? I'm exhausted from wandering around shops trying to get supplies for our voyage home. I'll need you tomorrow when the shops reopen.' He pushed the plate of sausage meat towards me. 'You deserve to starve but chew on this. It's *chouriço assado*: the house speciality, or so our host tells us.'

'What is it?' I gingerly picked up a strange lump of thick sausage meat.

'It's cooked and it had four legs in its youth. Ask no more questions if you're hungry.' He turned to the Second Officer. 'Mr Walton, can you explain to this young buckaroo the difference between shore leave and desertion?'

Mr Walton raised his wine glass to me in greeting. Shay Cullen was right: he had been drinking heavily. 'I'm off-duty: all sailors are equal on a licensed premises.'

I sensed that not everyone at the table agreed or was comfortable with his presence. Mr Tierney had pirouetted around the elderly dancing couple, holding aloft an empty wine glass as if it was his waltzing partner. He reached the table in time to hear Mr Walton's remark as he presented the glass to me.

'Men are only equal in two places.' Mr Tierney reached for a half-full wine bottle on the table. 'The first is on a mortuary slab. The second is at the bottom of the sea.' He poured wine into my glass. 'You look frozen, Jack: this will put some colour in your cheeks.'

'I don't drink wine,' I said.

He sat down and pushed the glass towards me. 'Trust me; the wine here is safer than drinking the water. At least in Lisbon you won't get served weak porter topped up with slops behind a sailor's back. This is a decent wine from the Douro Valley. Would you agree, Mr Walton?'

Mr Walton sipped from his glass. 'I wouldn't have taken you for a wine connoisseur, Mossy.'

'You don't need to be a canon lawyer to be able to enjoy mortal sin.' Mr Tierney turned to me. 'Drink up, Jack.'

I raised the glass gingerly to my lips. The wine tasted sour, reminding me of vinegar. But perhaps this reflected my mood at feeling trapped. Until this morning I would have loved to be allowed to sit among my shipmates in a crowded *tasca* in the Bairro Alto. Now I longed to be back out walking the narrow streets, imagining Katerina's look of surprise if I managed to keep my promise and track her down.

'I'm sure my ma would be pleased at how you're minding me,' I muttered sullenly.

'Don't be an ungrateful pup,' Mr Tierney replied. 'I can only keep an eye on you if you're having a drink with the rest of us. It took you a while to find your sea legs on the ocean but you were quick off the mark adjusting to a sailor's life in port. Two hours in Lisbon and you're already walking out with a young lady.'

'I'm doing no such thing.' I used indignation to hide my embarrassment.

'That's not what our spies told us.' Mr Tierney winked at the Second Officer.

Mr Walton gave him a sharp look, more of benign tolerance than reproach. 'You have a vocabulary strong enough to make a nun keel over, Mossy. So do me a favour: call me any foul-mouthed term of abuse you like, rather than label me a spy.' He gazed around the *tasca*. 'Especially in this city.'

'A figure of speech with no derogatory intent,' Mr Tierney said hastily. 'I'm merely saying that you provided an account of seeing Jack engaged in what Father O'Gorman in Wexford calls "the sin of keeping company".'

'I observed that the boy looked happy: as did the girl in question. Happiness may be classified as a sin in Father O'Gorman's fevered imagination, but it's not one in mine.' Mr Walton raised his glass. 'Drink to happiness, Jack. Savour it every chance you can, because holding on to it is like trying to hold water between your cupped fingers.'

As I clinked glasses with Mr Walton I realised how drunk he was. He seemed like a different man. Could some of his gruffness on board the ship stem from shyness? He held my gaze and then looked away, retreating into private thoughts so that he seemed to be seated among us and yet cut off by more than just his naval rank. Sipping my wine, I wondered if I could ever understand this complex man.

Mr Tierney leaned towards me. 'Drink slowly, lad. After a while it tastes like mother's milk.'

Myles Foley spoke for the first time. 'Wine is fine in its place, but its place is really in a priest's hands in a chalice. I'm tired of the sea but I feel no late vocation for the priesthood. It's time we switched to brandy.'

'I agree,' the Cook said. 'Priests spend seven years in seminaries being specially trained in how to drink wine. Portuguese brandy is more of a sailor's drink, though, of course, I only drink brandy on two types of occasions.'

'When are they?' I asked.

'When I'm on sea and on land.' Raising a hand to catch the *tasca* owner's attention, he looked around the table. 'What's the Portuguese word for brandy?'

'Brandy,' Mr Tierney replied. 'Ask for brandy in any port and they know exactly what you want.'

'God protect us from ignorant pillocks,' Ernie Grogan interrupted. 'Any swabbie knows that the Portuguese word for brandy is *conhaque*.'

Mr Tierney addressed the entire table. 'I know all there is to know about ignorance. Haven't I to listen to nonsense being spouted down in the engine room by this ignorant old fool? My only consolation is that nobody who wasn't born, bred and buttered in Bethnal Green can decipher what he's rabbiting on about. The word for brandy in any language is brandy. Am I correct, Mr Walton?'

Mr Walton didn't seem to hear him. He was staring at two teenage girls who had slipped in through the door. They tried to merge with the crowd and catch the eye of the Irish sailors without attracting the owner's attention. A local man near them made a snide remark. Other drinkers laughed while the girls tried to ignore him. But I saw how his insult stung, though they defiantly tried to hide it, just like they tried to hide the fact that they were cold and hungry. Mr Tierney followed Mr Walton's gaze.

'We'll be long enough looking at the scenery in Cais do Sodré,' he said in mild disapproval, 'without the scenery from Cais do Sodré coming looking for us.'

'Those girls don't belong in Cais do Sodré,' Mr Walton said quietly.

'Where do they belong?'

'At home on Christmas Eve: where they would be if there was food on the table.'

'Plenty of girls go hungry in Wexford, but I don't see them lining the walls of public bars,' Mr Tierney remarked.

'Maybe Wexford has an absence of foreign sailors who have money but lack the proper word for brandy,' Mr Walton replied. 'Or maybe starving girls who step out of line in Wexford get rounded up by our own secret police.'

'And who might our secret police be?' Mr Tierney asked.

'The nuns who lock away girls as slave labourers in laundries, starching the shirts of rich men.'

'Hold your horses now,' Thomas Bergin interjected. 'We'll have no disrespectful talk about nuns. My wife's cousin happens to be a nun. There's not every family in Wexford can make that boast.'

'I don't care if your mother was a nun, Bergin,' Mr Walton said sharply. 'Brandy means brandy in any language and free speech means free speech, even in this police state.'

Mr Walton's raised tone brought the *tasca* owner scurrying towards our table. Every drinker present now paid us close attention. People without a word of English stared in open curiosity, but I sensed that those who understood Mr Walton's remark were deliberately averting their gaze while listening to our every word. The appearance of the *tasca* owner forced the two girls to slip quickly back out the door. Mr Tierney and Ernie Grogan made a point of ordering drink in loud voices: Mr Tierney was telling the owner to fetch a bottle of brandy while Ernie Grogan kept interrupting, repeatedly using the word *conhaque*, even though the owner already clearly understood. The two engineers seemed on the verge of trading blows, but I knew they were secretly working in tandem – like they did in the engine room – creating a smokescreen of bluster behind which Mr Walton's last remark might be forgotten.

The owner hurriedly returned with brandy and fresh glasses. Mr Tierney poured a round for everyone present, careful to only half-fill my glass.

'A toast', he said loudly. 'António de Oloveira Salazar.'

'I'll drink to him,' Thomas Bergin said. 'People call him a dictator, but what has democracy ever done for us? Ireland could use a benign dictator too to take all the squabbling out of politics. Salazar kept his people out of this war and he's a God-fearing Catholic, unlike certain drinkers at this table.'

He glanced at Mr Walton: the only person – apart from myself – not to join in Mr Tierney's toast. Mr Walton had previously insulted my father and yet I felt a protective loyalty towards him. Mr Walton saw me hesitate about raising my glass.

'Clink Mossy's glass, Jack,' he said quietly. 'Don't bring trouble down on your head.'

'Only if you join in the toast first, Sir.'

Mr Walton raised his glass. 'Salazar,' he said loudly, his stern glance ensuring that I did likewise. '*Feliz Natal*: Happy Christmas.'

The other sailors sat back, breathing a collective sigh of relief. Mr Walton addressed Mr Tierney in a wry whisper.

'You'd sell your soul to the Devil if the price was right, Mossy.'

Mr Tierney's reply was equally low so that nobody beyond our table could hear it. 'The Devil probably already owns a down-payment on my soul. There are sins on it for which only a cardinal in his dandy purple socks could grant absolution. But I'm in no hurry to see my soul separated from my body because of drunken talk. Let's get safely from this bar and when we're sailing up the Tagus River I'll raise a toast with you to Salazar as the thuggish tyrant he really is.'

Mr Walton nodded apologetically. 'I stand corrected and confess to being more than a trifle drunk.' He turned to me. 'When you visit Lisbon, Jack, enjoy the view and keep your trap shut.'

'If Salazar is so evil, why do refugees pour in here from across Europe?' I asked.

Mr Walton leaned in towards me. 'Few people are totally good or evil: with exceptions like Hitler and Stalin, who are two sides of the same pure evil.'

Maybe it was the brandy loosening my tongue but I couldn't prevent resentment from surfacing. 'My father was pure good, despite your snide remarks about him.'

'Go easy, Jack,' Mr Tierney cautioned. 'You're addressing a ship's officer.'

'Let young Roche talk,' Mr Walton snapped. 'Like I said, free speech is free speech.'

'It's only free for them that can afford it,' Mr Tierney responded. 'We're all equal now because we've having a few drinks on Christmas Eve. But we won't be equal when we wake up tomorrow with hangovers. You'll be an officer and Jack a mere cabin boy.'

'You forget, Mossy, I began my life at sea as a cabin boy.'

'And if you were still one I'd give you the same advice: a shut mouth catches no flies.'

'Whatever's said at this table stays here.' Mr Walton looked at me. 'I don't recall making any snide remarks about your father.'

'You talked about his impatience and insubordination.'

'Did I not also mention his courage?'

'Maybe you did.' The brandy made me want to say more, but Mr Tierney's eyes warned me to shut up.

'Insubordination takes courage: the courage to speak or act when you see something wrong.' Mr Walton raised his glass. 'To the memory of Able Seaman Sean Roche, God rest his soul – a sailor I was proud to sail with.' The others raised their glasses and repeated my father's name. I drained my glass. Only after Mr

Walton downed his brandy did he add – in words so quiet as to be barely audible: 'And a man I gravely wronged.'

The awkward silence was broken by Mr Tierney. 'If Sean is gazing down from heaven he's surely thinking that we're a shower of gobdaws, sitting with empty glasses and the bottle still half full.' He poured another round, topping up my glass with an even smaller measure. 'Your mother would murder me if she could see us,' he muttered. 'I gave her my word.'

Mr Walton surveyed the other customers who were covertly observing him. 'But you made a good point, Jack,' he conceded. 'There are far worse places in Europe for refugees than Lisbon. Salazar never wished to let them in, but to his credit, he's made no effort to expel them, even though few ever manage to secure bunks on ships bound for Palestine or America. Maybe they exist in limbo here, but that's safer than being herded into Nazi death camps.'

'Hold your horses,' Thomas Bergin whispered angrily. 'We know nothing about death camps: there's nothing about them in any paper I read.' I couldn't decide if the helmsman was affronted or scared by such talk.

'Because you only read Irish papers,' Mr Walton said. 'Our newspapers are so censored that they've bred a nation of ostriches: men like you, with your head stuck in the sand and a superior swagger on your backside because you've a nun in the family.'

Thomas Bergin pushed back his stool, enraged. 'I've told you before: insult the good nuns and I'll stretch you across this floor – ship's officer or no ship's officer.'

Myles Foley gently placed a restraining hand on Bergin's shoulder. 'Go easy, Tommy, we're all friends here. Besides, I wouldn't be so quick to take offense on the nun's behalf: if I remember right she's only your wife's *second* cousin, once removed.'

'Removed to a convent,' Shay Cullen interjected. 'I wouldn't mind removing a few of my squawking cousins there too.'

The laughter defused the tension. Thomas Bergin had to sit down, though he remained incensed. 'It's a queer class of ship's officer who's reduced to drinking with the rank and file,' he needled. 'Why aren't you off with the Captain and the Chief Officer?'

'When a sea captain is negotiating a deal the last thing he needs is a more experienced captain looking over his shoulder,' Mr Walton replied.

'An ex-captain,' Thomas Bergin reminded him, emboldened by brandy. 'Ex-brewery worker, ex-cabin boy; ex-sea captain; is there anything you're good at?'

'I try to be a good provider for my family,' Mr Walton replied quietly. 'I'm also a good helmsman if you keel over drunk and the locals flog your body to hotel chefs here looking to cook ostrich steaks for rich guests living the high life.'

'I'll not be called an ostrich,' Thomas Bergin retorted.

'Then educate yourself here where the Irish censor doesn't rule,' Mr Walton replied. 'Cafés in Black Horse Square have uncensored American papers and you'll even find German government shops selling the vilest propaganda. It would sicken your stomach, but at least the Portuguese allow their people to read newspapers on both sides and make up their own minds.'

'Who'd want to read that class of stuff?' Thomas Bergin asked, riled. 'This war has nothing to do with me. I mind my own business and you'd still be a captain if you could have minded yours. Up de Valera, I say: like Salazar, he's kept us out of this war.'

'That's true,' Mr Tierney remarked. 'Thanks to Dev, there's nothing to keep us from the safety of our beds in Wexford, beyond U-boats, Luftwaffe pilots and mermaids.' He turned to Mr Walton, anxious to steer the conversation on to less argumentative ground.

'Has Captain Donovan tracked down our American cargo of phosphate?'

'He has,' Mr Walton replied. 'The bad news is that it's on a Yankee ship two hundred miles away, east of the Azores.'

The Dazzler Kehoe, who had let the conversation pass him by, whistled softly. 'I don't mind braving U-boats, but it would take a greater act of bravery to break that news to the Staffords.'

'Do we wait until the American ship arrives?' I asked.

'The Staffords aren't overly fond of berthing fees,' the Dazzler explained. 'The Lisbon Harbour Master starts his clock ticking the minute you toss a rope over a bollard.'

'The Captain and Mr Valentine were making inquiries before the shipping offices closed,' Mr Walton explained. 'Two ship's officers look like men on business: three officers crowding into a shipping office look like beggars. The phosphate will need to wait until another Irish ship arrives. We just have to hope that Captain Donovan can salvage this trip by finding a cargo of convenience.'

'What's that?' I asked.

'It's any cargo Captain Donovan can lay his hands on cheaply,' Mr Tierney said. 'A cargo the Staffords won't want to throw overboard after we dock in Wexford and throw us all overboard after it.'

Myles Foley chuckled softly. 'Wouldn't that be a laugh: to survive the U-boats and drown within sight of Pierce's Foundry?'

'We could swim for the quay,' I said.

The grey-bearded sailor shrugged. 'I never learnt to swim and nor did most crews I sailed with. I reckon that if you're shipwrecked, once you hit the water you're as good as dead. You can splash around for ten minutes in terror, but it won't make any difference: you're going to meet your maker. Swimming only prolongs the agony. What do you say, Dazzler?'

'I don't mind your conscientious objections to splashing around in the ocean,' the Dazzler joked. 'But as I sleep in the next bunk to you, I'm less happy about your conscientious objections to splashing soap under your oxters.'

'If God didn't intend us to stay warm, he wouldn't have given us the natural protection of a thin lining of dirt to ward off germs,' Myles Foley replied, not even remotely offended. 'Besides, I always take a hot seaweed bath any time any ship I'm on docks near Enniscrone in Sligo.'

'How often do ships dock near Enniscrone?' I asked.

The Dazzler scratched his head. 'The last ships to land near Enniscrone belonged to Napoleon, after he sent them miles off course to aid the Wexford rebels in the 1798 Rebellion.' He looked at Myles. 'You're hardly that old, are you?'

Myles Foley stared at his empty glass. 'A bishop wouldn't ask me my age. I'm older than my teeth and that's all I'm saying.' He winked at Mr Tierney. 'Thank God you're a qualified engineer, Mossy, because you make a lousy barman.'

Taking the hint, Mr Tierney shared out the remaining brandy, pouring the dregs into my glass. The men drank in silence: the only sound being Myles Foley's lips making a soft smack of satisfaction as he savoured the taste. The alcohol made me feel light-headed, but I was still alert for any chance to resume my search for Kateřina. I tried to imagine the journey she had undertaken to reach Lisbon from Czechoslovakia. I didn't rightly know where Czechoslovakia was. I suspected that Mr Walton knew, but I wasn't going to mention anything about Kateřina as it might give these sailors a chance to rib me. So I tried to pry for information more subtly.

'If Salazar didn't want the refugees, how did they get in?' I asked.

Mr Walton swirled the brandy around in his glass. 'In Ireland truancy officers threaten parents whose children don't attend school.

In Portugal the secret police warn parents not to be getting notions above their station if they try and keep their children at school. Salazar browbeats the poor into thinking they've a patriotic duty to remain ignorant and let a few privileged families rule over them, like company directors expecting the poor to meekly turn the pages of dusty ledgers every time they nod their heads.'

'Grant me patience,' Thomas Bergin muttered. 'We're drinking fine Portuguese brandy and this Jackeen still can't lose the chip on his shoulder about his first job in Guinness Brewery.'

Mr Walton ignored the interruption. 'But even in privileged elites you can find the same qualities your father had – decency and insubordination. When Paris fell to the Nazis, Bordeaux was flooded by Jewish refugees desperate to escape. The Portuguese Consul there was overwhelmed, with Salazar's bureaucratic hurdles making it virtually impossible for refugees to get transit visas to enter Portugal. Some say the diplomat had a nervous breakdown: why else would an aristocrat sacrifice his career to save the lives of strangers? But I like to think that insubordination and decency made him walk down the queue of terrified refugees outside his office, all of whom knew their doom was only days away. He handed each refugee a transit visa, regardless of religion, nationality or class. He saved thousands of lives, knowing that Salazar would sack him and his kin shun him as a traitor. He's a real man of courage to toast: Aristides de Sousa Mendes.'

But before he could raise his glass to repeat this name, Mr Tierney grabbed his wrist. 'We'll toast him to high heaven – along with Jack and the Beanstalk and Uncle Tom Cobley and all. But only after the *Kerlogue* sails past the Tower of Belém, out of earshot of snitches, informers and spies.'

Mr Walton stared at his wrist pinned to the table. 'I'm surely drunk as a skunk when the biggest reprobate I know starts lecturing me about social etiquette.'

'The place for social etiquette is drinking tea with nuns in a convent parlour,' Mr Tierney replied. 'My social skills are more attuned to extracting myself from foreign bars without a broken bottle being pointed at my throat.'

'Don't you start mocking the poor nuns as well,' Thomas Bergin spoke up, annoyed and seriously plastered. 'Why can't you leave the nuns alone? Leave the Portuguese alone too: they're a darling race and a decent, God-fearing people.'

'Lift your head out of the sand,' Mr Walton snapped. 'Do you think they fear God or the Police for Vigilance and Defence of the State?'

'You've no cause to mention the PVDE,' Mr Tierney said, aware of a silence descending on the *tasca*. All conversations ceased as drinkers strained to listen more closely. 'Leave the PVDE alone and please God they'll leave us alone. It's time to leave this bar.'

'Who are the PVDE?' I asked.

'A grand bunch of lads,' Mr Tierney whispered tersely. 'Like the Spanish Inquisition, but with a sharper dress sense.'

Mr Walton unclasped the Engineer's restraining hand. 'Behind your bluster, Mossy, you occasionally know how to cut to the heart of things.'

Mr Tierney's voice was barely above a whisper. 'I also know when to keep my trap shut and so the hell should you. A secret police is like a sailor's mattress: it only comes to life when you let your guard down and doze off. Suddenly every parasite hidden in the straw eats you alive. You may think there's no way for the poor to get ahead in Lisbon, but information about loud-mouthed foreigners translates into escudos. You of all people should know this. Maybe nobody else here knows, but I know what Sean Roche did for you.' He raised his glass in a loud toast: '*Deus, Pátria, Família.*'

This reference to my father perturbed me, but I knew not to ask questions just now. I joined in with my crewmates, noticing how other drinkers nearby dutifully raised their glasses, anxious to out-do each other in a display of fidelity. Mr Tierney kept his glass aloft until Mr Walton clicked his against it.

'That's twice you've sold your soul to the Devil,' Mr Walton muttered.

'I'm not selling my soul,' Mr Tierney said. 'I'm putting as much blue water between it and the Devil as possible.'

'I don't need reminding of what Sean Roche did for me,' Mr Walton said quietly. 'I think about it every day. How can I not when the man has sent his own son to judge me?'

Mr Tierney glanced at me, his eyes warning me to stay shtum. 'Leave the young lad out of this. Jack's here to earn a few shillings like the rest of us, not to judge anyone.' He reached across the table to place a friendly hand on Mr Walton's shoulder. 'The crew are wandering down to Cais do Sodré: nothing untoward now, just sightseeing. You're welcome to join us, but you're a ship's officer, and you'll have to lay down the law to some sailors here on our voyage back to Wexford. So we both know that when you wake up tomorrow you'll be glad I escorted you back to the ship before I rejoin the others.'

'I'm capable of making my own way back to the *Kerlogue*.'

Mr Tierney spoke with deliberate respect. 'I don't doubt it, Mr Walton, Sir. But I'd sooner have young Jack and I accompany you, Sir, rather than find you were followed by anyone in the pay of a pipsqueak dictator.'

The calculated use of the term 'Sir' sobered up Mr Walton. He looked around the table, aware of the awkward situation he had created. 'I've imbibed not too wisely, but too well. You're a good crew. I hope you'll allow me the pleasure of standing you these few drinks.'

'There's a kitty,' Ernie Grogan said. 'Every man pays with his own brass – except for young Jack.'

'I insist.' Mr Walton looked suddenly very ill. The reference to my father had shaken him and he seemed to be trying to restore a sense of seniority. 'I'm the only officer present.'

'But not the only father,' Mr Tierney said quietly. 'You can't afford to buy drinks for a shower of ruffians when you've a sick daughter at home.'

'Leave my daughter out of this!' His words seemed to be spoken in anger but I soon realised that they revealed a deep pain. 'My private life is not your concern, Tierney!'

There was silence: every man was aware of the potential discomfiture of the voyage home.

Then Ernie Grogan spoke up: 'This is the way it is, Sir. There's no more annoying geezer on earth than Mossy Tierney. But I rely on him to watch my back when we're in the engine room or out having a few tiddlywinks. I watch Mossy's back too: like Myles Foley looks out for the Dazzler and the Dazzler keeps a butcher out for Myles. There isn't a night in a port when the Cook doesn't say to me, "we'd best keep an eye on Tommy Bergin, he's hitting the gargle hard", or Tommy Bergin doesn't whisper "keep an eye on the Cook or he'll be under the table". That's how a crew works and you know it. Right now, because there's no mate looking out for you, we're all keeping a weather eye on you. Every shipman here knows that you shouldn't be making this voyage. You belong in the sickbay, Mr Walton, but you've a responsibility to earn brass because a father works through any pain if he has a poorly child depending on him. You're an officer and let's not pretend we'll ever be equal at sea. But many of us here are fathers and we're equal in that regard. I'm looking out for you, as a fellow father, so we pay our own way and depart as mates. Let that be an end to it, Sir.'

Mr Walton looked down at the table: all fight gone. He fingered his empty glass. 'I've made a fool of myself,' he said, 'and not for the first time in a bar in Lisbon. You're right, Ernie. I've too many responsibilities and not enough time left to fulfil them. Maybe you're wondering why I'm wasting money drinking brandy: but the brandy here numbs the pain in my guts and is cheaper than the Laudanum my doctor prescribes. My race is run, lads. If the Nazis don't kill me then cancer will: I'm riddled with it.'

'You're not God and nor is your doctor,' Thomas Bergin said. 'Only God decides when your race is run. I'll ask my cousin in the convent to pray for you and for your daughter too.' He held out a hand. 'No hard feelings, Sir.'

Mr Walton shook Bergin's hand. 'Happy Christmas, Tommy. Anything we said is forgotten when we leave this table.'

'Maybe by you,' the Cook said, anxious to break the solemnity, 'but I'll never be able to look at Tommy's backside again without thinking of an ostrich.'

Even Thomas Bergin joined in the laughter as Mr Tierney beckoned for the bill. The *tasca* owner scribbled sums on one corner of our paper tablecloth, totting up the cost of the wine, the plates of food and the brandy. He reached a final sum and, with a flourish, tore off this strip of tablecloth and handed it to Mr Tierney with equal ceremony, as if presenting him with a printed bill from a fancy restaurant. Mr Tierney passed it to me.

'You're the scholar,' he said. 'Do the maths and leave yourself out. You drank less than a sparrow would drink and ate even less.'

What I drank may have seemed little to Mr Tierney but I could feel the alcohol course through me and I wasn't sure how steady I'd be on my feet. I divided up the bill and a jumble of notes and coins were piled onto the table. The owner swept the money into a leather purse and produced a bottle of some liqueur, insisting that we enjoy a Christmas drink on the house.

'I don't want any more,' I told Mr Tierney, reaching for my sack of presents. 'I'll slip away and clear my head before making my way back to the ship. I might even attend midnight mass.'

'We're all attending a sailors' mass at six tomorrow evening,' he murmured. 'Now do me one favour. Walton may prove a handful on my own. Walk with me as far as the ship. After that Lisbon is your oyster.' Looking around at the other customers still covertly observing us, he winked and startled everyone by slamming his fist down on the torn paper tablecloth. '*Vivo Estado Novo!*' He raised his glass. 'Long live the New State.'

Glasses were dutifully raised around the *tasca*, although I sensed the owner growing wary of Mr Tierney's enthusiasm for the ruling regime.

'I'd leave it there if I were you, Mossy,' Myles Foley said quietly, downing his liqueur and standing up to leave. 'When they report back to the PVDE about how much you love Portugal, the fellows might decide it would be unfair to force you to ever leave it again.'

Chapter Sixteen

December 24, Bairro Alto & Alcântara

WE ALL STAYED TOGETHER AT first, carousing boisterously through the narrow streets of the Bairro Alto that sloped steeply towards the river. Yet our revelry was hushed by an intuitive consensus when we passed the open doorway of a *tasca* where a woman's voice floated out onto the street. She sang in a fashion I'd never heard before. I could not fathom the words but they seemed to brim with melancholia and a desperate longing for someone lost beyond reach. I peered inside. The drinkers were paying her attention but not undue reverence, as if this extraordinary singing was part of the backdrop to their lives.

There was nothing remarkable about the middle-aged woman's clothes, but her face looked transformed by the words she sang; her eyes were closed, as if they contained a private message only she understood. A man seated at a wooden table watched her intently; his hands following the pacing of her words as he plucked notes on a twelve-stringed rotund guitar. Mr Walton paused at my shoulder.

'That's Fado singing,' he said.

'What does it mean?'

'You don't need to understand things to appreciate their beauty.'

'The song sounds sad.'

'That's where the beauty is: in the sadness. Sadness is like a tossed coin.'

'I don't follow you, Mr Walton.'

He placed a hand on my shoulder. I couldn't tell if it was a friendly gesture or done because he needed to steady himself in the night air. 'Sadness can lie on either side of every coin you ever spin in the air. Life is about taking risks and hoping that half the time – if you're lucky – your coin lands face-up on happiness.'

The other sailors had moved on; their voices growing loud again once beyond range of the singing. I felt uneasy being alone with Mr Walton, especially after the references to my father, and suggested that we hurry on in case we lost sight of the crew. There was no danger of this: they had paused at a corner. Their heated argument about which direction to go in abruptly halted when Mr Walton reached them. The others nodded to him sheepishly and sloped off down a side street, leaving the pair of us standing with Mr Tierney.

Mr Walton stared after them. 'No disrespect, but they won't get far in Cais do Sodré,' he said. 'A madam in any knocking shop would need to be blind not to see that their pockets aren't stuffed with silver. On Christmas Eve them ladies are looking for big spenders.'

'Whatever meagre pickings the lads have will stay in their pockets,' Mr Tierney assured him. 'Tommy Bergin hasn't spent his communion money yet and hardened ladies of the night generally take one look at poor old Myles and have a whip-round for him.'

'You don't get to be a madam in such establishments by being kind-hearted,' Mr Walton observed.

Mr Tierney nodded. 'Business is business. But those madams are engaged in more than one business. Their bread gets buttered by richer men than sailors. The secret of a good night out lies in knowing which doors to knock on. Ernie Grogan was only put on this earth to test my patience, but it's useful to have a crewmate with a thick cockney accent. I've told the others to sing dumb and let Ernie do the talking. They'll only knock on the doors of madams in the pay of German spymasters. Ernie's accent gets us invited in, with a round of drinks offered on the house while the madam gets her nicest working girls to drape themselves around Ernie, thinking he must be on shore leave from an Allied ship. They want to get him polluted with cheap drink and dupe him into revealing details of whatever convoy he's about to cross the Atlantic in. On a good night the charade can last half an hour, with the rest of us getting well-oiled and eyeing the prettiest sights this side of New York. Then the madam realises that Ernie has sailed from Ireland in a rusty bathtub and we get thrown out with a string of curses. After that we head home for our cocoa unless we can persuade Ernie to chance his arm again.'

'Does it ever turn nasty?'

Mr Tierney shrugged. 'Shay Cullen is nifty with his fists and Tommy Bergin threatens them with his Rosary beads.'

Mr Walton laughed. 'You're missing the fun, Mossy. Join the others, but it's no place to bring the young lad.'

'I'm going nowhere near Cais do Sordé,' I said hastily. 'I'm just enjoying being out and about.'

'And you will be,' Mr Tierney agreed, 'once we escort Mr Walton back to the ship.'

'I made a fool of myself, Mossy, didn't I?' Mr Walton said.

'Any man is entitled to his few drinks,' Mr Tierney replied tactfully.

'Officers are meant to drink like priests, alone in our quarters. But I need no escorting: I know my way.'

'No one doubts it,' Mr Tierney said. 'But some ruffians from that *tasca* might be following us. We're only a few minutes from the dock and I could use some fresh air. Jack doesn't mind tagging along, do you, Jack?'

When Mr Tierney phrased it like that I could barely complain. Mr Walton decided to also humour him. We walked in silence: our boots echoing on the uneven pavement. I wanted to ask what they meant when they referred to my father earlier, but I sensed that neither man would welcome that question. Our silence remained unbroken even after we turned down the steps that led to the plaza where – despite it being Christmas Eve – people still queued outside the closed shipping offices. Families hunched on the ground, sharing any warmth afforded by old army blankets wrapped around their shoulders. Some people seemed asleep, perhaps accustomed to nights in the cold. Others silently watched our movements. We reached the wharf at Alcântara where there was no sign of the passenger ship beside which passengers had queued this morning. The wharf was deserted except for two harbour policemen who checked our papers and waved us on towards where the *Kerlogue* was berthed. Mr Walton ascended the gangplank first. I whispered to Mr Tierney that I wanted to slip away.

'Wait a few minutes, Jack,' he pleaded quietly. 'I feel responsible for Walton. I don't want him wandering off again. Stay with me till we clap eyes on the Captain. He won't be our responsibility then.'

As we boarded the vessel Mr Tierney contrived to stumble and make a loud clatter. This alerted the Captain, who climbed up on deck. He took in Mr Walton's condition and glanced at Mr Tierney.

'It's early for you to be calling it a night, Mossy.'

'If this was a hurling match, Captain, I'd call this half-time.'

Captain Donovan looked at Mr Walton. 'Is it half-time for you, Frank?'

'I seem to be among the walking wounded, though Mossy kindly ensured that I didn't have to be carried home on my shield.

Good night to you, Captain, and – even if I'm an hour early – Happy Christmas.'

'Sleep well, Frank.'

With surprising dignity for a drunken man, Mr Walton descended the ladder and retreated to his quarters. Neither the Captain nor Mr Tierney referred to his condition.

'Have we a cargo, Captain?' Mr Tierney asked.

Captain Donovan nodded. 'They don't know it yet, but the Staffords have entered the fruit importation business.'

'What class of fruit?'

'Oranges were the best cargo of a bad lot,' Captain Donovan said. 'Nobody in Ireland has seen an orange since 1940. The Staffords may throw them at me, but at least I'm giving them a cargo to throw.'

'It could be worse,' Mr Tierney said. 'Last time I risked my life sailing here to collect phosphate we wound up bringing back sheets of cork for stoppers for the tops of Guinness bottles, and crates of altar wine.'

'I hope the publicans and clergy rewarded you.'

'I'm sure the priests remember me in their prayers but I can't recall any publican sticking a free bottle of Guinness under my nose.'

Captain Donovan smiled. 'Happy Christmas, Mossy, and don't lead the young lad astray.'

'No fear of that, Captain.'

When the Captain descended the ladder I turned to Mr Tierney.

'Can I go now?'

'Come below deck for one second,' he said. 'I've got you a Christmas present: the finest nylon stockings. I figured you might feel embarrassed going into a shop yourself. I promise not to tell Ellie that I actually bought them.'

I didn't like the thought of Mr Tierney handling my gift for Ellie, but I was grateful to him.

'What do I owe you?'

He waved his hand benevolently. 'They're a thank you for how you handled that copper in Cardiff. Go down to your bunk and take a gander.'

I descended the ladder and Mr Tierney followed me along the passageway to the cramped cabin. He watched from the doorway as I put down the small sack of toys that I had been carrying for hours. On top of my father's old blanket lay an unopened packet of nylon stockings and beside it an American *Superman* comic. I looked back but the cabin door was being slammed shut. I ran towards it but knew instinctively that Mr Tierney had it locked from the outside.

'What are you playing at?' I shouted.

'I'm sorry, Jack.' He sounded genuinely apologetic. 'But I made a solemn vow to your mother.'

'Open the door or I won't tell you what I'll do with this comic.'

'Any child in Wexford would kill to get their hands on a *Superman* comic.'

'I'm no child. You said when I boarded this ship that I was to act like a man.'

'I know you're a man.' His voice was cajoling. 'The problem is that your mother doesn't.'

'Mention my ma again and I'll kill you, you blaggard,' I shouted.

'Kill me tomorrow, Jack, but I'm missing all the fun. I've a right to get drunk on Christmas Eve without being a babysitter. Now if you bang on that door you'll only bring Captain Donovan down here with a face like thunder. He's a man under stress and you'd be wise not to cross him. You've had a long day, so take the weight off your feet and enjoy the adventures of Superman. When you finish reading it I'll take a loan. Don't tell anyone, but I'm fond of a good comic myself.'

His footsteps retreated. I wanted to pound the door. I wanted to curse, and I felt close to tears. Somewhere in this city, Kateřina was scrubbing down a café counter, chairs piled on tables to allow her to mop the floor. I could imagine her glancing towards the window, wondering if my face would appear there. Tonight had been my one chance to find her. Tomorrow she was off work and I'd have no idea where to look. I could imagine her putting the cloth back in the sink and buttoning up her coat before, with a flick of a switch, the light in the café window went out. Mr Tierney was right. My banging on this door would only disturb the Captain. This was something I didn't dare to do.

I scrunched up the comic and flung it at the wall. Then I thought of how my brothers would love it. I picked it up and smoothed the pages out and then placed it carefully in my sack, along with the presents that Kateřina had helped me pick. I put a pillow over my face so I could pretend there were no tears there. Then, pent-up with frustration, I prayed that sleep might come.

Chapter Seventeen

December 24, Alcântara & Rossio, Lisbon

I LOST TRACK OF HOW long I lay in that cabin with the pillow pressed to my face. Every minute of confinement dragged like an hour. Then I heard footsteps along the passageway. These were softer than Mr Tierney's had been, softer than if the crew had returned and were drunkenly heading back to their bunks. I remembered the harbour policemen who checked our papers. They had seen Mr Tierney leave again but not Mr Walton or myself. Had the Second Officer said something seditious in the *tasca* which had been reported to them or were they – or an intruder who slipped past them – simply interested in robbing any valuables the crew might have in their kitbags? But maybe it was the police who had boarded the ship at dawn; men who had bided their time to question me about whether I had kept any documents from the pockets of that dead sailor found at sea.

The footsteps stopped directly outside my cabin. My first instinct was to call out. But I held my breath, terrified, praying that the footsteps might move on. Instead the bolt was drawn back. I had turned out the light and only a faint glow came from the passageway as the door swung open. A man stood there in uniform, but not a uniform I recognised. Then I realised that it was actually a pair of striped pyjamas. The footsteps had been quiet because the man wore bedroom slippers. He said nothing at first and I said nothing because Mr Walton looked so odd dressed like this. What could he want? Finally he spoke.

'I'll have a sore head tomorrow: I've a sore head already. People think that alcohol helps them to sleep. It knocks you out and wakes you again suddenly with a thump. I woke just now with something bothering me. Then it came to me. Mossy Tierney is capable of doing a shipmate a good turn, but no man so devious does anything for one reason only. He's a good man, Mossy, and smarter than he lets on. But he's always juggling more balls in the air than a circus performer. I suddenly realised what that charade of bringing me back to the ship was about and that I'd find you locked in here. Was a solemn vow to your mother mentioned?'

'Several times.'

'I saw in the *tasca* that you were restless to be gone. Is there a girl involved?'

'I had hoped I might run into her.'

'Is it too late now?'

'She's probably long gone. There was no guarantee I'd find her anyway.'

'There's only one way you'll ever know.'

'It's late.' I was unsure now about whether I wanted to face into the big city again.

'And you're young.'

'I'd be scared of making a fool of myself.'

'You'd have to work hard to make as big a fool of yourself as I did tonight. There's no guarantee of your coin landing face-up on happiness, but you'll never know unless you risk it.'

'Would you let your daughter out at this hour?'

'I'd die happy if the only danger that my daughter was facing was a midnight stroll with a lad like you.'

'The crew tell me she's gravely ill. I'm sorry to hear that. '

I sensed him bristle. 'My daughter is none of their business. Now do you have your father's courage as well as his impertinence, or do you just intend to lie there and mope?'

I pulled on my boots, angered by his remark. I made for the door and stopped. 'In the *tasca* you said you did my father wrong.'

'That's between Sean's ghost and me. Soon it will be between his ghost and mine.'

I brushed past and had reached the foot of the ladder before he spoke, so quietly that at first I wasn't sure if I was meant to hear.

'My daughter is facing a race against time with tuberculosis. I want her to live and I'll work for as long as I can in any job that will pay for her care. But if she did die tomorrow, then I could stop fighting this cancer that's eating my innards. But she's lost so much that I don't want her to endure losing a father as well. That's my race: her illness against mine. Time waits for nobody. This evening won't come again, no matter how often you sail into Lisbon. If you find this girl, treat her well.'

I didn't know how to reply, and I sensed that he didn't expect me to. I had one foot on the ladder when a stubborn impulse made me turn.

'What happened between you and my father?'

He shrugged. 'What happens at sea stays at sea.'

'I'm here in his place, so it can stay between us.'

Mr Walton was silent and I didn't think he was going to reply. Then he looked up. 'This isn't the time, Jack. It's Christmas Eve. Maybe you're heading out on a fool's errand but take the chance. Nothing is more pointless than regrets. Now go.'

I climbed up the ladder and crossed the deck. Clambering down the gangplank I showed my papers to the sleepy-looking harbour police stamping their feet by a fire to stay warm. In front of me

Lisbon rose, arrayed on its seven hills, with neon advertising signs bolted onto the walls of crumbling buildings. I set my face towards that pulsating beacon of light and began to run.

I had only spent one day in Lisbon, yet it felt like I already possessed a map of the city in my mind. I passed the refugees outside the shipping companies with barely a glance and they barely bothered glancing at me. I ran along the long avenue which hugged the riverside with the array of ships and wharves giving way to train tracks and rolling stock shunted into sidings. Uniformed men guarded municipal buildings. They gave me one look and paid no farther heed. It was obvious that I was no saboteur: I had the look of a boy racing at breakneck speed, late for a date with a girl. Could I call even this a date? Especially as Kateřina wasn't expecting me to find her. I'd never even had a proper date with Ellie, having only kissed her once at dawn before my ship sailed.

In the past year I had barely found the courage to hold a proper conversation with Ellie. I realised that this was what I was seeking tonight – not kisses, but a chance to learn how to openly talk to a girl. Kateřina wasn't just attractive, she was vivacious. This was a word I once read in a magazine. I wasn't precisely sure what it meant: I just know that whoever coined the word had someone like Kateřina in mind. Ellie was equally attractive: but Ellie's beauty was a wonder I understood. With Kateřina there was something extra, not just foreign and exotic, but a shimmering quality too, as if part of her was an optical illusion. This observation made no sense, but our single encounter had left me intrigued. I sensed that I barely understood her at all and would have found it impossible to describe her character. There seemed to be an innocent openness in how she embraced the simplest pleasures, like letting her hair blow backwards when hitching a lift on that tram. At times this gave her a childlike appearance. Yet behind her seemingly carefree nature there lurked a wounded vulnerability, as if she had already witnessed more of life than someone three times her age.

I loved Ellie but I understood Ellie. Ellie was rooted in Wexford life, able to decipher any nuanced glance or casual but barbed remark in that goldfish bowl where neighbours felt a divine right to look over everyone else's shoulder. Wexford was dominated not by fear of an all-seeing God but by a terror that neighbours might think you lacked respectability. To be poor in Wexford was no sin, though this didn't prevent people looking down on you. But every day in Wexford felt like judgement day. It was a cardinal offence there to stand out by being unconventional: it meant you were not keeping up appearances and had ceased to be respectable.

Kateřina seemed liberated from this burden of respectability, though her liberation was gained at a terrible price. She had no appearances to keep up in Lisbon, because it seemed from our conversation as if nobody here really knew her beyond her immediate family. She was as much a stranger in this city as I was. We were both only passing through, except that she could not pass: she was trapped here and was stateless. Her waitressing job was different from any life she must have envisaged when growing up in a privileged family. I wondered if her family had been among the terrified queue of refugees in Bordeaux when the Portuguese Consul destroyed his own career prospects by handing out transit passes to everyone fleeing the Nazis. How did her parents spend their days now? There were a hundred questions I would probably never get to ask her, because she was surely gone home by now; almost every café had their lights switched off in the streets that I was running through.

I reached a part of the riverbank where a maze of streets led away from the train station. From the charged atmosphere here and from how hard-eyed women watched me from the open doorways of buildings, where coarse laughter and loud gramophone music escaped from upstairs windows, I knew I had entered the red light district. A girl emerged from the shadows. I was shocked to see that she was younger than me. She laughed and said something suggestive. Even though I could not translate her words I understood their implied promise. What would it be like to lie with a girl and finally know the secrets that older boys boasted about with superior winks and smirks? I might have enough money in my pocket – the money saved for Ellie's stockings. I did not mean to halt but this girl deliberately blocked my path, brushing her body up against mine, aware that my eyes could not stop taking in the provocative way that she was dressed.

She smiled. It was a distortion of every girl's smile I'd ever known: the callous, triumphant smile of someone confident that I was too weak to resist her power; that my curiosity could not hold out against temptation. Then I heard drunken shouts from a side street. The voices were not Irish, but they restored me to my senses. I did not belong here, no matter how much I yearned to know what it must feel like to lie with a woman. Ellie's single kiss meant more than any tainted experience I could purchase here. So I brushed past the girl and ran on, afraid of bumping into my crew being ejected from some bawdy house: men not out for sin but for harmless devilment, determined to enjoy the camaraderie of this drunken evening, knowing that it might be among their last on this earth. We might soon endure a different form of camaraderie: our skeletal bodies lying together forever, strewn throughout the *Kerlogue's* sunken cabins. The crew would look after each other here in Cais do Sodré, but if they caught sight of me it meant the end of my freedom to roam these streets.

I ran on, down the length of the Rua do Arsenal until I entered Black Horse Square. Other parts of Lisbon might have closed for

Christmas Eve, but these streets leading out from here looked like they never closed. I didn't know how late it was but crowds still moved about: well-dressed couples hailing taxis that sped off down side streets, drivers beeping horns in their impatience to whisk away such important passengers. A river mist was creeping in but I could still discern the looming walls of the Castelo de Sáo Jorge on a hill to my right. The rich diners had long since finished eating in the Café Martinho da Arcada on the corner of Rua da Alfándega, but through the porticos I glimpsed them still relaxing at tables covered in elegant white cloth, savouring coffee, cognacs and cigarettes. Waiters hovered like statues waiting to be summoned to life. Policemen guarded the government buildings lining this square, their doorways protected by sandbags, while more policemen patrolled temporary bomb shelters built as a precautionary measure near the steps down to the river.

I stepped beneath the triumphal arch that led on to Rua Augusta: the pavement of this main street was laid out in such opulent marble tiles that I expected a policeman to question what business I had walking up past the expensive shops and restaurants that eventually led to the square at Rossio. Kateřina had said that the café where she worked was near here. This felt like a different city to the homely *tasca* where I had drank with the crew. Down a side street I glimpsed the Pan Am ticket office that Kateřina had lingered outside, as if staring in at the locked gates of Paradise. Each time I passed restaurants still open on Rua Augusta I peered in through the windows. These were too imposing to be described as cake shops, but perhaps Kateřina had downplayed the grandeur of the eatery where she worked.

In some windows a trick of the light meant that not only could I see the diners inside but I could also see my own reflection being reflected back at me. I looked so shabby compared to the men in elegant suits and the women in expensive dresses set off at the neck by fox furs. It was like peering at a brightly lit film set, where I played the part of a waif at the window. Occasionally a woman diner would glance up with pity or irritation or her companion would make a dismissive gesture, as if brushing me away. Several times tuxedoed waiters appeared in doorways, ordering me with silent glares to move along. But I refused to budge until I checked the face of every waitress inside.

Not only was I on a wild goose chase but as I drew closer to the square at Rossio I became increasingly conscious of my poverty compared to most people moving about. The smaller cafes up at Rossio itself remained packed, despite this late hour. There remained a slim chance that Kateřina might work in such a café or might simply pass through Rossio on her way home, because so many tram routes converged here. Passengers were still descending the steps down from the main train station. The same shoeshine boys who I had seen earlier were still working and I sensed that they would not go home until the last café closed. I spied a space among the crowd sitting on a circular low wall that surrounded a large fountain, which threw up a tall spume of water into the night sky. I sat there to catch my breath, suddenly aware of how exhausting this day had been and aware also of the long walk back to the ship. If the crew had already returned, I would face an interrogation from Mr Tierney and all for what? Had I ever possessed any realistic chance of finding Kateřina? Even if I did, what could I have said to her? My reflection in those restaurant windows made me acutely conscious of how poor I looked. I didn't feel like a sailor just now: I felt like a homesick child abroad for the first time at Christmas.

I knew that it was time to admit defeat and begin the long walk back to the Alcântara quayside. Yet I still couldn't so do. Instead I made a continuing nuisance of myself by peering through the doorway of every café in that square. I could not work out what languages were being spoken in there, though I could spot when customers were not Portuguese. The rich foreigners spoke loudly, as if this war was a boring inconvenience, forcing them to enjoy an extended holiday here. Poorer foreigners were shabbily dressed and spoke in whispers as if frightened of being overheard. The Lisboetas were more measured in dress and speech, the women very conservatively dressed. I heard American accents at one café table and German being spoken at the adjoining one. These enemies coexisted in an uneasy truce, each pretending to ignore the other.

I knew it would be hopeless to continue my futile search by walking up the Avenida da Liberdade. Every sharply dressed man who passed reinforced my feelings of poverty. The wine and brandy I had drunk earlier were making me feel ill. I returned to the fountain to splash water over my face. I must have looked a pathetic sight, with my wet hair sticking up, because I saw an elegant young woman stare at me as she emerged from the splendour of the Hotel Metropole on the arm of an older man. This sophisticated enchantress stood still, as if in shock, amid the crowds on the pavement while her companion unlinked her arm to summon a taxi from a nearby rank. I heard him tell the driver their destination in a German accent: the Estoril Casino. Then he glanced back impatiently and called her name.

But she was not being called; she was being summoned and summoned by the wrong name. He was calling her Natasha when her name was Kateřina. At least I thought it was Kateřina. This creature had the same eyes as the shop girl I had spent the afternoon with; the same coloured hair, even if now piled up in an elaborate style that emphasised the elegance of her long slender neck. For a moment I wondered could it be Kateřina's older sister, because this young woman – you could not call her a girl – looked much older, her figure almost bursting out of the silk dress. But if it was not

Kateřina, then why did she stand there as if caught out; why did she stare back at me in pained recognition? Was this man her father? Then he summoned her again and I knew that he was not her father. No man would address his daughter in such an authoritative voice. It was the impersonal tone used to summon a paid servant who could be summarily dismissed if she displeased him. This man was not used to being kept waiting.

He followed her startled gaze, but did not see me among the crowd: I was too far beneath his contempt to notice. He barked her name one final time – Natasha. It was not just a summons, it was an order. I saw how Kateřina wanted to say something to me. She wanted to explain but she couldn't and didn't need to. Instead she turned and walked obediently to the waiting taxi. The older man spoke sternly and she looked up at him and smiled meekly, almost pleadingly, until he condescended to smile back. She leaned forward and kissed his cheek before compliantly disappearing into the back seat. The man climbed in after her, slammed the door and the taxi sped off.

Chapter Eighteen

Christmas Day, Alcântara & Rua do Arsenal, Lisbon

I DIDN'T SLEEP THAT NIGHT, though I pretended to be asleep when my crewmates drunkenly descended the ladder, conversing in quarrelsome whispers as if already anticipating the excruciating hangovers they would endure after whatever slumber they could cadge before dawn. Mr Tierney was first to enter the cabin. I sensed him look down at my bunk, puzzled by how the door stood ajar, despite him leaving it locked. He didn't know if I had left the ship and I was in no mood to enlighten him. I was in no mood for anything except to be left alone, but my conflicted thoughts refused to grant me a moment's respite. The crew grumpily settled into their bunks, their breath adding a dense layer of alcohol fumes to the stale air in that claustrophobic space.

Within moments they were asleep, possessing that ability of sailors to snatch rest whenever they could, regardless of how atrocious conditions were at sea or what clamour was occurring nearby. In contrast, I stared up at the low ceiling, because every time I closed my eyes I saw Kateřina – or Natasha – in an elegant silk dress being herded into that taxi. Did everyone have secret identities in this city of subterfuge? Walking with her yesterday I had felt like a grown up, sufficiently well-travelled to be able to decipher this city. Now I felt like a child who had still naïvely believed in fairytales.

184

I barely knew Kateřina and had no right to feel this jealous flush. That German officer was not a jumped-up butcher boy like Pascal Brennan, strutting down Green Street to escort Ellie Coady to the Cinema Palace. He might actually be Kateřina's – or Natasha's – father for all I knew. But her distress when she spied me suggested a more complicated truth. Her eyes had seemed desperate to convey a message in the seconds before being ordered into that taxi. I'd never know what she wished to say because I would surely never find her again.

Despite my fevered thoughts I finally fell asleep because I suddenly became aware of the Cook shaking me awake.

'I could have sworn my cabin boy slept in this bunk,' he said. 'Now all I can find is a layabout snoring like a trooper and stinking like a brewery.'

'What time is it?' I asked groggily.

'Half an hour since you were meant to be scrubbing plates in the galley. I did the crew a slap-up fry for Christmas. But maybe you'd like me to bring you your breakfast on a tray with a special pot of tea?'

'I slept in,' I said. 'My head hurts like someone kicked it.'

'Then welcome to life at sea. Getting drunk doesn't make you a sailor. You'll have only earned the right to call yourself one when you can get up the next morning and do a day's work.'

Gingerly, I surveyed the empty bunks around me. 'I didn't hear the others get up: they looked half-dead a few hours ago.'

'They might be half-dead but they're walking around doing their jobs. So shake a leg: you and I need to visit every fishmonger on the Rua do Arsenal. If your stomach feels bad now, wait till you smell the stacked boxes of fish lining the pavement there. Our cargo of oranges is being loaded. Once the hatches are sealed we sail. You'll go home to Wexford smelling of dried Portuguese cod and fresh oranges. You can charge folk a penny just to sniff you.'

After he left I dressed quickly, splashing cold water on my face. It made little difference: my head throbbed as I entered the galley where Mr Tierney was draining a mug of weak tea, brewed with leaves that were already used twice. I headed towards the breakfast dishes piled in the sink, not bothering to greet either man.

'There's Christmas cheer for you,' the Cook said. 'Whatever drink you poisoned this young boy with last night, Mossy, he's like a bag of cats.'

'I'm not a young boy,' I remarked sourly.

'Maybe he's a midget doing impersonations so,' Mr Tierney teased.

'Go to hell, you old racketeer,' I countered gruffly. 'All you're good for is locking people into cabins.'

'You're an escapologist then, because you had the lock picked open by the time I got back.' Mr Tierney's tone grew more concerned. 'Don't tell me you went down the town, despite the promises I made to your mother.'

'Mention my mother again and I'll brain you.' I savagely scrubbed at the frying pain. I was furious at Mr Tierney's ribbing but mainly furious with myself for feeling so close to tears. I was hungover and vulnerable and homesick – just a stupid kid unable to recognise what was staring me in the face: that Kateřina had allowed me to only see whatever version of her I wished to see. I knew nothing about women and less about life. 'Happy Christmas my arse,' I muttered darkly. 'You pair of mocking blaggards.'

'That's no ordinary hangover,' Mr Tierney observed. 'It sounds like woman trouble.'

'Mind your own blasted business!' I picked up the heavy pan and might have flung it if the Cook had not gripped my arm.

'I don't care if you've contracted every disease that a good-time girl in Lisbon can donate to sailors: nobody throws pots in my galley, except me. I generally aim them at snot-nosed cabin boys. Get some air on deck and calm down. We've work to do. You're going to be my Sherpa when I bargain for supplies. There's a fry here if you want it, but otherwise get out of my sight. You'd test the patience of a saint this morning and I'm in no mood to be canonised.'

Grease had congealed around the sausages and black pudding on the plate he pointed to. I couldn't face it and climbed up on deck, glad to emerge into the fresh air, although so much activity was occurring there that there was barely room to stand. I had thought that the activity on the quay would stop for Christmas Day, but at dawn a consignment of oranges had been transported onto the dockside. The *Kerlogue's* hold was open and dockworkers bustled about on deck, shouting in Portuguese at the crane operator who was hoisting pallets, stacked with orange crates, from the quayside. An army of outstretched hands steered each pallet down into the hold where more workers unstrapped the ropes and stacked crates. Mr Walton stood next to a clerk from the shipping agents: both keeping a separate tab on the number of crates being deposited. The Dazzler Kehoe busily moved about, examining repairs he wished to attend to before we sailed again. The Captain and First Officer stood at the gangplank, laboriously examining reams of paperwork with harbour officials.

The dockside seemed as chaotic as ever. Beyond it – up the steps – I could imagine the queues still formed outside shipping company offices that might not even open today. The answer to their request for news of any berth would be the same as yesterday. But they would still queue as if the task of making futile inquiries leant a purpose to their day? Had Kateřina ever stood among them, or was everything she told me yesterday a mockery? Perhaps she was the daughter of a German officer and slept in a luxurious embassy compound. Maybe by day she wandered the streets, inventing personas out of mischief. Maybe our apparent friendship was a standard trawling exercise and she charmed any visiting sailor to see if we could be tricked into divulging information.

I felt a hand on my shoulder and turned to see Mr Tierney.

'I didn't mean to tease you in the galley, Jack,' he said quietly. 'But you know what buffoonery happens when men are together. I'd feel like an eejit asking you how you're really feeling when the Cook was there. Your first Christmas away: it can't be easy.'

'I'm just a bit hungover,' I said apologetically.

'We're all brain-dead today. But you have to knock a bit of pleasure out of life when you can. We'll have a tough voyage back.'

'If we make it back.'

'Oh, trust me: we will.'

'What makes you so sure?'

He glanced across at Mr Walton, still diligently counting the number of crates with the shipping clerk. 'We're sailing with a man who'd dearly love to die at sea. But the sea reserves the right to pick the moment of our death. It gives a sailor no say in such matters.'

'Why would Mr Walton want to die at sea?'

'The same reason we're all here: money – or a lack of it. Now head down to the galley: the Cook is chomping to go shopping. You can always spot a ship's cook: they're the only sailors who love shopping. Every time a cook sees a row of shops in a new port he's more excited than a dentist's wife traipsing up to Dublin for the Christmas sales.'

Mr Tierney was right: the Cook had donned a suit. His sharp Fedora hat, pinched down on both sides, made him look more like someone engaged in espionage than all the genuine spies on the dock. His normal workday outfit was baggy white trousers and a succession of white tops splattered with stains that reflected the meals he had cooked. Now he was as dapper as a dandy sauntering off to a dance. He had even scrubbed away the granules of flour that generally gave his moustache a silver tint. On the ship he was the butt of complaints and jokes, but as we descended the gangway he became someone else: a foreigner with money to spend. It didn't matter to any shopkeeper who already knew him that he was merely buying provisions for a small ship. A customer was a customer and, wherever we stopped to inspect foodstuffs, he would be treated with equal respect, as if he was the chief purser of a New York-bound liner crammed with passengers.

Today he was only buying supplies for ten men, but these traders knew that, on his next trip, he could have changed vessels and be tasked with purchasing vittles for fifty men on a transatlantic journey. Or, if they made the right impression, he might recommend their shop to fellow cooks when drinking in distant ports, using a beer mat to draw a map to their door. And, regardless of the size of his current order, he still possessed one thing that few local customers carried in their wallets: sterling banknotes. If Germany won the war, this British currency might prove worthless. But if the Allies won, then all the Reichsmarks that these Lisbon shopkeepers hoarded in metal boxes would lose their worth and sterling would soar in value instead. As he accepted respectful salutations from each trader whose store we visited (although he seemed disinclined as yet to make any purchases), the Cook explained how shopkeepers liked to hedge their bets. Any currency we spent today would remain squirrelled away until the chance came for them to barter it to their best advantage.

'Ireland is the only neutral country gaining nothing from this war,' he said. 'The Portuguese happily trade with the British and, at the same time, they flog tungsten to the Nazis to armour-plate their tanks. The Swedes supply the Germans with iron ore and Swiss banks can barely close their vaults, they're so crammed with looted Nazi gold.'

My nose told me when we reached the fishmongers along Rua do Arsenal. Not all shops had reopened but I was assailed by the pungent smells of fish on all sides: the raucous cries of scavenging gulls added to the clamour. Most fish looked so fresh that it might have only been landed moments ago. But the box which the Cook paused to inspect contained decidedly unappetising fish: they looked more like rigid slabs of cardboard than anything that had ever swam in the ocean.

'What's this stuff?' I asked. 'Are you trying to break our teeth?'

The Cook picked up a piece to thoughtfully sniff its strong smoky aroma. 'Fresh fish is no use to a crew because it will soon start to stink. Meet the best friend that any ship's cook can have: *Bacalhau.*'

'I'm not sure I want to meet it.' I doubtfully sniffed the stiff slab.

'If you want to become a ship's cook then listen and learn,' he said. '*Bacalhau* is dried and salted cod. Lisboetas eat it as a delicacy. It's inedible now but leave it soaking in water for two days and add a few spoons of milk. Then I promise that you'll never taste anything as sweet as its flaking white flesh. There's a dozen ways to cook *Bacalhau*, and between here and Wexford I'll teach you them.'

The fishmonger emerged through his open doorway, brushing his fingers on an apron before proffering an arm to formally shake hands with the Cook. The Cook politely accepted his handshake but placed the sample of dried cod back in its wooden box with an apologetic but dismissive shrug. He lifted his Fedora respectfully and gestured for me to move on. The fishmonger politely blocked his path and beckoned the Cook into his shop, indicating that superior fish was available inside. Making a courteous attempt at polite conversation, the Cook casually inquired about the price of the *Bacalhau*. He tut-tutted in mild disapproval at the quoted price and made to move away again. The fishmonger impatiently shouted into the semi-darkness of his shop. His assistant hurriedly appeared, bearing a tray with a bottle of port and two glasses. Olives, cheeses, pieces of sausage meat and bread were also hastily arranged on the tray. The Cook respectfully declined this snack but the fishmonger acted deeply hurt at seeing his hospitality spurned. Beseeching the Cook to linger as an honoured guest, he angrily shouted again at his assistant. I realised that the fishmonger's anger was because there was no glass for me. But the Cook wagged his finger to indicate that any drink or any ensuing conversation should be confined to men of an appropriate professional standing.

'You speak some English?' he asked the fishmonger.

'A little only, but enough,' the man replied with cautious modestly.

'Your face reminds me of a store owner I bought supplies from once when I took a tram to Graça…' the Cook paused, as if summoning up a forgotten name. 'José Pedro da Sliva.'

The fishmonger beamed in surprise. 'José Pedro is my brother. Only last night our families celebrate together…' He stopped, realising that the Cook had not halted outside his shop by accident. 'Any fish you need … anything you need … I can supply. If not, I ask José. Anything you see on display, but also anything you don't see…'

'You are José's brother?' the Cook feigned suitable astonishment.

The fishmonger nodded. 'José and I…' He entwined two fingers to demonstrate their closeness. 'Tight lips too … never speak…' Unsure about what the Cook actually wanted to buy, he played for time by beckoning his assistant to bring a third glass. 'Your boy … he must wet his lips on Christmas Day…'

'I never discuss my business in front of underlings.' The Cook turned to curtly dismiss me, his authoritative tone impressing the fishmonger. I meekly played along, realising that my role on this excursion had never been as a Sherpa but as a prop. The fact that the Cook had a cabin boy at his beck and call exaggerated the size of our ship. I meekly addressed him as 'Sir' and listened straight-faced to his instructions about the numerous tasks which I – along with two other imaginary cabin boys – were to perform in his absence.

I started to humbly walk away and he brusquely summoned me back, pointing to the tray of food the fishmonger's assistant was holding.

'Take a morsel for the road, boy. It is discourteous to refuse Senhor da Sliva's generosity on Christmas Day.'

Grateful for the food, I selected two chunks of dry bread and two pieces of cheese. The Cook frowned.

'Don't insult the Senhor's hospitality. You make him look like a poor man.' He pointed to the tray. 'Take some of these and these.'

Senhor da Sliva did not look like a poor man: he looked like a man in a state of shock at the amount of food disappearing. But he now needed to play along to emphasize his big-heartedness by insisting on me taking additional pieces of cheese and dark sausage and olives and slices of a special ring-shaped cake called *bolo rei*, which he said was only cooked at Christmas. My hands could barely hold all this bounty. Finally the Cook steered me on my way.

'Get along with you now, boy,' he ordered, giving me a fierce glower, followed by the longest wink I'd ever seen. I walked away, realising that not only did I have the finest of lunches but also the freedom of the city. I was starving but I didn't want to eat yet. It seemed crazy after having last seen Kateřina emerge from a luxury hotel in a silk dress, but I didn't know if she – in whatever life she truly led – was back walking these streets and if she was hungry. I knew nothing about her: I just knew that I could not eat this food alone until I made an effort to find her. When I reached Praça do Comércio I saw a paper bag blowing across the cobbled plaza. Carefully I transferred each delicacy into this bag. Then I walked the crowded streets towards Rossio, hoping against hope that I might meet her again and yet unsure about what to say if our paths did cross.

Chapter Nineteen

Christmas Day, Bairro Alto, Lisbon

I DON'T KNOW HOW LONG I continued my search for Kateřina around the square at Rossio and along the Avenida da Liberdade before I began to try the shabbier side streets that sloped down towards the Bairro Alto. I grew increasingly hungry and thirsty as I walked in the bright winter sun: my head was still throbbing with a severe headache after last night's wine. I would never find the street she claimed to live on by her description of it as the shabbiest one in Bairro Alto: every narrow shabby street led to another smaller one that looked even shabbier. Nobody who possessed a dress like she had worn last night could possibly live amid this poverty. I became convinced that everything she told me was a lie until – two hours into my search – I found the second-hand bookshop she had described. The windows were crammed with spines of books in languages I could not understand. It was obvious from the leather bindings that these were expensive editions, but obvious too, from the low prices displayed, that refugees had been forced to sell them for a fraction of their value.

This bookshop was real, if nothing else. I never strayed too far from it as I continued to wander through warrens of lanes, always returning to keep an eye on that shop. Several times I sat on a low wall to open my bag of food. But always a shawled old woman would appear from a doorway to gaze at me with open curiosity, or else famished children gathered around as if I was an exotic exhibit in a zoo. I couldn't eat in front of them and so I strode on, suspecting that privacy was impossible on these streets.

Another two hours passed before I rounded a corner and spied Kateřina standing alone at the bookshop, gazing in at the books displayed in the window, like she had said she often did. I watched her for several minutes before she became aware of me. I was observing someone I didn't know. This was not the carefree girl I had met yesterday, nor the young courtesan obeying a German officer last night. Here was somebody different: someone impoverished and alone. All pretence was gone; every fabrication used to shield herself from the world removed. I could see how lonely she looked and I knew from how she wearily allowed herself the respite of those few moments staring at the bookshop window that she had no destination except to walk in a loop around these streets. I knew this feeling: it was like watching myself pretend to have business to conduct while aimlessly traipsing through the streets of Wexford.

Eventually Kateřina sensed that she was being watched. She looked around to stare directly at me, and then ducked down a side street, intent on fleeing. There was no time to think. I quickly followed, knowing that if I hesitated she would give me the slip in this maze of streets. I kept her in my sight for two minutes, during which she changed direction a half-dozen times, flitting down tiny alleyways until she succeeded in losing me. I emerged into a small square with five narrow streets leading away from it. Three of them fanned out, falling steeply towards the river. The other two climbed upwards. There was no sight of Kateřina. She could have slipped into an alleyway or be watching from an open tenement doorway, ready to slip away once she saw me choose which street to continue my wild goose chase on.

Then it came to me where she must be hiding: the exact sort of place where I would hide if someone pursued me through Wexford. Kateřina would not have enough time to run down any of these streets and be confident that I wouldn't spot her. Instead, she had tried to sow confusion by giving me no time to think, hoping to make me panic and choose a wrong route at random. Turning around, I slowly walked back up the street I had run down. It was steep and winding, its tall buildings perched precariously on outcrops of solid rock. Not every house had a door opening directly onto the street. Some buildings were only accessed by rows of uneven steps which climbed up to doorways virtually hidden from the road. Kateřina stood in one such high doorway, her body pressed against the flaking paint on a huge door. When rushing past, there was no way I could have spotted her unless I had stopped to look back. The steep steps would have given her a vantage point from where she could watch me disappear if I had picked a street leading downhill. These steps she had scrambled up were steep and uneven, with no rail to protect her if she stumbled. I felt nervous for her up there, but it was clear from her expression that she felt terror and fury.

'I just want to speak to you,' I said.

'That gives you no right to chase me. How you know how it feels to be chased? One day in Lisboa and you are already a sneaky spy.'

'I wasn't spying on you.'

'Then what were you doing?'

I struggled to explain my tangled emotions. 'I wanted to know that you're all right.'

'That's not your business.'

'Yesterday I thought I knew you. Then I discovered you were someone different.'

'Who?'

'I don't know. That man last night at the hotel … was he your father?'

Kateřina's laugh was incredulous. 'Go home, Jack; you don't belong in the big world.'

'Okay, I know he wasn't your father. Is he your lover?'

Her expression changed. Any good humour was replaced by a bewildered hurt.

'How you can think I love such a man?'

Helplessly, I searched for the right words. 'I don't know what to think.'

Kateřina sat down on the top step. She looked weary. 'Have you been in love, Jack?'

'I am in love.'

'Not with me, I hope: that is all I need.'

I hesitated, trying for once not to be too tongue-tied to say what was in my heart. I owed it to Kateřina, and to myself, to find the right words. 'If I wasn't already in love with a girl in Wexford, then I would think I was in love with you. My feelings for you are so strong that I'd think they were love if I didn't already know what love feels like. I'm not in love with you, but I care deeply about you. I just want to know you're okay.'

The oak door behind Kateřina opened. An ancient woman emerged, dressed entirely in black. Our voices had attracted her attention. She scolded Kateřina sharply in Portuguese for disturbing the family celebrations going in inside. Trying to muster what dignity she could, Kateřina stood up, brushed any dirt off her dress and carefully picked her way down the uneven steps. The woman watched her. I recognised the look in that woman's eyes: the disdainful look that women of a certain class often directed at me when condescending to look in my direction. Her contemptuous gaze seemed to rob Kateřina of any self-esteem. When Kateřina reached the bottom step I impulsively clasped her hand and glared up at the old woman with such a glacial stare that it was she who looked away, cowed by my defiance. Meekly, she retreated inside and slammed the door.

'Don't mind that snooty hag,' I said. 'She probably hasn't the price of a loaf of bread to put on the table: the only thing keeping her alive is spite.'

'I trespass on her doorstep,' Kateřina replied. 'No matter where I walk in this city, I'm always a trespasser.'

I released her hand, awkward at having had the audacity to take it. She leaned forward and surprised me with a kiss.

'What was that for?' I asked.

'To thank you.'

'For what?'

'For saying you don't love me in words with more truth than the words other men use to pretend they love me, when there is only one thing they want. No one here loves me: but some men think they can use lies to advantage. I kiss you to thank you for nearly falling in love with me but being truthful to say you didn't.' Then she slapped me across the face with sufficient force to emphasise her point. 'Now my slap is for making me scared by chasing after me.'

'I didn't mean to scare you.'

'It wasn't you make me scared: it was the memories.'

'Are you really a waitress?' I asked.

She shrugged ruefully. 'Where would a refugee like me get a permit to work? Even if a café owner gave me work out of pity, the Secret Police would visit his café to tell him how a Lisboa girl could use that job. Lisboetas are not unkind at Jews; not like in some countries. They tolerate but don't encourage us to stay. This city only has one type of work for a girl like me.'

'Was that what you were doing last night?'

She flushed with annoyance. 'You know nothing about my life.'

'Then what do you do?'

'I pretend. When you saw me on the tram, who did you think you see?'

'A carefree girl.'

'Because that what I became for you yesterday: I lived out your illusion.'

'Is that all you were yesterday: an illusion?'

'You see the girl I would like to be. But I don't have the luxury to be only one person.'

'How many Kateřinas are there?'

She looked down the deserted street.

'What you really want, Jack? All men want something. Why did you come looking for me today?'

I held out the brown paper bag. 'I wanted to share my lunch with you,' I said honestly. 'I didn't know if you were rich – you looked rich last night – and I didn't know if you were poor – you looked poor when I first met you. There's not much to eat here and it's hardly a Christmas dinner, but it didn't feel right to eat alone if there was a chance that you were hungry too.'

Kateřina went silent, staring at the bag. It seemed a pathetically small offering: a few morsels of bread, cheese, sausage meat, olives and cake. When she looked up I feared that her gaze might contain mockery. Instead, I saw her blinking back tears.

'There is a room near here,' she said quietly.

'Is it your room?'

She shook her head.

'It is just a room where we can eat and, for once, have no prying eyes.'

Chapter Twenty

Christmas Day, Bairro Alto, Lisbon

THE HIGH BUILDING WAS ON a side street that I knew I would never be able to find again. The fact that it had a locked front door elevated it above many of the slum dwellings we had passed, most of which didn't have any signs of a front door left – the wood having been chopped up for kindling during harsh winters. This house was quieter: no squadrons of children raced down the stairs. Indeed, nobody was about, and Kateřina seemed anxious not to attract any attention as we climbed endless flights of wooden steps until we eventually reached a landing with two attic doors. Kateřina used a key to open the door to the left and discreetly closed it behind her once we entered the small room. Attempts had been made to cover up damp stains on the walls with pictures of Hollywood film stars cut from magazines. The only other adornment was a chipped wooden crucifix: it looked like it had been nailed above the door decades ago, untouched by any occupant who had arrived or departed since then.

'Is this where you live?' I asked again.

'I wish I live here.'

'Where do you live?'

'Some nights I can sleep here if I do not overstay welcome. Some evenings my friend – the girl who pays rent – has company. I must walk around the streets until her boyfriend is gone. We signal: she opens the curtain so that I know I allowed back in.' Kateřina sat down on a small sofa. 'I can only dream to have such a room but I am more lucky than some: I have a key and I can sleep some nights on this sofa, if I don't disturb her.'

Kateřina patted the sofa. I was uncertain if this was an invitation to sit beside her or if she was showing me how comfortable her makeshift bed was.

'She let me keep a suitcase under the sofa and I can use the last piece of clothes rail we rig up along the wall to hang what clothes I have. If any occasion is special then I am sometimes allowed borrow a dress from her and she always can borrow anything of mine.'

She stood up and walked over to a counter where a jug was covered by a cloth. Pouring two glasses of water, she beckoned for me to sit on one of two chairs at the tiny table. 'You brought bread. Now I bring wine for our Christmas feast.'

I sat down, tearing open the bag to reveal its contents. 'It's hardly a feast, I'm afraid.'

'It looks like a feast to me.' Sitting down, she passed me a glass of water. 'I can not offer real wine.'

'I only drank wine last night to feel like one of the crew,' I said. 'But I hate wine.'

Kateřina selected a piece of cheese. 'I do not eat sausage meat: you have sausage.'

'Why don't you eat sausages?'

She seemed amused at my ignorance. 'We Jews do not eat pork. Are there no Jews in your town?'

'I'm not sure,' I said. 'Wexford has Protestants all right but we're not encouraged to mix with them.'

'Are you afraid you will go to hell?' she teased.

'No,' I replied honestly. 'I'd be afraid to get beaten by my old teacher – Brother Dawson – if he caught me talking to a Protestant. Can you eat bread and cheese and olives and this cake?'

'I can eat my share.' Kateřina smiled. 'But you eat yours.'

'I couldn't face another bite of cheese or bread,' I lied. 'I ate so much already when helping the Cook to shop. I'll have the sausage: you take the rest.'

She protested, but even though she tried to eat slowly, I saw how famished she was. I tried to disguise my hunger, knowing that I would at least be fed rough and ready food en route back to Ireland.

'Who is the girl who rents this room?' I asked.

'She is my only real friend,' Kateřina said. 'She comes from a village near Évora where there is nothing only olives and cork-oak trees and barefoot children. She is a waitress: sometimes I borrow her life like I borrow her clothes. She work every evening till her feet ache, but for her Lisboa is an escape from poverty. Some nights when she gets home I pretend to sleep so she will not have to talk if tired. But other nights she shakes my shoulder and we sit talking till dawn. She tells me what men in her café say and how the owner stares at her body when she must bend down to wipe tables clean. Each time it happens the owner's wife looks at her angry, as if my friend wants to steal her fat husband and not just fight off his grubby fingers when he catch her alone.'

'What do you talk to her about?' I asked.

'Anything that happens in my day, but often I have nothing to tell because I speak to no one all day. I just walk the same streets and avoid the same people, trying to make myself tired so that I will fall asleep when I climb these stairs at night.'

'Who are the people you avoid?'

'People who knew me at one time: people who spend all their day walking from embassy to relief agency to post office, looking for news that they know will not come.'

'Where do you sleep when you cannot use this sofa?' I asked.

A resigned note entered her voice. 'I join some queue outside a shipping agent. It is safer in numbers. But sleep is not easy on cold pavement. So some nights I go back to Ericeira. Somebody there always has a spare blanket and a hundred questions.'

I remembered the woman in the post office who tried to attract Kateřina's attention.

'Where is Ericeira?'

'It is a town with forty beaches,' she said. 'Forty places to feel lonely in.'

Kateřina gestured for me to take the final piece of cheese. I shook my head, though I was as hungry now as when we commenced our paltry meal. She ate it slowly, trying to savour the taste.

'Last night the German embassy official you saw me with drove me to Estoril Casino. Estoril is the seaside resort where foreign millionaires now spend the war gambling and drinking champagne in safety. Some gamblers like to stroke a rabbit foot before they roll dice. That German liked to stroke my bare arm in public, before he rolled dice on the craps table. You would not believe the luxury in Estoril any more than you would believe the despair in Ericeira. Ericeira used to be the seaside resort where ordinary people holidayed before the war. But the hotels there are now empty so Salazar has sent many Jews who reached Lisboa to live in hotel rooms there. Everything is run down in Ericeira: even the children. You know how the steel spring inside a child's toy sometimes breaks? This is how refugee children look sitting on Ericeira's empty beaches: like forgotten, broken toys.'

'Is that where your family lives?' I asked.

Kateřina stared wistfully at the shabby sofa. 'I have a bed here on most nights. I have a suitcase and a rail for dresses.'

'That's not what I asked. You must have some family: you couldn't have reached Lisbon alone. Is Kateřina even your real name?' I felt a stab of irrational jealousy. 'That German last night called you a different name.'

Kateřina became more guarded, the atmosphere now tense. 'I been called so many names that names no longer hurt me. I was named Kateřina when I was born. But my father needed to find new names for us all. He spent our savings on forged papers when the Nazis marched into Prague. I had a new name to remember when we crossed into Hungary. But Hungary was not safe: Hitler's puppets there want to tear us limb from limb, they were worse than the Nazi's themselves. I needed to become invisible, to hide in a car boot as we crossed to Yugoslavia, but that place was not safe either. *Táta* used his contacts to smuggle us into Italy and then France: each time with new papers and a new name to remember. Every country feels different but the weight of fear always feels the same. Fear is like a shard of ice, always pressed against your neck: the fear that someone will call me by my old name on a street and I turn around and give our secret away if I forget that this no longer my name. I have learnt the true meaning of fear by always having to remember what name I am meant to be today.'

'I can't imagine anything worse,' I said.

'Then you barely lived. *Táta* wrote in newspaper what will happen after Hitler marches into Sudetenland. But my aunts and uncles did not believe him. Now I do not know if they are alive or dead.'

'Your father has no contact with them?'

'I have no contact with *Táta*. After we reached Ericeira he went to Lisboa one night to look for passage to any country that might take us; where we could start again – with no money but with no fear of late-night knocks at our door. But *Táta* is a marked man: *politický radikál*, his name in a Gestapo file. People often disappear in Lisboa and the police shake their head. Nobody knows who the police work for. After *Táta* disappear, my mother started to go to

Lisboa late at night, walking all the way if nobody would stop to offer her a lift. *Matka* was safe: Lisboa is a safe city provided no Gestapo agent has put thirty silver pieces on your head. The dangers for *Matka* came from inside her mind. It was so hard to travel this far and then lose her husband when it seemed that we were safe for now at least. Friends would find her alone in the synagogue or sitting at the fountain at Rossio, as if she was patiently waiting for *Táta* to find her. Her brain … it was like a ship … sinking. She no longer really knew me or the friends who brought her safely back to Ericeira. To her I was just a kind stranger trying to get her to eat what little food we had or sip water when her lips were parched. She would thank me but her mind was gone back to before I was born. I always tried to stay awake and lock our bedroom door, but the moment I fall asleep she would be gone again.'

'Where is she now?' I asked.

'She is safe now. If all that she is able to do is to sit and wait for her phantom date, then maybe it is better that she sits in an asylum where no harm can happen. There were too many times when she was found sitting alone in expensive restaurants, refusing to move, telling in Czech that she was waiting for boyfriend, a handsome young *radikál* and trying to explain that she cannot understand why he is so late. *Matka* no longer knows that she is now in Lisboa. In Lisboa if you become a nuisance on the streets they lock you up. I go to visit her but she does not know me. I make her feel uneasy because I sit too close, and she breaks my heart.'

Shyly I reached for Kateřina's hand. 'I don't know what to say.'

She squeezed my hand. 'A boy who brings cheese and *bolo rei* has no need to say anything.'

I wanted to comfort her. I wanted us to just sit in this small room and say nothing because there was nothing that could be said: at dawn I could sail away and Kateřina would be left in this purgatory. But the immature, small-town boy within me couldn't prevent a festering sense of having been duped yesterday from spilling out in clumsy words.

'How can you let a German official bring you to a casino after what they did to your father?'

Kateřina looked up, as hurt as if I had slapped her. She angrily snatched back her hand.

'Who are you to judge me? You know nothing of my life!'

'Then what were you doing, leaving the Hotel Metropole with him?'

'Last night I was being somebody else.'

'Natasha?'

She shrugged. 'Natasha. Ingrid. Erika. Dorothy. Name no matter.'

'Were you selling yourself?'

'Grow up. What do you think girls do in Wexford?'

'Nothing like that.'

'How you know? Maybe they are just not so open in your backward village.'

'Wexford is a town,' I said defensively. 'We have a mayor.'

She raised her eyes scornfully. 'Have you music conservatory? An art gallery? How is Wexford not like all the other ... what are the words a man once said to me ... one-horse dunghill villages?'

'We have a public library.'

'Wexford is a damp stain on edge of Europe: so small nobody would notice if it vanished,' she snapped. 'But what happens between men and women all over the world still happens in Wexford. Maybe it is cloaked in nice words there; but it is same bartering; the same yielding of one inch of skin or slapping a hand away. Maybe the deal gets done in silent looks on dance floor or by fathers bartering land or cash to sell their daughter's body and seal her future. But at end the decision is all about money, just like in Karl Marx. Have you not read your Karl Marx?'

'I'm a Catholic,' I protested. 'We're not meant to actually read things: we're meant to just accept things on faith.'

'Then open your eyes when you go home. Maybe you will not see girls shiver on street corners in your dungheap town. But watch grandmothers haggle over dowries behind closed doors and you will see that they are pimping the same thing that hungry girls sell in Cais do Sodré.'

I swallowed hard. 'Were you selling your body last night?'

Kateřina stared at me with sullen haughtiness. 'I not some girl in Cais do Sodré. I do not say I am better: but what I offer is different.'

'What do you offer?'

'Portuguese girls can only be themselves. But I can be anyone. It is easy for me to pretend to be somebody else, when I barely know who I am any more. I will not tell you if I have ever sold my body or not. But if a man just wants a girl's body, then he will find that easy in Lisboa. But I can give a man more: I can give him the disguise of being respectable. In Prague, my drama teacher said I would act on great stages one day. But here I need to create my own stage in this city where I stand out – a girl who speaks enough Italian and French to act as if I am from Milan or Paris.'

Kateřina tilted her head sideways. Her facial expression changed as she gazed at me with timid eyes. 'How old do I look now?' she demanded.

'I don't know, far younger than you really are.'

'Even Nazis do not like to bribe Portuguese officials in open. They play out a game instead. Some days I am paid to pretend that I am the young daughter of a German embassy official whose family is going back to Berlin. This German takes me with him to visit an important civil servant. He pretends he must sell his motor car for a pittance, because it is too expensive to take back to Germany. Then three days later I sit in that civil servant's office again in different clothes, pretending to be the daughter of a different German who has just arrived in Lisboa. This new German needs to buy a motor car and is willing to pay huge price for one. The civil servant has only owned this car for three days, yet he makes a fortune from buying and selling it in that time. I have lost count of the number of times I have seen that same car sold to that same civil servant. He finds it easier if the German pretends to have a daughter. It makes it look like they are honest family men.'

'What role were you playing last night?'

Her expression betrayed such vulnerability that I knew she was not acting.

'Is this why you track me down?' she asked. 'To call me vile names?'

'I've haven't called you anything.'

'I see you judge.'

'I don't know enough about life to judge anyone,' I said. 'I'm just trying to understand.'

'Last night I let myself be pawed by a Nazi who needed a giddy girl to bring to the Casino so that while there – seemingly by fluke – he would encounter an important government official who also has a dizzy girl on his arm. People watching would think that she and I were the goods being sold; these men buying our bodies as Christmas gift for themselves. But we were only there to camouflage what was really being sold: information between the two men. I was told in advance that when I see the government official's girl across the crowded casino I would run towards her like we were old friends. In this way the two men just seemed to be dragged together by chance. We two girls drank champagne on empty stomachs and we talked loudly to provide a smokescreen, so that it looked as if the two men were just exchanging polite chit-chat while they patiently waited for us girls to finish our giddy gossiping.'

'What did you and the girl talk about?'

She shrugged. 'We were not listening to what the other was saying, while the government official gave this Nazi the information he has paid for. I was too busy wondering how much the other girl was being paid and for what services.'

'What happened afterward?' I had no right to ask but couldn't stop myself.

'Afterwards is not your concern,' Kateřina replied warily. She paused, deciding whether to confide. 'Afterwards is when I try to make sure I am paid at least some of my promised money. Afterwards is about thinking quickly and hiding a hairpin between my knuckles. If you stab a man in his thigh with a hairpin it can slow down his greedy fingers. I have learnt the hard way how to mind myself. Afterwards is about making my choice and living with consequence.'

'So everything that you do is an act?'

'Me sitting here with you now is no act. I am not lying to you about this sofa bed and there are no lies in my suitcase full of keepsakes of no value to anyone else or I would have had to sell them in desperation long ago.'

I hesitated, aware that I was straying into dangerous territory. 'We both lost our fathers to the Nazis. I'm filled with hatred for the men who killed my father. I understand what it feels like to be hungry and cold. But I still don't understand how you can bear to be around such men.'

Kateřina went quiet, lost in private thoughts. When she spoke she sounded exhausted. 'Sit with me on the sofa, Jack. I can't face the loneliness of walking streets on Christmas Day, but I don't want to sit at this table any longer.'

The sofa was so small that when we sat down our knees touched. She would need to curl up at night to sleep on it. 'That question was unfair,' I said. 'I didn't mean to upset you. When I'm nervous I talk too much and ask stupid questions.'

'Why you nervous?'

'I've never talked this openly to a girl before: I've rarely been this close to a girl for so long.'

'Not even with Ellie in Wexford?'

'When we were young, yes. But right up until moments before I sailed I barely knew what to say to her.'

'Or do with her?' A teasing quality entered her voice, but also a note of genuine curiosity.

I felt myself blush. 'I've only ever kissed her once.'

'But she will let you watch her put on nylon stockings.'

'I should never have told you: I knew you'd tease me.'

'I not teasing. I will help you buy nylons.'

'A crewmate already bought me a pair to give her. It was his way of apologising for locking me into my cabin last night.'

'But you escaped.'

'I wanted to see you.'

She smiled. 'You didn't expect to see me like you did: I certainly didn't expect to see you.'

'I'm glad I did see you.'

'I shattered your illusion.'

'I don't want to see any illusion: I want to see you.'

Kateřina gazed at me. Her voice was bereft of mockery. 'Do you?'

Her gaze contained such vulnerability that it felt as if any answer I gave would cause hurt. In this moment my body felt like glass. It was as if her body was also made of glass and the slightest movement might shatter us into a thousand shards. 'I know what I'd truly like,' I replied hesitantly. 'But that's different from what I want.'

'Don't speak in riddles.'

'I would nearly sell my soul for a chance to see you – to see all of you. I can't even describe how much I long for that right now.'

'Are you scared for your soul? Because of whatever nonsense your priests drum into you?'

'I'm scared, but not for my soul. I'd be scared that I'd make a right eejit of myself because I wouldn't know what to do.'

'There must be a first time for everyone.'

I took her hand and brushed her fingers softly. 'I know that. And I know I'm the biggest fool alive because it will probably be an eternity before I ever get this chance again. It may be years from now, but when this chance comes around again, I want to make an eejit of myself with a special girl whom I have been in love with for most of my life, and I want that moment to be new and special for us both. Here with you, now, it would also be truly special … but I just worry that the next time … it might not be as special because of that.'

She squeezed my fingers. 'It's not because of who I am?'

'It's because you're special. If you were someone ordinary whom I could just forget about after my ship sails, then maybe it would feel different.'

'Will you tell Ellie about me?'

'I need there to be nothing that I have tell her about or, worse still, conceal from her. And yet when I go home I will be changed because of having met you.'

'You not even know me.'

'Before this, whenever I was even near a girl, I felt trapped in a cage of shyness. But you've unlocked it.'

Kateřina smiled. 'You are the strangest boy. You want nothing. I've never met a man before who, deep down, did not want something from me.'

'I do want something,' I said, speaking quickly as the idea entered my head. 'I want to help you to stow away. I can sneak you on board the *Kerlogue* and hide you among the crates in the hold. By the time the Captain finds out we'll be halfway to Ireland and it will be too late to turn back. I'd probably lose my job but the Irish authorities … they couldn't send you back … where could they send you, when you have no country left that you belong to?'

Kateřina took my fingers and raised them to her lips to kiss them once, before releasing her grip. 'You are sweetest boy,' she said sadly.

'I'm serious,' I insisted. 'The crew are all attending mass at six o'clock. The ship will be empty.'

'It is guarded by harbour police.'

'Them fellows pay me no heed as I come and go. I could show them my papers and go on board for a moment to change into my spare clothes and then sneak these clothes I'm wearing back out. If you change into these clothes and hide your hair under my cap, then all you'd need to do is just slip quickly past them and they'll think that it's me returning to the ship again.'

Kateřina rose and walked to the makeshift clothes rail. In one sweeping movement she pulled her dress over her head and turned to face me in her undergarments.

'This who I am: what I look like. Would you mistake me for a cabin boy?'

Mesmerised, I swallowed hard, trying not to stare at the curves of her body. 'No.'

'But you think that harbour policemen who are trained to look out for people trying to stow away will think me a cabin boy?'

I shook my head.

From the rack Kateřina removed the silk dress she had worn outside the Hotel Metropole. She pulled it over her head and shook her hair loose.

'Do you like this dress?'

'It's beautiful.'

'That man last night bought it especially because he wanted to see me wear it. Then after – after plying me with champagne on an empty stomach because we had no food, because he had taken his wife to dinner earlier – he wanted to see what I looked like when not wearing it. We tussled in the taxi back to Lisboa and I feared that he would bribe the driver to pull over and help him to pin me down. But the taxi driver only stopped when we reached a police checkpoint: long rows of cars in front of us. I scratched the German's cheek and scrambled from the taxi. Strangers stared out from car windows, amused at the sight of me on that dark road, breathless and scared, carrying my high-heels because I could not run in them. It took me three hours to walk back here, with none of the money I was promised to go with him to the Casino.' She paused and stood before me, letting me take in the fullness of her figure in that dress. 'Now let me ask you a question. Is Ellie the same size as me?'

I nodded.

'Bring you her back this dress because I never wish to see it again. It is new; worn once only. You can pretend that you buy it in same shop where you bought the nylons.'

'I can't take your dress.'

'It all I have to give. I want give you something.' She lifted the dress above her head and walked towards me, holding it out until I accepted. She knelt in front of me in her undergarments, bending her head and letting her hair cascade down to reveal her bare neck. 'When the moment comes that you and Ellie are alone like this, you kiss her gentle here on nape of her neck, because all girls like this. Do it very gentle. Take your time with this and with everything you do. Men are stupid to think they must impress us with strength, but it needs far greater strength to be patient, to be slow and let a girl get as much pleasure as you.' She looked up and leaned forward to kiss my forehead. 'Now you know as much as you need know to begin: all the rest you will have to find out for yourself.'

She rose and took a step back. I put one hand out so that it caressed the warm flesh of her stomach. We stayed like that, neither speaking, until she lifted my hand away and placed it back on the dress on my lap. She walked back to the rail and donned the ordinary dress she had worn when we met on the street. 'You must hurry if you wish to attend six o'clock mass with your crew.'

'Come with me.'

'I am a Jew. What would I do inside a Catholic church?'

'Have you ever been inside one?'

Kateřina nodded. 'I have sat in every church in Lisboa. I love the silence and how people leave you alone there. I go in when too tired to walk or I have money to light a candle for *Táta*. Next time I light two candles: one for your father, one for mine.'

'I'll do the same,' I promised. 'Maybe it will do us some good.'

'One day a distinguished-looking German saw me light a candle in Church de São Roque,' she said. 'Because I am in a church he never thought that I might be a Jew. He needed someone to pretend to be his niece that afternoon. He told me what café to wait in: the café where they now leave messages when they wish to find me. My Italian and French pronunciation and my air of sophistication impressed him. I knew exactly what lies to feed him And he fed these lies to his colleagues. This is why I can not be seen with other Jews. I am not proud of some things I do, but I do what is necessary to survive. You ask me how I can stand to be among Nazis. Like every refugee here, I am waiting, but I waiting for something different. The Nazis who buy my time do not know that I speak fluent German. Often they barely notice I am there at all, except as an actress in their little bribes and schemes. I smile and look bored as if I don't understand a word when they talk away in German but I listen all the time because one day they will let slip my father's name. I have an extra-long sharp hairpin. Like I told you, at times I need to dig it into man's thigh if he gets out of hand. But I keep it for a more important reason. One day they will let slip the name of the man who tortured and killed *Táta*. When they do, I will wait my chance to plunge that hairpin into his heart.'

Kateřina looked fragile, yet her eyes were so fierce that I didn't doubt her words.

'They'll hang you for that,' I said.

'I don't care, once my father's murder is avenged.'

I chose my words slyly. 'I don't believe you have the courage to plunge a hairpin into a Nazi's heart.'

'Don't talk me about courage,' she replied. 'You not know what things I've had to do.'

'Then how come you don't have the courage to be a stowaway?'

'I told you, it is impossible and too dangerous if I am caught.'

'I think you're too scared.'

Kateřina looked near tears. 'I don't care what you believe. Never doubt my courage.'

'Prove your courage: stow away on the *Kerlogue*.'

'It cannot be done.'

'You won't know until you try. What have you got to lose? Try it for your father's sake. If you die avenging his death, then all his efforts to keep you safe will have been in vain. I know what my father would want for me, and I think your father would want the same for you. Your *táta* wouldn't ask you to die for him; he'd want you to live.'

Chapter Twenty-One

Christmas Day, Alcântara, Lisbon

WHAT MIGHT HAVE HAPPENED IF I had not entered the Church of Nossa Senhora da Conceição, to double check that the crew were attending mass? I was so fired up in my determination not to abandon Kateřina that I refused to let logic ruin my plan. Due to her precarious existence, Kateřina was used to men trying to seduce her into suspending misgivings and doing whatever they desired. My attempted seduction was different: I wanted her to do nothing more than allow herself to get caught up in my grand scheme to rescue her.

Kateřina looked dazed when we entered the church, as if unable to believe that she had been lured into this. But maybe she was simply so lonely that she couldn't bear to be left alone to wander through the streets for the rest of Christmas Day. She knew the ruthlessness of the Secret Police who watched the Lisbon docks and understood better than I did the consequences of getting caught. But she had been alone for too long, surviving on nothing more than her wits. Just this once she relaxed her guard and was swept along by my enthusiasm and conviction that nothing could go wrong.

To ensure that nobody had stayed behind to guard the ship, I needed to count my crewmates. They stood out among the devout

Portuguese worshippers, not just by their clothes but by their unmistakable foreignness. They were not alone in this. Other knots of foreign sailors knelt among the congregation: hardened seafarers lost in private prayer while contemplating the fraught voyages ahead.

I had already come to realise that Lisbon was a city of contrasts: any building that didn't resonate with grandeur generally reeked of neglect. The two extremities met in this ancient church. Its sheer scale would be unimaginable in Wexford: high vaulted ceilings decorated in murals of rich gold and blues. Yet despite these sumptuous overhead panels, the gutters were cracked and rain had seeped through the windows to mark the plaster carvings in a mosaic of water stains. The scent of charcoal and incense spread by the altar boy swinging the golden thurible could not disguise an underlying odour of damp. Everything about this church felt alien except for the Latin phrases intoned by the priest with his back to the people. I didn't understand their meaning but found something comforting in hearing these familiar words that were part of my childhood. My father had once said that hearing Latin at mass in any foreign port made him homesick.

I longed to be safely out in the vastness of Biscay and knocking on Captain Donovan's door, ready to receive the force of his fury at my revelation of a stowaway. I wanted to be frogmarched to the hold where, when the hatches were opened, I would reach down for Kateřina's hand to help her climb up, blinking in the light. But before this could happen, I needed to ensure that all the crew were here. Being a Protestant, Ernie Grogan had no duty of obligation to attend mass, but I suspected that he liked to share in this ritual before we sailed. He was so small that I needed to creep halfway up the side aisle before I spotted him among the kneeing men and knew that the coast was clear.

The crew seemed to be following the mass devotedly, but as Kateřina and I silently retreated down the side aisle, Myles Foley turned his head as if conscious of being watched. His sight was so poor that I was sure he would not spot me but he said something because both Mr Walton and Mr Tierney turned to look at me. Ignoring their gazes I quickly left the church and hurried down the steps, taking Kateřina's hand. But something about how Mr Walton and Mr Tierney had glanced at Kateřina clearly perturbed her: her brittle veneer of confidence shattered as we neared the dockside. When she looked at me it was with the eyes of a frightened child needing reassurance. She had brought no belongings: we agreed that her small suitcase would attract attention. I kept whispering that if we just looked confident the harbour police would think that nothing was untoward: if she could trick her way past doormen at luxury hotels then she could easily do this. Kateřina wanted to believe me but looked increasingly unnerved as we reached the plaza with its queues arrayed outside the closed shipping companies.

One refugee there seemed to recognise her: a man in a white suit and matching Panama hat who stood up to silently observe her progress. Kateřina released my hand and maintained a discreet distance between us so that neither this man, nor anyone else watching, would automatically suspect us of being together. I descended the steps to the wharf, which reeked of tar and seaweed. Kateřina followed a few paces behind.

A passenger liner must have been due to dock from America because a queue of passengers with tickets to freedom was already formed on the quayside. It might take days for the ship to be readied for its return voyage, but intending travellers seemed anxious to put a distinction between themselves and the hordes still trapped in Lisbon. This queue was quiet, conscious of the long wait ahead, but any hushed voice that spoke possessed a quality I had not previously heard in Lisbon: an awestruck optimism.

I whispered for Kateřina to join this queue where no official was yet bothering to inspect travel papers. Then I sauntered alone towards where the *Kerlogue* was dwarfed by bigger ships in adjoining bunks. The same two harbour policemen warmed themselves at a small fire in an oil drum. Pulling my cap down low, I raised my hand in a relaxed greeting, reaching into my pocket for my Seaman's Identity Card. One policeman recognised me and gestured towards the fire, inviting me to warm myself. When I declined with a friendly shake of my head, he waved me on, not bothering to check my papers.

I walked up the gangplank with more confidence than I felt. But once out of the policemen's sight I sank to my knees on deck, trying to stem my involuntarily shaking. I had broken no law as yet and had barely considered the consequences of what could happen to me here in Lisbon if I was caught, or back in Ireland where the Staffords would most likely ensure that no shipping firm ever employed me again. A cowardly impulse urged me to stay on board until the crew returned and we made ready to sail. After an hour alone on the wharf, Kateřina would realise that I lacked the courage to go through with our plan and would trudge back to the sofa in her friend's flat.

But I couldn't do this. Insubordinate was the term that Mr Walton used to describe my father. I had mistaken it for an insult but perhaps he meant it as a backhanded compliment, an expression of admiration in my father's ability to think for himself. It didn't seem right to pray to God for advice about how to break the law, so I prayed to my father's ghost. I don't know if he gave me the courage, but I hurried down to my cabin where, before doing anything else, I took Kateřina's silk dress, which I had hidden under my coat, and folded it carefully beneath my pillow. I then changed into my spare clothes and placed the clothes I had been wearing in my kitbag, embarrassed at their raggedness, because I was about to ask Kateřina to wear them.

Donning my cap and coat again to conceal my new outfit, I descended the gangplank. The harbour police seemed surprised at my reappearance. I wandered towards them, offering again to show my identity papers, gesturing that I had left something behind on the wharf. They waved me on, too preoccupied with staying warm to follow my progress down the wharf or notice a figure step forth from the queue to join me.

Kateřina looked both scared and relieved that I had returned. I beckoned her to follow me into the dark shadows under the steps that led up onto the plaza. Anyone watching would mistake us for a courting couple. I handed her the kitbag and turned my back to allow her the privacy to undress. When I turned around she wore the clothes I had worn a few moments previously. They didn't fit her but I hoped that in this light nobody would notice. Her clothes were hidden in the kitbag. I wanted to kiss her just once; not a lover's kiss but the kiss you might bestow on a younger sister for reassurance. But there was no time: we needed to be quick for this to work.

I gave her my coat and she tried to conceal her long hair under my cap. Glancing back along the wharf, I saw sailors from an adjoining ship approach the checkpoint. The harbour police left the warmth of their fire to check these men's papers. I pushed Kateřina forward and she hesitated, looking back, wide-eyed, as if unable to believe she had let herself be talked into this. But unless she wished to attract attention, she needed to walk on unobtrusively. Her teacher in Prague was right about her acting abilities. With every step she became the embodiment of a sailor boy. She mimicked my walk and the jut of my shoulders. Although she was two inches shorter I had the eerie sensation of watching my double. As she approached the checkpoint she never quickened her pace, but kept close to the water's edge, as far away as possible from the flickering fire. When one policeman glanced up, her friendly wave was a replica of my earlier one and she reached into her pocket, like I had done, as if to produce identity papers. The policeman waved her on. Quickly she ascended the *Kerlogue's* gangplank and disappeared from sight.

The other sailors had also passed through the checkpoint. I needed to let time pass before attempting this walk myself, but I wasn't sure how long I had until my crewmates returned. I felt too paralysed with fear to do anything except lurk under those steps. Then I heard more voices approach. They were too far away to distinguish what language they spoke but, if this was Captain Donovan returning, my plans were doomed. Even so I might have stayed there, crippled by indecision, if the policeman who had waved Kateřina through didn't nod to his companion and disappear into the shadows to urinate. I knew that this might be my only chance.

I had kept my identity card which the harbour police had not yet properly examined. As I emerged – hatless and coatless – from the shadows, I prayed that the Harbour Police didn't know exactly how many cabin boys the *Kerlogue* possessed. I walked in a slightly drunken fashion, deliberately drawing attention to myself. Reaching the solitary policeman at the checkpoint, I handed him my papers and warmed my hands at his fire. He looked puzzled and asked me a question in Portuguese. I shrugged in casual incomprehension. Because my hat was pulled down when I first passed, he had not been able to get a clear look at my face. Peering again at the photograph on the card which matched my features, he glanced back towards where his colleague had disappeared. The voices I had heard were coming closer: more sailors from the bigger ship. One sailor had a pillow-case crammed with cigarette cartons. The policeman drew himself up to his full height and shouted for his colleague. His interest switched from me to this possible contraband. No cigarettes were getting past this checkpoint until a proportion was handed over to the policemen in exchange for turning a blind eye. Greedily, he beckoned me on. I walked up the gangplank, listening to the confrontation with the foreign sailors, who protested at being stopped. When I reached the deck Kateřina stood up from where she was hiding. She had changed back into her own clothes.

'I'm more scared now than during all the border crossings with my parents,' she whispered. 'This time I'm truly alone.'

'You're not alone,' I promised. 'I'll put food and water in the hold and once we're far enough out to sea I'll come for you.'

The dock was so dark that we could barely see each other, but there was enough light for me to glimpse the loneliness on her face. 'You're a good boy, Jack. No – you're a good man. But truly, I am alone.'

There was no time to reply: the Irish voices coming down the wharf were unmistakable. I needed to prise open one of the heavy doors wide enough for Kateřina to peer down into the hold. With the crew returning, there would be no time to provide her with food or water. There was just about enough time for her to summon the courage to lower her body down among the stacked crates of oranges. I had hoped to rearrange them to create a nest for her but the Irish voices had reached the police checkpoint and were waved on as the policemen continued to haggle over the contraband cigarettes. Kateřina lay on top of one stack of crates as I lowered the steel door back into place, so intent on not letting it bang that I barely had time to glance down one last time at her scared face. The hold was now closed, but I needed to step away from it in case I looked suspicious. I grabbed my kitbag and climbed up to lean against the wheelhouse, trying to look casual as I heard bootsteps

221

on the gangplank. Mr Walton and Mr Tierney appeared. They both stared at me.

'Where's the rest of the crew?' I asked.

'We took Communion and left early,' Mr Walton said. 'That was a lovely girl with you in the church.'

'She was.'

'I saw you with her yesterday in Black House Square.'

'And that's where I left her,' I said.

'A wise place to leave her,' he replied. 'Somewhere public, because nowhere is private in this city of prying eyes. You know that, don't you?'

'I do.'

'Do you really?' Mr Walton advanced towards me and, grabbing my jumper with both hands, pressed his face close to mine. 'Before it's too late, tell us where you've hidden her.'

'I don't know what you're talking about,' I said. But my eyes betrayed me by glancing down towards the hold, anxious to check if the doors were properly closed. One furtive glance was enough. Mr Walton pinned me against the wheelhouse while Mr Tierney went down to quickly open the hatches and reach a hand into the darkness. His voice was courteous but firm.

'If we could bring you with us, Miss, we would, but you know that we can't. I'm sorry, but for your own sake, please come up.'

Slowly Kateřina clambered from the hold, her hand clasped in Mr Tierney's grasp.

'Leave her alone, Mossy,' I begged. 'She has no one here. What is it to you if she's a stowaway? I'll go to the Captain when we're at sea and take all the blame. He need never be aware that either of you knew.' I stared at Mr Walton. 'For God's sake, Sir, won't you help her? You have a daughter the same age. Imagine if your daughter was trapped here.'

Mr Walton tightened his grip. His face flashed with anger. 'Mention my daughter again and I'll break your blasted neck and hang for the privilege. Do you hear me, boy?'

'I meant no offence, Sir. I'm just trying to help her.'

'So are we. If you think Lisbon is purgatory then you've never seen a Portuguese women's prison, and you have no clue what happens to refugees when they're deported back to France for breaking the law. So shut up and do as you're told.'

Kateřina stood trembling on the deck, crying so silently that you would barely notice. Mr Tierney bowed apologetically. 'Begging your pardon, Miss, and please excuse any liberties I take, but there's only one way to get you safely off this ship.'

Swinging an arm around her waist, he pulled her close and broke into a bawdy song while steering her towards the gangplank. At first she resisted – insulted not so much by his effort to force her off the ship as by the lewd way he pawed at her. But halfway down the gangplank she realised the necessity of this scenario. Even though I suspected that her tears were still silently flowing, she gave a vulgar drunken laugh and kissed his cheek. The harbour policemen were startled by her appearance but Mr Tierney's good humour pacified them. Soon they were laughing at the audacity of a common prostitute to have slipped past them; one who was now obviously being led away by the man who had purchased her services. But I sensed a note of caution enter the voice of one policeman who called out as if wishing to question her. Still, there was no better man for bluster than Mr Tierney, who raised his voice in such raucous singing that the policeman gave up trying to interrogate anyone. Mr Tierney's voice retreated into the distance, guiding Kateřina towards the anonymous safety of the waterfront.

Mr Walton kept me pinned to the wall. 'You little fool,' he said. 'You were being watched.'

'How do you know?'

'Because we were watching the sneaky tout who was watching you.'

'I wanted to save her.'

'Life doesn't always give us a say in who we're allowed to save.'

I thought he would loosen his grip. Instead, with surprising strength for a sick man, he dragged me down onto the amidships deck and towards the open hold.

'I'm not going down there,' I protested.

'For just once in your life, boy, do as you're told.'

He released his grip and I fell backwards. The hold was so crammed that I hadn't far to fall. I landed on a crate and felt a searing pain in my shoulder. The hatch doors were closed over and locked. I have never known such darkness. I knew that I would not be trapped here for long – Mr Tierney would never allow it – but it was impossible not to feel overcome by claustrophobic panic. What would it have been like for Kateřina to spend two days in this airless space? But maybe she had hidden in worse places when fleeing across Europe. I was relieved to hear Mr Tierney ascend the wooden gangway, certain that he would insist on my release. But although the two men talked quietly, the hatch doors remained closed. Just when I was about to shout to Mr Tierney for help, I heard the rest of the crew return. I stayed silent. Much as I hated being confined in this darkness, I had no wish to explain my presence down here to Captain Donovan, who arrived on deck and spoke briefly before moving off to his cabin. I heard Mr Valentine talking to Myles Foley and Mr Tierney. I'd had few dealings with the First Officer. Mr Valentine seemed a decent sort, but this was not the moment to get better acquainted.

Finally his voice moved away. I was about to shout for someone to release me when more footsteps ascended the gangway. Voices shouted angrily in Portuguese. Mr Walton's voice demanded to know their business on board. A long reply came in Portuguese, followed by a shorter one barked out in English. 'We search ship.'

Pandemonium was breaking out above me. I couldn't tell how many intruders had boarded the ship but they were obviously policemen – some of them being dispatched to search below deck. I heard footsteps on the ladder. It was the Captain demanding to know what was happening. The doors to the hold were thrown open and I was blinded by a bright light shining directly into my eyes.

'There she is,' a man's voice said. 'The young Jew.'

'Get the hell off my ship.' Captain Donovan grabbed the arm of the man shining the torch. Its beam was directed elsewhere, and I could make out the scene above me. 'That's our cabin boy and his papers are perfectly in order.'

A hand reached down to help me up. It was Shay Cullen. The man holding the torch wore no uniform, but I immediately knew from his manner that he was a member of the *Polícia de Vigilância e Defesa do Estado*. He turned to a man in a white suit and Panama hat standing nervously behind him. I recognised him: this man had stood up in the queue in the plaza when Kateřina and I passed by. She had instinctively distrusted him: I remembered her untangling her fingers from mine.

'She is definitely down there,' this man insisted. 'I was watching through binoculars. The boy was closing the hatch when I left to summon you.'

'If you are going to use using informers, don't waste your money on drunks, drug addicts and fantasists,' Mr Walton said cuttingly. 'This man was either too stupid to realise what he was watching or too greedy to get paid. This is the boy's maiden voyage. The Second Engineer and I locked him into the hold. It's the second part of the standard initiation ritual for any lad making his first voyage on a Wexford ship.'

'The harbour police say they just saw a girl leave the ship,' the detective said, not fully convinced.

Mr Tierney laughed. 'And what do you think was the first part of his initiation ritual? All the crew chipped in a few escudos and I escorted her off the ship when she was finished opening his eyes like she was paid to. You can take a witness statement if you can find her in Cais do Sodré.'

The detective addressed a question in Portuguese to the uniformed policemen who came back up on deck after searching the cabins below. They shook their heads. He glared angrily at the man in the Panama hat.

'They're telling lies,' the informer protested. 'How could a prostitute get onto this ship without the harbour police noticing?'

Mr Tierney laughed. 'A herd of elephants could get past them lads; they're only interested in warming their hands at the fire.'

The man in the Panama hat went to reply but the detective silenced him with an abrupt curse. He stared at us and then, without farther word, descended the gangplank alongside the other policemen. The man in the Panama hat followed, beseeching the detective to listen, but the detective walked away as if the informer didn't exist. The silence on deck was broken by Captain Donovan.

'I won't even ask what's going on. If I want to hear fairytales I'll read a book to my daughter. But one of these days I'll wring some necks on this ship and I'll do it strictly by rank.'

He glared at Mr Walton who nodded with apologetic respect. 'Sorry for any disturbance, Captain. We'll be ready to sail at dawn.'

The Captain took a deep breath. 'It wouldn't be Christmas without at least one rumpus. Now down to your bunks.' He descended the ladder and most of the crew followed, knowing this was not the time for questions. Only the Cook, Mr Walton and Mr Tierney remained gathered around me as I sat shivering on deck. The Cook reached down to ruffle my hair.

'You'll get over it, Jack, people always do. Now wipe away those tears and get some sleep.'

He left us and I looked up at the two sombre men.

'Go on,' I said, 'tell me what a right eejit I've been.'

'You're no eejit,' Mr Walton said. 'You're well-meaning. That's a good quality in anyone.'

'Do you know a town called Ericeira?' Mr Tierney asked.

I nodded. 'I've heard of it.'

'The girl said to tell you she's going back there. She said to say that if she's going to be lonely, she'd sooner be lonely from now on among her own people.'

I picked up my kitbag and descended the ladder. The men in my cabin were asleep or at least pretended to be. I lay staring at the ceiling. Then I remembered the silk dress. I took it out from under my pillow and pressed my face against it in the dark, breathing in her smell. I kissed it once, then folded it carefully and placed it in my kitbag.

Somehow I fell asleep because the next thing I remember was waking up to find light filtering through the cabin. By then we were miles out from Lisbon, sailing towards the mouth of the Tagus River.

Part Three

THE HOMEWARD VOYAGE

Chapter Twenty-Two

December 28, Afternoon Watch, Bay of Biscay

FOR THREE DAYS WE SAILED in a terse and vigilant quietude. The slagging and banter that usually occurred among the crew was strangely absent. The men took turns at the Middle Watch and Forenoon Watch and the Dog Watch, which they divided in two to let all hands enjoy a hot meal. But even when off duty, they seemed drawn to survey the grey expanse of waves, where any danger might lurk. In Lisbon you could see the people who spied on you. Out here it was easy to miss the trailing periscope through which prying eyes might decide our fate.

The Cook kept me busy, trying to give me little time to brood over Kateřina. But lying awake at night I realised what her fate might have been if the PVDE had found her in the ship's hold. I suspected that every crewman – except perhaps the Captain and Mr Valentine – knew what I had attempted, but nobody referred to it. This was partly to spare my feelings, but it also allowed them to deny all knowledge if questioned. Captain Donovan was no fool, but was wise enough to know not to ask: if he was told the facts there would be an onus on him to report me to the Staffords. Only Mr Tierney ever made a reference to the attempted stowaway and this was so oblique that nobody could have guessed what he was talking about. But seeing me stand at the stern of the ship one morning, gazing backwards after I emptied the slops bucket, he put his hand on my shoulder and murmured, 'You have a good heart, Jack. Never lose that.' In this moment I knew that, no matter how drunk he got after we returned to Wexford, he would never mention Kateřina to another living soul.

Towards dusk on the third evening I took a break from my chores and climbed up on deck to take one last look back at the horizon before the wintry sun set. After a moment I became aware of Mr Walton standing quietly beside me at the gunnel.

'You're still thinking about that girl in Lisbon,' he said.

'It's hard not to, Sir. The men surely think I made a right eejit of myself.'

Mr Walton shrugged. 'It would be a shame to go through life without making an eejit of yourself at least once. Lisbon is a city that can catch you sideways, knock you off guard. But you're young: you've every right to make a fool of yourself. I'm too long in the tooth to have any excuses left.'

His tone was different from any previous occasions on which we had spoken. It sounded sombre and so confessional as to make me uneasy. I sensed that he possessed an ulterior motive for halting to talk to me.

'You just had a few drinks on Christmas Eve, Sir,' I said hastily. 'Nobody on board would think any less of you for that.'

He followed my gaze back towards the horizon. 'Christmas Eve wasn't the first time I made an *amadán* of myself in Lisbon. Brandy kills the pain but loosens the tongue. Did your father ever mention a voyage on the *Irish Poplar*?'

'He served on it eighteen months ago,' I said. 'Ma was scared because it wound up sailing all the way to Angola. A tough voyage, if I remember right.'

Mr Walton nodded. 'I was Captain on the *Poplar* back then: the biggest heap of junk I ever sailed on. It was a Greek merchant ship that Spanish fishermen found abandoned out on Biscay after being bombed. The Spaniards looted anything of value from it and sold the rusting shell to the Irish government who gave it a lick of paint and a new name. Beggars can't be choosers and all de Valera cared about was whether it floated.' He paused. 'Did your father ever mention my name?'

'You asked me that before, Sir. I can't say he did.'

He nodded quietly. 'That would be Sean's style: a touch of class always.'

'Me and Ma hadn't a clue where Angola was, Sir, but we couldn't figure out why an Irish ship needed to sail all that way.'

Mr Walton made a point of being spruce in his appearance each morning, but now, in the floodlights lighting up the deck, I saw just how tired he looked by this time in the late afternoon.

'We sailed because we were told to,' he said. 'We were pawns in a game of bluff between de Valera and Churchill: both too stubborn to yield. Churchill wants to starve Ireland into giving him back our Treaty ports. He keeps whittling down the list of what we're allowed import. Last October he used soap as his latest weapon and banned us from importing it. When I nursed the *Irish Poplar* into Lisbon our American cargo of grain hadn't arrived. Instead a telegram ordered me to pick up the most inconvenient Cargos of Convenience ever: five hundred tonnes of oils and animal fats waiting on the dock in Luanda, in the colony that Salazar calls the Portuguese Province of Angola. If I could manoeuvre the *Poplar* down the coast of Africa, and back across Biscay, Ireland could make enough soap to ration it out and prevent an epidemic of infections.'

'How far is Angola, Sir?' I asked.

The Second Officer smiled grimly. 'Thousands of nautical miles past Lisbon: way too far for a ship tacked together by a handful of six-inch nails. Our cargo was a gift from Salazar plundered from his grubby African allotment there, provided we paid him cash before we set off. The beauty of Lisbon was built on human misery. Angola was the centre of Portugal's slave trade to Brazil for three hundred years. I never saw such human misery as in Portuguese Angola, Jack. I didn't plan to dock in Lisbon on our return voyage, but the *Poplar* was so decrepit that our mainmast capsized off the coast of Morocco. It was a miracle that we managed to limp back there to patch up the vessel.'

I nodded to indicate that I understood his story. What I didn't understand was his motive in telling me all this. But I sensed how these words did not come easy.

'You'd think we'd be glad to see Lisbon again after a six-week voyage to Angola and back. But we were sick of the sea and sick of the sight of each other. Every extra day in Lisbon ate into any profit we might turn from the voyage. My crew were morose, drinking heavily; knowing that if the repaired mainmast didn't hold, there was a fair chance of not making it back to Ireland. As you've seen, drink loosens the tongue. We were down in the Bairro Alto: another shabby *tasca* full of wine caskets and prying ears. This was my first voyage since a doctor diagnosed my cancer. It was only a matter of time before my ill-health became obvious to the owners of Irish Shipping.' He paused and shivered. 'It's one cold night, Jack, isn't it?'

'It is indeed, Sir.'

'I've gone for walks in winter and seen songbirds fall dead from hunger and thirst, when the frost is so thick that even roadside puddles freeze over. But I never saw a bird succumb to self-pity. Self-pity is a human weakness only, Jack, and I have to tell you, that night in the Bairro Alto I gave into self-pity, shouting off my mouth while I was using brandy to numb the pain.'

He shook his head as if finding the memory painful to relive. 'God alone knows what I said about that Portuguese fascist who hides behind Catholic piety while treating his subjects in Angola worse than a farmer would treat an animal. But not only God heard what I said. Word reached the police about a foreign sailor cursing Salazar in a land where dissent is forbidden.'

He looked away. I knew not to say a word, though I dreaded where this conversation might be leading. 'Ernie Grogan was right on Christmas Eve to say that every sailor needs another sailor to look out for him in a foreign port. That's what your father did for me when the police turned up to search for *o Comunista, o bolchevique*, the Bolshevik agitator. Their informant had been vague, not saying if the rabble-rouser was a skipper or deckhand. Your father read a lot, I remember: anything from Zane Grey to politics. He had poems and recitations in his head, and not just the usual "Dangerous Dan McGrew" guff, but real poets. You'd be hard-pressed to get him to say them aloud, but if he could be persuaded to recite John Masefield's "Sea Fever" in some bar, you'd see a whole table of sailors fall quiet, the hair on their necks standing up. I liked that about him. I liked his innate sense of decency too.

'He was the only person in Wexford to read the *Observer* newspaper,' I said, remembering my weekly walk – even when he was at sea – to meet the Dublin train, on which a copy was always sent down to him from Eason's in Dublin after their stock arrived on the English mailboat. Often my father took two or three back issues with him when returning to sea.

Mr Walton nodded. 'He stood out and yet he was one of the crew. Everyone accepted him for what he was: an intelligent man. That's more than I was on that night in the Bairro Alto. It was your father who spied the PVDE arriving. He knew at once why they were there from the stony silence of other drinkers. He'd barely opened his mouth all night, but he suddenly started talking gibberish: the same gibberish I'd been blathering. It took me a moment to realise what he was doing. He wouldn't shut up when I shouted at him to stop being insubordinate and to let his Captain speak. But he knew where his talk would lead and that took real courage. He took a risk; but he was betting that all an ordinary sailor would get was a beating and a night in the cell.'

Mr Walton looked away: hands gripping the gunnel so tightly that his knuckles turned white. 'But if a sea captain was caught spouting sedition – that would be a catch for the PVDE and a bargaining chip. A diplomatic cable might be sent to Dublin, discreet favours sought for my quiet release, because even a few paragraphs in a Portuguese newspaper about an Irish captain being deported would embarrass de Valera's neutrality. That night in the *tasca* I was so drunk that I was angry with Sean, but he didn't care. He knew that once the PVDE put handcuffs on me, my seafaring career was over. I may have been a bloody eejit but to him at that moment I was a shipmate in poor health with a sick daughter. He showed courage and insubordination and I showed him no thanks, shouting at him so furiously that the police thought I was admonishing him. The crew cottoned on to Sean's trick because the PVDE barely had him dragged out the front door before they manhandled me out the back door of the bar. Out on the street, I saw something in their eyes that sobered me, because I'd never thought to see it in any crew of mine. They said nothing but I saw their contempt. I'd been a tough skipper but a fair one. I minded any crew out here at sea, but now one of my crew was getting beaten in a police cell because I had succumbed to self-pity. There was barely a word spoken on our walk back to the *Poplar* and barely a word said the next day when I donned my uniform and went to the police station where your father was held. I stood bond for him, which is to say that I paid a bribe to make the police forget the matter, because to them he was just an ignorant sailor of no value and in Lisbon US dollars can make most charges disappear.'

'I remember his face being bruised when he finally got home,' I said. 'He told us he was jumped by two youths down a side street in Wales but gave them back as good as he got. He never said a word about you or Lisbon.'

Mr Walton nodded. 'They battered him in that cell. If it happened to me, I'd have told any superior officer what I thought of him but Sean was a better man than me. He was as uncomfortable with the fact that his Captain owed him a favour as I felt uneasy at being in a sailor's debt. A ship needs a strict hierarchy. Lose it and order falls apart. Our voyage back to Dublin was the most difficult I've ever known and not just from the stink of animal fat in the hold. I'd lost my crew's respect. Yet none of them would breathe a word about what happened, because, if they did, I'd never captain another ship. A dozen times on that voyage I wanted to summon Sean to my cabin and thank him, but I've a stubborn streak I'm not proud of.'

'Why are you telling me all this?' I asked, acutely uncomfortable but also seething with an anger that I found difficult to conceal.

'Because you're his son and you asked me on Christmas Eve. Yet I see that you're your own man. I'm not asking forgiveness, Jack; I'm telling you because someone needs to tell you. When I step away from this rail I'll become a ship's officer again and you'll be the Cook's gofer. But right now I'm talking to you, man to man, the way I should have talked to Sean on our voyage back.'

'I'm not a man,' I said. 'I'm a boy.'

Mr Walton shook his head. 'That's a luxury you've been robbed of. So feel free to call me the greatest gobshite on God's earth, right here at this rail, and it will stay between us. But I'm saying to you what I never got a chance to say to Sean. Oh, I planned to apologise in my own time, when we were back in some foreign port, having a drink as temporary equals. But we never sailed together again. The *Poplar* went into dry-dock in Dublin to have its mast examined and one night your dad went for a few drinks in the Liffey Bar with a crewmate named Codd – the slowest drinker on earth. They say your father kept urging Codd to finish his pint, afraid they'd miss the last bus down to dry-dock. And that's what happened. If they'd left ten seconds earlier they wouldn't have been chasing down Eden Quay after a departing bus, while an old Wexford sea captain leaned on the quay wall and laughed at them. He was the skipper of the *Kyleclare* and he was a crewman down because a young able seaman by the name of Brown from Arklow had slipped on the accommodation ladder when it was docked at North Wall and busted his hand. Brown was desperate to sail despite the pain he was in, but an X-ray showed that he had bones broken and no shipping company wants a man who can't do his work. Sean signed on the *Kyleclare* that night in Brown's place. Maybe its captain offered Sean better money to change ships, but I doubt it. Your father did the decent thing by leaving my crew because he knew that we'd both be more comfortable on different ships. I was relieved, until word came through that the *Kyleclare* was missing out here in Biscay. Now there isn't a day when I don't think that maybe I put your father under these waves.'

'Maybe it was the fault of Codd for not finishing his pint in time.' I tried to keep my voice neutral. 'If they caught that last bus, maybe they'd never have met the *Kyleclare*'s captain.'

'That's a lot of maybes.'

'Maybe it is.'

I added no 'sir' to that sentence, but my tone displayed no disrespect. I was representing my father and he would not have wanted that.

'The irony is that if he stayed on the *Irish Poplar* he wouldn't have had to rub shoulders with me,' Mr Walton said. 'Irish Shipping realised that my health was too poor to command a ship. They offered me a desk job, but you can't earn danger money at a desk. I was grateful to the Staffords for being decent enough to ask no questions about why I'd accept a post as a Second Officer. They're good people, the Staffords. But the day I discovered that Captain Donovan had signed on Sean Roche's son, it felt like Sean had come back to condemn me. Feel free to do so, but there's no need: I condemn myself for what happened to Sean.'

'Did you issue the order to launch the torpedo that sank the *Kyleclare*?' I asked.

He shook his head. I was lost about what to say, feeling helplessly out of my depth. I could only ask myself what my father would say and I didn't know the answer because I realised just how much of his life was kept hidden from us at home – this other seafaring world that I was only now glimpsing. No advice entered my head from my father. I needed to pick my own words.

'I don't know what my da thought about when the torpedo hit the *Kyleclare,* but I'd lay any odds that he wasn't thinking of you or blaming you. I reckon his thoughts were about Ma and me and my brothers, Eamonn and Tony, and Lily who was his pet. I reckon it broke his heart to know that his death would break our hearts. I reckon he didn't think about you at all and I bet he didn't even think about himself when the ship capsized because I don't think my da ever gave in to self-pity.'

Mr Walton remained quiet for what seemed the longest moment. Then he touched my shoulder for a brief second. 'You're your father's son,' he said. 'You've just quietly pardoned me and equally condemned me in the same sentence. That's no easy trick to pull off.'

'I wasn't playing a trick,' I replied.

'I know.'

'Can I go back to being a cabin boy again?'

'You can start by addressing me as "Sir".'

I knew that this was no reproach, but a reprieve: he was releasing us from the awkward intimacy of a conversation never to be mentioned again.

'I should probably go down to the Cook, Sir,' I said with careful formality. 'He has a string of chores for me.'

'You'd better go so. Nobody else will do them for you.'

We didn't shake hands or make any gesture to give anyone watching the slightest clue as to what we had discussed. But our eyes met and we bestowed upon each other a barely detectable nod of acknowledgement. I went below deck and left Mr Walton staring out at those dark waves, beneath which so many ships lay buried.

Chapter Twenty-Three

December 29, Morning Watch: 260 Miles South of Fastnet

THE FOURTH MORNING OF OUR homeward voyage dawned with a clammy grey mist: its unearthly coldness colonising every part of my body. There was little light in the cabin when I woke but I could see my breath being transmuted into a thick vapour every time I exhaled. Putting on my worn boots, I longed to stamp my feet to get the blood circulating in my toes. But the men snoring nearby had completed long shifts in the wheelhouse and engine room and would curse me if I woke them. So I put my good jumper on over my second, ragged pullover and touched the wool gently, remembering that the last person to wear it was Kateřina. Where was she now? I hoped she had returned to Ericeira where at least some people knew her, but I suspected that, even if I returned to Lisbon a dozen times, I would never find out.

Although due in the galley to help serve breakfast, I climbed up on deck first, thinking that some exercise might inject warmth into my limbs. It was a bad idea. While conditions were freezing below deck, down there it was at least dry.

Although there was no rain on deck, the mist lay so thick that my clothes grew damp within seconds. I stamped my feet to try and generate some warmth and then quickly retreated down the ladder.

The Cook acknowledged my arrival by nodding his head towards the huge urn of stewed tea, indicating that I should help myself to a mug. From its weak taste I knew that the tealeaves had already been recycled three or four times, but at least the pale liquid was hot and helped quench my thirst.

The only other soul in the galley was Myles Foley. He had just finished a shift on watch and, having eaten some breakfast, remained seated at the table. If the cold was seeping deep into my limbs, I dreaded to think about how his old bones must feel. Not that Myles complained. It was hard to imagine Myles making too much fuss in any situation, short of the Captain needing to amputate his toes from frostbite. His fingers cupped the steel mug of tea. Occasionally he sipped from it, but he seemed to be trying to ration out whatever heat emanated from the mug, using it to unthaw his frozen fingers. Myles didn't nod when I arrived but his weak eyes were so expressive that they conveyed a welcome and also his unspoken opinion of the weather. I drank my own mug quickly and washed it.

'How was the tea?' the Cook broke the silence.

'Like dishwater,' I said.

'You'd be so lucky.' He handed me a cloth, indicating which surfaces I should start scrubbing. 'The dishwater is reserved for officers only.'

We worked silently for a time. Myles Foley finished his tea and had no reason to remain, but I was glad that he did. We enjoyed his companionable silence as much as he enjoyed ours. He reminded me of an old sheepdog, content to be allowed to rest quietly in a kitchen corner. It felt too cold for words but the silence was never going to last. Footsteps clamoured along the passageway, accompanied by grumbles of discontent and curses against the biting cold. Mr Tierney entered, followed by Ernie Grogan and Shay Cullen.

'It's brass monkeys out there,' Shay Cullen exclaimed.

'There's a nip, all right,' Myles Foley agreed.

'It's taters, man,' Mr Tierney replied. 'Polar bears on ice floes are paddling past us, looking for some warmth at the North Pole. The mercury in the glass has fallen so low, it's barely higher than Ernie's bald forehead.'

'Go to hell.' Ernie Grogan grumpily eased himself into the seat besides Myles Foley. 'On second thoughts stay here: you don't deserve the warmth of the fires down there. Besides, the Devil wouldn't put up with you.'

'Five minutes of Mossy's yakking and the Devil would run off to sea,' Shay Cullen said.

'He wouldn't last long on this ship.' I risked joining in the banter. 'A few sips of that tea and he'd swim back to hell.'

Surprised eyes stared at me in the sudden silence.

'I'm part of this crew too,' I said, although I felt less cocky under their scrutiny. 'I'm allowed to crack one joke on every voyage.'

'Not about my tea,' the Cook warned. 'Serve the men their grub and be careful that when I next throw a bucket of slops overboard I don't throw you in after it.'

'Leave the boy alone,' Myles Foley said. 'I sailed with a Mormon from Utah once: wherever Utah is. This is the sort of tea he'd be delighted to have served to him.'

'And why exactly would that be?' the Cook asked, handing me two plates to give out.

'Mormons aren't allowed to drink tea: it's against their religion. But there's so little tea in this liquid that he'd be in no danger of being sent to hell and being forced to endure listening to Mossy concocting plans to smuggle cartons of American cigarettes into the Devil's lodging house.'

Mr Tierney accepted a plate from me and started to devour the meagre breakfast on it. 'I wouldn't know what a carton of American cigarettes looks like,' he said, straight-faced. 'Whatever you're insinuating, Myles, you're slandering the character of a wronged man.'

'I withdraw my remark about Mossy going to hell,' Ernie Grogan said, wolfing down the food I handed him. 'The Devil can hardly offer Mossy digs in hell when the man is close to becoming a Catholic saint.'

'Mind your tongue,' Myles Foley warned. 'Ship's rules: no feet placed up on the table and no mentioning a man's religion.'

'I'm only saying that Myles's bunk is six inches higher off the ground since we left Lisbon. There's either a stash of American cigarettes under it or Mossy has become a mystic and acquired the gift of levitation. Indeed, he's so holy that he can make his bed levitate, even when his scrawny carcass isn't snoring on top of it.'

The laugher cloaked the approach of footsteps. Captain Donovan appeared in the doorway before any of us realised he was there. All laughter stopped. He stared around as I handed Shay Cullen a plate.

'A man could die of thirst on this ship,' Captain Donovan observed.

'I'm just about to brew a fresh pot of tea and have the young lad bring it up to you, Captain,' the Cook said apologetically. 'I was polishing off the dregs in this urn first.'

'The dregs will do me grand.'

'I've good tea leaves set aside for you.'

'Set them aside for everyone.' Captain Donovan scrutinised the assembled company. 'Did I hear mention of cartons of American cigarettes?'

'Only jokingly, Captain,' Ernie Grogan said, 'I was using them as a punchline; a figure of speech, you might say.'

'You all know that our Navicert requires us to stop at Fishguard for British customs inspection before we sail on to Ireland to be cleared by customs there,' the Captain said. 'Before we reach

Fishguard I'll be searching this ship in advance for illicit contraband. I don't expect to find any. Do I make myself clear, Mossy?'

'Clear as a bell, Sir. There's nothing on board that shouldn't be on board, Sir.'

'Good. You make sure that everything that isn't on board stays well hidden.' The Captain grimaced as he sipped from the tea that the Cook handed him. 'Mother of God, it's like dishwasher reheated twice over.'

'I offered to make tea fresh,' the Cook said, offended. 'I don't mind sailing with windbags, but I was never before on a ship where the crew set themselves up as restaurant critics.' He pointed to a bucket of slops. 'Jack, toss that over the side. Wait a few minutes and bring me back a list of any complaints the seagulls have about it.'

I grabbed the heavy bucket, happy to escape from the galley. The morning light had grown slightly brighter but low clouds made visibility difficult and it still remained as cold up on deck. I dumped the contents of the slops bucket into the sea and stood, listening to the waves and the engine's throb. I knew that, just a few yards away, Mr Walton and Thomas Bergin were observing an uneasy truce, on duty together in the wheelhouse. But gazing out at the empty waves and at the oppressive banks of cloud made me feel a melancholic loneliness, as if I was drifting on a ghost ship, cut off from the rest of mankind. No seabirds even appeared out of the half-light to raucously scavenge what they could find among the floating slops.

I was alone, listening to the howl of the biting wind and to a low whine from the ship's engine. But as this sound slowly registered, I realised that it did not emanate from our engine or from anywhere on board. It was the noise of another engine, coming from high up within that thick mass of cloud. The sound was drawing closer but, with the wheelhouse door shut, Mr Walton or Thomas Bergin could not hear it yet. They were the people I should have alerted, but fear made me drop the steel bucket and run for the ladder. The Captain was still in the galley, the two engineers and Shay Cullen finishing their breakfasts. Myles Foley remained content to keep his own counsel among the assembled company. The Cook looked at my panicked face.

'You've dropped my bucket overboard, haven't you?' he demanded. 'If you've lost my slops bucket...'

'To hell with your bucket: there's a plane.'

'What class of plane?' Captain Donovan asked.

'I don't know. But it's heading directly towards us.'

No more questions were asked: the men rushed past me so fast that soon only the Cook and I remained in the galley.

'Remember one thing,' he warned. 'If we survive this attack I want my bucket back.'

Then he disappeared down the passageway too. When I climbed up the ladder the entire crew had materialised from different parts of the ship. Only Gary O'Leary was left, manning the engine room. I had only seen a plane once before in my life, when a funfair visited Wexford and people bought raffle tickets to win a ten-minute flight that swooped down over Main Street, where shopkeepers came out to wave, caught up in the novelty. No one was waving on deck now. Mr Walton had handed the wheelhouse binoculars to the Captain. But there was nothing to see yet: the cloud was too low. Nobody spoke and nobody moved. Watching them silently stand together, I felt that this was how Judgement Day would feel, with everyone summoned to account for their lives. The plane's engine was so loud now that it seemed impossible we couldn't see it yet through the low clouds.

'I don't like the feel of this.' Mr Tierney broke the silence.

'Let's wait till we see the whites of the pilot's eyes and the colour of his wings, Mossy,' Captain Donovan replied.

Another ten seconds passed – it felt so long it could have been ten minutes – before the plane suddenly appeared through the clouds. There was no mistaking its German markings.

'This bucko has no intention of bombing us,' the Cook said. 'He's coming in too low. He's going to machine-gun the deck.'

Everyone else ran for whatever cover might offer protection from the bullets. Men crowded into the wheelhouse or crouched beneath the funnel or tried to scramble down the ladder. I was the only one who didn't flee: I had my own reason for not running and the shame of this reason outweighed even my fear of death. I stood alone at the gunnel, watching the pilot approach. The plane was so low that I could see his eyes peer out from the mask covering his face. I raised my fist in fury and cursed at him and at every German who had killed my father. I called them cowards and curs, all this time hearing the Captain and Mr Walton shouting at me to run for shelter. But I was going nowhere. Then – just as the plane passed above my head without yet opening fire – I felt Mr Tierney's arms wrap around me. He picked me up, dragging me towards the wheelhouse.

'Stop struggling, Jack,' he said. 'Are you gone daft or what?'

'Leave me alone. I don't want to be with the others.'

'And what do you intend doing? To fight his bullets by shaking your fist, is it?'

'Maybe that's better than crouching like cowards waiting to die.'

Mr Tierney released his grip so that I stumbled forward and almost lost my footing. He slapped me hard across the face.

'That slap is from your dad and grandfather,' he said. 'Listen to me, you scut. There are no cowards on this ship: just ordinary men risking their lives to feed their families.'

'There's one coward.' I prayed to God that tears wouldn't come. 'The second I saw that plane's markings I pissed myself with fright. My pants are soaked through. That's why I'm standing out on deck, Mossy. I don't want the other men to make a mockery of me.'

Mr Tierney placed both hands on my shoulder, ignoring Captain Donovan's order for us to run for the wheelhouse. 'Braver men than you and I have wet their pants, and worse, when faced with danger at sea. You were brave enough to step onto this ship. What happens on board stays on board and no man here will think any less of you.' He looked after the departing plane and shouted towards the wheelhouse. 'That pilot is heading home for his breakfast, Captain. He either recognised our neutral markings or heard about the dishwater tea.'

'Mention my tea again and I'll shoot you myself.' The Cook's annoyed shout came from farther along the deck.

Mr Tierney was right in that the plane had almost disappeared but something worried me about the angle at which it re-entered the clouds. My fears were confirmed when the plane re-emerged, having looped around. Maybe this time the pilot would approach at a different height that allowed him to drop his bombs.

'He's coming back,' I shouted.

The Captain reached into a wheelhouse cupboard to produce an Irish flag. 'Mossy, wave this at him: it may be our only chance.'

Mr Tierney stared at the approaching plane. 'If this buck eejit can't see the huge Irish tricolour painted across our deck then he's in no mood to heed a neutral flag. I'm willing to die a martyr, but I'm damned if I'll die as a flag-waving majorette.'

A flash came from the plane. I flinched, thinking that a rocket had been fired. But no explosion occurred, instead he used the formation lights on the tops of the wings to create a farther series of flashes.

'He's signalling, Captain,' I said. 'You can just about make it out in this light.'

Mr Walton hurried from the wheelhouse, the Captain and Mr Valentine following. The plane was coming in so low that the engine almost deafened us. We could see its formation lights flash: three short flashes, three longer flashes and three short ones again.

'SOS,' Mr Valentine said. 'Save our souls.'

'Save whose souls?' I asked.

'That's what I'm wondering,' Captain Donovan replied. 'By the way he's tipping his wings he's asking us to swing around south-easterly.'

'It could be a trap, Captain,' Mr Tierney said, 'a U-boat waiting there to sink us.'

The plane passed overhead. The remaining crew emerged from hiding, watching as the pilot made another loop and headed back towards us.

'We're a hundred and fifty miles from the Fastnet Rock, Mossy. If a U-boat is lurking out here to sink us, there's no point trying to outrun it in this sardine can.'

'There's little point in sailing into the jaws of death, either, Captain.'

The pilot was making his third approach, this time coming in so low that I feared he would crash into the deck. His flying mask had made him look sinister, but now he removed his mask so that he looked like a scared young man, barely older than Shay Cullen. He did not try to flash in Morse code this time. Instead, just before passing overhead, he stared directly at us and lifted one hand from the joystick. At first I thought it was a greeting, but then – as his fingers pointed south-easterly – I recognised it as a desperate plea for mercy. The plane flew onwards, but as it did it dropped two red flares away to our starboard bow, illuminating the direction he wanted us to go in. This time we knew he wasn't turning back. We stood in silence in the curious coloured light briefly radiating from those flares until the aircraft disappeared from sight.

'SOS my backside,' Thomas Bergin said. 'This blaggard has used up his ammunition. He can't cause our deaths, so he's trying to cause mischief. He knows that if we stray into the Allied Sink on Sight zone, a British submarine will do his dirty work for him.'

'You could be right,' the Captain said. 'But what happens if you're wrong?' He turned to his Second Officer. 'What do you say, Mr Walton?'

'I'm not captain here and wouldn't presume to give advice to the man who is.'

'But I'm asking your advice.'

Mr Walton looked out across the waves. His voice was matter of fact. 'If this was my ship, I'd swing us around south-easterly.'

'I tell you, Captain, the whole thing is a trap that stinks to high heaven.' I knew from Thomas Bergin's panicked tone that he was frightened. I didn't blame him: every man on deck was scared.

'This pilot just issued a distress call,' Captain Donovan said. 'I can't tell if it's a hoax. I just know that when my ship was sunk last spring I spent eight hours in a life raft, praying that someone would answer our SOS. That's what the Nazis did to me, Thomas. Every sailor here has friends at the bottom of the ocean because of them. But I only know one way to live my life at sea. If I see a distress call, then no matter who it's from, I can't ignore it.'

The men were pensive, weighed down by this decision. It was Thomas Bergin who spoke.

'That plane was low on fuel, Captain. I reckon he's heading for France. He'll not risk coming back out here to check on us.'

'What are you saying?' Mr Walton asked.

'I'm just saying we're two days from Fishguard in high seas with a storm brewing. We're civilians from a neutral country. This isn't our war.'

'So you'll get your wife's cousin in the convent to pray for their souls, will you?'

Thomas Bergin angrily squared up to Mr Walton. 'Officer or not, mock the good nuns again and I'll deck you.'

Captain Donovan stepped between them. 'How long have you been at sea, Thomas?' he asked quietly.

'Thirty years, as boy and man.'

'And your decision would be for us to turn our backs on a distress flare, hitch up our skirts and head for home?'

Uncomfortable with the attention, Thomas Bergin looked away. 'I'm only a helmsman on this vessel: I'm not paid to be its captain.'

'You haven't answered my question.'

Thomas Bergin shuffled awkwardly. 'Every side in this war keeps taking potshots at us. It's a miracle the *Kerlogue* has survived this long. Our instructions are to steer a course of 12° west and not deviate until we're level with Land's End.' He looked around. 'Is it such a crime to want to focus on saving our own souls?'

The Captain looked at Mr Walton. 'Who had the wheel when the plane appeared?'

'Thomas Bergin was steering.'

'Then go back to your work, Thomas. Steer our original course.'

Thomas Bergin shifted uncomfortably. 'Is that an order you're giving, Captain?'

'No. I've just made you acting Captain.'

'That's not fair.'

'Neither is the sea.'

Thomas Bergin stared around at the circle of faces. 'To hell with this, Sir. You know well that if I turned my back as a captain on an SOS call, I could never sail into any port. How could I face a fellow seafarer or look at myself in a mirror? South-easterly we go, but God blast that pilot for flying over us.' Thomas Bergin entered the wheelhouse. 'If there's a U-boat waiting we'll die like dogs, but at least we didn't slink away like them.'

The rest of us stood in silence. Mr Walton opened a packet of cigarettes and handed them around. It was the first time we'd stood together since our conversation on deck last night. I accepted a cigarette from him with a nod of thanks, still unsure of how I felt. Ernie Grogan lit one and then took a second cigarette.

'This is for Gary O'Leary who is still on duty in the engine room, Sir. I'd better let him get away to his bunk.' He walked towards the ladder. 'It's all right for you gentlemen to stand around airing your quiffs, but I've an engine room to run.'

'And I've fresh tea to brew,' the Cook said. 'I'll use the good tea leaves. If a U-boat is waiting south-east of here it would be an awful waste of good tea, not to mention eleven lives.'

Mr Tierney took a drag of his cigarette. 'And of six bottles of good bourbon, five hundred smuggled American cigarettes, a stone of white flour and several pairs of nylon stockings that would win me more favours in dancehalls that my heart could cope with.' He looked at the Captain. 'Not that these things are on board, Sir.'

The Captain looked at him wearily. 'Just get on with your work, Mossy. And any of you with no tasks to do, keep your eyes peeled on the waves. I don't know what we're looking for, but let's hope we find it before it finds us.'

The huddle of men broke up. As I reached the ladder, Mr Tierney put his hand on my shoulder. 'Change out of your trousers,' he said quietly. 'You'll find a grand pair of black trousers in my kitbag that I wore to Christmas mass. Tighten the belt, roll up the legs and they'll fit you fine.'

'I have a spare pair of my own,' I said. 'They're your good Sunday trousers you're giving me.'

'Let's worry about that if we see another Sunday.'

I looked at the waves stretching away. 'What's out there, Mossy?'

'I wish to God I knew,' he said grimly. 'But I suspect we'll find out.'

Chapter Twenty-Four

December 29, Forenoon Watch, The Western Approaches

WE PLOUGHED SOUTH-EASTWARDLY IN A watchful silence, straying from our designated course into a zone that we had no right to be in. No one spoke unless it was absolutely necessary. I suspected that in the engine room, even Mr Tierney and Ernie Grogan worked in silence, knowing there was no point in speculating about what we might find or what fate awaited us. The Captain and his two officers went down to their cabins and returned up on deck, dressed in uniform: buttons polished, peaked caps brushed. Mr Walton and Mr Valentine both occupied the wheelhouse. I realised that this was the first time I had seen these two officers together and that – although they shared a cabin – I had never heard them exchange a single word. They silently rotated the tasks of steering the ship on its new course and scanning the waves through binoculars. They positioned me at the bow of the ship, reckoning that I had the sharpest eyesight and that while their binoculars would pick up objects in the far distance, my eyes might spy any periscope discreetly popping up in the mid-distance. Shay Cullen was positioned to keep watch at starboard, where Gary O'Leary joined him, despite not having got any sleep. Thomas Bergin and the Dazzler Kehoe were positioned to port, with the Dazzler positioned at stern to keep a weather eye on the waters we had just sailed through in case a submarine surfaced in our wake. The crew smoked precious cigarettes, feeling there was little point in rationing them out any more. Myles Foley joined me at the bow: more to keep me company than to keep watch, because with his cataracts he was half-blind.

We all stood within hailing distance of each other, yet nobody seemed able to break the silence. It weighed upon us just as much as the low clouds which reduced visibility to such an extent that it felt like a morning that had never truly dawned. A soft rain began to fall. Then a harder rain came, soaking through the thick material of Mr Tierney's good trousers, the bottoms of which I needed to roll up before they came even close to fitting me. I had made an extra notch in my belt, but the waistband was so wide that they seemed in permanent danger of falling down.

How far ahead could I see in the incessant drizzle? It was impossible to measure distance or time in this half-lit netherworld. It felt like we were ghosts, drifting through limbo. My hands were so cold from gripping the gunnel that all sensation disappeared from my fingers. The only person moving around was the Captain, but he flitted between our look-out posts with such quietude that I never heard him approach until he appeared beside me at intervals. Normally he only lingered for a moment to share our mute vigil, but on one occasion he spoke.

'Can you see anything, Jack?'

'Not a dickey-bird, Sir.'

'Keep your eyes peeled. Remember, you're looking for the second hardest thing to spot out at sea – a periscope.'

'What's the hardest thing to spot?' I asked.

Myles Foley provided the answer in his usual quiet tone: 'A torpedo speeding under the waves.'

The morning – if it was still morning – grew colder; the rain became heavier. The ocean had never seemed a lonelier place. The Captain issued quiet instructions to the Dazzler Kehoe and Garry Roche. He came over to place a hand on Myles Foley's shoulder, indicating with a nod that the old sailor should follow the others down to the galley. The Dazzler and Garry were barely gone ten minutes before they reappeared: Shay Cullen and Thomas Bergin being dispatched in turn to get some hot soup. The Captain took over my watch before Myles Tierney came up on deck.

'Get some warmth inside you, Jack,' he said. 'I'll stay at the bow. There's no point in leaving Myles stationed here alone. Myles is like a bat. I don't just mean that he's half-blind: I mean he has developed an inbuilt radar system like a bat. It lets him steer around a ship by pure instinct. He'd find a thru'penny bit if it rolled between two planks on a ship: just don't expect him to notice a dreadnought coming straight towards us through the waves.'

I entered the galley where Shay Cullen and Thomas Bergin were finishing their soup. Mr Tierney joined them. The Cook handed me a brimming bowl. I only realised how ravenous I was when I tasted my first spoonful. The Cook lit a cigarette.

'This is the first bit of silence I've enjoyed in my galley all voyage,' he observed. 'It's just a pity that it took the Luftwaffe to stop you all complaining.'

Mr Tierney pushed back his empty bowl. 'If we die at least our final meal was hot. It might have been nice to have figured out what the soup tasted of, but you can't have everything.'

He tipped his cap to the Cook and sauntered down the passageway. I finished my soup, surprised and grateful for the extra hunk of buttered bread that the Cook placed beside my empty bowl. When I rose he put an affectionate hand on my shoulder. I glanced at him and he shrugged, embarrassed at betraying emotion.

'Away to your post, you wee scut,' he said gruffly. 'Tell the Captain there's more soup for anyone who wants it.'

I went back up on deck. Mr Tierney – who had joined the Captain and Myles Foley at the bow – watched me struggling to keep his spare trousers from falling down.

'You shouldn't be up on deck in that fancy outfit,' he remarked. 'You should be dancing a foxtrot in the ballroom of the Ritz Hotel.'

'Go to hell, Mossy.'

He glanced out at the waves. 'There's a fair chance I'm heading there.'

Myles Foley was staring out to sea with a look of such fierce concentration that I wondered what he was actually gazing at. Nothing real, because there was nothing visible; but perhaps in his near blindness he was imagining the ghosts of dead shipmates. He barely seemed aware of us any more.

'I'll take over the watch, Captain,' I said. 'Not that there's much to see in this light. How long more do we keep looking?'

'Until it's so dark that we can't see anything. Then we revert to our original course. I wish to God I understood whatever cat-and-mouse game that German pilot was playing.' He went to walk away but stopped, perturbed by the intensity on Myles Foley's face as the old man squinted through the waves. 'Are you all right, Myles?'

'Look to starboard,' the old sailor replied.

'What's to starboard?'

'I haven't a clue, but there's something. I'm not able to see it but I feel it in my bones.'

The Captain scratched his head and turned to me. 'Take a good look to your left, Jack.'

'It's where I'm looking, Sir. There's nothing out there.'

'If Myles says there is, then there is. Even if Myles went totally blind, he'd still be the first crewman I'd sign up for any voyage.' He turned to Mr Tierney. 'Grab the field-glasses off Mr Walton, will you, Mossy?'

Mr Tierney hurried away and I raised a hand above my eyes to try and focus better. But the only thing far out to starboard was a seabird perched on the waves, a long distance away. After a few moments I made out what appeared to be a small piece of driftwood bobbing alongside it. Mr Tierney returned. I tried to describe to the Captain what I could see.

'It's white and bobbing about. Maybe you'll be able to tell what class of bird it is when it takes flight.'

Captain Donovan focused the binoculars in the direction I pointed to. If it was a bird then its head was tucked under its wing because nothing protruded from its body. But a change in the Captain's demeanour told me that it wasn't a bird.

'Can you see it, Sir?' I asked. 'Near that bit of driftwood?'

The Captain lowered the binoculars: his face solemn. 'That's not driftwood: it's wreckage. And it's no bird: it's a sailor's cap.' He handed Mr Tierney the binoculars. 'What do you think, Mossy? A Royal Navy cap?'

Mr Tierney was silent for a moment, staring through the lens. 'The poor sod who wore that cap never enlisted in the British Navy, unless the Brits have started attaching long ribbon to the back of their hats. That's a German naval cap floating on its lonesome, and what's floating beside it is a smashed tea chest.'

Both men were so focused on this one tiny patch of sea that they hadn't noticed the other small items of wreckage starting to come into view.

'There's dozens of tea chests,' I said, steering Mr Tierney around to focus the binoculars in the right direction. 'On the horizon: can you see them?'

Mr Tierney lowered the binoculars and made a sign of the cross. 'They're not tea chests, unless tea chests can magically grow arms to wave at us.' He handed the binoculars to Captain Donovan. 'There's a flotilla of men out there, Captain. I can't tell who are they, but whoever they are, they're drowning.'

Chapter Twenty-Five

December 29, Afternoon Watch, The Western Approaches

WE SAILED INTO A SCENE from hell. It reminded me of a book I saw once in Wexford Public Library, called Dante's *Inferno*. I'd been unable to understand the text, but the nightmarish drawings had stayed locked in my memory: faces of lost souls contorted with pain, eyes pleading, hands helplessly reaching out. The only difference in the reality I was encountering out here at sea was that not everyone's hand was stretched out towards us as we reached the floundering mass of men. Some bodies floated facedown. They were already dead and only held aloft by a sodden lifebelt or because their corpses were still preciously perched on top of pieces of driftwood they had died clinging on to. The wash caused by our ship as we approached caused one plank of wood to capsize. A man had been clinging on to it. His lifeless body slipped into the water. He rolled over in the heavy waves and I glimpsed his face, blue with cold and streaked in blood. His opened eyes stared unblinkingly upwards as he sank without a sound.

In those seconds while he disappeared I experienced absolute silence. This must have been my mind going into shock, momentarily blocking out everything except his eyes vanishing from sight. A moment later I became aware of a desperate cacophony of cries on every side, with frantic pleas of 'Comrade, comrade'. Men didn't just shout for help in German or in broken English. Many shrieks had moved beyond any identifiable language to become primeval articulations of pain. Some men did not even realise they were screaming: they seemed barely aware of where they were. Many sailors were blinded or had grotesque scorch marks across their burnt faces: their hair singed or entirely burnt away to expose raw scalp. It looked like they had been caught up in a huge fireball explosion, the force of which sent everyone hurtling through the air. The lucky ones had been thrown clear into the freezing waves: others had probably remained trapped on the bombed ship as it sank in a blaze of flames and billowing smoke.

But looking at some floating corpses I wondered if these initial survivors had been the unlucky ones; they had been forced to endure agonisingly slow deaths bobbing about in the icy waves, when it might have been better to quickly drown inside the capsized vessel. Had my father's death been mercifully quick or had he struggled for hours to stay afloat on the waves? I leaned over the gunnel and got violently sick in great heaves that brought up everything inside my stomach. These were the first German sailors I had ever laid eyes on: members of the Navy who had callously sank unarmed Irish ships, as well as slaughtering thousands of people on Allied convoys. They were the invincible Kriegsmarine: sailors I had fantasised about killing on nights when I lay awake, spooned between my sleeping brothers, grieving my loss. My father was a good man and I hated every Nazi who participated in his death, yet I couldn't bring myself to hate these pathetic wretches struggling to survive amid the waves.

In this poor light it was hard to know how many survivors were out there, but they didn't look like a fearsome killing machine. Many looked little more than boys, scared and exhausted, desperately calling for help. I was so busy gazing down at the individual faces that I was scarcely conscious of what was happening on board the *Kerlogue*. Now I became aware of how my crewmates had busied themselves. The ship was rolling heavily in the swell of each wave. The Dazzler Kehoe had fetched grappling hooks from the storeroom. All the crew not needed in the wheelhouse or the engine room lined the scuppers from mid-ships to aft. Each time the ship dipped – having crested a heavy wave – they leaned over the gunnel, working individually or in pairs. Some used grappling hooks to grab hold of a body and try and haul it up onto the deck before the ship rose again on the next wave. Others knelt and used their bare hands to grab hold of sailors who had drifted close enough to be able to reach up and attempt to grasp the hands being proffered.

Often the German survivors hadn't enough strength to hold on and fell back into the water. But as each huge wave washed over the gunnel, several more saturated, exhausted German bodies were plucked from the sea and lay strewn on the deck. The sea water that splashed over the gunnel swirled around their bodies before being washed out through the scuppers. The Irish crew braced themselves to lean forward again as the ship dipped down into the relative calm of the brief trough that heralded the imminent arrival of the next wave. Captain Donovan appeared at my side, agitated by my inaction.

'Are you a sightseer? There's work to be done, boy. Work alongside Myles. He can barely see what he's doing, yet he won't stop while there's one soul left in those waves. He'll tire quickly and if we're not careful, when he tries to pull some man out, the fellow will haul Myles into the sea instead. I'm making you responsible for him. Do as he says and mind him. If you see him about to stumble into the waves, break the grip of whatever German wrist is grasping his hand. I don't care if it means the

German gets crushed against the side of our ship. I'm saving who I can but I'll save my own crew first.'

The ship was now besieged by floating bodies. Every survivor who had clung onto an upturned lifeboat or a floating scrap of wreckage frantically tried to propel themselves towards the *Kerlogue*. It was not yet dusk but almost no daylight penetrated the thick rain clouds. Mr Valentine fired an emergency flare: not to attract attention but so that its trail of blazing light could allow us to try and estimate the numbers of bodies in the sea. The flare shot up through the clouds and its rays filtered down, illuminating the clouds with an unearthly brightness. Captain Donovan's sharp intake of breath told me that he was equally shocked by the number of survivors visible in that eerie light.

'How many do you think there are?' I asked the Captain.

'I wish I knew, Jack. I reckon there were twice as many men in the sea twelve hours ago and if we hadn't altered course, then only a couple of dozen would still be alive by dawn tomorrow. You don't just drown at sea: your limbs seize up until you literally freeze to death. There are more sailors out there than the *Kerlogue* can hold.' He shook his head. 'Only God should have to make this choice.'

'What choice, Captain?'

'Between how many poor souls we can drag on board without capsizing the ship and how many we have to leave behind to drown.' He turned to me. 'Now look after Myles in case we lose him.'

I ran to take my place at Myles's shoulder. The old man nodded to acknowledge my arrival but seemed too exhausted to speak. The ship started to tilt steeply downwards in the trough between two waves. The *Kerlogue* was a coaster, built for short costal trips. It was never designed to withstand seas this rough. The angle at which we rode the next wave was so severe that it felt as if the ship might topple over, but it brought us within reach of more stranded men. One such man was only a few feet away, trying to paddle closer but fearful that the ship might crush him. His right hand stretched out but Myles's reach was too short. I motioned for Myles to stand aside and offered my own outstretched hand. A gash across the man's forehead was clotted with blood. His eyes were bloodshot. His face, ravaged by the cold, had the growth of two days' stubble. But the brass buttons on his midnight-blue jacket and on his shoulder epaulets displayed the insignia of a Nazi officer. He saw my hand hesitate in mid-air and his expression changed. Although his eyes hardened with fear and not with haughty impatience, it brought back memories of how that German official in Lisbon had imperiously beckoned Kateřina like she was his slave. The *Kerlogue* breached the low point of the trough. As the vessel rose again in the swell that heralded the next wave, I missed the man's fingers by inches and he disappeared from sight. Myles Foley fixed me with a glare.

'You could have reached him,' he shouted.

'I tried,' I shouted back, shocked to feel a guilty thrill of revenge.

'You didn't try hard enough.'

'I tried to rescue the Nazi murderer.'

Myles Foley gripped my soaked jumper. 'Before his ship sank he was a Nazi: now he's a drowning sailor. Out here, we're all sailors. Your father and grandfather understood that about the sea. Are you going to disgrace their memory?'

The brutal force of the next wave hit us, smashing against the gunnel and spraying the deck with icy water. It soaked through our clothes, almost knocking us off our feet.

'These sailors murdered my father.'

'They followed orders,' Myles Foley said. 'If they hadn't they'd have been put up against a wall and shot.'

'And you want me to follow your orders, is it?' I asked, so overwhelmed by everything that I could barely distinguish between right or wrong any more.

The ship was tilting steeply again in the trough before the next wave. The German officer resurfaced in the water. His face was bleeding even more profusely from where it had smashed against the ship's side. Myles Foley leaned over the gunnel, trying to reach him. But the German seemed too dazed to stretch out his hand. 'I don't give orders,' the old man snapped. 'Run off and play with marbles like the child you still are. I'm not following orders either: I'm following my conscience and my conscience tells me to haul this poor bastard out.'

Myles Foley leaned out so far that I needed to grab his jacket before he toppled in. Mr Walton, who was working alongside us, paused for breath and leaned against the grappling hook he was using. I grabbed the hook from him and swung it out towards the German officer. It struck his shoulder and caught in his embossed epaulet. The force of the blow roused the dazed man from his stupor. He clung to the end of the hook with what strength he could muster in his numb fingers. His weight was too much for me and I had delayed too long: the next wave was already approaching. But I felt Mr Walton and Myles Foley each wrap one arm around my shoulder to anchor me and use their other hand to strengthen my grip on the grappling hook. Between the three of us we dragged the officer closer. Shay Cullen knelt at our feet and grasped the man's shoulders, trying to haul him up before the gigantic wave swept over us. We managed to hoist him almost all the way over the gunnel before the wave struck. It knocked us backwards so that we clattered against the side of the wheelhouse and landed on the heap of bodies already piled on deck.

The wave washed over us and was sluiced out the scuppers. I wasn't sure if the bodies I landed on were alive or dead. I tried to scramble to my feet. As I did so, fingers reached out to latch onto my hand in a fearsome grip. I looked down. It was the German officer. One eye was so badly bruised that he could not possibly see out of it, but his other eye stared fiercely at me. I tried to pull my hand away but he held it firm until certain that I understood his silent expression of thanks for having saved his life. Myles Foley had already returned to the gunnel. Mr Walton lingered beside me.

'Give me back my grappling hook,' he said.

'Sorry, Sir.' I handed it to him.

'You didn't want to save that man's life, did you? You wanted revenge.'

'That's none of your business,' I snapped, resenting the question. 'No matter how I felt, I did save his life, didn't I?'

Mr Walton gazed at the survivors slumped on the deck: their teeth chattering, their breath coming in rasping gasps. 'I'm not speaking as an officer; I'm talking man to man. His death wouldn't bring your father back. Revenge and hatred dragged the world into this war. I'd gladly give my life to save my daughter's life, and you'd have given anything to rescue that girl in Lisbon. But we can't always save the people we love; we can only save the people we're able to.'

The deck was suddenly ablaze with light. Mr Valentine had readjusted our night security lights and pointed them seaward. Each face in the waves was starkly illuminated.

'There's too many out there,' I said. 'The Captain says we can't save them all.'

'We pack every inch of space until one more body will capsize us.'

'What will happen to the others left alive in the water?'

Mr Walton lifted the grappling hook and gestured for me to join Myles Foley at the gunnel. 'The sea is a cruel place. Everyone who goes to sea knows it. That's what these men told themselves every time they aimed their guns on a ship and needlessly sent good men to their deaths. If they face the same fate, then so be it. All we can do is save as many souls as we can.'

Chapter Twenty-Six

December 29, Last Dog Watch, The Western Approaches

FOR PERHAPS ANOTHER FIVE HOURS I laboured alongside Myles Foley in the scuppers, both of us using our bare hands to try and haul bodies from the waves. But in truth I lost all sense of time. Was it really only at dawn that I had climbed up on deck to empty the slops bucket and heard an approaching plane? Since then there had been little sense of an ordinary day passing: the rain and clouds had never yielded more than a feeble half-light until the seascape became transfixed by arc lights trained on the waves. Beneath their dazzling glow it was hard to have any sense of the darkness of dusk descending. I could only gauge the passage of time by the deepening rope burns on my palms. My throat was hoarse from shouting and I desperately needed a drink of water, but there was no time for anything beyond dragging bodies from the sea. I had passed beyond exhaustion into a state where my drenched and aching limbs functioned without thinking.

I needed to act as Myles's eyes, scanning the massive breakers for bodies to point out to him. Myles seemed able to communicate with those sailors in the sea, although they couldn't hear him above the buffeting waves and screams of drowning men. Even if they could hear what he shouted, we possessed no common spoken language. But he shared with those sailors an unspoken language of the sea. The sight of this elderly mariner calmed them. I had never considered what God looks like. In any religious paintings I had ever seen, God's face was always suffused by a halo of golden light: His robes blinding in glimmering opulence. But maybe in the minds of drowning sailors God looked nothing like this: maybe His face was personified by the countenance of this old seafarer who had witnessed everything, both good and evil, that can occur at sea and who, rather than sit in judgement, was quietly beckoning them home.

For whatever reason these jaded men gazed at him and seemed calmed by his serenity. If Myles had intimated that he was summoning them to join their forefathers in the next world, I think that many sailors would have ceased their long struggle and surrendered themselves to death. But instead he summoned them towards our ship with all the passion he could muster. He didn't just want them to live: he was insisting on it. And so, although unable to hear or understand what he was shouting, they intuitively followed his instructions – paddling towards us, still clinging to whatever driftwood kept them afloat. Then, at his nod, they took an enormous leap of faith by letting go and swimming towards our beckoning arms with the last reserve of strength they could summon. These few seconds, when they blindly propelled themselves through the water, seemed to last an eternity. I always doubted whether I would be able to reach them. Then I would feel the force of their fingers desperately clutching hold of mine and feel Myles wrap his arms around my midriff to prevent me from falling in. When I was sure that I had their hand grasped tightly, Myles and I began to haul them from the sea, inch by agonising inch, in a race against the oncoming wave. If we could not drag them over the gunnel before the wave broke, I could be swept back into the ocean with them, because once those men grasped my hand, nothing short of death would persuade them to relinquish their grip.

While most of the crew focused on hauling bodies from the sea, Captain Donovan and Gary O'Leary tried to treat the wounded. Every blanket was stripped from our bunks and placed around the shoulders of survivors who hunched down in any available space. Kitbags were raided and our spare clothes distributed to allow some men at least to strip from their saturated uniforms. But we lacked sufficient clothing to cater for even a fraction of these men. Many shivered violently in the grip of hypothermia while others moaned in pain from burns to their faces and hands that not even all those hours in the freezing ocean had cooled. We possessed no doctor and only a rudimentary first-aid kit. But the most precious resource we were running out of was space. The crew had no time to examine the condition of the men they dragged on board. Most of the German sailors were too dehydrated and paralysed with cold to do anything beyond lie down wherever they could. Some attempted to help in the rescue but the deck was so slippery and overcrowded that they quickly realised they were only getting in our way.

The *Kerlogue* was sinking lower in the waves, struggling to stay afloat under the extra weight. Myles and I tried to pool our strength, but we were just an old man and a fourteen-year-old boy. Each time we managed to haul another survivor on board we needed longer to catch our breath. Even hardened sailors like Mr Tierney and Shay Cullen seemed drained by this ceaseless, back-breaking work. Watching Myles as he fought to summon the stamina to stand up again, I knew that he would never stop working until his heart seized up. If this heart attack occurred while holding onto me, I would most likely topple into the sea.

Captain Donovan obviously realised this too, while recognising that there was no point in ordering the old man to rest. Therefore he assigned us another task. Our new job was less dangerous but we accepted it with the gravest reluctance, because it seemed too terrible to contemplate. But it needed to be done so that the sailors still alive out there on the waves might have a chance of survival.

The Captain had placed the most seriously injured survivors in his own cabin. Others who needed medical assistance were crammed into our sleeping quarters: men lying two-a-bunk on straw mattresses. Others were tightly wedged on the narrow floor space between bunks. The passageways and store rooms were also overflowing. Myles and I were allotted the responsibility of kneeling beside prone figures to decide which sailors had ceased breathing. Often their bodies were still warm but others were so stiff that they must already have been dead when they drifted close enough to be plucked from the sea. The survivors grimly looked on, aware of the necessity of our grim cull. Some even feebly raised a hand to indicate that the sailor beside them was dead.

The first body we picked up was of a boy who looked barely older than myself. His hair was matted into knots and the parts of his face not streaked in dried blood had turned blue from cold. No matter what way I held his stiff shoulders, his wide-open eyes kept staring at me as we made that first sombre trip to the stern to hoist his dead body onto the gunnel and let it slide back into the ocean. I went to speak but what came out was a gush of bile that shocked me because surely to God there could be nothing left inside my stomach by now. It happened so suddenly that some of it stuck to my clothes. I began to tremble and might have collapsed if Myles had not placed his hands on my shoulders. He stared into my eyes and quietly nodded. I took three deep breaths and nodded back: neither of us said a word because nothing needed to be said. We returned to find our next corpse – a small man in his forties with one side of his face so badly burned that part of his cheekbone was visible. As we lifted him over the side and let him fall, we paused to rest for the few seconds that it took his body to bob about before sinking beneath the waves.

I felt we should say a prayer for each dead sailor or at least allow them a small moment of ceremony, but we had no time: this terrible sifting was necessary to create more space for those survivors still in the sea, those men the rest of our crew were continuing to haul in, using hooks and ropes or their by now badly blistered bare hands. After our ninth trip we returned to the main deck to find our path blocked by four German sailors who had gathered enough strength to rise. I thought they intended to protest about our actions. Instead one man placed an arm on my shoulder and bestowed upon me a sober nod of thanks. I looked at Myles, whose hand was being shaken by another German.

'They're saying that this job belongs to them,' he said. 'We need to let them say farewell to their comrades in their own way.'

Hearing a commotion near the wheelhouse, we pushed our way up through a ruck of bodies to find Captain Donovan and Mr Walton being confronted by a German leutnant. A star and two gold stripes were arrayed on his sleeve and he had not lost his braided cap while drifting with fellow survivors in a wooden lifeboat, to which Mr Tierney had managed to throw a rope. Mr Tierney stood mutinously beside the Leutnant, having obviously been instructed by this German officer to take him to whoever commanded the *Kerlogue*. The Leutnant nodded at Mr Tierney, dismissing him back to his duties. Mr Tierney stuck his hands insolently in his pockets and stood his ground. Having been in a lifeboat, the Leutnant looked fresher than the survivors nearby who wearily struggled to their feet and stood to attention to salute.

'Who is Skipper here?' he asked.

Mr Walton replied before Captain Donovan could speak. 'We have no skipper; we have a captain. You speak English?'

The Leutnant smiled. 'I studied English literature and philosophy at university before devoting myself to music.'

'I left school at fourteen,' Mr Walton said. 'But I enjoy a good book. German authors especially.'

'Really? Which ones?'

'Heinrich Mann, Joseph Roth, Friedrich Engels.'

Any goodwill vanished from the Leutnant's smile. His tone was condescending. 'I see why you are not skipper: a self-educated man can only rise so high. Any educated man would know that those authors are not German – they are Jews or degenerates.' He turned to Captain Donovan, his voice more conciliatory. 'I take it you are in command, Sir. My compliments to you and your men: their efforts will be rewarded. But they look exhausted. Stand your men down and I will organise my sailors to take over this rescue.'

He issued a command in German to the exhausted sailors. However, their eyes were no longer trained on him, but on a bedraggled figure who climbed up from amidships. This man lacked a cap. His face was scratched and his uniform torn, but I could tell – from the braided insignia on his sleeves and the quiet authority he radiated – that here was a more senior officer.

'The Devil blast it,' Myles Foley whispered. 'These lads outnumber us a dozen to one. All they needed was a leader. Now they have one.'

'Who is he?'

'A big cheese, whoever he is, and we're small fry.' Myles turned to Mr Tierney. 'I don't like the look of this, Mossy.'

'Check your watch,' Mr Tierney replied grimly. 'The wage clerk at the shipping company will want to know the exact hour that we are cast adrift in the lifeboat.'

271

The Leutnant saluted and stood smartly to attention. *'Mein Kapitänleutnant*, I feared we had lost you.'

Ignoring his salute, the Kapitänleutnant said something sharply in German that made the Leutnant bristle. The Leutnant replied in German and then repeated his words in English, as if determined to defend his honour, even in the eyes of Irish onlookers.

'I assure you, I thought every officer had left the destroyer before I ordered the last lifeboat to row away.'

The more senior officer shrugged and then saluted the Captain and Mr Walton.

'I am Kapitänleutnant Joachim Fleischer, of the Destroyer T26, Captain. We are in your debt: you have strayed into a dangerous zone.'

The Captain did not salute back but offered his hand in greeting. 'I'm Captain Thomas Donohue. One of your planes flashed an SOS: we could hardly ignore such a signal.'

The Kapitänleutnant shook his hand warmly. 'The British cruisers who sank my destroyer left the survivors for dead in the water. You could have ignored that SOS and done likewise. I fear you have endangered the lives of your own crew.'

'And I fear you have lost most of yours.'

The Kapitänleutnant nodded in sombre agreement. 'Their loss weighs heavily on me. I don't recognise many survivors: most here are not from my destroyer. Where have you sailed from?'

'Lisbon.'

'And what is your cargo?'

'Crates of oranges.'

The Leutnant's laugh was halted by a sharp glance from his Kapitänleutnant.

'You have made a remarkably dangerous voyage to buy oranges,' the Kapitänleutnant observed.

'We were meant to collect a different cargo. Luckily for you that ship from America was delayed, because not even our Cook could feed half-drowned sailors with phosphate fertilizer. He is breaking open the crates, brewing a concoction of boiling water and orange juice to try and get some heat into your men.'

'He's calling it the Kerlogue Cocktail,' Mr Tierney added. 'You'd swear he was a Manhattan bartender.'

'We are short of mugs, fresh water, blankets and medicines,' Captain Donovan said. 'The only thing we are not short of is oranges.'

Mr Walton stepped forward. 'We were saving one blanket, Kapitänleutnant Fleischer. You are shivering with cold. It might be wise to wrap yourself in it.'

The Kapitänleutnant looked around. 'I see sailors in a worse state than me. Please give it to whoever needs it most.' He issued a command in German and the sailors gratefully hunched back down again, having obviously been told to be at ease. He turned to the Captain. 'But my throat is parched ... is there some water you can spare?'

'Fetch a mug of water from the kitchen, Jack,' Captain Donovan ordered. 'As quick as you can.'

Mr Tierney put out a hand to restrain me. 'Try my kitbag instead,' he said. 'It contains fire-water – the finest black-market American bourbon available in Lisbon.'

I descended the ladder. The scene below deck was unlike anything I had ever witnessed. Exhausted men leaned against both walls in the passageway: so tightly packed that some bodies only remained upright because there was no space to collapse into. I squeezed into the tiny cabin where Mr Tierney's bunk was near mine. I needed to point to his bunk and make drinking gestures before the men jammed in there eventually understood. The sailor who located the bottle gave a sharp intake of breath, having obviously unearthed the Aladdin's cave of contraband that Mr Tierney had assembled to supplement his income. The bourbon passed from hand to hand until it reached me. I knew that nothing else there would be touched.

Back topside the Kapitänleutnant was explaining how his destroyer – along with two other destroyers – had sailed from the port of Brest, hoping to rendezvous with a merchant ship carrying German war supplies. This had covertly sailed from Japan, hoping to slip through the Allied blockage at Christmas time.

'The British must have tracked our signals,' the Kapitänleutnant said. 'When we reached our rendezvous point the Japanese vessel was already sunk and Royal Navy Cruisers lay in wait. Our position was hopeless. The cruisers could outrun us and their guns have a longer range. My sailors manning our four-inch guns knew we were only providing a fireworks display. The cruisers stood to, beyond our range, watching our shells land harmlessly in the sea – all the time lining up their six-inch guns.'

'Sounds like you need a drop of this, Kapitänleutnant.' Mr Tierney opened the bourbon. The German officer accepted it with a nod of thanks and drank deeply as if trying to blot out the horrific images. His hand shook as he held the bottle out towards Mr Walton.

'Will you share a drink, Sir? You look more exhausted than most of my men.'

Mr Walton took a swig before offering the bottle to Captain Donovan, who declined. He offered it to the Leutnant who also declined, and then handed it back to Mr Tierney. Mr Tierney drank deeply and passed the bottle on to Myles Foley, who gratefully accepted. Kapitänleutnant Fleischer nodded his appreciation to Mr Tierney.

'The Kerlogue Cocktail is stronger than I expected.'

'This one is called Tierney's Tonic. It was being smuggled home for a Wexford doctor.'

The Kapitänleutnant smiled. 'I fear we have drunk your smuggler's profit.'

'That's all right.' Mr Tierney accepted the bottle back from Myles. 'The good doctor paid in advance. He'd be too tight-fisted to drink it: he only wanted to show off the bottle to impress his friends at Rosslare Golf Club. He can now boast that his bourbon was drunk by a shipwrecked Kapitänleutnant. Is your leutnant sure he won't share a sup?'

'We do not permit smuggling on our vessels,' the Leutnant replied.

'No,' Mr Walton agreed. 'But you permit the killing of innocent seafarers.'

The Leutnant went to reply but Kapitänleutnant Fleischer's restraining hand silenced him. Mr Tierney knelt to offer the bourbon to a German sailor shivering in a blanket, indicating that he should pass on the bottle.

'We have all lost friends in this war,' Kapitänleutnant Fleischer said. 'I knew I would lose many good men when I saw those British cruisers. There is no feeling more terrible than sensing that you are doomed and you can do nothing about it.'

'I am familiar with that feeling,' Captain Donovan replied grimly. 'And with how it feels to be left to my fate in a lifeboat.'

The Kapitänleutnant nodded in sympathy. 'I am sorry to hear that: accidents happen.'

'Your U-boat commander knew that the last ship I was on was unarmed and neutral. We were target practice.'

The Kapitänleutnant shrugged, reluctant to concede the point. 'We were target practice for those British cruisers. Within minutes my engines were down and the bridge suffered a direct hit. If I had been at the wheel I would be dead. But I was trying to save as many souls as I could. One destroyer had already disappeared: the other was sinking in a ball of fire. Five hundred men were floundering in the sea. I gave orders to lower all lifeboats. The first one overturned. Leutnant Krausser oversaw the launch of the last boat so efficiently that it had disappeared by the time I returned to board it.'

'There was fire and panic everywhere,' Leutnant Krausser said defiantly. 'I had no idea you were still on board. Hard choices must be made in hard wars.'

A hand touched my hand. I looked behind me. The bottle was drained. The sailor holding it spoke in German. I thought he was asking me to fetch more bourbon. Then I realised that he was asking if he could keep the empty bottle. It felt odd for an adult to request my permission for anything. I nodded and he placed it inside his jacket. Only then did I wonder whether he intended to use it as a weapon.

'I don't know how much longer those of your men still in the sea can survive, Kapitänleutnant,' Mr Tierney said. 'Our lads are exhausted. If six strong men could work with us it might make all the difference.'

'I already ordered the Irish Skipper to stand down his men,' Leutnant Krausser said. 'This rescue is a task for the Kriegsmarine.'

Ignoring this remark, the Kapitänleutnant addressed a tall sailor nearby who stood up and nodded before moving away. The Kapitänleutnant turned to Mr Tierney. 'This man, Josef, speaks no English but is an excellent sailor. I have ordered him to select experienced men to assist you in any way they can. Now your Captain and I must speak.'

As Mr Tierney turned away with Myles Foley he whispered to me: 'If it looks like they're going to seize the ship, you find me, Jack.'

Then there was just myself and the Captain and Mr Walton besieged by Germans. They didn't seem to deliberately close in, but with more bodies being brought on board there was nowhere else for people to stand. Most were dishevelled and barely had the strength to stand up; but they were still the dreaded Kriegsmarine. My eye was drawn to the Leutnant's cap: it bore the symbol of a gold eagle with outspread wings, its talons proudly perched on a swastika. There was silence, broken only by one plaintive German voice calling out from near the scuppers: *'Friedrich? Wo bist du, Friedrich?'* This quietude was interrupted by the Cook's arrival.

'I've surely died and gone to heaven, Captain,' he said. 'I'm handing out hot drinks and for once nobody is whinging.' He glared at me. 'When did you stop being my cabin boy?'

'I'm busy.'

'You don't look it.'

'I'm busy.' This time I invested sufficient intonation in my words for him to grasp their implication.

He turned to the Captain. 'Can you ask this officer if there are a couple of deckhands strong enough to peel oranges?'

'My men will gladly help you,' the Kapitänleutnant said. 'Historically our two races share much in common, including a common enemy.'

The Cook sighed in exasperation. 'I need men to peel oranges and I get a history lesson.' The only thing we share in common is that we're all sure to be starving tomorrow.'

Kapitänleutnant Fleischer called out names and four men stood up and listened to his instructions in German. They swept up the Cook in their midst as they moved down towards the opened doors of the hold. It was impossible to tell if they had been ordered to assist or detain him.

'How big was your destroyer?' Captain Donovan asked.

'Thirteen hundred tonne, with a speed of thirty-three knots.'

'The *Kerlogue* has a speed of nine knots if we're lucky. So many men are packed into our wheelhouse that my helmsman can barely steer. My cabin is overflowing with seriously wounded men; some burnt from head to toe.'

'The Kapitänleutnant is right: we share a common enemy,' Leutnant Krausser said. 'For centuries Britain committed atrocities when occupying your country. Think of your famine dead in mass graves and then tell me how neutral you really are.'

'Mossy Tierney had a brother shot dead by the British,' Mr Walton replied. 'Myles Foley, our oldest crewman, spent two years sleeping on bare boards in Lincoln Prison for IRA membership – not that he mentions it. I know many Irishmen who fought against the British and many of their sons are fighting in this war. If I was younger I might do likewise. But don't you find it strange that, despite the animosity between Ireland and England, no Irishman has chosen to wear a Nazi uniform in this war?'

Tension was heavy: the moment balanced on a knife-edge. The only sound was that grief-stricken German sailor still calling: '*Friedrich? Wo bist du, Friedrich?*'

Finally the Kapitänleutnant spoke. 'You have done my Führer a great service, Captain. I ask you to complete that service by sailing for the port of La Rochelle in France. I promise to reward every man on board. Name any cargo and it will be provided free of charge. This ship's owners will not thank you for returning to Ireland empty-handed.'

Captain Donovan shook his head. 'I cannot do that: you're asking me to commit an act of collaboration with Germany.'

'I'm asking you to commit a humanitarian act. Some of my men are dying. Land them at the nearest port, which is La Rochelle.'

'Landing you at La Rochelle would breach Ireland's neutrality.'

'Do you think Britain will invade Ireland over one small act of mercy? The British cruisers presumed that my crew were drowned. When Germany wins this war it will be wise for Ireland to have stored up some favours with the Führer.'

'To hell with your Führer,' Mr Walton said quietly.

Leutnant Krausser stepped forward. 'Insult my Führer again and I will personally arrest you.' He addressed his commanding officer. 'We have one hundred and fifty men on board, Kapitänleutnant. *Die Leute müssen sich ausruhen, sie haben doch ihre Verletzungen gesehen! Geben sie den Befehl, und ich übernehme das Kommando des Schiffs!* Give the order and I will assume control.'

'I do not give the orders on this ship, Krausser,' The Kapitänleutnant said.

'You don't expect me to take orders from this Irishman?'

'You will take your orders from me, as will every German sailor on board.' He turned to the Captain. 'Captain Donohue, I'm making a last formal request for you to land my men at La Rochelle.'

'And with respect, Kapitänleutnant, I cannot comply. Britain only allows Irish vessels to sail in Biscay if we obey a Navicert to land in Wales so their officials can inspect our cargo before we sail on to Ireland.'

'So your intention is to hand us over to the British as prisoners of war?'

Even the voice of the unseen sailor plaintively calling out seemed faint suddenly. The tension was such that every sailor leaned forward, straining to hear Captain Donovan's answer, despite being unable to follow this conversation in English. But they sensed that their fate was being decided.

'If I disobey my Navicert I may never be allowed to re-enter a British port,' the Captain said. 'But there won't be any cargo left to inspect. Your sailors will have eaten it before we reach any port.'

'You haven't answered my question,' Kapitänleutnant Fleischer said quietly.

'I have seriously wounded men on board my vessel: some will not survive this night. When they manned your destroyer they were the Kriegsmarine. But once a man jumps into the water, I don't give a damn about his nationality: he becomes just another drowning sailor. When the Irish ship, *City of Bremen,* rescued thirty-three Dutch sailors in the North Sea it didn't ask their nationality, no more than The *Kyleclare* asked the nationality of fifty-two British survivors it rescued off the Mayo coast.'

The Kapitänleutnant shook his head. 'I have not heard of either vessel.'

'A Luftwaffe Junkers 88 bomber blew *City of Bremen* asunder last summer, for the crime of trying to bring home a cargo of grain from Lisbon. Our Cook was on board. He's only here, boiling up oranges for your men, because a Spanish fishing trawler recognised him as just another drowning sailor when they picked him up from these waves. I cannot tell you what happened to the *Kyleclare,* but maybe you can tell me. One of your U-boat commanders sent eighteen unarmed Irish seafarers to their deaths on that ship – including the father of our cabin boy here.'

The Kapitänleutnant bowed in my direction. 'If such a mistake occurred, young man, I apologise and sympathise.'

I was trembling so much from fear and anger that I was surprised to find the courage to reply. 'Only my father can accept your apology and his body was never found.'

The Kapitänleutnant conceded the point. 'I cannot compensate you for your family's pain. But I can compensate every man here for their endeavours today.'

'We didn't pick you up for compensation; we picked you up because any sailor drowning in the ocean becomes a fellow seafarer,'

Captain Donovan said. 'Your men are in my care. My duty is to get them urgent medical attention. I am refusing your request to land at La Rochelle on humanitarian grounds, but I am also ignoring my Navicert. When the British authorities haul me over the coals I'll tell them that I acted purely on humanitarian grounds in getting your men medical attention by sailing for the nearest port: Cobh in County Cork in Ireland.'

'We have heard enough nonsense,' Leutnant Krausser said, impatiently, 'You will sail where you are told.'

Kapitänleutnant Fleischer turned to his Leutnant: cold anger in his voice. 'Do not interrupt a conversation between two superior officers.'

'This Skipper is a glorified fisherman in a tin bucket.'

'He is a sea captain like I am.' Kapitänleutnant Fleischer turned back to the Captain. 'As this is your vessel, I respect your decision while deeply regretting it. Any German who questions your authority will be court-martialled should we be lucky enough to see dry land again.' He paused to ensure that the Leutnant understood, and then addressed Mr Walton. 'What is your rank, Sir?'

'I am Second Officer.'

'How many more men can you pick up, and still have a chance of reaching Cobh?'

Mr Walton looked around. 'That's one terrible decision but we need to make it soon. We're massively overloaded already, only inches above the waterline. The scuppers can't clear the waves splashing over the deck fast enough: we'll need men with buckets to bail out excess water. We need to get lucky and hope the ship doesn't get totally submerged or break asunder in these waves. And our crew need to rest: they've been hauling bodies from the waves for hours now.'

The Kapitänleutnant turned to the Captain. 'With your permission, I would visit the most badly wounded. Have you medical supplies?'

'We are out of bandages so we have started to strip down the rolls of gauze used to grease the engines,' Captain Donovan replied. 'We dip the gauze into seawater first, in the hope that the salt might ease the wounds. We have bed sheets that your men might tear up into strips to bandage wounds if they can find space to work in.'

'I possess a small personal supply of strong painkillers,' Mr Walton added. 'These men are under your command so you should decide who needs that laudanum most.'

'Do you not need it?'

'Their wounds of the men in Captain Donovan's cabin will kill them quicker than my cancer will kill me.'

Kapitänleutnant Fleischer offered Mr Walton his hand. 'I suspect there is little that you and I would agree on. But I am glad of this chance to sail with you. I have seen too much evil in this war to believe in God. But if He exists, then I wish you a place in heaven.'

Mr Walton accepted his handshake. 'Like you, Kapitänleutnant, I have no idea if a God watches over us. But if we reach Cobh without capsizing we'll have witnessed a miracle.' He looked at Leutnant Krausser. 'What do you believe in, Leutnant?'

'I believe in the Führer.'

Mr Walton nodded as he led the Kapitänleutnant away. 'I'll tell him that when I meet him in Hell. I've a berth booked down there, alongside all those great writers you label as Jews and degenerates.'

Chapter Twenty-Seven

December 29 & 30, First Watch and Middle Watch

HOW MANY MORE HOURS DID we linger in that nightmare location, our arc lamps illuminating small patches of ocean amid the darkness? We would drift in a following sea where strong waves pushed us on, and then swing around in a Starboard tack into a head sea, the wash from enormous whitecaps crashing directly over our bow. For long spells we would find no more survivors as we backtracked through tumultuous breakers. Then, as we crested an enormous wave, our lights would uncover another clutch of freezing sailors clinging onto drifting wreckage. Sometimes it was just a solitary hand raised in the desperate hope of attracting our attention. Often it was the German survivors now assisting us who shouted out, pointing towards former shipmates who drifted facedown in the waves: men for whom this rescue had come too late.

I worked where and when I could. There was a sense of chaos on board, as it became increasingly too crowded to move about the deck. Yet simultaneously there seemed a curious acceptance as wearied survivors succumbed to sleep in any position they could find. When I fought my way down to the galley, the Cook shouted at me to assist the handful of Germans assigned to retrieve any remaining crates of oranges from the hold. But when I struggled back up through the crowds to reach the hold, I found that those sailors with enough strength to stand up had already formed a human chain to pass the crates by hand all the way down into the galley. After eventually forcing my way back down, the Cook – who looked increasingly harassed and exhausted – cursed me for my slowness. He continued to angrily issue orders, like a man who felt he was losing control of the private fiefdom in his galley. I was told to assist with peeling oranges or to check what little remained of our diminishing freshwater supplies or do various other tasks which I would find were already being done by helpful German sailors. Finally he dispatched me to retrieve empty mugs or any container that could be used as a makeshift drinking utensil, shouting at me to ensure that every man on board had at least one hot drink inside them.

Naturally I discovered that the German sailors had already devised a system to return these containers. When I told the Cook this, he threw his eyes to heaven and shouted that I was a useless cabin boy. Could I not see how the empty wooden crates cluttering up his galley needed to be smashed into pieces? Had I not enough sense to take them up on deck and toss them overboard? And if I couldn't do this one simple task, then I could throw myself into the waves too, for all he cared. I set off in a sulk, so laden down with broken crates that I could barely see where I was going. As I tried to push my way yet again through the bodies lining the passageway, I felt a hand on my shoulder and discovered that the Cook had followed me out from his galley.

'Don't mind one word I say, Jack,' the Cook said apologetically. 'I get angry when I'm flustered and because there isn't even a blasted dog to kick to a ship, you're getting the brunt of it. I've not been this rattled since the morning I got married, when my wife's relations all descended from the Wicklow hills for our wedding breakfast, eating and drinking all before them, like they hadn't seen a square meal in a month of Sundays. These Germans keep reminding me of my in-laws at the wedding.'

'Because you have to feed them all?'

'No: because my wife's relations were all bogmen with such thick Wicklow accents that I couldn't understand one word of what they were spouting at me, just like these fellows.'

I stacked the broken crates at the bottom of the ladder and men handed them up to me. Reaching the gunnel, I began to scatter wooden slats into the ocean. They hadn't far to fall: I had never seen a ship so low in the water. Myles Foley was among the crowd standing at amidships. At first I thought the old seafarer was finally resting. Then I realised that he was bent over the hunched shoulders of a German sailor, trying to comfort this man who was frantically staring out to sea. The man raised his voice and I realised that I had been listening to him for hours, although his voice was so hoarse now that his words came out in barely more than a gravelly whisper: *'Friedrich? Wo bist du, Friedrich?'*

Myles beckoned me over. 'This is Herr Müller: he's calling his brother's name. They were conscripted together and bunked together. They jumped from the destroyer together and got separated in the water. They both managed to cling onto something and shouted encouragement to each other for hours as the waves forced them farther apart. I can't get the poor blighter to move, even just to get a hot drink or see if there's a scrap of dry clothing left. He keeps calling his brother's name. He's convinced he can occasionally hear Friedrich calling back.'

Herr Müller grasped my hand so ferociously that it reminded me of the desperate grip of the men whom Myles and I had rescued. He was beseeching me with manic eyes and a stream of words I could not understand.

'He wants you to help him keep watch,' Myles Foley explained. 'I said you have the sharpest eyes on board. Stay with him. It's only human nature for the poor man to need to feel that he's doing something. Having you here will give him some comfort. Keep your eyes peeled. We're finding fewer survivors but we still spot the odd poor soul in the water. Even if it's not his brother you find, it will be someone's brother.'

'How can you understand what he's saying?' I asked.

'I sailed on ships out of Hamburg years ago. A sailor picks up bits of lingo – pidgin German, pidgin Italian, pidgin Greek. Not enough for a proper conversation, but enough to recognise grief when it's staring you in the face. Now be a good lad: stay with Herr Müller. If you do see anything move out there, shout for Mossy at the top of your lungs.'

The German gripped my wrist, leaving me with no option but to kneel beside him on the flooded deck. Myles Foley disappeared and I was left alone with this stranger, both of us staring out to sea. The man nudged me and gestured. It took a moment to realise that he wanted me to shout his brother's name: his own voice being too hoarse to carry any distance. When I called out tentatively he squeezed my hand fiercely, urging me to shout louder: "Friedrich!' Every few moments he beckoned me to be silent and we'd listen for any answering cries: our eyes surveying the floodlit waves. Then he would nudge me to begin shouting Friedrich's name again.

This forlorn task unnerved me more than any other job done all evening; even more than when Myles and I had let dead bodies slide back into the sea. That grim chore had at least served a purpose by creating space on board. Earlier, when labouring with Myles at the scuppers for hours during this rescue, I was propelled by a frenetic energy, a rush of adrenaline and fear engendered by the urgency of our task. My terror of being pulled into the sea had kept me alert every time I reached down to grasp an arm protruding from the water. Although my muscles ached, the exhilaration of knowing we'd saved another life had always given me a renewed surge of energy. I had never known such a sense of purpose as when gladly pushing my body beyond endurance, with no time to think about what I was doing.

But now, kneeling beside Herr Müller while freezing sea water sluiced around my knees, I had too much time to think. Every horrific incident witnessed over the past ten hours hit me and I experienced such a sudden bone-weariness that I could barely keep my eyes open. Helplessly staring out to sea with this grief-stricken sailor became exhausting, because it felt like the most futile task I had done all night. How many hours was it since we had rescued Herr Müller? How far away had we sailed from the spot where we found him and where his brother presumably should be? Maybe Mr Valentine knew our exact position as he tried to steer in the crowded wheelhouse. But I had lost all sense of time and direction, during the endless circling that the *Kerlogue* had been doing for hours. If Herr Müller's brother was still alive, he could be drifting anywhere within a nautical mile of our position. But the awful truth – which I lacked the words or the courage to tell Herr Müller – was that Friedrich was almost certainly dead.

Not that I blamed Herr Müller for refusing to give up hope while there remained a chance of his brother being found alive. But his relentless hope triggered memories of how I once clung to a similar yearning after the *Kyleclare* disappeared. For weeks after it became obvious that my father was never coming home, I had walked down to the Wexford quays every evening, to stand alone and stare out across the water, convincing myself that if I patiently waited there for long enough his vessel would miraculously appear.

The longer I had stood on the quays each night, the more an irrational conviction had grown that my solitary vigil was keeping him afloat somewhere at sea. If I gave up and turned to walk home through the dark streets, then his last thread of hope would snap and the lifeboat, which I had kept fervently hoping he was stranded in, would sink beneath the waves and take him to his death.

I had been too busy during this rescue to think about my father. But being trapped with Herr Müller, who seemed oblivious to how his fingernails dug into my skin, rekindled every emotion I had felt when news reached Wexford: grief, bewilderment, denial, and such a fearsome anger that I remember swearing to murder any German sailor I ever encountered. I could explain none of this to Herr Müller: even if he had understood English he had worked himself up into such a pent-up state of anxiety that there was no room in his mind to comprehend anyone else's feelings. Several times I tried to prise away my hand but he refused to relinquish his grip, even during the increasingly rare occasions when Mr Tierney and Mr Walton managed to locate and drag another body on board. Herr Müller always pushed his way through the knot of onlookers to stare down at the newly-rescued man, firstly in hope and then in abject despair. Once he established that it was not his brother he seemed indifferent as to whether the man was alive or dead. He would push his way back to the gunnel, dragging me behind him, while I desperately looked around for Myles. Herr Müller's voice was almost totally spent, yet I always understood his rasping whisper. It was an order for me to start shouting his brother's name again and try and listen for a reply from out at sea, amid the hubbub of noise on deck. In truth, at times when I stained to listen, I swore that I could hear a voice call back from somewhere out there; that, at the very extremity of my hearing, a voice was pleading for help, although the sound was so faint I could not tell if this unseen – or probably illusory – man was calling in German or English and if he possessed a Lübeck or a Wexford accent.

I was so exhausted that I could barely distinguish between what was real and imaginary any more. I may have briefly blacked out into sleep, but I must have done so with my eyes open or else Herr Müller would have shaken me awake. I just know that, after a brief lapse into unconsciousness, I was woken not by a sound but by a sombre silence. The atmosphere had subtly changed on deck. I looked up, suddenly aware that Captain Donovan and Mr Walton stood behind me, alongside Kapitänleutnant Fleischer. Mr Tierney joined them and Myles Foley reappeared. For the first time, Herr Müller relaxed his grip. I could barely lift my right arm, which he had been grasping: all feeling had disappeared from my fingers, with the blood barely able to circulate. Herr Müller tried to address Kapitänleutnant Fleischer, but his voice was completely gone.

'He's convinced his brother is still alive out there,' I explained. 'He thinks he can hear his brother's voice calling back.'

'Can you hear anyone, Jack?' Captain Donovan asked.

'Sometimes I think I do, Captain, but it may be inside my head. I've never been so dog tired in my life.'

'You've done your best, lad.' The Captain turned to Myles Foley. 'What do you say, Myles? Are there still survivors out there?'

The old man stared out at the floodlit waves and nodded. 'Oh yes, don't ask me how I know, but I'm certain there are, God help them. Hundreds possibly, who have drifted in every direction. But those poor sods are too far away or simply haven't the energy left to wave. I couldn't say if Herr Müller's brother is among them, no more than I could tell you what direction to steer in to save them.'

'How do you know they're out there?' Kapitänleutnant Fleischer asked. His tone was not interrogatory but genuinely curious. I spied Leutnant Krausser approach us through the hordes of weary men.

Myles Foley shrugged, uncomfortable at this attention. 'I can't explain it no more than I can explain how a dog smells fear: I just know that a dog can. Likewise, I can smell the blind terror of drowning men out there. I just know it in my heart, like I know that death will visit this ship at least once more tonight. I couldn't tell you how many are left in the water or how many more we can haul on board without capsizing. But I know in my soul that it's time to turn this ship around.'

Leutnant Krausser saluted his commander. 'I have completed a roll call, Kapitänleutnant. We have one hundred and sixty-eight German sailors on board. Ninety-six are crew from your vessel. This leaves one hundred and ten crew from T26 unaccounted for. The other sailors on board are from the destroyers T25 and T27. This means that four hundred and fifty of our men are dead or clinging to life out there.'

Mr Tierney blessed himself. 'May they find peace in heaven.'

The Leutnant turned to him. 'We do not leave one man alive out there. I estimate that this ship has not reached full capacity. Even if it has, another man died from his injuries some moments ago. If we put his body overboard, it makes room for at least one more survivor.'

'We might find one more or a dozen more and be forced to pick which one to haul on board,' Myles Foley said. 'But maybe we'd search for hours and find nobody. I just know that we've spent ten hours in this spot and it's time to get back onto our designated route. We're easy prey here for any trigger-happy U-boat captain looking to add another notch to his belt. If you tell me there's a hundred and sixty-eight survivors crammed on this ship, then, with deep regret, I'm telling you that it's time to go.'

'I am not telling the likes of you anything,' Leutnant Krausser said. 'I wish to speak with my Kapitänleutnant and your Captain.

But I ask you not to spread false rumours about U-boats. I know the Kriegsmarine, and we would never open fire on a ship so obviously full of German sailors.'

'You knew the Kriegsmarine when you were an officer in it,' Mr Walton said. 'But when we pulled you from the water you ceased to be one of the hunters and joined the hunted. Welcome to our world, Krausser.'

'You will please address me as Leutnant,' Leutnant Krausser insisted. 'Even if I am being made a prisoner of war, I refuse to be stripped of my rank.'

'You'll be no prisoner of war,' Mr Walton replied. 'If we somehow limp back to Ireland you'll be interned as an alien refugee. Refugees get robbed of their titles and everything else they possess. You should know: your forces have stripped enough refugees of their identities. If a U-boat commander encounters us, he may raise his periscope and spot German uniforms on desk. But more likely his radar will simply reveal a ship's hull beneath the waterline and he'll blast a hole in the *Kerlogue* for devilment or to extract revenge for your Kriegsmarine having lost three destroyers. He may decide to send the Allied cruisers who sank you a message by sinking us.'

Captain Donovan turned to the Kapitänleutnant. 'It's a terrible decision, but I think we've done all we can do.'

Herr Müller could not understand these words but he sensed their meaning because he turned to me, insisting that I start calling his brother's name again. But I was too jaded and overwrought and shook my head. Releasing my hand in disgust he gripped the gunnel and tried to shout, although what emerged was a barely audible croak: *'Friedrich? Wo bist du, 'Friedrich?'*

'I am not in command of this ship, so I cannot make the decision for you,' the Kapitänleutnant said. 'But you are dangerously overcrowded. It pains me to leave men behind, but unless the wounded survivors get medical attention soon, the number of injured men we are likely to lose will be higher than the number of additional survivors we are likely to find. You must do as you see fit, Captain.'

He spoke quietly in German to Leutnant Krausser, but in response the Leutnant ignored his own Kapitänleutnant and directly addressed our Captain. 'I beseech you, Captain Donovan. Look at this poor man still searching for his brother. We cannot leave while we have a chance of saving even one more human life. Can you imagine what it is like to be out on those waves?'

'I know exactly how it feels,' Captain Donovan replied grimly. 'But I need to save the souls on board this ship.'

Even Herr Müller recognised the finality in the Captain's tone. He turned to me, unable to hold back his tears any longer, and tried to grab my arm. I shrugged him away, feeling utterly wretched. All my crewmates felt the same: I saw it in their faces. Any pride in having saved lives was obliterated by a sense of guilt at leaving even one sailor behind. Leutnant Krausser saw my brusque gesture and admonished me.

'Why won't you help this poor man, while there still might be time?'

'You help him,' I snapped. 'I've helped him for hours. I'm so tired I can barely stand up.'

'Tiredness is no excuse for letting a man drown,' Leutnant Krausser said.

'Don't talk to me about drowning!' I could no longer control my temper. Herr Müller's tears reminded me of the tears I silently cried in Wexford, trying not to wake my brothers. 'Damn you to hell, Leutnant! And damn Müller's brother too!'

'That's enough, Jack,' Mr Tierney cautioned quietly.

'Damn every blasted German on board!' I felt so close to tears that cursing seemed like my only defence mechanism to keep them at bay. Herr Müller stared at me, bewildered by my newfound anger. Myles Foley addressed him in some halting words of German. I doubt if they made any grammatical sense but they seemed sufficient for Herr Müller to grasp their meaning. He looked at me again but this time there was something different in his stare: a look of compassion and shared grief. He understood how I felt better than anyone on board. I also understood his terrible onslaught of emotions, having lived through them. He reached out a hand, this time not to grip my wrist but to touch my shoulder in a gesture of condolence and solidarity. In that moment he ceased to be German: his mute gesture brought back the touch of all the men who had attended the mass for my father, awkward in their Sunday suits, saying nothing because no words were sufficient. Herr Müller glanced back out to sea but the fight was gone from him. He did not sit down, because there was nowhere to sit. His shoulders slumped and during those few seconds, when he let go of the last sliver of hope, he aged before our eyes. Herr Müller shivered as if only now realising how exhausted and famished he was. I looked at Myles.

'What is the German for "I am sorry for your loss"?' I asked.

The Kapitänleutnant replied, not just telling me the words I needed to say, but addressing those words to me, conveying his sympathy for my own loss. *'Es tut mir leid für Ihren Verlust.'*

I knelt beside Herr Müller and pronounced the words as best I could. He took my hand and squeezed it – gently this time – and nodded. In that moment it felt like we were in a private world. Then Mr Tierney stepped forward. The old coat he wore was soaked and streaked with blood from having hauled out men who were bleeding. It would offer Herr Müller little protection against the freezing night air, but Mr Tierney placed it around the man's shoulders because this was the only human gesture he could make. Myles Foley encouraged Herr Müller to rise. 'There's nothing more you could have done for him, Jack,' he said. 'I'll find him somewhere quiet and stay with him.'

The men nearby silently parted as the old sailor led Herr Müller away. Mr Tierney shivered without his coat. He gave a last look out to sea. 'Blast this war to hell,' he said and looked at the Captain. 'What do I tell Mr Valentine, Sir?'

Captain Donovan removed his cap to bless himself. His lips moved in a silent prayer. 'Tell him to steer a course back towards our designated route,' he said. 'And if we ever reach Wexford alive tell him to lodge a complaint with the company that fixed our ship's radio after the RAF bombed the *Kerlogue*. The blasted thing has stopped working.'

'When did our radio stop working?' Mr Tierney asked.

The Captain put back on his cap and prepared to busy himself organising the ship. 'Two minutes from now when you accidentally turn off the knob without noticing. Our Navicert orders me to obey every instruction issued by the British authorities on Land's End Radio. But, like Nelson who raised his telescope to his blind eye, how can I follow instructions if I can't see or hear them?'

Chapter Twenty-Eight

December 30, Morning Watch, The Western Approaches

WE SAILED ON IN DARKNESS, in a silence broken only by involuntary cries of pain from wounded men. Everyone else seemed too bone-weary to have anything left to say, or maybe nobody knew the words to express their emotions. I had no way of knowing what the Germans surrounding me were thinking about: comrades they may have left to die in the sea; their families or sweethearts back wherever they called home; their fate if we reached Cobh alive. But maybe they were too tired to think; maybe they just stared into space, neither awake nor asleep, conscious of nothing except coldness and hunger. I was used to the *Kerlogue* being brightly lit at night: a beacon of neutrality for air crews to hopefully recognise. But in the hours before dawn we wanted nobody to notice our existence in this dangerous zone. The quietude on board was such that it already felt like a ship of ghosts. If we were spotted, so far off-course, this was what we might truly become.

The faintest flicker of light came from the wheelhouse. I counted fourteen German sailors squeezed into the tiny space where Shay Cullen tried to man the wheel. As I manoeuvred my way past it I heard breaking glass and realised that Shay had deliberately broken a small side pane. I looked in through it and he shrugged.

'I know it's freezing out there, Jack,' he called out, 'but it stinks in here and I need fresh air. I don't know how to ask these lads to open a window in German. I can barely move or breathe and, I swear to God, I can't see a thing in front of me. I could be steering directly towards a U-boat for all I know. I just look at the compass and hope for the best. Set my mind to rest, will you? Can you anything in the sea ahead of us?'

'Just darkness,' I replied, trying to peer over the shoulders of the men crammed on deck.

Shay Cullen nodded. 'At sea there are two types of darkness: good darkness and bad darkness. Fingers crossed it's good darkness, eh?'

I picked up the larger shards of broken glass and, with difficulty, negotiated my way to starboard to fling them overboard. Mr Walton stood there. At first I thought he was keeping watch. But when, even in the almost negligible light, I saw how fiercely his fingers gripped the gunnel I realised that he must be in intense pain.

'Can I fetch your painkiller from your cabin, Sir?' I asked.

He looked at me. 'I don't have a cabin any more, Jack. It's now a field hospital and any laudanum is long gone to men who needed it more.'

'Is there anything I can do for you, Sir?'

Mr Walton gazed into the darkness. 'You could solve a puzzle, Jack. Your dad and I once discussed whether our lives spent at sea were wasted lives. Any bunk at sea is a lonely bunk and whiskey becomes a bothersome companion. We miss out on so much that ordinary men take for granted. We work hard to raise our children, yet when we get home we feel like strangers to them. We're king of the castle walking through the front door all right, our pockets full of sweets and everyone running to hug us. But we're outsiders in our own homes. Life at home has its own pattern and we know we're no longer truly part of it. Naturally, you and your brothers and sister were always sad to see your dad go back to sea, but one part of you must have been glad because it meant your lives could return to normal.' He tried to smile but there was a pain within his smile that he couldn't hide. 'That's an unfair question, Jack. Don't even bother trying to answer; I'm just thinking aloud.'

'It's a fair question,' I said. 'It's just one I never wanted to think about. I feel grief for my da but there's guilt too there. You see, once I waved him off at dawn, I always had Ma to myself again. Not fully to myself because of Lily and the boys, but I'm the oldest and when he wasn't home she'd ask me for advice on things. When Da came home she was so happy that she only really had eyes for him, and I was no longer the most important man in her life any more.' I paused, anxious. 'Did Da feel that we didn't want him at home?'

Mr Walton shook his head. 'Your da knew you loved him.'

'Did you and my da talk much, Mr Walton?'

'Before our last voyage ended badly, we did. Sean was an intelligent man and I liked his company. That's rare for me because I generally prefer my own company.'

I looked back at the silent men packed on every side of us. 'He might have changed ship anyway, even if that stuff between you in Lisbon had never happened. He was a terror for changing ships; Ma always scolded him for it.'

'We'll never know the answer to that one, Jack.'

'No, but I know that bad things happen every day in this war, Mr Walton. A man who suffers from self-pity doesn't give away every painkiller he has. Da would be fierce upset if I spoke out of turn in anything I said to you the other evening.'

He nodded his head softly in the moonlight. 'You didn't speak out of turn, Jack, you spoke your mind. And there's one thing you could do for me, though it may be a hard ask as there probably isn't an ounce of tea left on board, but I'd kill for a cup of scald just now.'

'I'll do my best, Mr Walton.'

I was the only person moving around the ship. It meant I had to constantly step over people, yet nobody complained. As the youngest on board, I had a licence to roam. I descended the ladder. The men lining the cramped passageway neither complained nor commented on my progress past them. Most seemed asleep on their feet. A few nodded, others stared at me with bloodshot eyes. The Cook was asleep on a chair at the table. I realised that this was the first time I'd ever seen him sit down in his galley. There was a ladle in his hand, and from how he sprawled forward I knew that sleep had caught him unawares when he took a moment's rest. Three Germans slept on the other chairs, heads cradled in their arms resting on the table as they all somehow found enough space. More sailors slumped in corners or sprawled on the floor, all sleeping so deeply that it looked as if nothing could wake them. I knew where the Cook kept a secret stash of tea leaves. There was just about enough left to make one good pot. It would need to be served black, but I also knew the location of his small stockpile of sugar.

I set a kettle to boil, bolting it securely onto the cooker, although the ship was not rolling as much now as during the rescue. It felt as if the waves themselves had grown lethargic at this hour. The galley reeked of oranges, the basin clogged with a mush of pulp. Mounds of orange-peel littered every surface. I remembered when I was young my father bringing home an orange in his pocket after a voyage. It was years since anyone in Wexford had seen one. But standing in this galley felt like being trapped inside one vast orange. I knew that the damp clothes drying into me would soon stink of that fruit. As the kettle began to boil a noise made me turn. Mr Tierney leaned against the doorway.

'Sure I'll have a cup as well, just to be polite,' he said.

'It's the last cup you'll get on this voyage.' I whispered, nodding towards the snoring Cook. 'I've raided his secret stash.'

Mr Tierney snorted. 'That fellow has more stashes than Ali Baba and the Forty Thieves.'

I poured hot water into the pot and carefully stirred the precious handful of leaves. 'What are our chances of finding clean cups?' I asked.

'About the same as our chance of getting a Christmas bonus after we dock with an empty hold smelling of oranges.' He picked up two used mugs from the table. 'These mightn't be called clean in the Ritz Hotel, but this isn't the Ritz. Pour me a sup: I'm parched.'

I poured some tea into the mug that Mr Tierney held out. 'I promised to bring Mr Walton up a drop. Should I bring a mug to the Captain too?'

Mr Tierney shook his head. 'Leave the Captain to his own business. He's walking a dangerous tightrope, especially with that powder keg of a leutnant on board. Actually we have two leutnants on board, though I fear we'll only have one by dawn.'

'What do you mean?'

'Do you not remember the first chap that you and Myles hauled on deck: a badly wounded officer? The Captain and Kapitänleutnant are with him, but it's a priest or a Lutheran minister he needs to steer his soul towards heaven.' Mr Tierney looked up, aware of sudden tears in my eyes. 'What ails you, Jack?'

I was remembering that uniformed man stretching out his hand in the water: blood covering the gash on his forehead. I had seen his Nazi insignia and deliberately let my fingers miss his. Even though I gripped his hand at the second attempt, after another wave brought him back within reach, by then he had collided with the ship's hull.

'I could have grabbed him sooner,' I said. 'I wanted to make him suffer.'

'He was only in the water for an extra minute, Jack. You saved his life: that's what's important.'

'If he's dying now then I saved nothing.'

'He's dying in a warm cabin surrounded by seafarers, with his head on a pillow and his lips not cracked from salty water. I don't know if he still knows where he is, but he knew he was rescued. He's among his own kind and his body will be prayed over. You saved him from drowning alone. Don't underestimate that.'

'I caused the cut on his face to reopen.'

'That cut isn't what has him at death's door.' Mr Tierney put down his mug and gripped my shoulders. 'Look at me, Jack. Did you put him in the water?'

'No.'

'Six-inch shells from an Allied cruiser put him there. The gunners who fired those shells aren't beating themselves up about it, no more than that Leutnant beat himself up when he inflicted the same fate on Allied sailors or unfortunate passengers in convoys. People die in wars, Jack. You lost your da and you're not a saint who can forgive everything. There wasn't one of us manning the scuppers who wasn't remembering some friend killed by the German Navy, and there's not one of us who didn't quietly think that it served them right to get a dose of their own medicine. But we put that thought from our minds like you put it out of your mind. Maybe you could have dragged the Leutnant from the water a minute earlier, but he has such serious internal injuries that it's a miracle he was still alive when you did rescue him. Now, you need some rest. Pour yourself a mug of tea and find a corner to grab a kip. Do you hear me?'

'I'm just making this tea to bring it up to Mr Walton.'

'To hell with Walton: get some hot scald inside you before you go back up on deck. Mr Walton can wait: he's not going anywhere.'

Mr Tierney stared at me so insistently that I poured tea into a cup that stank of orange pulp and only realised how parched I was after the first swallow.

'Do you want to bring Ernie Grogan a cup?' I asked.

My neighbour shook his head. 'I'll tell him there's a sup left here in the pot. He wouldn't enjoy drinking it in the engine room with two dozen thirsty men watching his every move. It's like being part of a silent movie. We can't reach our instruments: we have to make hand signals to pass a message along to the man nearest whatever valve we need to turn. The engine room is more crowded than on the dance floor of the Cornmarket Ballroom during the final jitterbug of the night.'

Mr Tierney drained his tea and was gone. I drank my own cup quickly: I wanted some warmth to remain in Mr Walton's mug of tea, although I probably spilled half of it when climbing back up to the ladder to reach him. Mr Walton hadn't moved from the gunnel. He accepted what was left in his mug with a nod of thanks and sipped it slowly.

'Orange-flavoured tea,' he observed.

'The whole ship is orange-flavoured, Sir.'

He smiled. 'I'm grateful for it, and I've drunk far worse.'

Dawn was starting to break in the east, turning the heavy rain clouds grey. Everything around us was being slowly tinged with faint light.

'It's been a long twenty-four hours since that pilot flew overhead,' Mr Walton said.

'I've never known a longer day, Sir.'

'Well, you're about to. Yesterday was all about frantically trying to rescue men. The next twenty-hour hours are all about sitting in silence, hoping against hope that we don't hear an aeroplane approach and wondering if we'll ever see land again. For your sake, I hope we do, Jack.'

'And your sake too, Sir. Surely you want to see your home again?'

Mr Walton stared at the horizon as it slowly became more visible. 'I've watched the sun rise over so many oceans that by now this deck probably feels more like my home than any other place.' He raised the cup to his lips. 'All men want to die at home, but I've a good reason why I want these waves to be the home that I die in.'

Chapter Twenty-Nine

December 30, The Forenoon Watch,
The Western Approaches

I WOKE SUDDENLY, WITH NO recollection of having gone to sleep. The sky was not quite blue, but it was less cloudy. I lay on the deck, near the bow of the ship. Somebody had placed a roll of canvas sacking under my head. Another piece of canvas covered me like a makeshift blanket, but I still felt chilled to my bones. German sailors sat up around me, talking quietly. I had no idea if I had fallen asleep in this spot or if someone had carefully placed me there. I could ask nobody. Some sailors acknowledged the fact that I was awake with a brief nod, but nobody addressed me. Gazing around, I saw similar huddles of men occupying every space. They reminded me of a pod of grey seals I once saw basking on rocks near the Saltee Islands, ready to shuffle into the water at any sign of danger. This wasn't an option for us. My legs were so stiff from sleeping in a cramped position that it was a struggle to rise. Without looking up, men automatically put out their hands to steady me while I got my balance. Slowly I made my way around clusters of sailors and down the ladder, hoping there might be something hot to drink in the galley.

The Cook was awake and angrily complaining to Mr Tierney and Myles Foley. The Germans who had slept at the table were banished out into the passageway. The Cook fixed me with an irate glare.

'Some cabin boy you are. Where the hell have you been?'

'I must have fallen asleep on deck: I've no memory of it.'

'Herr Müller found you asleep standing up, like a horse in a field,' Myles Foley said. 'He got the other men to create space and made you as comfortable as he could.'

'Check your pockets if you slept surrounded by Germans,' the Cook said. 'I dozed off and some thieving bowsie stole a little stash of tea I was saving. If I knew which German flyboy it was, he'd feel the weight of my fist!'

Mr Tierney fixed me with a stare that advised me to sing dumb. The Cook gazed around the filthy galley. 'You risk your life dragging them from the ocean and once your back is turned they pilfer everything that isn't nailed down. I've a good mind not to cook them another bite of grub.'

'Can I have a mug of water?' I asked. 'I'm parched.'

The Cook gestured towards a saucepan. 'I think there's some orange juice left.'

'Mention oranges and I'll throw up.'

He shrugged as he poured me a tiny mug of water instead. 'It's spoilt you're getting: you hadn't seen an orange in years before yesterday.'

'And I hope it's years until I see another one. Anyway, I don't think there's food left to cook: the larder looked empty last night.'

'Officially, the ship's larder is as bare as old Mother Hubbard's cupboard,' the Cook agreed. 'But contingency supplies might have found their way on board in Lisbon.'

'For what sort of contingency?'

'A contingency that might involve Wexford shopkeepers parting with ready cash or a small sack of flour being delivered into the hands of a certain Garda Sergeant.'

'It's hungry work being a peeler, cycling around hunting innocent smugglers,' Myles Foley observed wryly, 'especially when you're as fat as the particular ignorant gombeen in question.'

'That same gombeen broke every regulation by processing Jack's Seaman's Identity Card at a few hours' notice before we left Wexford,' Mr Tierney added. He turned to me. 'It's the spoils of the sea, Jack: our own compensation fund for the fact that we might get shipwrecked or bombed.'

'And what particular spoils of the sea do you have?' the Cook inquired.

Mr Tierney looked affronted. 'A bishop wouldn't ask me that in confession.'

'I'm not a bishop. What have you got stashed, Mossy?'

'I wouldn't say that I've stashed anything away personally,' Mr Tierney replied. 'But it's possible that I might be warehousing certain items in my capacity as the chairman of a syndicate. But I'm not at liberty to disclose our assets without consulting my various shareholders scattered around this ship.'

'I've been called a fair few names,' Myles Foley said. 'But I was never called a shareholder before.' He turned to Mr Tierney. 'The truth is, Mossy, this ship is crammed with famished seafarers.'

'I'm not denying that, Myles. But if our Cook wants to play poker, then he won't mind me asking him what cards he is holding behind his back.'

'The Cook ran his hand lightly along the top of a small press. 'There's a hidey-hole behind this, known only to God, the carpenter who built it and me. The Germans found a twist of hidden tea, but they never found the eight-stone sack of white flour intended as the mother of all Christmas presents for my missus. Or the pound of sugar purchased on the black market in Cardiff as an insurance policy to sweeten the cough of any overzealous customs inspector who chanced across my hiding space.'

'Customs officials are partial to sugar,' Myles Foley agreed.

The Cook nodded. 'Their sweet tooth causes them temporary blindness.' He looked at Mr Tierney. 'What can you add to the pot, Mossy?'

'Nothing significant,' Mr Tierney said warily. 'Twelve batteries intended for wireless sets; two dozen bicycle tubes – people go mad for them since the British banned rubber imports. Likewise, a dozen golf balls that my missus can use to barter with the doctor next time one of the children gets sick.'

'Keep talking,' the Cook said. 'I'm not cooking golf balls.'

'You won't cook much either with fifty candles or two boxes of bars of soap or a bale of fine cloth acquired in Lisbon for a dressmaker to knock up some frocks from.'

'You're listing a very selective inventory, Mossy. Don't pretend you haven't got a stash of food hidden on board.'

Mr Tierney shrugged defensively. 'I've nine hungry mouths to feed at home.'

'And I've scores and scores of hungry mouths to feed here and now. Even if the Germans stole tea behind my back, I'm still Cook on this ship. Now what are you smuggling that can actually go in my oven?'

'Two sacks of white flour,' Mr Tierney said ruefully. 'One promised to my missus and the other to be divided between Shay Cullen and Thomas Bergin. Bergin wants to donate his half to his wife's cousin, the nun who looks down her nose at him. Also some sugar, Bovril, yeast, a few tins of Lyle's Black Treacle and two pounds of coffee. I've no idea what class of concoction you can conjure with all that.'

'You just bring it here and leave the choice of menu to me: you can either have Chef's Surprise or The Last Supper.' The Cook turned to me. 'I need every drop of fresh water on board, Jack. We're baking bread. It will be like the miracle of the Loaves and Fishes, except with no fishes involved.'

I accompanied Mr Tierney into what was once our cabin. It was impossible to count the sailors corralled in that space. No man there had been unaffected by their hours spent in the freezing ocean. The cabin stank of stale air, damp clothes and vomit. Men shivered under blankets or sat upright, unable to gain any respite from the hacking coughs that racked their bodies. Several men lay virtually naked, swamped by fever and running such high temperatures that they could not bear to be covered by anything. Their companions tried to keep them cool by sponging down their limbs, using strips of torn uniforms and a bucket of sea water.

'What's the German for bread?' Mr Tierney asked me.

'How would I know?'

'Bread,' Mr Tierney called out loudly, miming the motion of tearing open a loaf and eating it. The sailors stared blankly until someone deciphered his gesture and said, '*brot*'.

This single word silenced the cabin. Every eye focused on us, as if expecting bread to miraculously materialise. The sailors tried to create space for Mr Tierney to root under different bunks. He reminded me of a conjurer at a funfair, mumbling strange incantations as he transferred unseen items between unseen sacks. Occasionally his arm appeared from under a bunk to hand me an item of food. The atmosphere in the jammed cabin changed as the men realised that the promised bread had yet to be baked. They were famished and the long wait would feel like torture. Mr Tierney sensed their dejection when he stood up because he paused and then disappeared again beneath his bunk to root in another sack. He re-emerged, holding two packets of American Lucky Strike cigarettes, and looked at me ruefully.

'If I ever reach Wexford again I'll be skint,' he said. 'Any profit from this voyage has gone down the Swanee.' He handed the cigarettes to a sailor, indicating that he pass them around. 'If the smoke doesn't kill them it may at least fumigate the room.'

We parted in the passageway; Mr Tierney going to relieve Ernie Grogan in the packed engine room while I returned to the kitchen, where the Cook was already mixing up a huge mound of dough.

'Have you any yeast?' he demanded. 'I swear to God, if Mossy forgot to give you the yeast, I'll strangle you.'

'You're like a bag of cats.' I tried to put down the various sacks and tins without dropping anything.

'You'd be like a bag of cats if you had all those hungry eyes watching from the passageway.' I looked back. There was silence among the men there, their minds too consumed with a craving for food to speak. Word must have spread: two burly men clambered down the ladder and approached. The Cook looked up, perturbed by the territorial way in which they entered his galley. He scrutinised them in suspicious silence until both men rolled up their sleeves and, with a respectful nod to him, took their place at the table and began to help him mix the dough. He inspected their workmanship. When they looked up again it was he who nodded in respect.

'These lads are the real McCoy,' he said. 'Ships' cooks are like priests – we'd recognise each other anywhere. Get some rest until I call you. This is a closed shop: qualified professionals only.'

Chapter Thirty

December 30, Afternoon Watch and First Dog Watch, The Western Approaches

THE KERLOGUE SLOWLY SAILED ON through the overcast afternoon. Our speed rarely exceeded seven knots. It was cold up on top and almost as chilly below deck. The only things that contained any warmth, the sole prospect that nourished our jaded spirits, were the loaves being continually baked by the Cook and his two German compatriots. I was recruited into the baking process, at first as a distributor but then to guard the galley doorway: my presence supposedly meant to deter the hungry sailors who stared in at the cooks busy at work, their clothes and hair streaked with flour. The Cook lacked a single word of German and neither of his German counterparts spoke English, but this minor inconvenience did not prevent them from incessantly chatting as they worked. I don't know if the German cooks understood anything about the recipes for stews that the Cook described, pronouncing key ingredients loudly as he mimed cooking actions and outlined the shapes of vegetables with his hands. Similarly, I had no idea how much he grasped of their talk, that I presumed must be about the difficulties of cooking for hundreds of men, even when their destroyers had been sailing into violent confrontations.

But perhaps it was unimportant that they understood any of the actual words being spoken: each of them seemed to be acknowledging that a ship's galley – even one as tiny as the *Kerlogue's* – was an independent fiefdom where crew members left their rank at the door. Or maybe they talked so loudly to keep fear at bay. All three were aware that, down in the galley, they would be among the last to know (and the most likely to drown) if our ship was attacked. But I liked to think that they understood one another at heart without needing a shared language. They knew, from the inflection in a speaker's voice, when his story about mishaps and misappropriations reached its punchline. They laughed uproariously because, if they could not grasp every nuance of the story being told, they sensed that it echoed similar culinary disasters they had endured.

For me the greatest wonder was how all three managed to work in that cramped space: each inch of space was requisitioned as a mixing surface for dough or a resting place for loaves to cool. The unrelenting heat was in direct contrast to every other cabin on board. But even on the freezing deck the shivering men seemed warmed by the smell of baking bread that wafted upwards: its aroma containing such strong memories of home that it seemed to alleviate the gathering darkness. After much debate the three cooks would eventually pass each new batch of loaves as being cool enough to eat. Some loaves were fortified with treacle, or any other available ingredient, before being divided into thin slices. Then – with more instructions than if being entrusted with gold – I was dispatched to dispense the baskets of bread.

I needed to keep a mental list of which cabins I had visited and what parts of the deck I had yet to reach. With so many to feed, these morsels were never going to fill anyone's stomach, but what mattered was that the bread was warm and comforting. Each sailor savoured it, chewing every mouthful slowly in silence. Even wounded men seemed to find solace in this most modest of meals. I lost track of the numbers I fed but I genuinely believe that no man took a second share: primarily out of decency but also because his compatriots would beat him to a pulp if caught committing such a selfish act. I found it impossible to distinguish between most Germans; but because I was the youngest person on board they seemed to know me and also know my story. As I distributed these pitiful slices, each sailor nodded and said '*danke*'. But many added the phrase: '*Es tut mir leid, dass Sie ihren Vater verloren haben!*' which I gradually understood to be an expression of sympathy at the loss of my father.

One man sat alone in the bow of the boat. The deck was so crowded that it was impossible to sit in isolation. Yet I sensed other sailors were deliberately maintaining a small exclusion zone around Leutnant Krausser. If he was aware of being shunned, he ignored it, his gaze fixed on the darkening horizon. When I approached with my tray of bread he shook his head, insisting that I should serve the other men first. But I stayed where I was, holding out the tray. Even though I feared everything this man stood for, I recognised that he was starving too. He hesitated, and then selected the smallest piece of bread left before bestowing on me a curt '*danke.*'

The wheelhouse remained so crowded that I used up an entire basket of bread on the men packed into it. Shay Cullen was trying to steer. He took a bite from his slice and gave a low whistle of appreciation.

'I've never tasted sweeter bread. Tell the Cook I must have struck lucky and got part of a loaf baked by a German.'

'Tell him yourself when you haven't the protection of all these sailors between you and his fist,' I replied. 'Are we making headway?'

'We're still afloat, aren't we? That's headway. Hopefully by dawn we'll reach the Fastnet Rock. If you think this sea is rough, trust me, you won't know the meaning of rough till we round the Fastnet. Have you been down to the engine room?'

'It's next on my list.'

'Tell Mossy and Ernie to open up the engine. They must be playing pitch and toss for all the speed I'm getting. Ask Mossy if he's afraid that he'll have to buy a round of drinks if he gets us to Cobh by New Year's Eve.'

When I brought my next consignment of bread down to the engine room, it was too crowded for me to get inside the door. I let the sailors pass the tray over their heads, each man taking a slice. Within a minute the empty tray was returned to me. I had no way of knowing how many men remained unfed.

'Did that bread reach you, Mr Tierney?' I shouted in the general direction of where I knew the Second Engineer was trying to work.

'Devil a bite,' he shouted back. 'I wouldn't mind, but legally speaking, the flour was illegally smuggled by me. A hundred and fifty men are destroying all evidence of my smuggling and I'm still going hungry. Tell the Cook to send another batch down here or there'll be ructions, do you hear?'

'Shay Cullen is wondering if there's any chance of more speed.'

This time Ernie Grogan replied, though I couldn't see him through the crowd. 'If Cullen's in such a hurry, tell him to damn well swim. I won't miss having to sleep in the next bunk to a man who only ever changes his socks every September, whether they're dirty or not.'

The three cooks bristled when I relayed Mr Tierney's message back to them, protesting that the next batch was too hot to cut. But when I mentioned how impatient Mossy sounded, the Cook reluctantly divided a hot loaf into slices that were smaller than usual. He looked at me.

'What have you eaten?' he demanded.

'Nothing,' I replied defensively. 'I've been too busy.'

'I'm not accusing you,' he said. 'I'm ordering you to eat: you're a growing lad. This is your last chance.' He cut an extra-large slice and handed it to me. 'Warm your own stomach before dancing attention on Mossy Tierney. Tell him that if he gives us any more lip I'll boil up his wireless batteries to make soup. After you take these loaves to the engine room, hurry back. There's only three loaves left and they're to go to the Captain's cabin. Then you can close this galley door because my colleagues and I are on strike.'

After visiting the engine room I collected the final loaves to bring to Captain Donovan. When I knocked on his cabin door his voice instructed me to enter. The words brought me back to standing with Mr Tierney in this passageway when the *Kerlogue* was still moored in Wexford, trying to summon sufficient courage to persuade the Captain to let me sign on. That memory felt like it belonged to a different life. This voyage had only shown me a small glimpse of the outside world, but it was more than most of my neighbours would ever see. But it did not make me feel like a seasoned sailor. This trip merely taught me how little I knew about life, and how much I had still to learn. A month ago I would have passed Myles Foley on the street and paid him no heed, beyond fearing that if I paused to nod at such an old man, he might bore me with tales I had no interest in. This voyage had made me see beyond his age and realise what he could teach me. It had taught me to look beyond Mr Tierney's bluster and see a man whom you could trust with nothing, and yet whom you could trust with your life. These crewmen were subservient to the Captain and yet, at their core, each was his own master. While Mr Walton and Thomas Bergin would agree on nothing; on board this vessel they silently agreed to disagree, working together as if their lives depended on it. In truth, many more lives now depended on them.

I was just a kid, yet they had made me one of them. I knew I would find it impossible to share a narrow bed with my two brothers again. If we reached Wexford safely then I would bring home this ship's blanket that once belonged to my father and sleep wrapped up in it on the stone flags by the kitchen fire. I was now the breadwinner and I needed my own space. There was no guarantee of us reaching Wexford, but at that moment – maybe due to the smell of the bread I was carrying – I longed to see my mother again. More than anything I wanted to shield her from the pain of being bereaved by the sea a second time. During every night of this voyage I suspected that she had lain awake, incessantly praying for my safety. Those prayers would not just be entreaties to God to keep me safe: they were also her bulwark to keep fear at bay – easing her sense of helplessness by giving her something to do, even if just to recite decades of Hail Marys late into the night. As a child I could always make her smile by singing her favourite song:

> *I love the dear silver that shines in your hair,*
> *And the brow that's all furrowed and wrinkled with care.*
> *I kiss the dear fingers so toil-worn for me,*
> *Oh, God bless you and keep you, Mother Machree.*

I was in such a state of nervous exhaustion that I only became aware that I was singing this song aloud when the Captain's door swung open and Mr Walton stood glaring at me.

'Is this a music hall?' he asked. 'Did you not hear the Captain summoning you?'

'Leave the lad alone, Frank,' Captain Donovan called from inside. 'He looks asleep on his feet: we all are.'

Embarrassed, I entered the cabin. The scene could not be more different from the ordered world that had greeted Mr Tierney and I two weeks ago on the Wexford quays. badly wounded men commandeered any available floor space, being tended to by the Captain and Kapitänleutnant Fleischer. Mr Walton resumed assisting them. Maybe it was because he had not slept in so long or because he had sacrificed the laudanum that kept his pain at a tolerable level, but he now possessed the stoop of a far older man. It was evident to everyone how ill he was. He nodded his thanks when I handed him a slice of bread. I placed a slice down beside Myles Foley, who was neatly stitching up an old blanket. I knew without being told that it contained the body of the Leutnant I had helped pull from the waves. Captain Donovan accepted the portion of bread and paused to savour a bite.

'I won't even ask how this white flour materialised.' He nodded towards where Myles was finishing the makeshift shroud. 'We're too far from Ireland to keep the Leutnant's body on board. Besides, as a sailor, we thought he might be happier with his own kind beneath the waves than lying in a grave in Ireland that nobody will ever visit. Have you been to the engine room yet?'

'Mr Tierney is in a foul mood with folk complaining about how slow we're going,' I replied.

'It won't improve his mood, but tell Mossy to bring the ship to a halt for a moment. We're taking this poor man up on deck before the last of the daylight is gone. I don't care if every submarine in the Atlantic is pursuing us: a burial at sea is still a burial, and we'll do it in stillness and with dignity.'

When I returned to the engine room to shout this command in over the heads of the men, I expected Mr Tierney to grumble. But he obeyed and made the sign of the cross. Perhaps it was the noise of the engine stopping, but as I hurried up on deck I noticed

315

the sailors from the engine room following me. Some knocked on cabin doors and called out in German. I felt like the Pied Piper as I climbed the ladder and looked back to see men crowd into the passageway and wait their turn to follow suit.

Captain Donovan and Kapitänleutnant Fleischer had already carried the body up on deck, sealed inside the stitched-up blanket. They stood at the bow where Leutnant Krausser had sat alone. The Leutnant had merged in with the men who stood in silence all the way to amidships and right back to stern. Mr Walton noticed the men following me.

'Your German must be improving,' he said wryly, before adding, in a more sombre tone, 'Kapitänleutnant Fleischer wants a word.' He paused. 'You're your own man: do only what feels right in your heart.'

Myles Foley was kneeling to inspect his handiwork, anxious that no stitching came loose until the body had sunk several fathoms, with the weights placed in the man's pockets. He gestured for Herr Müller to help check the needlework, primarily just to give the grief-stricken man a role in the proceedings. Kapitänleutnant Fleischer watched me approach.

'Young man, are you familiar with Psalm 23: The Lord is my Shepherd?'

'In English, yes,' I replied.

He turned to Captain Donovan. 'The last light is almost gone, Captain. You will not be offended if I conduct the service in German?'

'No,' Captain Donovan replied. 'But this is a civilian ship. If there are Nazi salutes, neither I nor my men will join in.'

'This man was a civilian long before he donned a uniform. We were all civilians until war brought us to this place.' He turned back to me. 'Before his body enters the waves I would like if you could recite Psalm 23 in English. I would then ask Matrosengefreiter Müller to recite it in German.'

'What does "Matrosengefreiter" mean?' I asked.

'A sailor: Second Class. Will you do this for me?' He paused and then looked towards the body stitched into the blanket. 'Not for me: will you do it for him?'

I glanced back at the watching men, aware that the Irish crew were vastly outnumbered. I felt so inexperienced compared to these seafarers. But Mr Walton's words stayed with me. I didn't know if it counted as insubordination to disobey a request from a foreign commander, but I could only remain true to my own instincts.

'I willingly risked my life to try and save every sailor,' I said, 'and it broke my heart when we needed to leave men behind to drown. But it's a different thing to ask me to pray for an officer who was part of the same Navy who murdered my father.'

I don't know where Mr Tierney appeared from, but some protective instinct had caused him to leave the engine room. He stood directly behind me. Mr Walton stepped forward too. Our Second Officer was so ill that he had barely enough strength to stand up, but he was ready to strike the first man who raised any objection to whatever decision I made.

'I'm not asking you to just pray for the Leutnant,' Kapitänleutnant Fleischer said. 'I'm asking you to say a prayer for all the men who have gone to their deaths on Biscay during the war, with nobody to pray over them. Your father and Matrosengefreiter Müller's brother included.'

'With respect, Sir,' I replied defiantly, 'my father wasn't part of your war. Leave him out of this.'

'What age are you?' the Kapitänleutnant asked quietly.

'Sixteen.'

He gave a sad half-smile. 'What is your real age?'

'On this ship, I'm sixteen.'

'I have a son aged sixteen. He has been conscripted and sent to fight on the Russian front. He had no say in the matter, like I had no say in what orders I was given when I commanded my ship. My son loves books and music. There is a girl he is sweet on. I hope he got to kiss her before he left for the front; that – just once – he knew the pleasure of a girl's lips. But he is so gentle that I'm not sure he found the courage to kiss her. My son is now a man, or at least is forced to wear a man's uniform. But to me he is still a boy. I cannot imagine him hurting a fly, but out on the freezing Russian front, he must kill or be killed. Conscientiousness is not an option. He must advance through the snow into the teeth of Soviet machine guns or be shot by a German officer for cowardice if he hesitates. Perhaps you are so morally superior that you would kill nobody. If you are, then I respect your courage. But before you make that claim, I only ask you to imagine what it feels like to have an officer stand behind you, ready to shoot a bullet into your skull if you refuse to kill.' He looked around at the silent men. 'Do my sailors look like killers? Do they look any different from your crewmates? They are hungry and tired and sick of war. They miss their homes and children. None wish to be out here on these waves, except for some fanatics. But this is where we were sent with a stark choice: kill or be killed. We have hunted and now we are the hunted. We killed good men and lost good men. Before we bury our comrade at sea I will ask my men to bow their heads in silence. Everyone has someone they need to remember. You may wish to remember your father or you may wish to walk away. That is your decision.'

He gave a command in German. Although the men were silent already, a deeper quality entered their silence. He nodded to Herr Müller kneeling beside Myles Foley, but before that bereaved man could stand up and pray in German, I stepped forward. Raising my voice, I thought not just of my father but of the lost Wexford sailors whom I only knew through his stories: his crewmates and friends now missing beneath these waves:

The Lord's my Shepard, I'll not want.
He makes me down to lie
In pastures green; He leadeth me
The quiet waters by.
My soul He doth restore again,
And me to walk doth make
Within the paths of righteousness,
E'en for His own name's sake.
Yea, though I walk in death's dark vale,
Yet will I fear no ill;
For Thou art with me, and Thy rod
And staff me comfort still.

As I spoke, other Irish voices joined in. When I was finished Herr Müller recited this same psalm in German. I looked back at Mr Tierney and Mr Walton. Their faces were sombre in whatever light remained, but both nodded in silent approval.

Chapter Thirty-One

December 31, Afternoon Watch, The Western Approaches

ANOTHER NIGHT PASSED WITH US huddled in silence on the freezing deck. It was hard to believe that only ten nights ago I had voluntarily left the warmth of my bunk to try and sleep up here, too preoccupied with seasickness to worry about the cold. I doubted if even the harshest storm would make me seasick now, but if it did, my stomach had nothing to throw up. The miracle of yesterday's bread was a distant memory. No cooks – not matter how ingenious – could conjure a meal with no foodstuffs left on board. All we could do was carefully ration out the tiny amount of drinking water left and hope to sight land before a U-boat commander sighted us.

However, it wasn't a submarine that chanced upon us in the late afternoon, but a plane. I was below deck and didn't hear the engine, so when I climbed the ladder I found the scene on deck utterly disconcerting. Half the German sailors seemed to be missing. Then I saw them being urged by Captain Donovan and Kapitänleutnant Fleischer to jump down into the empty cargo hold. The air of weary silence which had pervaded the ship for thirty-six hours was replaced by tension. Mr Walton was helping the Dazzler Kehoe and Thomas Bergin to unroll huge sheets of tarpaulin, with the remaining Germans lying down on the deck to let it cover them. Men pushed past me, trying to descend the ladder. But it was so crowded below deck that there was no room for anyone else down there. The ship's hold also became so packed that no more men could jump into it. Those who remained above deck looked around in search of any hiding place. Then I heard the sound that was causing their panic: the distant but unmistakable drone of a plane approaching through low clouds. Shay Cullen looked anxious when he appeared at my elbow.

'Is it an Allied or a German plane?' I asked.

He shrugged. 'The only thing certain is that it will have mounted machine guns. If it's RAF, they'll want to know why our course suggests we are heading directly for Ireland. If it's the Luftwaffe, then our guests won't be slow about emerging from hiding to urge the pilot to convey our position to U-boat command. We'll soon find a flotilla of U-boats emerging from the waves to transport then back to France.' Shay Cullen nodded towards Leutnant Krausser. 'I know which air force this geezer wants it to be.'

Leutnant Krausser had spent hours cleaning his officer's cap and uniform. Even the buttons on his jacket were now buffed up.

'He's waiting for his chance to seize control of this ship,' Myles Foley whispered, having joined us so silently that neither of us heard him approach.

'At least a Luftwaffe pilot won't bomb his own men, will he?' I asked, scared.

'No,' Shay Cullen replied. 'But if the Germans here can get taken on board a rescue vessel then the decision about whether or not to sink us won't be made by Kapitänleutnant Fleischer.'

Myles Foley nodded. 'A sunken ship tells no tales. Herr Hitler might prefer to destroy any evidence that this ever happened. It would avoid international newspapers reports that members of his mighty Kriegsmarine needed to be rescued by a ragtag of sailors in a tin bucket.'

Kapitänleutnant Fleischer helped the Captain to close the hatches over the hold, leaving the men below in darkness. He looked up and, seeing the Leutnant on deck, barked an order. Leutnant Krausser stood in mutinous defiance, as if deciding whether to obey. The Kapitänleutnant shouted more forcefully. The Leutnant reluctantly retreated into the wheelhouse and hunched down out of sight. The deck looked bizarre, crisscrossed with sheets of tarpaulin, beneath which the men surely found it difficult to breathe. The plane emerged from the clouds. Its wing markings showed that it was clearly an RAF aircraft. Kapitänleutnant Fleischer was bare-headed, but his tattered navy tunic was still identifiable. He looked around, but there was nowhere left to hide. Several German sailors still trapped on deck hastily stripped to their waists and dumped the remnants of their uniforms in the sea. The Kapitänleutnant seemed unsure of what to do. He struck me as a man who would refuse to crawl beneath tarpaulin. Walking towards him, Mr Walton removed his greatcoat and presented it to the Kapitänleutnant, who donned it gratefully and stood with the Captain, watching the pilot approach. The airplane made one low sweep over our deck and then swung around to return for a closer look.

'This fellow knows there's something afoot when he sees men stripped to their waists in the depths of winter,' Myles Foley said grimly.

'Let's hope it's not the Polish air crew from six weeks ago,' Shay Cullen added. 'If they machine-gun our deck again, they'll kill a lot more men than they expect to.'

The plane came in towards the *Kerlogue* again, this time even lower, the spine lamps under its fuselage beginning to flash in amber and white.

'It looks like he's trying to order us to change route,' Shay Cullen said. 'He knows there's something suspicious: we're miles off course for a ship that he knows has to dock in Wales for inspection.'

'Can he make us change route?' I asked.

'He can do what he likes,' Myles said. 'Once we veer off our designated route we're fair game for anyone who fancies taking a pot shot at us.'

The plane was so low that we could see the pilot's face as he made another pass overhead. Even with his mask on, he looked barely older than me. The aircraft flew past but I could see it already being angled to swing back. I felt scared, but my fear was surely nothing compared to the men lying beneath the tarpaulin or crouching in the black hellbox of the swaying hold. At least I could see what was happening. Captain Donovan beckoned to me.

'Run to the wheelhouse, Jack. Ask Mr Valentine for the signal flags and be quick about it.'

I raced to the wheelhouse and opened the door. Leutnant Krausser grabbed my jumper, pulling me inside to stare into my face. 'What are your instructions?' he demanded.

'Leave the boy alone or I'll hurl you back into those waves,' Mr Valentine shouted.

'I need the signal flags,' I said.

'What are you signalling?' the Leutnant hissed.

Mr Valentine made a move towards the Leutnant. So many bodies were hunched between them that it would be impossible for him to reach Krausser, but the First Officer's expression contained such menace that the Leutnant relinquished his grip. Mr Valentine opened a locker and bundles of flags passed from hand to hand until they reached me. I ran back across the deck and was about to hand them to the Captain when Mr Walton stepped between us.

'Allow me, Sir. The pilot mightn't like your message. If he shoots the messenger, you'll need all your authority to keep command of this ship.'

Mr Walton didn't wait for a response but strode to the prow. He faced the approaching plane and held aloft three flags in succession.

'What's Mr Walton signalling?' I asked.

'That we need urgent medical attention,' Myles Foley said.

The plane flew directly overhead, flashing the same sequence of lights.

'This pilot is not interested in anything we have to say. He sees that we seem to be heading directly for Ireland and are therefore off course. He's instructing us to revert to our designated route,' Shay Cullen told me. The plane turned again in a loop. The game of bluff was over. This was the pilot's last pass: he would either accept our course or fire a barrage of warning shots. Mr Walton held aloft a different selection of flags. He mounted one foot on the gunnel and leaned forward so much that he was in danger of toppling into the waves. The aircraft's approach was so low that it seemed to head directly towards him.

'What's he signalling now?' I asked.

'That because it's a medical emergency we have to make for Cobh,' Shay Cullen replied.

The plane was only yards away from Mr Walton, who suddenly stood up on the gunnel, balancing precariously on the edge. Standing at his full height, he waved the signal flags even more violently. Something had to give: it seemed certain that either Mr Walton would fall into the waves or the Allied plane would riddle him with bullets.

'You'd swear he wanted to be killed,' I said.

'Men provide for their families any way they can,' Myles Foley replied quietly.

But the gunner didn't open fire. As the plane passed above Mr Walton, the force of its slipstream blew him backwards. Or maybe an instinct for self-preservation caused him to step back so that he fell onto the slippery deck. Captain Donovan and the Kapitänleutnant ran forward to help him.

'Mr Walton has been paying into an insurance policy for years,' Myles Foley added. 'It guarantees his family a lump sum, but only if he dies at sea. You're looking at a gravely ill man whose sole remaining wish is to die on board a ship. But God doesn't let us choose the timing of our death.'

The plane was moving away, its angle of elevation suggesting that it did not intend to turn back. Everybody on board sensed this: there was movement beneath the tarpaulin as men struggled to push it away and gasp for fresh air. Shouts came from the hold: trapped sailors desperate to see daylight. Leutnant Krausser emerged from the wheelhouse.

'That fool came in so low that even one bullet fired into his fuel tank would have crippled him,' the Leutnant said. 'I can't believe this ship does not possess a single gun. What sort of fools sail unarmed into a warzone?'

'The sort of fools who picked you up,' Shay Cullen retorted.

Leutnant Krausser turned to Captain Donovan. 'It is not correct to allow an ordinary sailor to address me like this. Please remind this man that I am an officer.'

'You're a guest, Leutnant.'

'And where do you plan to deliver your guests? I don't know what signals you exchanged with that British pilot. I demand to see a chart of our course.'

'This ship's course is not your responsibility, Krausser,' Kapitänleutnant Fleischer said.

'The fate of my comrades is, especially when they receive no leadership.'

Kapitänleutnant Fleischer turned to the Captain. 'The pilot issued you with a command, Captain.'

'I considered it more of a request. He's flying off, with his duty done.'

'And what's your duty, Captain?'

'I steer my own course.'

Leutnant Krausser grasped the Kapitänleutnant's shoulder. 'It is not too late to steer for France. If that plane returns to bomb us, at least we'll die sailing into the war instead of running like cowards. I demand that we seize this ship and take our chances.'

The Kapitänleutnant examined the hand on his shoulder. 'Standing orders allow you to take command, if your Kapitänleutnant is incompetent, medically impaired or senile. Get every man on deck who supports you to stand up.' Looking around, he shouted loudly in German. *'Alle Männer, die dem Leutnant Gehorsam leisten wollen, vortreten!'*

There was silence. Not one sailor stepped forward. The Kapitänleutnant looked at the Leutnant.. 'There's your answer, Krausser. These men are not cowards, but they have fought their fight and it's over. I only wish that my son was as safe on the Russian front. Now remove your hand from my shoulder.'

The Leutnant glanced around at the sullen circle of sailors. No one spoke, but I could sense their loathing towards him. He turned and walked to the furthest end of the deck. The men silently parted to let him pass and closed ranks again. A sailor with youthful features, but whose hair had turned grey, saluted Kapitänleutnant Fleischer.

'*Mein Kapitän*,' he said.

Those two words were continually repeated as every German sailor on deck saluted. Kapitänleutnant Fleischer turned to the Captain.

'Is your course still set for Cobh, Captain?'

'Several of your men are critically injured. I can't guarantee that we can reach Cobh in time to save them, but we'll do our best.' He turned to Mr Walton, who was limping. 'You took a nasty tumble, Frank.'

'I was just trying to see what the plane was signalling,' Mr Walton replied. 'I couldn't decipher a word: it was probably in Polish.'

Chapter Thirty-Two

December 31, Midnight, Fastnet Rock

NONE OF US UP ON deck slept much during that freezing night which seemed to stretch into eternity. At one stage a bitter squall of rain lashed down on us but no sailor bothered to try and cover his head. We were already so soaked that one more drenching made little difference. Rather than shelter from the rain, many men lifted their faces and opened their parched mouths wide, trying to quench their thirst with the moisture of the raindrops. The eventual clearance of the rain did not provoke a single comment. Heavy clouds parted and a half moon threw a silver light over the huddled figures. This was when the deadly quietude began to be broken by a curious, rhythmic stomping. It started so quietly, and emanated from so many places – even echoing up from packed cabins below – that it was impossible to know who initiated this rhythmic slapping of hands on wood and stamping of feet, or what it signified.

The only thing certain was that this cacophony grew ever more ear-splittingly loud, with men standing up to beat timber slabs from the smashed crates against the gunnel. It felt menacing: like a prearranged summons to mount a mutiny. But why leave it so late – when we were only hours from Ireland – to seize control, unless their intention was to scupper the vessel: preferring to send us all to our deaths rather than be interned? It made no sense after the back-breaking hours we spent rescuing them. I saw that it made no sense to Captain Donovan either. He opened the wheelhouse door, alarmed and perplexed. Myles Foley emerged from the crowd. I didn't know how long it was since this old man had last slept. Apart from Mr Walton – who was in such pain that it was at mystery he could still walk – nobody had earned the right to look more exhausted than this old seadog. I had last seen Myles slumped on the deck, too jaded to raise his hand in greeting. But now he seemed intoxicated with energy. Wielding a stick, he banged it hard against the side of the wheelhouse.

'Have you joined everyone else in going stark raving mad?' Captain Donovan asked him.

'It's here,' the old sailor replied. 'Can't you feel it? It's only moments away.'

Mr Tierney had fought his way up from below deck, agitated by the noise. 'This is worse than being at home listening to my daughters caterwaul over who's wearing what dress to what dance,' he said. 'What's only moments away?'

'Sylvester.'

'Sylvester?' Mr Tierney gazed out to sea. 'Well there's always room for one more at a party. I just hope he's rowing out here on a boat stocked with whiskey.' He looked at Myles. 'You're talking more nonsense than a Kildare man. Who the hell is Sylvester?'

'We should greet him with fireworks,' Myles added.

'Has everyone on board lost their senses?' Captain Donovan snapped.

'With respect, Captain, you've lost track of time.' Myles Foley replied. 'What hour is it on your tick-tock? These sailors are farmers' sons, more used to operating a threshing machine than a battleship. They're driving out the evil spirits of the old year and welcoming in the new one. In Germany they give the coming of the New Year a name: Sylvester. If they were back on the farms where they belong, they'd be banging drums to make noise and sending great wooden wheels filled with blazing straw rolling down the hillsides, with younger lads chasing through the forests with flaming cudgels.'

'It sounds just like Tiger Bay in Cardiff on a Saturday night,' Mr Tierney said.

'Mock all you like, Mossy,' Myles Foley replied with a fierce intensity, 'but it's a wondrous sight. When I sailed out of Hamburg I was invited into the forests one New Year's Eve and saw it for myself: sheer pagan joy that not even Hitler's goose-stepping bullies can stamp out. We're moments away from 1944. These men are saying good riddance to the death and destruction they witnessed during 1943. They're driving out the evil spirits, just like their ancestors did. Even though they're starving and cold; they're starting the New Year afresh with hope: hope is the one thing that no-one can steal from us.'

The raucous pounding made by the men didn't seem threatening any more: I felt swept up in its exhilaration. I could imagine church bells ringing across Wexford town at midnight and my family standing in our doorway to shout New Year's greetings along the length of Green Street to the neighbours spilling out onto the street. Ellie Coady would be there, laughing and waving, and I hoped she was thinking of me. I wondered what Kateřina was doing at this moment. Was she alone in her small borrowed room, a candle lit as she prayed for her vanished father, or in Ericeira with fellow refugees, or mingling among the crowds surely thronging Lisbon's streets? I didn't want to think that perhaps she was dressed in a borrowed gown, being paid to accompany some braggart German official swaggering through the glistening casino at Estoril, with champagne flowing and Kateřina smiling meekly, paraded like a sacrificial trinket.

The boisterous clamour on board stopped at the sound of a harshly shouted command. Leutnant Krausser began to speak in a manner which suggested that he expected everyone's undivided attention.

'What's this geezer pontificating about?' Mr Tierney asked.

'*An tUasal O'Hitler, an amadán ainbheartach,*' Myles Foley replied in coded Irish, as Mr Walton emerged from the wheelhouse. 'He's telling the men that it's their duty to use this moment to re-pledge their support in the coming year to their Führer.'

'I'm not spending New Year's Eve listening to shite and onions,' Mr Walton said. 'Especially if it's probably my last New Year's Eve.' With difficulty he hoisted himself up onto a steel container beside the funnel. His surprisingly good – and loud – baritone voice carried on the night air.

> *Should auld acquaintance be forgot*
> *And never brought to mind?*
> *Should auld acquaintance be forgot*
> *And days o' lang syne!*

Leutnant Krausser stopped in mid-sentence and glared at Mr Walton, annoyed by this interruption. But Mr Walton's singing was so raw that it was impossible for the Leutnant to continue. I was always too shy to sing properly in public, but I found my voice swept up as every Irish voice on deck joined in the chorus:

> *For auld lang syne, my dear,*
> *For auld lang syne,*
> *We'll drink a cup o'kindness yet*
> *For auld lang syne.*

Mr Walton sang the next verse on his own, his fingers outstretched as if extending the hand of friendship to every man present.

> *And there's a hand, my trusty friend,*
> *And give me a hand o' thine,*
> *And we'll tak a goodwill glass o' ale*
> *For the sake of auld lang syne!*

I couldn't tell if the sailors began to sing the chorus in the Scots dialect of Robbie Burns or in some strange German translation. But whatever words they sang, we were all singing in unison. They lifted their voices joyfully in the night air, remembering loved ones and lost ones at this turning point of the year. I have never heard a song sung with such passion as by these men, some wrapped only in old blankets. Maybe this was the last thing they had left: the power to raise their voices in song. When the last chorus ended, Mr Walton needed to reach out his hand for me to help him to slowly clamber down. He looked drained by the effort it had taken him to sing.

'They loved it,' I said.

He grimaced as he planted his feet back on the deck. 'I won't get a swelled head: they were the ultimate captive audience.'

'You did great,' Mr Tierney assured him. 'When I sing, half the pub walks out: you only had one walkout. Perhaps the poor Leutnant got caught short in the waterworks department because he was doing an awful lot of agitated jigging about.'

We looked across to where Leutnant Krausser had stood, but he was gone.

Mr Walton smiled grimly. 'I wish all auld tyrants were so easily forgot.' He extended his hand. 'Happy 1944, Mossy.'

'Happy New Year, Mr Walton, Sir, and may we share many a New Year's Eve to come in the best dog-rough bars of foreign ports.'

They shook hands. This acted as a spur for men around us to follow suit. A line of strangers shook my hand and gripped my shoulder to say '*Frohes Neues Jahr*'.

Mr Tierney laughed when it was his turn to grip my hand. 'It's the oddest New Year's Eve I've ever known, apart from the one your dad and myself spent locked up in a police cell in Cherbourg. We were still wet behind the ears and made the classic Irish mistake of deciding that instead of drinking alcohol we'd just stick to a few harmless bottles of wine.'

'I never heard that story.'

'Neither did my wife or your mother, and we'll keep it that way.' He looked around. 'We can't provide fireworks for these lads but we can light up the darkness just a bit.' He pondered his decision, and then sighed in a resigned manner. 'I may as well go bankrupt in style. Have a good root under Thomas Bergin's bunk. There's a sack up against the wall; you'll need to reach right in to find it. It was the last thing I was holding back – my final two hundred Lucky Strike American cigarettes: my last chance to knock an extra few shillings out of this voyage.'

'I wouldn't have taken Thomas Bergin for a smuggler,' I said, 'with all his talk about being related to a nun.'

'Shay Cullen and I felt it would be an unchristian act to trouble his conscience by letting him know that we'd hidden fags under his bunk. Two hundred glowing cigarettes will hardly outshine the Northern Lights but we'll pay homage to this Sylvester in our own way. Lucky Strikes are a good smoke. And it's just as well, because some of these lads look so ill that this may be the last fag they'll ever puff on.'

The air was so putrid in the cabin where Thomas Bergin's bunk was that I found it hard not to throw up. Others in the cabin had been less lucky: even hardened sailors were vomiting into a bucket being passed around. The cabin felt cold and clammy. It took me several minutes to locate the sack. I left one packet of Lucky Strikes with the men there and then moved between the other cabins, the engine room, the galley and up along the deck, dispensing packets and attempting to say *'Frohes Neues Jahr'*. There was such a shortage of matches that every cigarette needed to be lit from an already burning one being held by someone else.

Whenever I looked back I saw glowing patterns of red specks spread across the deck, all the way down amidships to stern.

I could also see another speck – this time of white light – ahead of us to starboard. This flash would disappear for five seconds and then reappear, blinking so quickly that it barely registered before it was gone. The Dazzler Kehoe was passing by and followed my puzzled gaze.

'What am I staring at?' I asked.

'The Fastnet Lighthouse, though crews on cargo ships call it the Lonely Rock. A chum of mine who worked the emigrant ships between Cobh and New York called it The Teardrop. You'd see hardened men line the rails with tears in their eyes to watch the flicker of the Fastnet disappearing. The next piece of land was Ellis Island in New York. This is the last bit of Ireland emigrants glimpse when they're America-bound.'

'And the first glimpse they catch when they come back,' I replied.

The Dazzler shook his head. 'For most, the crossing is their first and last time on a ship, after scraping together the fare. They know they'll not see this lighthouse again. I've known some rough voyages where I thought I'd never see it again myself.'

'Does this mean we're close enough to Ireland to be safe?'

The Dazzler shrugged. 'U-boat captains are slime rats who'll hug the coastline for easy pickings. There's also the danger of being blown to pieces if we strike a mine that has floated free from its mooring. But we're close enough for a technological miracle to occur.'

'What miracle?'

'Tell the Captain that we've sighted the Fastnet and you'll find out for yourself.'

In the wheelhouse, they had already identified the lighthouse. Captain Donovan and Mr Walton were joined by Kapitänleutnant

Fleischer and Leutnant Krausser. Mr Tierney had also squeezed in, along with a dozen Germans who had nowhere else to stand. They appeared to be asleep standing up. When I opened the door I half expected them to spill out like a shoal of mackerel from a net. I passed around a pack of cigarettes. Captain Donovan accepted one gratefully.

'I won't even ask where they came from,' he commented.

'Thomas Bergin was saving them for his wife's cousin in the convent,' Mr Tierney said. 'They enjoy a Lucky Strike after they rise before dawn to recite *Matins*.' He slyly plucked two cigarettes from the pack: one to smoke now and one to wedge behind his ear for future use.

Mr Walton accepted a cigarette and told me to pass the pack around the wheelhouse. 'I suppose nuns are only allowed to fantasise about two things,' he said. 'Burning heretics and burning Lucky Strikes.'

The Captain offered him a light from his own cigarette. 'Make a New Year's resolution, Frank; lay off the poor nuns and give our ears a rest.'

'Have you any New Year's resolutions yourself?'

'I was thinking of become more talkative with strangers.' He looked at Mr Walton. 'Would I be wise?'

'There's only one way to find out.'

Captain Donovan took a drag of his cigarette to steady his nerves before he flicked the heavy dial to turn on the short-wave radio set. The wheelhouse was filled by an indistinct hiss of crackle as he held the mouthpiece aloft.

'Come in, Radio Valentia,' he spoke into the mouthpiece. 'This is the MV *Kerlogue* of the Wexford Steamship Company calling Radio Valentia in Ireland.'

Everyone held their breath. We had been out here alone for so long that it seemed impossible to imagine anyone picking up the

Captain's voice across the miles of waves that separated us from Ireland's most westerly point: the remote island of Valentia off the Kerry coast. I could imagine the tiny radio station there, where the first telegram cables from America had reached Europe, beside a small pier from which generations of the same families still set off in a lifeboat to help sailors in distress. The island would be in darkness: seabirds nesting on its cliffs and seals stretched on rocks, one eye alert for danger. At this hour of celebrating the start of a new year, would there be anyone on duty, listening out for a stray voice to emanate from the dark Atlantic?

After thirty seconds Captain Donovan repeated his message. The crackle of static grew louder and then miraculously – or so it seemed to me – a voice from the outside world entered the wheelhouse: surprisingly loud and un-muffled.

'This is Radio Valentia receiving your signal, MV *Kerlogue*. Please report your present course.'

The Captain breathed a sigh of relief. 'This is MV *Kerlogue* to Radio Valentia: we will shortly pass the Fastnet Rock and swing inland. We are being forced to deviate from our course because of a medical emergency. We have taken on board one hundred and sixty-four shipwrecked sailors; many so badly burnt that they urgently need medical attention. I will therefore make an emergency stopover at Cobh before sailing on to Fishguard to discharge our Navicert.'

The radio silence which greeted these words continued for so long that nobody knew if we had lost contact with Valentia Island or if the radio operator was consulting with a superior. Finally a reply came.

'MV *Kerlogue*, identify who is speaking.'

The Captain pressed the knob on the handset. 'This is the MV *Kerlogue* of the Wexford Steamship Company.'

'Identify the nationality of the sailors taken on board?'

'German sailors found drowning at sea. We formally request you to inform the authorities at Cobh that we need a tender with medical personnel ready to board us and remove the most seriously wounded.'

This time we did not need to wait long for a reply. But the voice that resounded through the transmitter had a different accent: more authoritative and distinctively British.

'Come in, MV *Kerlogue*, this is Land's End Radio in Cornwall.'

The Captain and Mr Walton exchanged anxious glances.

'Land's End was quicker off the mark than I expected,' the Captain said.

'Your hearing is better than mine,' Mr Walton bluffed. 'I thought I heard something over the crackle but didn't quite catch it.'

'We'll catch it in the neck in Fishguard if we ignore their instructions,' Captain Donovan said.

A terse silence filled the wheelhouse. It was impossible to communicate farther with the Irish-based radio station without acknowledging that we could hear the message from Cornwall. It had become a dangerous game of bluff.

'Two men are lying dead in my cabin,' Captain Donovan said quietly. 'It's hard for other survivors there to have the corpses still beside them, but I've nowhere to put the dead bodies. Even if Mossy could get our engine up to top speed, I know that between here and Cobh I'll have to place coins over the eyelids of at least one more poor soul, to ensure that his eyes stay shut in death. Perhaps we wouldn't lose too many others if we extend this voyage for another seven hours by sailing direct to Fishguard, but my conscience won't allow me to risk seeing more men die on my watch.'

Mr Walton turned to Kapitänleutnant Fleischer. 'What would happen if we disobeyed an order from a Nazi wireless operator?'

Kapitänleutnant Fleischer looked at him stoically. 'I won't insult your intelligence by pretending there could be more than one outcome.'

The silence was broken by the Valentia operator. He had overheard the interruption from Land's End Radio and guessed at the game of brinksmanship being played.

'This is Valentia Radio calling MV *Kerlogue*. Your request for emergency medical assistance has been relayed to the Cobh Harbour Master. Well done, *Kerlogue*. Over and out.'

Nobody spoke in the wheelhouse, but the response from the Land's End Radio operator was instantaneous. 'Come in, MV *Kerlogue*. Your Navicert instructions are to proceed to Fishguard. I repeat, proceed immediately to Fishguard.'

Captain Donovan went to reply but was beaten to it by Mr Walton, who blew strongly into the handset, creating a harsh crackling.

'This is the MV *Kerlogue's* Second Officer, Frank Walton speaking. Please identify yourself: your message is breaking up. Is that Valentia Radio? Please repeat message.' He blew again into the handset. 'I repeat: message breaking up due to interference. Please identify yourself, Valentia.'

The British radio operator sounded exasperated. 'MV *Kerlogue*, this is Land's End radio in Cornwall. Proceed immediately to Fishguard. Confirm you have received this order.'

Mr Walton looked around. 'Can anyone hear a word he's saying?'

'Hand me the radio,' Captain Donovan ordered. 'I never gave you permission to use it.'

'Call it an act of insubordination: a quality I learnt from a fine seafarer who protected a far less wise captain than you one night in Lisbon. Every jumped-up desk-bound sailor in Fishguard will throw the book at you when you face the music there. If they blacklist you, the *Kerlogue* can't sail until a new captain is appointed. But if they arrest a mere Second Officer, that won't stop ten other crewmen from earning a wage on their next voyage.' He pressed the handset knob. 'This is Second Officer, Frank Walton, of the MV *Kerlogue* speaking. Repeat your last message; Valentia … your signal appears to be gone.' He switched off the radio before farther instructions could be issued.

'I salute you all,' Leutnant Krausser said. 'Every man on board has done his duty. When the war ends, this favour will not be forgotten.'

'My only duty is to my wife and kids who depend on whatever few bob I can rustle up from making a living at sea,' Mr Tierney said. 'Duty is the sort of word that men like you in uniform love because you can hide any crime behind it. We weren't doing our duty by hauling you from the sea: we were doing what was right. So don't cheapen it by calling it a favour to your Führer or to any blowhard Leutnant like you.'

'You know nothing about me,' the Leutnant replied. 'Before the war I studied piano at the *Staatliche Hochschule für Musik:* Cologne's finest music conservatory. Do you think I enjoy seeing people killed in this war?'

'I think you enjoy your status,' Mr Tierney replied. 'But you'll just be another ordinary internee in an army barracks after we dump you on the pier at Cobh.'

The Leutnant snorted, amused at the engineer's ignorance. 'I shall remain an officer in whatever camp we temporarily reside in until the Führer sweeps through Ireland in his final push to ensure a German victory. A sailor will be assigned to brush my uniform. Men will salute me in that camp and should any man address me with such familiarly as you are doing now I will have him disciplined, like your captain should discipline you.'

'That will do, Krausser,' Kapitänleutnant Fleischer warned.

'It needs to be said, Kapitänleutnant,' Leutnant Krausser said. 'I admire Captain Donovan's actions, but the Irish lack discipline. It is why England rightly occupied them for centuries. It was a calamity that the English never properly crushed their puny rebellion. It gave a mongrel race ideas above their station. The smallness of this boat shows how incapable the Irish are of governing their own affairs.'

'Seeing as you admire the English so much, you'll be eager to stay on board when we sail from Cobh on to Fishguard,' Mr Walton said. 'I suspect they will be most keen to hear your views and make your acquaintance.'

'We will meet the English around a conference table when they finally see sense. The tragedy is that we could have settled things with them in a civilised manner in 1939. We could have divided up the lesser breeds between us, if the Jews and Bolsheviks had not brainwashed England into embarking on this unnecessary war.'

'The English never looked too brainwashed to me,' Mr Walton said.

'Jews run their newspapers; Jews control their banks. When the ordinary Anglo-Saxon realises how he has been duped, Englishmen will rebel against their so-called leaders and we will finally see a civilised order imposed across Europe, with all the riff-raff and scum gone. No disrespect, but the English are a superior race to you. We can prove it scientifically and you cannot argue with science. You Irish may not be degenerates like the Gypsies and Jews, but you are still only half-breeds who belong working out in the fields alongside the Poles and Slavs.'

'Then surely it is beneath you to be forced to live among half-breeds like us,' Mr Walton insisted. 'I'll ask you again: why not stay on board and confront the British with your irrefutable scientific evidence after we dock in Fishguard?'

'I know my duty,' the Leutnant said quietly. 'I will not desert my men.'

'They are not your men, Krausser,' Kapitänleutnant Fleischer said sharply. 'These sailors remain under my command.'

'They remain one heartbeat away from being under my command, Kapitänleutnant, and you are not a well man.'

I had no right to speak up in such company, among men who barely seemed aware of my presence, but I couldn't stop myself. 'When this ship reaches Cobh it will be the happiest moment of my life.'

Mr Walton glanced at me, puzzled. 'Why is that, Jack?'

'I'll finally get enough space to swing a right hook and flatten this Nazi eejit.'

Captain Donovan threw his eyes to heaven. 'Get this child out of here, Mossy,' he snapped. 'Give him a colouring book to keep him occupied.'

Mr Tierney shoved me roughly towards the door. 'You're out of order entirely, boy,' he chided me. He only stopped scolding me when we were out on deck with the wheelhouse door closed behind us. He was so bent over that I thought he was winded. But when he looked up he had tears of laughter in his eyes. 'You're right out of order,' he repeated quietly. 'You'll need to queue up like the rest of us to punch that blasted eejit.'

Chapter Thirty-Three

January 1 1944, Middle Watch
and Morning Watch, Irish Waters

AFTER MY OUTBURST IN THE wheelhouse it seemed wise to keep my head down. I had never addressed an adult in such a fashion before and – for all of Mr Tierney's laughter – I had no way of knowing if I was in trouble with the Captain. I also wasn't sure how the German sailors whom I went to sit among on deck would react to news of a superior officer being spoken to like this. I sat in silence during the slow hours spent skirting the Fastnet and approaching the Irish coast, passing near Cape Clare Island and Sherkin Island, where distant flickers revealed oil lamps or candles in isolated cottage windows. Our route took us farther back out to sea then to avoid rocks and sand banks, but kept us within tantalising sight of the occasional lights of remote west-Cork towns like Castletownshend and Rosscarbery.

By the time we passed Clonakilty Bay and the Seven Heads, drawing ever closer to the Old Head of Kinsale, I was so drowsy as to be barely aware of my surroundings. But I felt a shiver of apprehension I when I became conscious of movement behind me. Myles Foley was manoeuvring a path towards me, accompanied by Herr Müller and another sailor whose face I didn't recognise.

This stranger lagged behind the other two, seemingly reluctant to approach. Had he been instructed by the Leutnant to assault me, to show how any future insubordination would be dealt with? Was Myles Foley trying to act as an intermediary, to intercede on my behalf with his limited German? Herr Müller quietly spoke to the sailors seated, half-asleep, beside me. These men shifted up on the cold deck to allow space for the new arrivals. The two Germans sat to my left and Myles Foley placed his hand on my shoulder as he lowered his old limbs to sit cross-legged to my right. This gesture was to give him some stability as he sat down, but there was also something fatherly in the act: it conveyed support and a covert warning that their visitation had a serious purpose.

'You know Herr Müller, lad,' he said. 'This second gentleman is a wireless operator by the name of Herr Oppermann.'

I nodded to them both. Herr Müller nodded back but his companion gazed into the distance as if finding it hard to look me in the eye. Perturbed, I glanced at Myles Foley for guidance.

'Is this about Leutnant Krausser?' I asked. 'Is something going to happen to me?'

Both Germans glanced up sharply at this mention of the Leutnant. Neither spoke but their faces betrayed that they were more scared of him than I was.

'Why would we want to discuss that pompous blowhard?' Myles asked. 'We're here because Herr Oppermann heard Herr Müller talk about why you're at sea so young ... about your father.'

I felt more uneasy now than when I had thought that this man was coming to threaten me. 'What about my father?'

'I told Herr Müller the name of the ship poor Sean died on. The *Kyleclare* meant nothing to him but Herr Oppermann has heard that name before.'

I stared at this sailor who still avoided eye contact with me. I was experiencing an odd mixture of emotions: a poisonous hatred and yet such tremulous apprehension that I didn't want the conversation to continue.

'Is he one of the crew who…?'

Again, Myles Foley placed a protective hand on my shoulder. 'This wireless operator says he was never been on board a U-boat in his life and I believe him. But in the naval base in France he drank with crewmen from a U-boat: sailors on shore leave who talked more openly than they should have.'

Herr Oppermann was now staring at me, though he couldn't follow a word that Myles Foley was saying.

'*U vier fünf sechs*,' the man said quietly.

Puzzled, I looked at Myles for guidance.

'He says it was U-boat 456,' Myles translated.

'*Kapitänleutnant Max Teichert*.'

'That was the commander's name,' Myles said.

'Is he taunting me with the name of the man who killed my father?'

'He's trying to tell you whatever you wish to know,' Myles replied. 'Isn't it better to know what happened to your father rather than be tormented by the questions eating your soul? I've spent my life watching hardchaws get drunk in dog-rough pubs, with their crewmates thinking they're tough nuts, afraid of nothing. But I look at such fellows, so quick to use their fists with strangers, and I ask myself, what unanswered questions have they bottled up inside that they're running away from?'

I gazed towards the distant scattered lights of Ireland and tried to collect my thoughts. One childish part of me still longed to cling onto the fantasy that by some tenuous chance my father was alive somewhere as a prisoner-of-war. Then I looked at the sombre stranger and I nodded for Herr Oppermann to say what he had come to say. I knew I'd lost any right to remain a child on the night that my mother placed my first pair of long trousers beside my bed. I had to know the truth so that she could know it and be allowed to properly grieve.

'*Einzelgänger*,' the man said.

Myles Foley looked puzzled. He spoke to Herr Müller, and both of them tried to break down this long word. Myles listened to Herr Mullen and nodded whenever he heard a word that he felt he understood.

'It's a dog that hunts alone … no, not a dog…' He nodded in sudden realisation. 'A lone wolf: that's how Kapitänleutnant Teichert operated … scavenging under the waves … making his own judgement calls. That's what Herr Oppermann is saying … or so I think anyway.'

'*Es war im April,*' Herr Oppermann said. '*Ich hatte mit einem der U-Boot-Besatzung viel zu viel gesoffen.*'

Myles Foley nodded to show that he grasped this sentence. 'Back in April Herr Oppermann spent a night drinking with the crew of U-boat 456.'

The wireless operator spoke again, repeating certain words slowly, while Herr Müller tried to chip in with smaller words. Perplexed, Myles listened and tried to interpret.

'This U-boat saw action up in the Arctic, attacking Soviet convoys. They gained such a murderous reputation that they were ordered down to Biscay to create mayhem.'

Herr Oppermann added something and Myles Foley looked puzzled.

'They were like fish?' Myles made a swimming motion but Herr Müller shook his head. He pointed to the veins on his wrist and shivered. Myles nodded.

'He's saying the crew of U-boat 456 were cold-blooded, like fish; cold-blooded killers. But something was bothering them that night they drank with Herr Oppermann.'

Herr Oppermann looked directly at me. For the first word he uttered that a word I recognised, though he pronounced it in such a foreign accent that it was like hearing it for the first time: '*Kyleclare*.'

I nodded for him to continue. His words now came in such a flood that Myles struggled to decipher what was being said. This conversation was straying beyond whatever rudimentary German he possessed. The old Arklow seafarer glanced around and saw Leutnant Krausser passing nearby, pausing to address clusters of men. Pointing towards the Leutnant, Myles said something in broken German, obviously suggesting that they ask the Kriegsmarine officer to translate their conversation. Both sailors shook their heads fretfully and Herr Oppermann grabbed Myles's hand, lest it attract Leutnant Krausser's attention. Only then did I understand the grave risk he was taking. Every German on board would be interned in an Irish military barracks for the rest of the war, but as Leutnant Krausser had indicated, this did not change the reality that they could be court-martialled there by superior officers for any infringement – most especially for betraying details of a naval engagement. Leutnant Krausser would be eager to make an example of someone, to re-impose discipline and emphasise how his rank still held sway. If Krausser realised what these two men were doing, they might be ostracised and endure a second layer of incarceration within the camp, by becoming shunned outcasts among their peers.

Myles Foley nodded unobtrusively to show that he had grasped their dilemma. Leutnant Krausser was eliciting cautious responses from the sailors he circulated among: his manner suggesting that he was covertly conducting an inspection. Myles deliberately looked away. If the Leutnant glanced towards us, nothing in our outward appearances would suggest that we were holding a conversation. Herr Oppermann gazed out to sea as he spoke quietly and Myles Foley's features never betrayed how he strained to understand each word. In a low tone Myles continually asked the wireless operator to repeat certain phrases that he struggled to grasp. Then from inside his tattered jacket Myles produced a betting slip and a tiny pencil stub picked up from a bookie's shop. He discreetly handed these to Herr Oppermann. The wireless operator hesitated and then began to cover the betting slip in a succession of small sketches, so simple that they might have been scrawled by a child. I desperately needed to know what he was sketching. But as the Leutnant still hovered nearby, I didn't want to attract attention. So I waited while Myles Foley examined each sketch and whispered farther questions. Eventually he nodded to indicate that he understood as much as he would ever comprehend of what this man wished to convey.

Myles turned to me. 'From what I gather, Kapitänleutnant Teichert deserved his reputation as a killer. The *Kyleclare* was his easiest kill but also his most hesitant one. His crew were used to encountering every class of ship, but they didn't know what to make of the *Kyleclare* when they chanced upon it. They'd never seen such a tiny vessel alone, so far out at sea. The *Kyleclare* was so overloaded with cargo that she was listing to starboard and lying as low in the water as we are now, with waves washing over her deck. The Kapitänleutnant wondered if she had been abandoned there as a booby trap to get them to surface. It made him cautious of betraying his position. So they only rose high enough for his periscope to crest the waves. Even then he found it hard to keep the *Kyleclare* in his sights. His periscope kept being washed by waves, making it difficult to see clearly. The waves breaking across her bows made it hard to identify any markings. The *Kyleclare* was so lopsided that he was only sure it wasn't abandoned when he saw the shapes of two men in the wheelhouse. But a lone wolf is always wary of danger. The U-boat crew told Herr Oppermann that Kapitänleutnant Teichert took an eternity to make his decision, staring through the periscope in silence. The crew were tense too: not a sound on the sub until he finally issued a command to fire three torpedoes. One for accuracy, I suppose, and another as back-up. The third torpedo was for pure wickedness, because even one direct hit would send the *Kyleclare* to the bottom of the ocean.'

Myles Foley paused. He suddenly looked exhausted. He had surely known many of the crew on the *Kyleclare*. His fingers fidgeted with the betting slip, turning it over so that I could see crude drawings of a tiny ship amid high waves, a drawing of a submarine under the surface filled with matchstick figures and a sketch of three torpedoes fanning out. The last sketch seemed to be of nothing. Then I realised that the undulating line drawn in faint pencil represented the empty waves with nothing left floating upon them.

'The crewmen claimed that Kapitänleutnant Teichert had barely issued his order, with the torpedoes unlashed from a range of five hundred metres, when a giant wave lifted up the *Kyleclare's* hull and its neutral markings became visible. I can't follow everything Herr Oppermann is saying, but it seems that the Kapitänleutnant shouted "Halt!" after he saw the tricolour and the word ÉIRE on the hull. But you can't stop a torpedo. The crew said that the next few seconds were the strangest they had ever experienced on a U-boat. Normally there was a roar of triumph at scoring a direct hit. Instead, was there total silence when two torpedoes struck the *Kyleclare*. The third torpedo missed. Not that the U-boat crew saw the two explosions, but they could feel them. The reverberations were so fierce that the U-boat was buffeted about. The Kapitänleutnant ordered the sub to surface afterwards. But there was nothing to suggest that a ship had ever been there, beyond some scraps of wreckage. Your father and his shipmates never knew what hit them; it was over in seconds. This is what Herr Oppermann wants you to know: it was certainly not a painless death, but it was a quick one. There were no survivors clinging to wreckage for hours until they drowned: there were no survivors at all.'

The two Germans gazed directly at me, their faces solemn. They weren't apologetic: this was a war and these things happened in wars, but I did not need Myles to translate the human sympathy in their expressions. I took the betting slip and stared at each drawing: childish in execution but deadly in its meaning. They were not drawn by somebody who had been present, but I didn't want to ever let these sketches go: they represented a final link to my father.

'Ask him something,' I told Myles. 'If the U-boat had found survivors, would this Teichert fellow have stopped to pick up my father and the others?'

Myles looked at me sombrely. 'You're not a child any more, Jack. U--boats stop for nothing: they don't take prisoners.'

I looked at the two Germans. 'Do they expect me to forgive Teichert because he had second thoughts after realising he made an error? One day I'll track down that murderous bastard and make him answer to me.'

'Kapitänleutnant Teichert has had to answer to a higher authority than you,' Myles Foley replied quietly. 'These matters are now between him and his Maker. He'll answer, like we all have to answer for our deeds. Teichert and his crew – the men Herr Oppermann drank with – were blown to smithereens by a Canadian vessel escorting an Allied convoy five months ago in the mid Atlantic. Canadian escort vessels don't stop for survivors either. Teichert's crew suffered the same death that they inflicted on your father.' He paused. 'Leutnant Krausser is glancing in our direction too often for my liking, so you'll do what your father and grandfather would do. Never grass on a fellow sailor, no matter what his nationality. I can't guarantee that these two sailors are good men, but I've no reason to suspect they are bad men. So shake hands with them both. Then stand up slowly to attract no attention and walk across the deck and scrunch up this betting slip and drop it discreetly into the sea so no evidence remains of what Herr Oppermann risked telling you. Do you understand?'

I nodded. Looking at Herr Müller, I asked Myles to translate. 'Tell him I'm sorry I couldn't spot his brother in the sea.'

The old seafarer spoke in German. Herr Müller nodded in appreciation and murmured a reply to Myles.

'He wants to thank you to looking for his brother. They were always together, even sharing a bed as boys. He feels lost without him: like the pain you still feel after a limb gets ripped from your body.'

I reached beneath the neck of my jumper and found the St Christopher medal which the constable had given me in Cardiff. It had protected me until now. I produced the string from around my neck.

'Will Herr Müller be safe in the Curragh?' I asked Myles.

'The Curragh camp is not without its dangers,' the old man replied. 'There's the danger of getting bitten by a sheep; the danger of dying of boredom and the danger that a damp sod might fall on their toes as they spend the rest of this war piling turf into stacks to dry. Otherwise they'll be safely guaranteed two meals a day, which is more than you or I are certain of. But they'll still be imprisoned a long way from home.'

'Tell him I want him to have this to keep him safe.'

After Myles Foley explained in German, Herr Müller accepted the medal and placed it solemnly around his neck. He whispered something.

'He wants to know if you have a sister,' Myles said. 'Don't take him up him wrong: he means a younger sister.'

I nodded. Herr Müller reached into his pocket to produce a hand--carved wooden doll, ten inches high. Her skirt was made from sacking that he had carefully transformed into a traditional German costume. He had stolen coarse yarn from a rope to create strands of hair, which he had managed to dye yellow. Although her clothing was crude, the carved features on her painted face were exquisite.

'He carved this for his daughter,' Myles Foley translated. 'Now he fears that his daughter will be too old to play with it by the time he sees her again. He wants your sister to have it.'

I could imagine the pleasure on Lily's face when I handed this doll to her, along with my small Christmas gift already purchased in Lisbon. I didn't know how my mother would feel when I brought a German doll into her home. But there was no time to think about this: Leutnant Krausser was striding towards us. I put the doll in my pocket and solemnly shook hands with both Germans. Then, for good measure, I shook hands with Myles too: it seemed the right thing to do. The betting slip was clenched in my left fist. As I rose I found myself face-to-face with the Leutnant.

His bearing reminded me of a younger, more autocratic version of Brother Dawson. The officer made an effort to sound friendly as he addressed me, as if he felt it beneath his dignity to acknowledge our previous altercation. But behind his spurious façade of friendliness I detected suspicion. He had seen me talk to the two sailors and, with his mania for control, yearned to know what we were discussing. Brother Dawson had always needed to know – and control with a leather strap – every whisper in his classroom. I brushed past the Leutnant, my left fist tightly closed. Behind me I could his tone grow interrogational as he quizzed

Herr Oppermann. I kept walking until I reached the gunnel. It was crowded there. We had long since sailed past Crosshaven and into the narrow estuary entrance that guarded the approach to Cobh. Men strained their eyes to catch a proper glimpse of Ireland. I longed to study the drawings on the betting slip one last time but I couldn't take the chance. Two small tenders were visible on the dawn horizon, steaming out from Cobh to meet us. When I felt certain that every man was watching the tenders, I discreetly let the crumpled betting slip fall into the waves.

Chapter Thirty-Four

January 1944, Morning Watch, Cobh Harbour

AFTER STANDING ALONE IN SILENT thought at the gunnel for a time, I sought shelter in the wheelhouse. It was less crowded now: the German sailors had anxiously moved out into the dawn light, alerted to the approaching boats. Captain Donovan held the wheel with Mr Walton and Mr Tierney beside him. Mr Tierney scrutinised my face.

'Are you okay, Jack? You're looking a bit shook.'

'I'm grand, Mossy,' I replied.

'You must be shook,' he observed. 'It's the first time on this damn voyage you've called me by my proper name. Did that jackass Krausser say anything to you?'

'Men are placing bets all over the ship,' the Captain observed. 'Mossy and Frank here have ten bob riding on you to floor Krausser in the first round after we erect a boxing ring on the pier at Cobh. Remember now, it's Marquess of Queensberry rules.'

Mr Walton and Mr Tierney laughed: their way of letting me know that I was in no trouble for my earlier outburst. I should have laughed along with this ribbing but I was too distracted attempting to take in the enormity of everything I had just been told.

'I'm boxing nobody,' I muttered. 'I'm just looking forward to eventually getting home and seeing my mother.'

'Your mother, is it?' Mr Tierney teased. 'And is it your mother you'll be bringing to the Cinema Palace, wearing the nylons you managed to hold on to on this voyage, despite everything?'

'I certainly won't be bringing you, Mossy.'

Captain Donovan laughed. 'If you decide to bring Mossy, be sure to tip me the wink in advance: we'd all pay into the shilling and fourpence seats just to see Mossy wearing a pair of nylon stockings.'

'The only way you'll see me wear a nylon stocking is if the Staffords refuse to pay our wages because the guests ate their cargo,' Mr Tierney said. 'You'll see me run down the Wexford quays with a nylon over my face and their petty cash box under my oxter.'

'They'll fork out their few bob,' Captain Donovan replied. 'They are good employees and where else will they find another crew of fools willing to sail to Lisbon again?'

I looked at the Captain. 'You said you'd see how I coped on this voyage. Will I still have a job after we dock?'

'That depends,' Captain Donovan replied thoughtfully.

'On what?'

'On whether I have one. The Staffords won't be thrilled to see their profit gone. The Irish government won't sing my praises for landing them with all these hungry mouths to feed and the British will tear strips off me for breaking my Navicert.'

'But do you still feel you did the right thing, Sir?'

The Captain shrugged, signifying that my question had no simple answer. 'If we'd handed them over to the British then every U-boat would lie in wait for us after word got out. Likewise, if we had landed them in France every Allied pilot would be itching to teach us a lesson out at sea where there are no witnesses. Sometimes you have to steer your own course.' He looked at me. 'But if I remain master of this vessel, then we'll need a lazy scut of a cabin boy. It's been one tough voyage, Jack. Are you sure you want to risk a second one?'

I remembered walking the streets of Wexford empty-handed in early December. It wasn't just the hunger and cold I recalled; it was my sense of worthlessness. A cabin boy was the lowest rank on a ship, but at least on this vessel I was somebody.

'I'd take the risk,' I said. 'I just wouldn't mind one night in Wexford first.'

'Would the reason be female?' Mr Tierney probed. 'And might she look good in a blue polka-dot dress?'

'The reason could be male,' I replied.

Mr Tierney scratched his head. 'You've lost me.'

'I might want to stand on the quays until a messenger boy passes by, so I can chuck him and his butcher's bike into the water.'

'Pascal Brennan?' Mr Tierney laughed. 'Why throw that pipsqueak into the waves? Just look at him sideways and he'll melt in terror. Doesn't he know you're Sean Roche's son? That alone would put him to flight.'

Mossy's tone was jocular, but I almost broke down: this mention of my da conjured up images of him shouting in dazed confusion as those torpedoes struck the *Kyleclare*. But I couldn't reveal his fate, not while Leutnant Krausser prowled this ship and might identify Herr Oppermann. I also sensed that the facts about my father's death were too enormous for me to properly take in just yet. I would need months to come to terms with the terror that had surely gripped the *Kyleclare* when those torpedoes stuck. I would need to continually relive my father's dying moments until they lost their power to hurt. Only then could I move on; shaped by him but needing to step from his shadow and chart my own course. The only person I would tell until then was my mother, who deserved to know the fate of the man she loved.

355

The wheelhouse door opened. Shay Cullen entered, stamping his feet for warmth. 'It's brass monkeys,' he said. 'Half of Cobh is swanning out to take a gawk at our Germans. You'd swear we were Fossett's Circus arriving in town with acrobats and an elephant.'

'Another sailor in my cabin died from burns an hour ago,' the Captain replied grimly. 'The sooner the others get medical attention, the better their chances. These tenders will escort us into harbour where soldiers will bring our uninvited guests to Collins' Barracks in Cork. You can bet there's a warm meal waiting for them. We'll be lucky to scrounge a cup of tea somewhere.'

'Speaking of uninvited guests,' Shay Cullen said, 'my mother's sister is married to a tight-fisted miser who farms forty-two acres just outside Cobh. They keep a mighty flock of hens. I can hardly see them killing two plump chickens for a prodigal nephew. But they might be cajoled into producing a fried egg for each of us, and something strong in the way of liquid refreshment.'

'They'd hardly welcome the whole kit and caboodle of a ship's crew arriving on their doorstep at dawn?' Mr Tierney replied.

Shay Cullen grinned. 'My aunt would. She loves company. She'd be thrilled skinny at any excuse to take out the good bone China in the parlour that normally only gets unlocked when the parish priest calls. And my uncle – a dour skinflint old enough to be her father – will absolutely hate us for it. That man wouldn't spend Christmas. But he'll grow wary and respectful when he sees Captain Donovan's peaked hat and uniform. He's terrified of uniforms on account of him being the biggest racketeer in Cork. Al Capone would have the morals of a Benedictine monk compared to him. I'm not sure which will give me the most pleasure: seeing my aunt enjoy a bit of company or watching the old misery guts silently suffering as he watches us eat every mouthful of his grub. Compliment him on his grand head of hair, by the way: he has the worst toupee in

Munster. Every morning he shakes the salt cellar over it, hoping that strangers might mistake the salt for dandruff and be fooled into thinking his hair is real.'

'The state we're in, Benedictine monks would turn us away as quick as Al Capone would,' Captain Donovan cautioned.

'Still, a fried egg is a fried egg,' Mr Walton mused quietly. 'And it might be a sin to deny Shay's aunt the chance to use her good China. I'd risk a refusal just to get a gander at the old miser's wig.'

Captain Donovan glanced towards him. 'What else would you risk, Frank?'

'That demands on what's being offered,' Mr Walton replied, the mood suddenly sombre.

'Would you risk another voyage?' Captain Donovan nudged the ship to starboard to align it with the approaching tenders. 'After we scrounge some fuel I need to push on to Fishguard so British Customs can through the motions of inspecting my empty hold. I'll wire the Staffords for instructions about whether to sail back to Lisbon with another load of Welsh coal and hope that our American cargo of phosphate is still there, or whether they want us to return to Wexford or to Dublin. Your priority should be to see a doctor in Cobh and get whatever pills or potions might ease that pain. You belong in your sick bed, but while I'm still captain there's a bunk here if you'd sooner stick with us.'

'I can still do my work,' Mr Walton said, his pride offended. 'I'm no invalid who needs looking after.'

'There's no one saying you are,' the Captain replied cautiously. 'I'm saying that I won't find a better Second Officer elsewhere.'

Mr Walton nodded: his honour appeased, though in truth he looked sicker than most of the German sailors in the Captain's cabin. 'Provided the Staffords post my wages to my wife, then if there's a last voyage going I'll take it.'

'What's this talk of a last voyage? You've years of sailing left,' Mr Tierney insisted.

Mr Walton smiled, though even he could not disguise his pain. 'You're full of wind, Mossy. I'll ask the doctor if he has pills to cure wind if I get to see one. Will we have the pleasure of your company on this next voyage?'

Mr Tierney shrugged. 'It might be wise to avoid folk in Wexford who paid in advance for the transportation of certain commodities.' He glanced at the skipper. 'If truth be told, Captain, there's talk that the chief engineer on the *Cymric* is retiring soon. If the money on offer was better… you know the score, you have children yourself. I hope you wouldn't stand in my way. But I'd gladly serve a few more months on the *Kerlogue* first.'

'I'll stamp your discharge papers V.G. any time, Mossy, though I'd be sad to lose you,' the Captain replied. 'Still, maybe we'd best see if I get another Navicert first. There's no guarantee the British will let me sail out of Cardiff again.'

'They will,' Mr Walton assured him. 'The naval officials who'll rag you will only be desk sailors: lads who would get sick-sea if they stepped too quickly into a bath. And even those jumped-up Napoleons won't refuse an offer from a coaster foolhardy enough to risk transporting three hundred and thirty tonnes of Welsh coal to Lisbon. Britain needs Salazar's gold. If we sink en route, it's no skin off their nose.'

The door opened again. Kapitänleutnant Fleischer stood there.

'The tenders are almost upon us,' he said. 'Do the soldiers know we are unarmed?'

'They do,' Captain Donovan assured him. 'There also should be medical staff on board.'

'I need to thank you for what you have done for all of us and for our Führer.'

'We did nothing for the Fuhrer,' Mr Walton said tartly. 'We simply helped fellow seafarers.'

The Kapitänleutnant nodded, conceding the point. 'I don't expect you and I to ever see eye to eye, Herr Walton.'

'I don't expect us to ever meet again, Kapitänleutnant.'

Kapitänleutnant Fleischer held out his hand. 'Then will you accept my thanks, as a fellow seafarer?'

Mr Walton shook his hand and the Kapitänleutnant proceeded to shake hands with us all, ending with the Captain. 'Your ship is so overloaded that I didn't think we would ever see dry land. You have my gratitude, Captain Donovan.'

'I lost a good number of souls along the way.'

'You've saved many more lives,' Kapitänleutnant Fleischer replied.

'All the same, they died on my watch.' The Captain paused and I saw how much this troubled him. Then he placed his hat carefully on his head. 'I suppose we'd better make ourselves presentable for these Corkonians.'

'You're shipshape and ready to greet a commodore,' Mr Walton assured him.

Captain Donovan smiled. 'It would be a brave man to wake a commodore at this hour. Come out, Frank, and let's see who we're dealing with.' He turned to me. 'If you want to knock a living from the sea, Jack, you'd best try steering us some of the way in. Shay Cullen will teach you.' He gazed through the wheelhouse door at the wretched German survivors crowding every inch of deck. 'This is the oddest cargo I ever landed. After you, Kapitänleutnant.'

The officers left the wheelhouse and Shay Cullen stepped back from the wheel. 'You heard the skipper, Jack. Hold this wheel gently like she was your sweetheart so that, when the seas get rough, she'll happily let you squeeze her good and tight.'

As I took hold of the teak spokes of the wheel a man's voice shouted from the first tender: 'Ahoy there, *Kerlogue*'. Captain Donovan instructed the Dazzler Kehoe to catch the rope thrown from this tender and secure it tightly. Dawn had not fully broken but there was just about enough light to see. I wanted to take in everything happening around me. Yet manning the wheel felt like such a responsibility that I was afraid to do more than stare ahead at the lights of Cobh. I couldn't even properly claim to be steering because Shay Cullen and Mr Tierney stood on either side of me, nudging the King Spoke more upright whenever they felt it necessary to keep the rudder aligned to the hull.

The handful of Irish soldiers who had boarded the *Kerlogue* gazed with open curiosity at their new captives. One lowered his rifle and took out a packet of cigarettes, which he passed around.

Mossy laughed. 'One packet of fags won't go far on that deck. It's a pity we didn't keep these Cork soldiers a few oranges for their troubles.'

'Oranges in Cork are as rare as orangutans,' Shay Cullen remarked.

'I suspect there are only two oranges left in Ireland.' Reaching into his jacket, Mr Tierney furtively produced two gleaming oranges. 'I have to bring something home for the little ones. It's all I've left from this trip.'

'Apart from two-dozen bicycle tubes,' I reminded him. 'And twelve batteries for wireless sets.'

Mossy clipped me around the ear. 'Don't be cheeky, you wee brat, and learn how to steer. Crash into one of these tenders and you'll drown a quarter of the Irish Navy. It's the only Navy on earth who cycle home every day for their dinner.' He turned to Shay Cullen. 'And this uncle of yours: you say he's the biggest racketeer in Cork?'

'The biggest blaggard and scoundrel anyway,' Shay Cullen replied.

'The sort of scoundrel who wouldn't be averse to conducting some business with a butcher in Cardiff? That is, if he found two middlemen to discreetly transport a few hams for him ... honest go-betweens who'd only deduct a smidgen of profit to cover our costs.'

'He'd sell his grandmother into a harem if there's money to be made,' Shay Cullen assured Mossy. 'And thankfully, he's so ignorant that he hasn't a clue what the going rate is for black-market hams in Cardiff.'

Mr Tierney nodded. 'When the Kapitänleutnant's Comanches get unloaded, nobody in Cobh will pay us a blind bit of heed. Let's walk out the road to his farm. I'd kill for a fried egg.'

They lowered their voices then to discuss the ploys and stratagems that an honest sailor needed to employ to supplement his meagre income. But I was overcome by such a sudden, profound tiredness that I found myself barely listening. I was staring ahead at the huge church that dominated the skyline of Cobh, and the tall terraces of shops and warehouses which lined the harbour and were just about visible in the light. But looking back now, I realise that I was gazing far farther ahead in my elevated dreamlike state, induced by a lack of food, water and sleep. On that morning, however I wasn't consciously aware of exactly what I was gazing towards. Overwhelmed by fatigue, all that I physically saw was the slowly decreasing expanse of waves that separated us from those imposing stone buildings in Cobh.

It is only now – writing these words seven decades later – that I fully comprehend just what I was trying to discern in my unconscious mind, amid the overwhelming exhaustion which so floored me that, for the eternity of those few seconds, I barely knew if I was awake or asleep. But during those seconds the empty waves became an indecipherable canvas that waited to be coloured in by the future. Without knowing it, I was envisaging an empty bed in a ward of the County Home in Enniscorthy, when I arrived home on shore leave five years later, in 1949, to be told that Myles Foley had died alone there two days previously: his death certificate left incomplete because nobody could hazard a guess as to the year of his birth.

I was seeing myself walk for miles through the streets of Swansea in 1944 to locate Spanish Joe's Café under the railway arches on Wind Street, where I sit in silence, drinking a bowl of Spanish Joe's pea soup in memory of Mossy Tierney, after word reached us in that port that *The Cymric* was sunk with no survivors, en route from Ardrossan in Ayrshire to Lisbon. That afternoon I would glance up to spy Ernie Grogan sitting alone at a corner table, as oblivious to me and the other sailors around him as he was to the silent tears streaking his face.

I was watching Shay Cullen and myself fail to comfort Mr Walton as his anguished shouts of pain petered out into whimpers and then a rasping death rattle, when we were two days out from Lisbon in the autumn of 1944 – on that trip when Captain Donovan waited patiently to see the British ambassador and persuade him to let Mr Walton be buried in the tiny English graveyard of St George's, close to the Basilica da Estrela – six graves away from Eoin Deasy, the Irish castaway we'd found dead in a rowing boat.

I was foreseeing Ellie Coady laughing as she put on Kateřina's silk dress that I brought home from Lisbon, and was I foreseeing her too slowly remove her wedding dress on our honeymoon night in 1951 in the Woodenbridge Hotel near Avoca: the hotelier so enraptured by Ellie's radiance that he presented her with a bag of apples as we were leaving, and his wife becoming so enraged by jealousy that she ran after us to charge me an extra half-crown for them.

I was seeing myself trawling for cod in freezing, dog-rough seas off the coast of Iceland to earn the deposit for the house where Ellie and I set up home in a new Dublin suburb – Ellie always lighting a fire in the front parlour, with the children banished from it, on my first night home on shore leave, laden down with sweets.

I was visualising myself shipwrecked on a sandbank on the MV *Cameo* on that stormy night when I needed to be winched on board a lifeboat moments before the vessel capsized, leaving all my possessions behind except a ragdoll that our eldest daughter christened Cameo when I presented it to her after I finally made it safely home.

I was picturing the departure lounge of an airport in Paris, during a brief stopover to change planes, on the only occasion that Ellie ever went abroad in her life – a diocesan pilgrimage to Lourdes – where she was fascinated by the foreignness of everything. Amid the crowds of passengers in transit, I became convinced that I glimpsed Kateřina for the first time since Mossy Tierney bundled her to safety off the *Kerlogue*. I had often searched Lisbon without finding any trace of her; but there she was – or else somebody who was her double – in Paris in 1967, as elegantly dressed as on that Christmas Eve night when she emerged from the Hotel Metropole at Rossio – only this time she linked the arm of a well-tailored man whom she plainly seemed to love. Was it wishful thinking, or was it really her, all those years later? All I know is that when that lady sensed my gaze and turned to glance back, she genuinely had no idea as to who I was or why I was staring at her, although she smiled politely before boarding a plane for some foreign land where she led a life that I knew nothing about.

I was envisaging my last glimpse of my beloved Ellie: her head shaved in preparation for the operation on a brain tumour that she never recovered from, dying on the shortest day of the year in 1969, and how our house no longer felt like home for years afterwards – dark years when I often recalled Mr Walton's remark that any bunk at sea was a lonely bunk and how whiskey became a bothersome companion. But no toddler wants to see their grandfather drunk, and often when I lay in my cabin with a book and a bottle of Bushmills during my final years as a ship's cook, the ghosts of Mossy Tierney and Myles Foley and Frank Walton crowded in to chide me to get a grip on my grief.

I was picturing myself, retired and ten years sober, on the Christmas morning when my youngest granddaughter – the same age that Lily was when I first went to sea – shyly handed me the gift that all my grandchildren had clubbed together to purchase at an auction in Adam's auction rooms, after my son-in-law noticed it listed in a catalogue. A hand-carved wooden doll: her traditional embroidered German costume conjured from a flour sack and her hair spun from rope that had been painstakingly spliced apart and dyed yellow so that it fell down to cover the delicately painted features on her face. The auctioneer's catalogue described it as having been in the ownership of a Kildare family who purchased it in the winter of 1944, from two German internees in the nearby Curragh Camp, who went from door to door, selling dolls for a pittance, carved from wood surreptitiously purloined from camp fittings.

That Christmas morning was the first time I cried since Ellie died. When I tried to give the doll back to my granddaughter she shook her head stubbornly and asked to be given a story instead. She demanded to know why I never talked about being at sea during the war, or about the times my ship was bombed, the lives I helped save or the lost friends I sailed with. I had shaken my head, like on every other occasion when my grandchildren asked me; like when they tried to get me to accept a medal for valour from some government minister. I told her: *We were no class of heroes; we were just a bunch of honest-to-God sailors, trying to feed our families as best we could. There's nothing more to tell, or maybe there are things I just don't want to remember.* But my grandchild had stared back at me – with eyes so fiercely blue and determined that were a mirror image of Ellie's whenever Ellie would put her foot down – and replied: *I want you to write it down.*

Maybe this is the last image that I foretold in my unconscious mind as I gripped the spokes of that heavy wheel while we edged our way slowly into Cobh Harbour: this vision of me as a man as old as Myles Foley lived to be, seated alone at this kitchen table to fill copybook after copybook in this copperplate handwriting that Brother Dawson hammered into me. But as I write now, I can recall again that freezing dawn on New Year's Day of 1944 when I was woken from my trance by Mossy Tierney thumping me on the shoulder and saying 'For the love of God, Jack, you'd best stick to leaning how to cook: you're after nearly ploughing into this next tender coming out to meet us.'

I felt Mossy's fingers gripping my right hand and Shay Cullen's fingers gripping my left as they helped to steer the *Kerlogue* to starboard to allow the next tender to come aside us and be made secure with ropes. With their hands holding the wheel alongside mine I could afford to look around. I saw nurses coming on board and stretcher-bearers and a man who – from the cut of his jib and his black bag – could only be a doctor. Captain Donovan led him down the ladder to his cabin as some German sailors started to board the tender to make more space on deck. The pilot of a tug some distance ahead of us signalled for me to follow him in. Mr Tierney released his hand from mine.

'You've been staring into space like a gobdaw for these past five minutes. You must have been thinking of Ellie Coady. She's going to look good in them nylon stockings when we get finally reach Wexford.'

'I've a silk dress for her as well,' I said.

'What dress?' Mr Tierney asked. 'You never told me about any silk dress.'

'I don't tell you everything, Mossy. But I tell you one thing – Ellie isn't going to look good in them: she's going to dazzle.'

Mossy laughed as both men stepped back to give me the space to grip the spokes of the wheel again, with renewed confidence, in the growing dawn light.

Postscript

THERE WERE TEN MEN ON board the MV *Kerlogue* on its voyage home from Lisbon with a cargo of oranges on December 29, 1943, when it received an SOS signal from a German reconnaissance aircraft and altered its course to spend ten hours rescuing one hundred and sixty-eight sailors from the sea – four of whom died on board.

The real-life crew on board that day were:
    Captain Thomas Donoghue from Dungarvin, Co. Waterford.
    Chief Officer Denis Valencie from Co. Dublin.
    Second Officer Patrick Whelan from Co. Wexford.
    Chief Engineer Eric Giggins from London.
    Second Engineer Joseph Donoghue from Co. Wexford.
    Third Engineer Gary Roche from Co. Wexford.
    Boatswain John 'Chum' Roche.
    Helmsman Thomas Grannell.
    Able Seamen Tom O'Neill.
    Able Seaman Jack Furlong.

When inventing my fictional crew, I tried to let the birth places of some of my imaginary characters echo the composition of the real-life crew. However, these characters are total phantoms of my imagination. Beyond saluting their bravery, I do not presume to speak in any way for the actual men involved in this rescue. Nor do I pretend to know what their thoughts were during this voyage or how they spent their time in Lisbon. I have no knowledge of whether this particular crew tried to supplement their meagre incomes by the minor smuggling that was endemic among lowly paid Irish sailors who undertook dangerous wartime journeys. Nor do I presume to know anything of their individual political opinions.

Their actions during the rescue speak for themselves and are outlined in Captain Frank Forde's fine non-fiction study, *The Long Watch: World War Two and the Irish Mercantile Marine*. Forde's book is an invaluable factual account of the fate of many small ships mentioned in this novel. Although in this novel the *Kerlogue's* voyage begins in Wexford, its actual starting point on this trip was Dublin Port.

The loose inspiration behind the character of Mossy Tierney was a Chief Engineer from Wexford named Michael Tierney: a neighbour of my father who persuaded my father – at sixteen – to visit the offices of the Wexford Steamship Company and pretend to the Stafford family that he had worked in the kitchens of St Peter's Seminary. This lie proved convincing enough to land my father a job as a cabin boy, which turned into a forty-four-year-long career at sea as a ship's cook. While my father rarely liked to speak of his experiences of being bombed by German planes while sailing to Lisbon on the MV *Edenvale* – the sister ship of the M. V. *Kerlogue* – or of how the *Edenvale* towed the stricken British ship *Palmston* to the safety of Milford Haven, he remembered with deep affection the mischievous nature of his Green Street neighbour, with whom he sailed until their paths diverged.

Less than two months after the *Kerlogue* rescued one-hundred and sixty-eight members of the Kriegsmarine, the Kriegsmarine took the lives of Michael Tierney and his ten unarmed crewmates on board the Arklow schooner the *Cymric* on that same dangerous Lisbon run. Six of the *Cymric*'s crew were Wexford men. I hope that Michael Tierney's ghost will excuse the small gesture of homage in using his surname when creating the fictional Mossy.

The *Kerlogue* would have been skippered on this voyage to Lisbon by Captain Desmond Fortune, if he had not been so badly injured, during the RAF attack on the *Kerlogue*, that he remained unable to walk unaided for the rest of his life. His replacement, Captain Thomas Donoghue, was fifty-nine years old when taking command. In 1945 the *Kerlogue* was skippered by forty-year-old Captain Richard O'Neill, who died while the ship was docked in Lisbon. He was buried in a small cemetery in that city, in the presence of his crew.

The diseased sailor discovered dead on a life raft with no clues as to his identity except for a British Navy identity disc, which gave his name, number and R.C. as his religion, was F. O'Rourke. He was actually found drifting by the crew of the ill-fated *Kyleclare*, en route from Barry to Lisbon, in June 1942.

Although other characters in this novel are imaginary and possess fictitious names, Brother Dawson was real, as were the sadistic acts which he was given immunity to commit and never had to answer for in his lifetime.

During the Second World War the Lilliputian Irish fleet saved the lives of five-hundred and twenty-one people of all nationalities, including German, British, Dutch and American survivors. Neutral Irish ships were attacked on forty-one occasions, resulting in one-hundred and forty-nine crewmen being killed and thirty-eight wounded.

In 2011 a set of seven handcrafted wooden dolls turned up for auction in Dublin. They had been made by German sailors rescued by the *Kerlogue* who, while interned in the Curragh Camp, crafted them from purloined pieces of wood and scraps of fabric transformed into traditional German costumes. They were given as a gift to an Irish army nurse who looked after the German internees.

An annual mass is now held in City Quay Parish Church in Dublin, after which wreaths are laid at a small memorial that commemorates Irish merchant seamen lost during World War Two. The National Maritime Museum of Ireland in Dun Laoghaire has a replica of the *Kerlogue* on display.

In June 2015 a limestone memorial inscribed with the names of the *Kerlogue's* crew was unveiled on the Wexford quays, in a ceremony attended by many of the crew's descendants, close to where the offices of the Wexford Steamship Company once stood.

Dermot Bolger,
6 February 2016,
Dublin.

Also by Dermot Bolger

Poetry
The Habit of Flesh
Finglas Lilies
No Waiting America
Internal Exiles
Leinster Street Ghosts
Taking My Letters back
The Chosen Moment
External Affairs
The Venice Suite
That Which is Suddenly Precious

Novels
Night Shift
The Woman's Daughter
The Journey Home
Emily's Shoes
A Second Life
Father's Music
Temptation
The Valparaiso Voyage
The Family on Paradise Pier
The Fall of Ireland
Tanglewood

Young Adult Novel
New Town Soul

Collaborative novels
Finbar's Hotel
Ladies Night at Finbar's Hotel

Plays
The Lament for Arthur Cleary
Blinded by the Light
In High Germany
The Holy Ground
One Last White Horse
April Bright
The Passion of Jerome
Consenting Adults
The Ballymun Trilogy
1: From These Green Heights
2: The Townlands of Brazil
3: The Consequences of Lightning
Walking the Road
The Parting Glass
Tea Chests & Dreams